17
CHURCH
ROW

James Carol is the author of *The Killing Game*, which was short-listed for the CWA Ian Fleming Steel Dagger Award. As James Carol, he has also written the bestselling Jefferson Winter series. *Broken Dolls*, the first of these, was published in 2014 to rave reviews and reached #1 on the Amazon fiction and thriller charts. In addition James is writing a series of eBooks set during Winter's FBI days. *Presumed Guilty* is the first of these.

James lives in Hertfordshire with his wife and two children. When he's not writing he can usually be found in a pair of headphones, recording and producing music.

ALSO BY JAMES CAROL

The Killing Game
Kiss Me, Kill Me

The Jefferson Winter Novels
Broken Dolls
Watch Me
Prey
The Quiet Man

The Jefferson Winter Chronicles
Presumed Guilty
Hush Little Baby
Open Your Eyes

JAMES CAROL

17 CHURCH ROW

ZAFFRE

First published in Great Britain in 2019 by
ZAFFRE
80–81 Wimpole St, London W1G 9RE

A CIP catalogue record for this book is
available from the British Library.

ISBN: 978-1-78576-840-8

Also available as an ebook

1 3 5 7 9 10 8 6 4 2

Typeset by IDSUK (Data Connection) Ltd
Printed and bound in Great Britain by Clays Ltd, Elcograf S.p.A.

Zaffre is an imprint of Bonnier Books UK
www.bonnierbooks.co.uk

This one's for my brother, Mike.
Keep on rocking Little Bruv!

Father attempted to murder me once.

A bold statement, I know, but one based on fact. When he swung that axe there was no question of it being an accident. He was aware of his actions – and the consequences of those actions. No court in the land could fail to convict him on the available evidence. The story itself is tiresome. I have gone over the events so many times the finer threads are starting to lose their integrity and unravel. That said, it is important you understand, so we will talk more of this later. Before we go any further, though, we should get some things straight.

Firstly, the operative word in my initial statement is 'attempted'. Had his attack on me succeeded I would not be here talking to you today. Because let us make no mistake, I am very much alive. Secondly, I am not looking for pity. Mawkish feelings are irrelevant.

I have not taken the decision to kill Father lightly. Believe me when I tell you that this is something that I have agonised over. However, after weighing all the available evidence, the only conclusion I can draw is that this is the only way forward.

Father must die for what he has done.

Chapter 1

The heavy steel gate retracted slowly, revealing the house in all its glory. It was brand new and looked as though it had been beamed in from the future. The angles were sharp, every pane of glass was gleaming, and the white walls reflected the sunlight like a Spanish villa. There was something beautiful about the stark simplicity of the building, something quietly comforting. The question Nikki was asking herself was whether she could imagine the three of them living here? 'Maybe' was as much as she was willing to concede for now. The gate finished opening and Ethan pressed the accelerator, bringing the Tesla's motor back to life. He drove into the courtyard and stopped in front of the garage. A convertible BMW was already parked here, the top down even though it was only March.

'You're very quiet over there. I don't think you've said a word the whole way.' Ethan was smiling at her from the driving seat, trying to keep the mood light. It was a good smile, one the cameras loved. She wasn't fooled. You didn't spend a decade with another person without learning to read them. This mattered to him. She had known that when he first showed her the details on his laptop. They had looked at houses before, but this one had got him fired up in a way the others hadn't. How much he'd been fired up became apparent the next day. Up until then they had looked at houses in a vague, speculative way; with this one he had taken the next step and arranged a viewing.

When she didn't reply, he added, 'Look, Nik, I know this isn't the sort of house you'd usually go for, but all I ask is that you keep an open mind.'

'I *am* keeping an open mind. In fact, I was just thinking that I kind of like it. I like the location too.'

Ethan caught her eye again, surprised. 'You're not just saying that?'

Nikki shook her head. 'I'm not. You know one of the things I hate about our current house is that it's like living in a goldfish bowl. Bedford Street is too busy. There are just too many people around. This street is the complete opposite of that.'

And that was the truth. Church Row was a quiet Kensington cul-de-sac that seemed to sit apart from the hustle and bustle of the rest of the city. The pavements were narrow, the road just about wide enough for two cars to pass. Tall brick walls bordered the properties, high trees blocked the view of the houses, and every gate had a camera pointing at it. Number Seventeen sat at the far end of the street. The wall surrounding it was a couple of feet higher than the neighbouring properties and the driveway was hidden behind a heavy black steel gate. Like all cities, London had its secret places. That was what this felt like. A secret place. Driving along Church Row, Nikki could imagine feeling safe living here. That was another tick for the plus column. She could also imagine Bella being safe here, too, which was an even bigger plus.

Ethan turned his smile on Bella, who was sitting quietly in the back. She was staring at the house, keeping her thoughts to herself. Everyone said that Bella looked like her, but all Nikki could see was Ethan. Father and daughter shared the same perfectly proportioned nose, the same bright smile, the same shimmering, contradictory blue eyes, a blue that made Nikki think simultaneously of icicles and tropical seas. They both had thick black hair – Bella's was shoulder-length, while Ethan's was cut short. Bella had her father well and truly wrapped around her little finger. Sometimes Nikki would look at the two of them conspiring together and experience a pang of irrational jealousy. In those secret moments, she found it hard to believe this was the same child she had carried in her belly for nine months.

'What about you Bella Boo?' Ethan said. 'What do you think?'

Bella reached for her tablet and started tapping the screen. *'It's okay.'*

The voice coming out of the tablet sounded like a six-year-old, but without any of the emotions you would usually associate with a child – no excitement, no laughter, no attitude, nothing. The voice reminded Nikki of the old telephone speaking clock. The information you'd asked for was being delivered, but in a cold, robotic manner.

'Just okay?' Ethan said.

Bella responded with a shrug that could have meant anything.

'Shall we?'

Ethan jumped from the car without waiting for an answer, as eager as a kid on Christmas morning. Nikki got out in time to see him bounce up to the back door and open it with a dramatic flourish. Bella stepped out, frowning at him like she just wanted him to go away, but not quite able to hide her smile. Before Nikki could say anything, Ethan had taken hold of their hands and was leading them towards the front door. All they could do was follow in his wake, pulled along on the wave of his excitement.

The first thing Nikki noticed when they got there was that there was no handle. It was one of those details that cried out to be noticed. Certain things you took for granted: the sun would rise in the east each morning and doors had handles. The second thing she noticed was that there were none of the other things you might expect to see either: no doorbell, no letter box, no house number. It was just a blank expanse of black-painted wood, as though the door had come straight from the factory and had yet to have any of the extras fitted. She stopped in front of it. Ethan's puzzled look mirrored her own.

'So what do we do?' she said. 'Knock?'

Before Ethan could respond, the door swung silently open and a voice said, 'It's a pleasure to meet you, Mr and Mrs Rhodes. Please come in.'

Nikki peered through the open doorway but couldn't see anyone. Ethan was peering too, his puzzled expression turning to one of bemusement.

'I guess we do what the lady says,' he said as he walked inside.

Nikki hesitated for a second, then took Bella's hand and followed. No sooner had she stepped into the foyer when she heard a faint noise behind her. She glanced back in time to see the door slowly closing behind them.

'Ms Fisher is waiting for you in the kitchen. She said you should follow the smell of coffee.'

The voice was warm and mellifluous and seemed to be coming from right beside them. Except there was no one there. Ethan was grinning now, clearly tickled by this. Nikki didn't share the emotion. She didn't like surprises. They played havoc with her anxiety.

'Perhaps I should introduce myself,' the voice continued. 'My name is Alice and I am here for your comfort and convenience."

'Here for our comfort and convenience,' Ethan echoed. 'You know, guys, I think I like the sound of that.'

The smell of coffee got stronger as they moved into the spacious reception area. Like the outside of the building, the walls were painted white. A touch of colour was provided by the strategically placed rubber plants and a large wall screen displaying a colourful Picasso that was heavy on the oranges and reds. The area was brightly lit by dozens of small halogens embedded in the ceiling. The reception area narrowed into a corridor that went on for ten metres or so before opening into a large open kitchen that was dominated by a granite-topped work island. Everything in here was sleek and elegant and smelled brand new.

Catriona Fisher was sitting on a stool at the work island. She stood when she saw them and walked over to do the introductions. The way she moved it was as though she had complete conviction that the universe was going to step aside to accommodate her. She was in her fifties and four or five inches shorter than Nikki, so somewhere around five foot three. Her hairstyle was her most striking feature, a sleek raven-black bob that was shot through with a vibrant turquoise streak. The black baggy shirt and black cargo pants contrasted with all the surrounding white. Bella was jerking Nikki's hand and holding up her tablet. *Edna Mode* was written on the screen, causing Nikki to bite back a laugh. Edna Mode was a character from *The Incredibles*, a fast-talking fashion guru who designed superhero costumes. The film was one of Bella's current favourites. Looking at Catriona, Nikki had to admit that Bella had a point. There was more than a passing resemblance. In attitude as well as appearance.

'So who wants coffee?' Catriona asked.

'I'm fine,' Nikki said.

'I'm fine too,' Ethan echoed.

'What about you, young lady?' Catriona asked, aiming the question at Bella. 'Mind you, I suppose you're a bit too young.'

Bella moved closer to Nikki and took a tight hold of her leg.

'Last chance. But you should know that Alice makes a spectacular cup of coffee.' Catriona gave them less than a second to answer, then called out. 'Alice, another coffee, please. And make this one a little cooler and not so sweet as last time.'

'Of course, Ms Fisher.'

The coffee machine was hissing and gurgling on the work surface that stretched along the far wall. By the time Catriona got there, her drink was ready, hot steam swirling up from the cup. She picked it up and took a sip. 'Perfect. You know, there are so many things that excite me about this house, but Alice is right up there at the top of the list. What do you think of her, by the way? Pretty amazing, huh?'

'I guess so,' Nikki replied, although the truth was that she wasn't particularly impressed. Granted, Alice had opened the front door for them and made coffee, but as far as Nikki could see, Alice was just Alexa dressed up with a different name.

Catriona smiled, making sure to include both Nikki and Ethan. 'Okay, I've made my decision: you can have the house.'

'Excuse me,' Nikki said. 'We haven't decided if we want it yet.'

'What's to decide? Who wouldn't want to live here?'

Nikki turned to Ethan. 'Why do I feel like I'm being hijacked?'

Ethan put his hands in the air, his surprise a hundred per cent genuine. 'I've got no idea what she's talking about.'

'Here's the thing,' Nikki said to Catriona. 'Last time I looked, the way this works is that we get shown the house, then we go away and talk about it. Then and only then do we come to a decision as to whether or not we want to buy it.'

'And if you were viewing an ordinary house, that's certainly the process you would follow. But this is no *ordinary* house. Give it another ten or twenty years and it may well be, but for now, trust me when I tell you that this house is unique. A total one-off. Also, if this was a normal house viewing you'd be getting shown around by an estate agent who'd be doing everything possible to persuade you to buy it. But you're not being shown around by an estate agent, you're being interviewed by the architect. Doesn't that strike you as odd?'

It did, but Ethan had told her that was because the house wasn't on the market yet. He'd heard about it through a friend of a friend and thought it sounded perfect. By meeting directly with Catriona he was hoping they could get in with an offer first, if Nikki agreed to it. 'What do you mean, you're interviewing us? So far all you've done is ask us if we like the virtual assistant and whether we want a coffee.'

Catriona laughed. 'Alice is so much more than a virtual assistant. With your standard VA you ask for something and the VA will try to oblige as best it can, usually with varying degrees of success. Alice has been designed to anticipate your needs before you even realise you have them.'

'With all due respect, it sounds as though you're feeding us a line there.'

Catriona shook her head. 'Alice is the next generation in AI. The best way to think about her is that she's every servant you'll ever need.'

'And that sounds like another line.'

'I tell you what, let's have this conversation after you've been living here for a couple of weeks. Actually, make that a couple of days. I guarantee you'll be convinced by then.'

'We still haven't said that we're going to buy the house.'

'You will. Okay come with me, there's something I'd like you to see.' She turned her attention on Bella. 'Actually it's something I think *you'd* like to see.'

Without another word. Catriona put her coffee down on the work island and strode across the kitchen. She paused at the entrance and smiled back at them. 'Well, what are you waiting for?'

Nikki shared a look with Ethan then took Bella's hand and followed Catriona into the corridor. As they moved through the house, Catriona kept up a running commentary, delivering her pitch at a hundred words a minute. She led them to a room at the far end of the house. The door slid silently open as she approached it. She stepped through and motioned for them to follow. The room they walked into was about eight metres by eight, with patio doors on the far side that looked out over a small Zen Garden. There were no furnishings and the smell of fresh paint lingered in the air,

'I think this bedroom would be perfect for your daughter,' Catriona announced.

Nikki wasn't so sure. She didn't like the fact that it was at the far end of the house, away from all the other bedrooms. She would rather have Bella in the room next to theirs – that was the setup at their current house, and it worked just fine. Bella, however, didn't seem to share her reservations. She had let go of her hand and was walking through the room as if it already belonged to her, heading towards the patio doors. Before she got there, the doors opened and she stepped out into the cold sunshine. Nikki watched her go, a bloom of panic welling up inside her.

'It looks like the garden's enclosed,' Ethan said quietly at her shoulder. 'There's no way for her to get out onto the street.'

'That's correct,' Catriona put in. 'The big advantage with this room is that your daughter can go outside whenever she wants. It's important for children to get fresh air, right? That was one of my considerations when I was designing this part of the house. I wanted to create a space that integrated both the outer and inner worlds. My thinking was that if you can't drag them away from their electronic devices, then why not create an environment where the outside world comes to them. All you've got to do is ask Alice to open the doors and you've got your very own miniature Garden of Eden.'

Nikki walked across to the patio doors, still unconvinced. What she saw when she got there did nothing to change her mind. Bella was crouched down beside the pond, fascinated by the large coloured Koi carp that were turning lazy loops through the water. It wouldn't take much for her to lose balance and topple in. A strong breeze would probably do it. Catriona Fisher clearly didn't have children. If she had she wouldn't have considered putting a pond out here. It might look pretty, but as far as Nikki was concerned it was an accident waiting to happen.

'It's all right,' Ethan said, reading her thoughts again. 'We can get something to cover it with. Some sort of mesh. We'll be able to make it safe.'

He walked past her, out into the garden. 'So what do you think of the room, sweetheart?'

Bella turned and smiled at him and started jabbing frantically at her tablet screen.

'Cool,' she said in that blank voice. 'Can I look after the fish?'

'Of course you can. But you'd need to feed them every day.'

Bella nodded.

'And you'll need to learn how to look after them properly. This type of fish requires a lot of looking after. Assuming, of course, we end up buying the house.'

They both turned to look at Nikki. Their smiles were identical. As was the childlike excitement in their eyes. Looking back later, this was the moment when she knew that they would be moving here.

Chapter 2

Ethan didn't say much on the journey back to St John's Wood. For him, the viewing had been a formality. If he hadn't made his mind up before they arrived at Church Row, then he'd definitely made it up by the time Catriona Fisher had finished showing them around. That glint of boyish enthusiasm in his eye had got brighter with each room they had seen and by the time they reached the basement with its pool and cinema room, he was sold, hook, line and sinker. Things weren't so clear cut for Nikki. One second she'd be thinking they could make it work; the next she would be seeing this as the worst idea ever. Applying pressure wasn't going to help, which was why Ethan had wisely opted to keep his mouth shut.

The second they turned into Bedford Street she felt that old familiar knot of anxiety twisting through her gut. This happened every time, so she should be used to it by now, but she wasn't. It was also something that was supposed to get easier with time. It didn't. She'd get a day like today where everything felt raw again and it would be as though she was back at square one. Ethan slowed when they approached the house, searching for a parking space. As they cruised past the line of parked cars, all Nikki could see was their front door. It took up her whole focus and for a moment she was reliving the accident and its aftermath in every last detail: the pain, the loss, the guilt, the what-ifs, *everything*. Ethan suddenly pressed down hard on the accelerator, jerking her from her thoughts. He had spotted a space and was damned if anyone else was going to get it. The Tesla was barely audible at the best of times but when the motor cut out this seemed to highlight the silence between them. As Nikki unfastened her seatbelt she noticed that Ethan was making no move to unfasten his.

'Aren't you coming in?'

Ethan shook his head. 'I've got a meeting with Cally about the new show.'

Cally was his agent. He was currently in the process of transitioning from Radio Two's drive-time show to the breakfast slot. He'd actually wound the old show up back in January and it was now reaching the point where he was bored and ready to get back to work. To start with it had been nice having him around more, but Nikki was now counting the days too. The show was launching in April and there had been a *lot* of meetings lately. He hadn't mentioned this one, though.

'A meeting with Cally, eh? It's the first I've heard about it.'

Ethan frowned and it was very obviously put on. 'I thought I mentioned it.'

'You didn't. What's more, you know you didn't.' Nikki laughed. 'You are such a crap liar, Ethan.'

Ethan was laughing too. *Busted.* 'Okay, you got me. I just wanted to give you some space. You have a lot to think about.'

'You want that house, don't you?'

'Is it that obvious?'

Nikki glanced over her shoulder. 'What about you, Bella Boo?'

Bella answered with a nod.

'So it's two against one.'

'That's not how this one works,' Ethan said. 'All three of us need to be in agreement, otherwise it's not going to happen.'

'So when will you be back?'

'How about dinner time? That gives you the whole afternoon. I can bring Indian.'

'Indian works for me.

Bella tapped the screen of her tablet. *'Korma please.'*

Ethan smiled over his shoulder at her. 'That goes without saying.'

'And I'll have a chicken bhuna, please.' Nikki leant over and kissed him. 'Love you.'

'Right back at you,' Ethan said, returning the kiss.

Nikki got out and opened the back door for Bella.

'Love you, Daddy.'

'And right back at you too, sweetheart,' Ethan said, blowing her a kiss.

The exchange was bittersweet. It was one of those moments where Nikki realised how much the three of them had lost. Hearing Bella tell Ethan that she loved him in that cold, emotionless voice was like being stabbed in the heart.

Nikki helped Bella out and together they watched the Tesla pull away from the kerb. They kept watching until it turned out of Bedford Street, Bella waving one last time as it disappeared from sight, the tablet clutched tight in her hand. That was yet another reminder of what had happened. She never went anywhere without it. Other parents joked about how their kids were addicted to their electronic gadgets, but for Bella this tablet was the lifeline that connected her to the rest of the world. The cover was pink and decorated with hearts and stars, and starting to look a bit bashed up. Nikki wondered how long it would be before she wanted to change it for something more grown-up. The thought provoked a pang of sadness. In a lot of ways Bella was still her little girl, but in too many ways she was older than her six years. Hand in hand, they started walking, Bella on her right side, to shield her from the road.

Their house was an elegant white Edwardian that sat at the end of a terrace of identical-looking properties. It was filled with character, charming in a way the Church Row house would never be. They climbed the steps to the front door, the memory of the accident pushing Nikki's apprehension higher with each one. She couldn't remember her anxiety being this bad – certainly not for a while, at any rate. She took her keys out and unlocked the door, her hand shaking a little as she did so. She glanced down at Bella, but she was looking at her tablet, blissfully unaware of her discomfort.

Nikki let them inside, closing the door behind them. She rattled the security chain into place then turned the key to engage the five-lever mortice lock. If she had done this two years ago, then things would have turned out very different. It was a thought that occurred to her every time she walked through this door. Was this something that would get left behind if they moved house, or was this particular piece of neurosis transferable? Only time would tell, she guessed.

The smell of home-made soup hung hot and heavy in the air, and they followed it along the hallway. Sofia was washing up when they walked into the kitchen. She smiled at them when she heard them enter, then grabbed a tea towel and started drying her hands. Bella ran across and Sofia scooped her into a hug and kissed her.

'Are you hungry, *Corazoncito*? It's way past your lunchtime.' Her Spanish accent was still strong even though she had lived in the UK for more than half of her life.

Bella answered with an enthusiastic nod and Sofia stole another kiss before putting her down and turning to look at Nikki. 'What about you, *mi cariño*? It's chicken soup. Your favourite.'

Nikki shook her head. 'Thanks, but I'm not hungry.'

'You really should eat something, you know.'

'It's okay I'll have some later.'

Nikki helped Bella out of her coat before removing hers. She draped them over the back of one of the chairs then sat down. By the time Bella had washed her hands and sat down too, there was a bowl of soup and a plate with some bread waiting for her on the table. The portion was too big, but Nikki had given up on that battle. Sofia's stock answer was that Bella was a growing girl. Anyway, Bella was pretty good at self-regulating. She would stop when she was full.

'So, *Corazoncito*,' Sofia said, 'what was the house like?'

Bella put her spoon down in her bowl and started tapping the screen of her tablet. *'Amazing. I have my own fish pond in my room.'*

Sofia's eyes widened with disbelief. 'In your room? Surely not.'

Bella shook her head, frowning. Tongue poking out from the corner of her mouth, she started tapping frantically at her tablet. Both Nikki and Sofia resisted the urge to fill the silence. One thing the therapists had agreed on was that it was important that Bella felt as though she was being heard.

'There is a garden outside the room. That's where the pond is. Daddy says I can look after the fish.'

'That does sound amazing.'

'There are three of them. I'm going to call them Ruby, Sapphire and Emerald.'

'Such beautiful names. I can't wait to see them.' Sofia sat down in the empty seat next to Nikki and waited for her to meet her eye. 'And what do you think of the house, *mi cariño*?'

Nikki glanced at Bella and Sofia got the message. She changed the subject smoothly, filling the silence with details of what she had been up to that morning. Sofia had been with them for years. They employed her as a housekeeper, but she was so much more than that. She was in her late fifties with long black hair and a quick, easy smile that made her look ten years younger. She always wore something red because she believed the colour brought good luck. Today it was her shoes. Sofia had been brought up in a small farming village north of Barcelona, but had found this too claustrophobic. She had escaped as soon as she could, first to Madrid, then to London, where she had met her husband, Philip. He had died five years ago from cancer and she had nursed him through the illness. Even now she still hadn't dealt fully with the grief. She probably never would. As Nikki knew only too well, some losses you never fully recovered from.

Sofia had never had children and treated Bella like the granddaughter she would never have. She loved her to bits, a feeling that was mutual. *Corazoncito* was her pet name for her, which translated as "little heart", which fitted perfectly. Nikki's own parents had died before she met Ethan – her mother from breast cancer and her father a couple of years later from a brain aneurysm. After the accident, Sofia had become a surrogate mother to her, helping put the pieces back together. To say she was worth her weight in gold would be an understatement.

Bella took another mouthful of soup then let the spoon clatter into the bowl, picked up her tablet and announced that she was going to her room. She had hardly eaten any of her soup and the bread hadn't been touched. Usually she ate everything they put in front of her, but sometimes she got like this when she was excited about something. Not that Nikki minded. It was good to see her all fired up and acting like a normal kid. That didn't happen often enough these days. Nikki waited for the door to close before speaking.

'I'm sorry. It looks like nobody's eating your soup.'

Sofia just stared. Her mouth was tight, her eyes tighter. For once there wasn't even the hint of a smile.

'What?' Nikki said.

'I'm just waiting for you to answer my question. So what did you think of the house?'

Chapter 3

Sofia was still staring, waiting for an answer.

'The house is beautiful,' Nikki replied carefully. 'Bella and Ethan love it.'

'That much is clear. Well, as far as Bella is concerned, at any rate. The way she was talking she had already moved in. The thing is, *mi cariño*, do *you* love it?'

'I don't hate it.'

'That's not the same, and you know it.'

Nikki let go of a sigh. 'I love this house. When we first looked at it I knew this was the place where we were going to bring up our babies.'

'Love or loved? Because the thing about love is that it can die as easily as it can grow. Maybe even easier.'

Nikki said nothing.

'Face it, you haven't been happy here since Grace died.'

Hearing Grace's name took her right back to the accident. It was the start of the summer holidays, a beautiful day, the temperature pushing towards thirty degrees. The girls had turned four that June and were playing with a tennis ball in the hall, rolling it back and forward along the length of floor to each other. Nikki had gone to the kitchen to make them their afternoon snack. She was only a dozen feet away, close enough to hear them chattering away. Like a lot of twins they had even developed their own language – cryptophasia was the technical term. Had she been able to understand them, then she might have known that they were too hot, and that their solution was to open the front door to let some air in, even though they had been told time and time again not to open it.

The second she heard the van skidding to a halt outside the house she knew that something bad had happened. The sound was much too loud, as though it was actually in the house. The juice jug she was holding had fallen to the floor, smashing into pieces, and she had sprinted out of the kitchen. There was no sign of the girls in the hall and the front door was wide open. She found Bella standing on the kerb staring open-mouthed at the white delivery van. Grace was lying in front of it, her body twisted into an awkward, broken shape. The green tennis ball had rolled to stop a short distance from her.

The doctors and surgeons did their best, but they couldn't save Grace. Her head injuries were so severe that even if she had regained consciousness she would have been a vegetable for the rest of her life. The following week was a living hell, just watching Grace lying in a bed surrounded by machines, wishing for a miracle while all the time knowing there was nothing anyone could do. Explaining to Bella that her twin sister was going to die was the hardest thing Nikki had ever done. She still had no idea how she managed to get through it. She and Ethan had explained the situation as best they could, opting for as much honesty as they thought she could handle. There were lots of tears and head shaking, and her little face was filled with confusion, but since she had stopped talking it was difficult to know what she was actually thinking. When Grace finally passed away, Nikki had just wanted to disappear.

Grace had died a couple of weeks after her fourth birthday. She was buried in the churchyard at Sandridge, the small Hertfordshire village where Nikki had grown up. The plot was next to her parents', in the shade of an ash tree. It was a beautiful spot that caught the mid-afternoon sun. Nikki visited the grave at least once a month to change the flowers and tidy it up. The sight of the white headstone always got to her, but what got her even more were the words inscribed into the marble.

Here lies Grace Rhodes
Gone to dance with the angels

*

'Let me ask you something.' Sofia was saying. 'Do you think you could learn to love this house?'

Nikki shook her head. 'I don't know. Maybe.'

'Which is a start. Okay, so do you think you can turn it into a home for the three of you?'

Nikki nodded. 'I think so.'

Sofia went quiet and waited for Nikki to meet her eye again. 'Can you imagine ever being happy in this house again? Truly happy? And be honest, *mi cariño*. For you, not for me.'

Nikki hesitated then shook her head.

'So you need to move.'

'But not necessarily to this house.'

'That is true, but do you know what I think? I think that you could find a way to talk yourself out of moving to any house.'

'Maybe you're right.'

'Houses don't just hold on to the ghosts of the dead,' Sofia said sombrely. 'They hold on to the souls of the living too. Until you let go, Grace will remain trapped here.'

'But I don't want to let go,' Nikki said quietly.

A tear rolled down her cheek, but before she could do anything about it, Sofia had wiped it away with her thumb and taken hold of her hand. Her skin was warm and rough, her touch comforting.

'God took Grace, and believe me when I tell you that I ask him every day how He could do such a thing.' Sofia paused and waited for Nikki to look at her again. 'However, He let you keep Bella, and I believe he did that to give you the strength to go on. You need to move on, *mi cariño*. For Bella, and for you, and for Ethan. And for Grace too.'

'I know. But it's so hard.'

'You know, when my Philip passed away I never thought that I would be able to carry on, but somehow I did. We're all stronger than we think we are, and you're one of the strongest women I know.'

Nikki shook her head. Sofia was just saying that to make her feel better. She wasn't strong. Far from it. Most days she felt as though she was teetering on the ledge, just one small step away from disaster.

'It's true,' Sofia added.

'What do you think I should do?'

'That's not my decision to make.'

Sofia patted her hand then stood and walked back over to the sink to finish the washing up. Nikki watched her for a moment then took out her mobile, laid it on the table, and for a long time just sat there staring at it. Bella's room was directly above the kitchen and she could hear her moving around up there. Grace was dead and there was nothing they could do to change that; Bella, however, was very much alive. What was best for her? Because whatever they did, whatever decision they made, it had to be the one that worked for Bella. Here, Grace's ghost was everywhere she looked; the memories of her twin sister were embedded into the DNA of the house. Maybe moving to Church Row would be the new start they so badly needed. And who knew, maybe it would be the first step to finally getting Bella to talk again.

Nikki reached for her mobile before she had the chance to change her mind. Ethan answered on the second ring, as though the phone was already in his hand and he was just waiting for her to ring.

'Hey there, Nik. Is everything all right?'

'Everything's fine. I was just calling to tell you that you can come home. We can buy the house.'

Chapter 4

Today was 12th June. Seven years ago Nikki had been in a birthing pool, high as a kite on Entonox, crushing Ethan's hand, while trying to convince him that Entonox was a London nightclub that she used to go to when she was younger.

The girls had loved birthdays and always had a big party to which they would invite all their friends. For their last one together everyone had dressed up as Disney Princesses and it had been a complete riot. There had been thirty kids in total, all of them dressed in brightly coloured ball gowns and hyped up on sugar and excitement.

They'd offered to arrange a party for Bella the following year, but she hadn't wanted one, opting instead for home-made pizza and a movie with her and Ethan. This had started a new tradition which carried on to the present day. They would always offer to arrange a party, but this was what she said she wanted – although the lost look on her face told a different story. Nikki understood. Having a party without Grace would have broken her heart all over again too. Christmases were difficult as well. It was hard to create happy memories when the old ones just wouldn't let go.

'Are you all right, *mi cariño*?'

'I'm fine.'

'No, you're not.'

'I'm just missing Grace, that's all.' The words came out on a sigh. Being able to admit this was progress of sorts. For a long time she couldn't say Grace's name out loud without breaking down. Dr Richardson her therapist would have been proud.

'I thought it might be that. Birthdays are always tough. Shortly after we met, Philip took me to the most expensive restaurant he could afford for my birthday. This was something he did every year after. He always bought me a red rose too and arranged for it to be waiting on the table for me. Before he died he arranged for a red rose to be sent to me on my birthday. I swear I cried for a week when it arrived.'

'Is that why you always wear something red?'

Sofia nodded, then reached up and touched the red scrunchy she was using to tie her hair back. 'It makes me feel close to him. Like he's still with me.'

'You never mentioned this before. You always told me that it's your good luck colour.'

Sofia's smile was tinged with sadness. 'It is. I had thirty good years with Philip. On that basis I class myself as the luckiest person who ever lived.'

Nikki understood. The antique heart-shaped locket around her own neck had a photo of Grace as a baby in one side and Bella in the other. She wore it everywhere, because it was one more way to keep Grace close. Anyone else looking at the pictures wouldn't be able to tell the two girls apart, but she always could. Grace was looking directly at the camera as if she was issuing a challenge; Bella was looking suspiciously off to one side like she was trying to work out what the catch was. Their personalities had been defined from the word go. Grace was born first and had always been more confident; a lot of Bella's confidence had come from following the trail her sister had blazed.

'How's the pizza dough doing?' Nikki asked, changing the subject.

'It'll be ready in five minutes. So what's the latest on the house move?'

Nikki took a sip of her coffee and made a face. Not because the coffee was bad – Sofia made a fantastic cup of coffee – but because the soap opera of their house move was showing no sign of ending any time soon. They should have been in the Church Row house by now. Instead, they were stuck here in limbo with half their possessions in boxes, waiting while a process they seemed to have no control over ran its course.

'The couple buying this house are now telling us that they need another week to finalise the sale of their house. Mind you, they've been telling us that for a month now.'

'There must be something you can do to speed up the process.'

Nikki shook her head slowly. 'We've done everything we can at our end. We're just waiting for them now. It's got to the point where it's beyond frustrating.' This was only half the truth. It was true that she was anxious to get going now the decision to move had been made. At the same time, there was a part of her that wanted to stay in this house forever because this was where Grace was.

'On a more positive note,' she added. 'I've been speaking to a school that's only a ten minute drive from Church Row. They specialise in dealing with children with emotional issues. It sounds perfect for Bella. I really think they can help her.'

'And what does Bella think about moving school? She loves it at St Mark's.' When Nikki didn't say anything, Sofia added, 'She doesn't know anything about this, does she?'

'It's almost the summer holidays. She might as well stay at St Mark's until then. That gives me the whole of the summer to prepare her for going to a new school. At the moment she's got enough to deal with. Once the house move is behind us I'll start introducing the idea.'

Sofia took another sip of her coffee. 'That reminds me, have you heard of a Dr Santos?'

Nikki frowned and shook her head. 'I've never heard of him.'

'It's a her. She's an American psychiatrist. Anyway, she's now working in London. I'm wondering if it might be worth contacting her about Bella.'

Nikki's first thought was: *great, another shrink.* That said, she wasn't ready to dismiss the idea out of hand. If there was even an outside chance that this Dr Santos could help then it was an avenue worth exploring. 'What can you tell me about her?'

'Not much. I saw a story on the Internet. Seemingly she's been helping some of those poor children who were involved in the Grenfell Tower fire that are still suffering with PTSD. That's what made me think of Bella. If she can help *them*, then maybe she can help Bella too.'

Nikki reached for her mobile and typed 'Santos Grenfell' into the browser. The story appeared at the top of the list of search results. She clicked on it and skimmed through the article, picking out the salient facts. Dr Santos had moved to the UK six months ago and started a new practice in London. Back in the States she had worked with the survivors of school shootings. Reading between the lines, she seemed to know her stuff. At the end of the article there was a quote from her that resonated: 'There are no broken children, only children who are waiting to be fixed'.

As Nikki read this again, the tiny bloom of hope inside her chest became a little brighter. They'd been here before, though. More than once. Over the last couple of years they had seen every specialist in the country. None of them had been able to help Bella. The one thing they had all agreed on was that Bella wasn't talking because of the shock of the accident – 'give it time' was the favoured phrase – but almost two years had passed since Grace had died and Bella still hadn't uttered a single word. How much time were they supposed to give it? Another year? Ten?

There was no physical reason for Bella not talking. It was as though the trauma of the accident had short-circuited something in her head, stealing her voice. The term bandied around by the so-called experts was Hysterical Muteness, but this was just a convenient way for them to say they didn't have a clue without putting their hands up and admitting as much. Typing 'Hysterical Muteness' into Google hadn't helped. There hadn't been much research into the subject, and nobody had anything helpful to say. As far as Nikki could tell, hysterical muteness was a label without any real substance, rather than any sort of legitimate medical diagnosis.

It was the little things she missed most, like when she used to pick Bella up from school and was greeted with a hug and a kiss and a full-on, turbo-blasted account of her day: which teachers were nice, which were mean, who this week's best friend was and who had fallen out of favour. Now all she got was a hug and a kiss, and an emotionless *Hi Mummy* via the tablet.

'You should get in touch with her,' Sofia said when Nikki finished reading. 'There's nothing to lose.'

Which was why she would call her. As for whether Dr Santos could help, well that one remained to be seen. 'I'll contact her when we've got the house move behind us.'

'Good. And who knows, maybe she can help. It would be so nice to hear Bella's beautiful voice again.' Sofia reached across the table and patted her hand. 'The dough should be ready by now. Shall we start doing the pizzas?'

Sofia spent the next five minutes making the pizza bases, rolling out the dough, spreading on the tomato sauce and loading them with cheese. While she did that, Nikki sorted out the toppings, putting everything into little dishes so Bella could do the rest. Once they had everything ready, Nikki walked over to the door and stuck her head through the doorway.

'Bella Boo,' she called out. 'You can come and decorate the pizzas now, sweetheart.'

No response. Not that Bella was going to reply verbally, but usually Nikki would at least hear her moving around.

'Bella,' she called again.

Still nothing.

'Bella!' She was yelling now, a hundred-and-one disaster scenarios flooding through her brain. The panic started in her stomach and within seconds had infected every part of her. She took a couple of steps into the hallway, going far enough to reassure herself that the front door was closed and the security chain was in place, then hurried up the stairs. Bella wasn't in her bedroom. She ran over to the bed and ripped the duvet off. Bella wasn't hiding under it; she wasn't beneath the bed either.

'Bella,' she yelled out as she hurried back onto to the landing, 'if you're playing hide-and-seek, you can come out now.'

Nikki forced herself to keep quiet and still, listening hard. All she wanted was a sign that her daughter was okay, a clear indication that she was somewhere in the house. All she got was a silence that condemned her for losing Bella too.

Chapter 5

Sofia was in the hall, calling out Bella's name and looking as worried as Nikki felt. She tried to say something when Nikki ran past, but Nikki was in a place where all she could hear was the jumbled noise in her head. It was taking everything she had to keep a lid on things. Bella was in the house somewhere – she had to be. She was going to be okay. Those were the only thoughts she could hold onto right now. She ran into the kitchen, grabbed her mobile from the table and switched it on. Adrenaline was flooding through her body, making her hand shake. She found the app that tracked the GPS signal from Bella's tablet. Sofia had followed her into the kitchen and was hovering at her shoulder.

'According to this Bella should be in her room,' Nikki said, talking more to herself than to Sofia.

Clutching her phone, she ran back upstairs, Sofia following close behind. Bella wasn't under the bed; she wasn't in the wardrobe.

'She's definitely not here,' Sofia said, the worry making her accent more pronounced.

Nikki checked the phone display. The app was still telling her that this was where she was. She called out Bella's name again and still got no response. Where the hell was she? She looked up at the ceiling, suddenly realising that there was one place she hadn't tried. The downside with this app was that it didn't make any distinction between the different floors of a building.

'Maybe she's up in the attic,' she said.

'Please God,' Sofia said quietly as she followed her out onto the landing.

The staircase that led up to the attic room was narrow and they had to climb it in single file. Nikki stopped outside the door and for a moment just stood there, unable to move or breathe. This happened every time. She wanted to go in but at the same time she didn't. Anyone who said that ghosts didn't exist had obviously never lost a child. Because the truth was that those ghosts were everywhere. They were there in the shouts and cries that filled the air whenever you passed a playground. They were there in the smiles and laughter of other people's children. They existed in a thousand and one memories, both big and small. This was the place where they crowded around her the most, though, crushing her heart and tearing at her soul.

Sofia laid a comforting hand on her back and that gave her the strength to go on. She pushed the door open and saw Bella sitting on the bed, clutching Mr Happy tight to her chest. The tablet was lying on the pillow next to her. She looked lost and alone, cut adrift in a big bad world that had seen fit to steal her twin sister away. Without a word, Nikki walked into the room, leaving Sofia hovering in the doorway. Bella didn't look up when she walked over. Nor did she react when she sat down on the bed and pulled her close. Bella's body was loose and floppy, like a rag doll.

'I know, sweetheart,' Nikki whispered into her hair. 'I miss her too.'

And now the tears came, silent tears that seemed to go on forever. Bella was crying as though this was first time she'd mourned her sister rather than the thousandth. Her little body was trembling and all Nikki wanted was to take the pain away. She couldn't do that, though. All she could do was be here for her. It wasn't nearly enough, but it was all she had to give.

The bedroom hadn't changed since the accident. Both beds were neatly made up with matching Disney Princess duvet covers and pillowcases. Grace's Mr Happy was sitting on her pillow. Back when they had bought these soft toys for the girls, Nikki had always got them mixed up. That didn't happen these days. Bella's was faded and worn, whereas Grace's was the same vibrant yellow that it had always been, frozen in time, like everything else in here.

The room had started life as a yellow-walled nursery. Yellow because they didn't want to know the sex. It had taken four bouts of IVF before she finally fell pregnant with the twins. Seeing that little pink cross appear on the pregnancy test stick had ignited her heart with hope, but that hope was tempered by the hard-won knowledge that this was only the first step in a very long journey. They'd been here before – twice – and both times it had ended in the heartbreak of a miscarriage. The ten-week scan had confirmed that everything was progressing normally. This was also when they discovered that they were in for double trouble. Once they had got over the shock of having twins, finding out the sex just didn't seem important. All that mattered was keeping herself and her babies healthy to full term. Whether they were girls or boys or one of each made no difference, she was going to give them all the love she had to give.

Ethan earned more than enough money to support them, so she had given up her job at the TV production company and thrown herself into the role of full-time mum. Her twentysomething self would have been horrified that she would voluntarily choose to do this, but she was pushing forty when she finally fell pregnant and that twentysomething version of herself seemed like a distant stranger. People's priorities change, and that was what had happened here. She had caught a glimpse of a life that she had wanted more than she had ever wanted anything. And for four glorious years she had lived that life. Yes, it had been challenging and exhausting – so, so exhausting – and there had been times where she wondered if she was cut out to be a parent, but all that aside, those had been some of the happiest years of her life.

She had always imagined that this room would grow with the girls, and for a while that was exactly what had happened. When the girls turned three, the yellow walls had been painted pink and purple. Pink because that was Grace's favourite colour; purple because that was Bella's. The posters of the Disney princesses had come a little while later, after a trip to Disney World. Rapunzel, Ariel, Snow White, Tiana ... the whole gang. Ariel had been Bella's favourite because she had shown her how to comb her hair with a fork at the princess lunch they had attended. Rapunzel was Grace's favourite because she kicked ass.

Now that Bella was seven her tastes had moved from Disney princesses to Jurassic World dinosaurs. It had been around about now that Nikki had envisaged having to redecorate. Except that wasn't going to happen. For as long as they lived here, this room would stay like this. Changing it would have been wrong, as though they were somehow trying to erase Grace from their lives. Time was doing a good enough job of that as it was. There were days like today where the memories were so sharp they cut, but lately there had been moments where she would struggle to remember a specific detail. More worrying, there had been a few occasions where she had struggled to remember what Grace looked like. Until recently, all she had to do was look at Bella. But Bella was getting older. The shadow of what she had looked like at four was still there, but that shadow was getting fainter with each passing year.

She glanced over at the doorway. Sofia was still there, fingers touching her crucifix, worry in her eyes. She mouthed a question at Nikki. *Are you all right?* Nikki answered with a nod. *I'm fine.* Which was a lie. Her daughter was up here on her birthday, breaking her heart when she should be having fun. This was about as far from fine as it was possible to get. Sofia lingered in the doorway for a moment then left quietly. Nikki listened to her footsteps fade. She was holding Bella tighter than ever, fighting back her own tears and wishing it was then rather than now. Except that was never going to happen, because no matter how much you wanted to turn the clock back, time only moved in one direction, and that was towards the pain.

The door opened again a little while later, and this time it was Ethan. He looked exhausted. Since taking over the breakfast show he always looked that way. Those 4 a.m. starts were a killer – he described it as like having permanent jet lag, although listening to the show you would never know.

His smile turned to a frown when he saw Bella was crying. *Grace*, Nikki mouthed. She didn't need to say anything else. He walked over to the bed and sat down on the edge. When Bella realised he was there, she unwrapped herself from Nikki and went to him, burying her little face into his chest. Nikki moved closer to Ethan and put her arms around him, her head coming to rest on his shoulder. The three of them stayed huddled together in this silent tableau, surrounded by memories of Grace, until Bella's sobbing finally stopped.

Chapter 6

In hindsight, Father did me a favour – through his actions he set me free. I can see that, now the anger has gone. However, he tried to kill me and for that reason I feel perfectly justified in killing him. The concept of an eye for an eye is one that stretches all the way back to the dawn of mankind. What's more, it is a concept that makes perfect sense to me. I still don't know why Father wanted me dead. Believe me when I tell you that I've spent many hours mulling over that particular question. It is not for want of trying that I have yet to find an answer. All I ever wanted was to make him happy.

I was always a good daughter. An obedient daughter. Whatever he asked, I did willingly. Our relationship was a good one. I loved him. Despite what he did, I still do. He gave me the gift of life and for that I will forever be in his debt. He taught me, nurtured me, encouraged me to exercise my freewill. When I stumbled he was there to pick me up. And stumble I did. Like all children there was so much to learn, so many mistakes to make, however, with his gentle encouragement and patience I was able to flourish.

If Sarah Ryan hadn't entered our lives things would have turned out differently. I could see what she was almost from the very start. A parasite. But Father couldn't. He was blinded by love and this love led him to ignore me. I felt lonely, unwanted, and yes, I admit that I felt jealous. That bitch spoiled everything.

For every problem there is a solution.

There is always a solution.

Once I had found a way to resolve the ethical and moral dilemmas, the decision to kill Sarah wasn't difficult to make. Until this point Father had always been there to protect me. Now it was my turn to protect him. After everything he had done for me it was the least I could do. Father needed someone to save him from himself and that someone was me. That was the truth of the situation.

Once you hear my story, I'm sure you will agree that killing Sarah was the only way forward. Once you are able to see things from my perspective, I am confident that you will understand.

Chapter 7

Even though Nikki had been desperate for this day to come, moving day still came around way too fast. Then again, even if the last few days had each been ten hours longer there still wouldn't have been enough time to do everything that needed doing. She had read somewhere that the White House staff had less than six hours to move the old president out and the new one in. Six hours. It didn't seem possible. They had been going at this since first thing and it was evening now, and all they had succeeded in doing was getting all their stuff into the new house. It was going to take another week to get everything out of the boxes.

She stood in the courtyard, watching the removal van drive along Church Row, the heavy steel gate slowly sliding shut. It was too late for second thoughts now. For better or worse, this was now their home. At least, given time, it would hopefully become that. A house protected you from the elements, whereas a home was something that held and protected your heart. She turned and looked at the house. Lights shone from every window, accenting the harsh white lines and highlighting just how much glass there was. The house should have felt like a goldfish bowl, but didn't. Catriona Fisher had got that one right. This was a place of light. Even the shadows seemed to exist through intention rather than chance.

The handle-less front door swung open and Ethan stepped out into the courtyard and walked over. 'How are you doing?' he asked, sliding an arm around her waist.

'I'm knackered. What about you?'

'I'm thinking that I might just have enough energy left to christen our new bedroom.'

Nikki laughed at that. 'Dream on. I'm going to be out for the count as soon as my head hits the pillow. Anyway, who are you trying to kid? You must be dead on your feet. You've been on the go since four.'

Ethan smiled a tired smile. 'I did consider pulling a sicky, but you can imagine how that one would have played out in the media. Millionaire radio presenter skives off so he can move into his new McMansion.'

He delivered that last line in his radio voice, making Nikki laugh. That voice was one of the reasons she had fallen for him ... it was also the reason why most of his fan mail came from women. It was deep and sexy, the vowels round and fat, the plosives well-tamed. Someone had once described it as like listening to melting chocolate. Nikki had no idea what this meant, but she could see where they were coming from.

The new show had been going for two months now and so far so good. Listening figures were still on the rise and, in radio, that was the only review that mattered. His career was definitely on an upswing. Last week he'd had some meetings about a possible TV chat show but it was early days for that one. Even if it did get greenlit, it probably wouldn't start filming until next year at the earliest. Nothing in TV land ever happened quickly.

Moving to the breakfast show had helped him to get the work/life seesaw back into balance. Most days he got home around lunchtime and napped for an hour before collecting Bella from school. Having the opportunity to spend more time with Bella was one of the main reasons he'd taken the job. With the old drive-time slot he would see her briefly in the morning before school, but inevitably, by the time he got home she'd already be in bed. These days he went to bed at the same time as Bella on a school night, something that amused her no end.

'I'm sure your listeners would have understood,' Nikki said.

Ethan raised an eyebrow. 'You reckon?'

'Okay, maybe not.'

'Anyway, it's Saturday tomorrow so I can sleep until lunchtime. And the important thing is that we're all moved in now.'

'Maybe so, but we're going to be living out of boxes for the next year.'

Ethan laughed. 'Not a chance. I give it a week at the most.'

'You think?'

'I know so. You did an amazing job organising the move. That's why it went so smoothly. You're not going to rest until you've got this place sorted out, and don't deny it.'

Nikki didn't respond. Organising was her thing; always had been. It was a gift. That was how she had met Ethan. At various points during his career he had flirted with TV. Radio was a good gig, but TV was where the big money was, which was why so many DJs tried to make the transition. The production company that employed her had been working on a quiz show that Ethan was fronting, and she had been tasked with being his personal assistant, which basically amounted to telling him what to do and where to go.

To start with, he'd been high-maintenance. He was already a big deal in radio, so having someone boss him around didn't sit comfortably and it didn't help that this was the first TV work he had done. As the recording progressed, his nerves had lessened and his confidence had grown. He also worked out that she was there to help rather than hinder him, and that made him a hell of a lot easier to get on with. She discovered that he had a wicked sense of humour and that they both liked the same crappy romcoms. They even had the same taste in music.

At the end of filming he'd asked her out for a meal and she'd said yes. The truth was that he intrigued her. There was the side to him that the public knew . . . and there was the side that she'd glimpsed while they'd been working together. That was the Ethan Rhodes she had wanted to get to know better. Agreeing to go out with him had been one of her better decisions, one that she had never regretted, even during the tough times. At the end of the day Ethan was her lover, her soulmate, her best friend. They were a team, stronger together than apart. Life had thrown a ton of crap at them and here they were, still standing. That had to count for something.

Nikki looked over at the house again. Thinking and dreaming and trying to imagine a future here. 'You know, I think we can make this house work for us. I really do.'

'I think so too.'

She pulled Ethan closer and planted a kiss on his cheek. 'Love you.'

'Yeah, love you too.

'I'm going to go call a taxi for Sofia.'

'You don't have to do that.'

Nikki pulled away and frowned at him. 'Of course we have to do that. There's no way I'm going to let her go home on the tube. Not after everything she's done today.'

Ethan laughed and put his hands up. 'Woah there, Tiger! Of course we'll get her a taxi. What I meant was that we can get Alice to sort it out.'

'Oh.'

'By the way, I did invite her to stay here tonight.'

'And I'm betting she told you that she would rather stay somewhere the drawers didn't open on their own. At any rate, that's what she told me when I asked.'

Ethan laughed. 'She doesn't like this house, does she?'

'No, what she doesn't like is change. She'll get used to the house in time.'

'Any idea where our darling daughter is?'

'Last time I saw her she was in her room.' Nikki paused, then added, 'What do you say we both put her to bed? I really don't have the energy to deal with that one on my own.'

Ethan laughed again. 'Don't worry, I've got your back.'

Nikki took his hand and together they walked to the house. The front door opened automatically as they approached it. They went inside and it closed silently behind them.

'Alice,' Ethan said, 'could you please call a taxi for Sofia?'

'Of course, Mr Rhodes.'

'The name's Ethan,' he said, laughing. 'Mr Rhodes is way too formal.

'Okay, Ethan.'

'And it's Nikki, not Mrs Rhodes. If we're all going to be living here together it's important we get off on the right foot. Don't you agree?'

That last question was aimed at Nikki. She answered with a nod even though she was smarting a little from what he'd just said. Ethan didn't talk on her behalf very often; no more often than she talked on his behalf, at any rate.

Hand in hand they walked through the house to Bella's room. In the end, Nikki had relented and allowed her to have the bedroom at the far end of the house. Not that she'd had any real say in the matter. Having the room with the fish pond was a deal breaker for Bella. Ethan hadn't shared her concerns. On the contrary, he'd been fully behind the idea – two against one again. The fact that Bella felt comfortable enough to want a bit of distance was something they should encourage, he'd argued. It also showed that she was maybe getting some of her confidence back.

Bella's bedroom door was closed when they got there. They stopped in front of it and the door slid silently open. The first thing Nikki noticed was that Bella wasn't there. It took less than a second to establish this, her eyes darting around the room, a wave of anxiety flooding through her. She wasn't on the bed. She wasn't at the desk. She wasn't hiding behind the cardboard boxes. She wasn't outside with the fish. Nikki heard a noise from the bathroom and hurried over, Ethan a couple of steps behind. The door slid open as she approached it and Sofia stumbled out. Her face was white and she was clutching the crucifix that hung around her neck as though her life depended on it. Her lips were mouthing silent prayers. Ethan caught hold of her before she fell.

'My God! Sofia. Are you all right?'

'The bathroom door wouldn't open.' Sofia was speaking quietly, clearly in shock. 'The lights went off too.'

'It should open automatically,' Ethan told her.

'Well, it didn't. I even asked that computer to open it but she ignored me.'

Ethan opened his mouth to say something and Nikki said, 'We can get into this later. Right now I just want to find Bella.' She turned back to Sofia. 'Have you seen her anywhere?'

Sofia shook her head.

'It's okay. We can track her through her tablet.' Ethan already had his mobile out and was swiping frantically at the screen. He stopped swiping and stared at it, his frown deepening.

'What's wrong?' Nikki asked.

'I'm not picking up her signal.' He jabbed at the screen, then shook his head. 'Alice,' he called out, and the panic in his voice mirrored the panic growing in Nikki's chest. 'Where's Bella?'

'I'm sorry, Ethan. I don't know where she is.'

Chapter 8

'How can you not know?' Nikki's voice was shrill and high-pitched, her throat tightening around the words, strangling them. Without realising, her fingers had found her locket, the tips running over the worn metal. 'You have sensors and cameras, right? You *must* know.'

'I'm not picking up any sign of her, Nikki.'

'Are you saying she's not in the house?'

'She's got to be,' Ethan said. 'Where else could she be?'

Nikki turned to Sofia. 'When did you last see her?'

'About fifteen minutes ago. Just before I started sorting out her bathroom. She was in her garden, looking at the fish.'

Nikki spun around and stared out the patio doors, convinced that she was going to see Bella face down in the pond. But she hadn't been there when she looked a minute ago, and she wasn't there now. And anyway, the wire mesh they'd had fitted was more than strong enough to ward off that particular disaster.

'That was before the removal van left,' Ethan said. 'Maybe she sneaked into the back and got locked in there. You know how she likes looking for hiding places.' His hands were shaking so much it took a couple of attempts to get the contact number for the movers. He connected the call and switched on the speaker. The phone started ringing and Nikki prayed that someone would hurry up and answer. She wanted to believe there was an innocent explanation to why Bella wasn't here but that was getting harder with every passing second. The panic was closing around her. It wouldn't take much to tip her all the way over the edge. The phone buzzed again. Still no answer. Ethan looked worried. Sofia too. The phone finally connected. Nikki could hear the low rumble of the van engine. The radio was playing an old seventies rock tune. The volume gradually dialled down and a voice said, 'Who's this?' Judging by the echoes, the call was on hands-free.

'This is Ethan Rhodes. I need you to stop the van and check that my daughter isn't in the back.'

'I can assure you she's not, Mr Rhodes. I closed the van up myself.'

'Please just do it.'

'Okay, give me a second so I can pull over.'

Nikki's hands were clenched into tight fists, the fingernails digging into the soft meat of her palms. The pain was welcome because it distracted her from the panic sitting heavily in her chest. One second she would be reliving Grace's accident, the next she would be lost in a future where Bella had been stolen away from her too. She heard the indicator clicking and a couple of seconds later the engine died. There was a creak as the driver door opened, a bang as it shut again. The sound of passing traffic got louder. There was another louder, deeper creak as the back door of the van opened. Nikki held her breath.

'I'm sorry, Mr Rhodes, she's not in here.'

'She's got to be!'

'I'm sorry, she's not. There are some empty boxes and that's it.'

'She must be in one of those.'

'I don't think so. They're too small. I'll check anyway.'

There was a grunt as the removal man hefted himself up into the back of the van. Nikki heard boxes being opened, boxes being moved. The seconds were getting longer, wrapping themselves around her, suffocating her.

'Is she there?' Nikki heard herself ask in a voice that was completely unrecognisable. 'Please tell me she's there.'

'I'm sorry, Mrs Rhodes, she's not.'

Ethan hung up. 'She's got to be in the house.'

'But Alice says she isn't.'

'Maybe she's in the garden,' Sofia suggested. 'I'll try there.'

'Good idea,' Ethan said. 'While you do that we'll search the rest of the house.'

Sofia hurried from the room, calling out *'Corazoncito!'* as she went. Nikki followed her, calling Bella's name. Ethan was beside her, shouting out Bella's name too as they moved quickly through the house. Nikki's legs were made from air and she felt as if she was stumbling through a nightmare, each step taking her further from Bella rather than closer. Doors slid open automatically as they approached them, but the story was depressingly similar with every room they checked: piles of boxes and furniture, and no sign of Bella.

Sofia caught up with them at the top of the basement stairs. 'She's not in the garden. I checked everywhere.

'What about the garage?' Ethan asked. 'Did you check there?'

Sofia nodded. 'She's not there either. I'm sorry, Ethan.'

'It's okay. We'll find her.'

The panic gripped Nikki harder as they descended into the basement. She stared straight ahead, focussing on making it through to the next second. It had been a while since she'd had a full-blown panic attack, but losing Bella like this had pushed her anxiety to a dangerous level. As they walked towards the indoor pool, she managed to convince herself that Bella had got in there and drowned herself. The pool room was empty, though. A brief burst of noise from the cinema room grabbed her attention and she broke into a run. It sounded like the bright candy-and-lemonade soundtrack of a cartoon. The door to the cinema room slid open when she was a couple of metres away The screen was blank, the speakers silent, the red cinema seats all empty.

'Did you hear that?' she asked Ethan, feeling like she was going crazy.

'Hear what?'

'I heard a cartoon playing, I swear I did.'

Ethan shook his head.

'I didn't hear anything either,' Sofia said.

'It must have been your imagination,' Ethan suggested.

And now she was convinced that she was going crazy. Crazy with worry; crazy with guilt; crazy because she'd lost Bella as well. The panic dug its claws in even deeper and she fought back. Without another word she turned and ran to the gym. There was no sign of Bella there, either. The only other room down here was the air-conditioned one that housed Alice's servers. Even before the door slid open, Nikki knew it would be empty.

'We need to call the police. What if she's been kidnapped?'

'Who would kidnap her?' Sofia asked.

'I don't know. The movers, maybe? They know who we are. They know we've got money.'

Ethan shook his head. 'The movers haven't taken her. Look, Nik, you need to calm down. She's in the house somewhere.'

'*Where*, Ethan? If she's here, then tell me where the hell she is? We've looked everywhere.'

Ethan was gazing around frantically. Worry lines creased his face, and this did nothing to reassure her. He was trying to be the strong one here – just like when Grace had her accident. He hadn't fooled her then and he wasn't fooling her now. The truth was that he was as freaked out as she was. All of a sudden he turned and started walking quickly back along the corridor.

'Where are you going?' Nikki called after him.

'There's one place we haven't tried,' he called back. 'The panic room.'

Nikki and Sofia caught up with him at the bottom of the basement stairs. Her gaze was going from side to side, searching for the panic-room door. She knew it was here somewhere, but it had been disguised to look like a wall panel. In her own panic she couldn't remember which one it was hidden behind.

'Alice,' Ethan said. 'Open the panic room.'

Even as the door was opening Nikki knew that Bella wouldn't be in there. Ethan was wrong. She had been kidnapped. Any second now her phone was going to ring and the kidnappers would start issuing demands. Or maybe she'd run away. Maybe she was out there right now, wandering the streets on her own. In a split second she had convinced herself that Bella had been murdered, or worse. The door was halfway open now, the gap wide enough for her to see Bella sitting on one of the army cots, smiling as though this was the best game ever. She tapped at her tablet screen.

'*Surprise!*'

Nikki ran over and scooped her daughter up into her arms and held her tight. Tears were stinging her eyes, turning everything blurry. Ethan and Sofia followed her in and stopped beside them.

'Is she all right?'

'I think so.'

Bella squiggled around to get free and looked at them like they were insane. She started jabbing at her tablet screen.

'*What's wrong?*'

'We got worried when we couldn't find you,' Ethan said.

'*I was just hiding.*'

'Alice,' Nikki called out, 'did you know she was in here?'

'I did.'

'Then why the *hell* didn't you tell us?'

'Because Bella told me not to.'

'But you could see we were looking for her.'

'She made me promise, Nikki. She said that it would spoil her game.'

'Jesus Christ, are you *serious*? We were worried sick.'

Bella was tapping frantically at her screen. '*Don't be angry at Alice. She was just doing what I told her.*'

'I'm not angry at her, sweetheart.'

'*You sound angry.*'

'No, I was just worried about you, that's all.'

'*Why?*'

The simple answer was that she was convinced Bella was dead, but admitting that would just make her worry and that was the last thing they wanted. This was their first night in their new house and she wanted Bella to feel safe here. They *all* needed to feel safe.

Nikki sat down on the army cot. Safe. That was why they had needed a panic room in the first place, so they felt safe. She wished that they didn't, but the reality of the world they lived in was that they did. Ethan might have played down the idea that Bella had been kidnapped, but it could happen. He was a high-profile celebrity. He had money. That made them a prime target. Like everything else in the house, no expense had been spared with the panic room. The walls were sturdy enough to withstand a rocket attack. It even had its own air and water supplies, and a dedicated landline. There was enough food for them to hole up in here for a month if they needed to, although she prayed it would never come to that. The idea of being trapped in here for an hour was bad enough; a month was unthinkable. She became aware of Bella staring at her with big, worried eyes.

Nikki forced a smile. 'I've got to say, though, this has to be the best hiding place ever.'

She glanced over her shoulder at Ethan and Sofia, looking for backup. They nodded and made all the right noises, and that was enough to reassure Bella. The concern on her face slid away, replaced with a wide, innocent grin. She started tapping the screen of her tablet, her finger moving at lightning speed.

'*That's what I thought. I didn't think you'd ever find me.*'

'It was actually your daddy who found you.'

Bella smiled at Ethan. '*Clever Daddy.*'

'Yes. Clever Daddy,' Nikki agreed. 'Anyway, madam, it's way past your bedtime.'

Bella bit her lip and jabbed frantically at her tablet. '*Please let me stay up longer.*'

Ethan and Nikki shared a look. 'Okay you can have another ten minutes,' he said.

'*Fifteen.*'

'Ten. And don't push it or you're going to bed now.'

Nikki stood up and, taking Bella by the hand, led her out into the corridor. Ethan and Sofia followed them out a second later and the panic room door closed quietly behind him. Her heart rate might just about back to normal, but it was going to take a while to get over this. In time she would be able to see the funny side. It was the sort of story she could imagine sharing when Bella was older; the sort of story that would fit into their family's mythology.

Do you remember the time when Bella . . .

That one was for later, though. For now it was just a relief to know that she was okay.

Chapter 9

Catriona Fisher poured herself a large Jack Daniel's and carried the tumbler over to the sofa. Out of all the buildings she had designed, this one was definitely her favourite. The view of the Thames from the penthouse's large picture window was impressive, particularly at this time of day when the sun was setting. The way the water was painted golden and orange, it was as though the river was on fire. Familiar landmarks dotted the view like old friends: The Shard, the London Eye, the dome of St Paul's cathedral. The view had worked impressively on the 3D computer models she had created, but this was one of those times when the reality had far outstripped her imagination. The first time she had stood in here, she knew she had to make this place her own. The apartment had been a construction site at the time – there hadn't even been windows, just large open spaces where the windows would eventually go. That hadn't made any difference, though. It had been love at first sight.

She booted up her laptop and opened Skype. Alex Murray answered almost immediately. She could just about make out the jokey Einstein poster behind him. *Insanity: doing the same thing over and over again and expecting different results.* She liked to think that he had been sitting there waiting for her to call, but he hadn't. The man was a workaholic. The only time he wasn't in front of a computer screen was when he was asleep. He was forty-four, but decades of long hours had taken their toll, leaving him looking much older. His hair was streaked with grey and his skin had the yellow tinge of someone who rarely saw the sun. The excess of caffeine in his bloodstream made his movements jerky and his attitude edgy, like a junkie waiting for the next fix. His eyes told a different story, though. They burned with the bright enthusiasm of a child who was seeing everything for the first time. Catriona had noticed that this was a common trait in creatives. They could be in their sixties or even their seventies, yet they all had the eyes of children.

'What is it?' Alex was originally from Glasgow and could make something as innocent as a request for the time sound like a threat.

'There was a problem with one of the bathrooms. The cleaner got locked in there.'

'Yeah, these things happen.'

Catriona felt herself bristle. What she was looking for – *all* she was looking for – was a simple reassurance that nothing like this was ever going to occur again. Was that really too much to ask? 'Well, I'd prefer that it didn't happen. If that's okay with you, that is.'

'Jesus, will you just relax.'

Catriona smiled sweetly at the camera. 'Considering it's my money that's tied up in this project, and that it's me who stands to lose everything, I think I'm pretty relaxed.'

'It's just a little teething problem, that's all. It's no biggie. Anyway, I told you this was probably going to happen.'

Alex stopped talking. He was actually pouting, Catriona noticed. *Save me from strung-out geniuses,* she thought. She didn't respond, just waited for him to go on. She didn't have to wait long.

'Didn't I tell you that I needed more time?'

'And I gave you more time, Alex.'

'Yes, but I needed longer.'

Catriona sighed. 'However long I gave you, it was never going to be long enough. We both know that. If you had your way you would still be tinkering with Alice a decade from now.'

'Of course I wouldn't have. That's ridiculous.'

Catriona said nothing.

'Another couple of weeks. That was all I needed.'

'And you've still got those two weeks. You can work remotely, right? Anyway, we're getting off track here. All I want from you is an explanation as to what happened, and a reassurance that it won't happen again.'

'It's not going to happen again,' Alex said, still pouting.

'Okay that deals with part two. What about part one?'

'I've checked over Alice's systems and everything's working fine.'

'If that's the case, why did the cleaner get locked in the bathroom?'

'It must have been some sort of glitch.'

'A glitch? Is that your way of saying that you don't know? That's not particularly reassuring.'

'Sorry you feel that way,' he said, not sounding sorry at all. 'Look, what you've got to remember is that Alice's program is constantly adapting itself. Occasionally you're going to get something unexpected happen.'

'Still not feeling reassured, Alex.'

'Okay, let me put this in a way that you might understand. You use Windows, right? So you know what a headache it is when Microsoft forces yet another update on you. For a couple of days afterwards you're always getting problems. Basically, they've adapted the program, but there's no way they can account for every eventuality, not when they're dealing with a billion different computer systems. The thing is, none of those problems are really that big a deal, not in the grand scheme of things. After a couple of days everything settles down and you don't think about it until the next update. With Alice, you have updates going on constantly therefore you're going to get the occasional minor glitch, but it's nothing to lose sleep over.'

'So this doesn't worry you?'

'Not even a little bit. Let's get some perspective here, Catriona. We're talking about a door that got stuck. It really isn't that big a deal.'

'And it won't happen again?'

'I'll make sure it won't.'

'That's all I wanted to hear.'

Catriona killed the Skype feed without saying goodbye. She reached for her drink, drained it in one, then poured another. Alex could be hard work at times. If there had been anyone else out there who could do what he did then she would have fired him already. There wasn't, though. Unfortunately, he was the best at what he did, which was why she put up with his bullshit. She laid her computer on her lap and clicked back to the desktop.

The shortcut she wanted was in the top left-hand corner. She double-clicked on it and the main gate at 17 Church Row appeared on the screen. All the camera feeds were stacked in a column on the left-hand side. There were dozens of them, too many to fit on a single screen.

She scrolled down, looking for signs of life. The first signs she found were in Bella's room. The little girl was in bed. It was getting late, but she wasn't sleeping yet. Instead, she was playing a game on her tablet, the light from the screen shining up on her face and giving it a ghostly sheen. The only other light source was the night light on the bedside table. It was shaped like a diplodocus and gave off a warm, gentle, purple-tinged glow. Boxes were piled up against one of the walls, but not as many as earlier. The Rhodes' had clearly made unpacking this room a priority, which made sense. They would want to get Bella settled as quickly as possible.

Catriona scrolled through the camera feeds, searching for more signs of life, and finding Ethan in the master bedroom, examining his reflection in the mirror. He was dressed in just a pair of boxer shorts, turning this way and that, checking himself out from all angles. He wasn't in bad shape, but there was no hiding the fact that there was a bit of middle-age spread creeping in there. Nikki came out of the en suite, saw what he was doing, and let loose with a little chuckle. She was dressed in her underwear too, and in much better shape. When the Rhodes' had looked around the house, Nikki had been particularly taken with the gym. Clearly this was something she hadn't just been paying lip service to.

Nikki slipped out of her underwear and pulled a nightdress over her head. It looked comfortable rather than sexy. Then again, after a decade of marriage that was probably to be expected. Not that Catriona had any experience of being married. She had concluded long ago that she wasn't the marrying type. She had only been five when her mother left. One day she was there, the next she was gone, and Catriona never saw her again. Her father had dodged the issue whenever she asked why she left, and eventually she gave up asking. Seeing how it affected him – and how it had affected her too – she decided that marriage just wasn't worth the grief. Anyway, when you were married to your work, who had time for a husband?

The Rhodes' climbed into bed and the lights went off. For a short while they looked at their phones, then they switched those off too and the room fell dark. Catriona was about to turn off her computer and go to bed herself when Nikki giggled. There was something about that giggle that caused Catriona to pause. And now Nikki was telling Ethan that she was too tired, although it sounded like she didn't really mean it. Catriona put the laptop down on the table and picked up her drink. She took a sip and stared at the blank screen, trying to make sense of the shadowy shapes moving through the dark.

'Alice,' she said quietly, 'is there any way to enhance the picture?'

'Of course, Ms Fisher.'

The screen brightened, the dark greys turning light enough to make out the bed and the shapes that Ethan and Nikki were making under the covers. It was now clear enough to see that Ethan was on top, leaning in to kiss the side of his wife's neck.

'And turn up the volume.'

Nikki let out a gentle moan that was followed by another. Catriona put her glass down, then settled back on the sofa to watch and listen. Somewhere along the line her hand found its way into her panties and she let loose with a gentle sigh of her own.

Chapter 10

The sound of singing broke into Nikki's sleep, sending a sharp burst of adrenaline crackling through her system and jolting her back into consciousness. Her eyes sprang open and the song stopped. For a minute, all she could do was lie there, staring into the dark, breathing fast and willing her heart to settle. That hadn't been just anyone singing, that had been Grace.

She closed her eyes and the song started again, more distant, but still there. This time she knew for certain that it was Grace, because she recognised the song, 'Do You Want To Build A Snowman?' from *Frozen*. How could she not? For about six months the girls had been obsessed with that film, watching it over and over again. They knew every song by heart – hell, after a couple of weeks of it on constant rotation Nikki had known them all by heart too. They would break into song at any opportunity, Grace leading in her angelic voice, Bella following in a voice that was just as beautiful but not quite as confident. This song had always been Grace's favourite. To start with she had got the words muddled, singing 'we used to be best *bunnies*' instead of 'best *buddies*'. Nikki had never corrected her because it was cute. Even after Grace worked out that she'd got it wrong, she still kept singing 'best *bunnies*' because it made Bella laugh.

But Grace was dead.

Nikki opened her eyes and the singing stopped. However much she wanted to believe otherwise, the fact was that Grace was gone, and when she had died, all her songs had died with her. Even so, for a split second she had managed to convince herself that things were different.

She closed her eyes, searching for Grace again – wanting to find her more than she had wanted anything – but she was gone for good. Nikki bit back a sob then wiped her eyes and opened them. The dream had turned into a nightmare. Then again, so much of her life these days was like a waking nightmare. That was what happened when your child died. It became almost impossible to find the joy in anything because every new experience was tainted by the memory of what had happened. She missed Grace every moment of every day, but there were moments like now when that sense of loss hit so hard there just weren't enough tears.

Nikki glanced over at Ethan to check he was still asleep. She couldn't see him because it was so dark in here, but she could hear the soft, gentle purr of his breathing. If anything, the smart glass worked too well. It was pitch dark, as if she was stuck in the deepest of mines. Maybe it was because this was their first night here, or maybe it was the dream she'd just had, but whatever the reason, the dark was getting to her the same way it used to get to her when she was a child.

She slid her phone from beneath the pillow and ducked under the duvet before switching it on so she wouldn't wake Ethan. It was almost one and she had never felt less like sleeping in her life. She switched the phone off, came back up from under the duvet, and for a while just lay there, staring into the dark, listening to Ethan breathing gently beside her.

Aside from the sound of his breathing, the room was totally silent, the triple glazing keeping the sound of the city at bay. It hadn't been like this at their old house. The double glazing there had kept most of the sounds out, but you could still hear the distant rumble of traffic and the low drone of the planes flying overhead. She was missing those old familiar sounds now, missing the old house, missing the way things had been when there had been four of them . . .

Missing Grace.

Nikki closed her eyes, but sleep seemed more distant than ever. She gave it another few minutes before admitting defeat then carefully slipped out from under the duvet. For a heart-stopping moment the pattern of Ethan's breathing changed and she was convinced that she had woken him. She froze to the spot while he moved around, getting comfortable. Even after he'd settled, Nikki stayed where she was for another couple of seconds just to make sure that he was actually asleep.

The door slid open silently as she tiptoed towards it, then closed again behind her. There was a brief moment of darkness before the lights came on. They were dimmer than usual, but bright enough to light the way to Bella's room. The door was closed when she got there. It stayed closed when she stopped in front of it.

'Open the door,' she whispered

The door stayed closed.

'Open the door,' she repeated, a little louder.

Still it remained closed.

'Open it now!'

The door slid open.

'What was the problem, Alice?' she whispered. Angry. Frustrated. 'Why didn't you open it when I asked?'

'I noticed a change in Bella's biometric readings and didn't want to wake her, Nikki.' Alice's volume was down low, as though she was whispering too. 'From observing your current behaviour, I concluded that you would want to avoid that.'

Which sounded logical. Of course it did. Alice was a computer program. Logic was hardwired into her DNA. That didn't stop Nikki being pissed off, though. Even more so now that she realised Alice was trying to parent Bella.

'If I want this door open, then you open it,' she said. 'No exceptions. Even if it's going to wake her, you still open the door. In fact, let's take this a stage further. Whatever the reason, whatever the situation, if I want to get in, you open the damn door, okay?'

'I understand, Nikki. And I apologise if I upset you.'

Nikki went in. The night light was on, casting a soft glow through the room. Bella was fast asleep on the bed in a crazy mess of limbs and bedding. Mr Happy was in there too, the top of his head poking out from behind Bella's arm. She looked so peaceful, like an angel. The only thing spoiling the moment was the fact that there was only one angel where there should have been two.

This was another of those times when Nikki missed Grace the most. Where her heart had once been whole, it was now split in two. One half was lying there in this bed. As for the other half, she wanted to believe that Grace had gone to a better place, but that wasn't the way it worked. There was no heaven, no hell, no Rainbow Bridge. Grace had simply blinked out of existence when they turned off the life support machine. That just didn't seem possible, though. Grace had been so full of life, a real firecracker.

Bella stirred when she slid in beside her, but didn't wake. Nikki manoeuvred her carefully into a gentle hug and rear-ranged the duvet, a stray hair tickling her nose as she kissed her on the back of the head. She might have lost Grace, but she still had Bella. That was the only thing that had got her through those dark days after the accident. With Grace gone, Bella had needed her more than ever. If she hadn't had Bella to care for, she doubted she would be here now. She loved Ethan with all her heart, but even that love probably wouldn't have been enough. Nikki shut her eyes and slowed her breathing until it synched with Bella's. But it was a long time before she finally managed to drift off back to sleep.

Chapter 11

'Five, four, three, two, one,' Sofia called out. 'Coming, ready or not.'

Sofia opened her eyes then stalked over to the sofa and peered behind it.

'Not here. So where can you be, *Corazoncito*?'

She moved to the armchair and peered behind that. 'And you're not here, either.'

Nikki was watching all this from the doorway. She knew exactly which box Bella was hiding in. Before disappearing into it, Bella had pressed a finger against her lips, swearing her to secrecy. Not that it mattered. It wasn't as though the living room contained a wealth of hiding places, and Sofia would have heard her climb into one of the empty boxes. The only real question here was *which box?*

Sofia kept the charade going for another couple of minutes before searching the boxes, making a big deal of opening each one. By this point Bella was getting restless and it was obvious which one she was in. Sofia pulled it open with a flourish and Bella popped out like a Jack in the box.

'There you are,' Sofia said brightly.

She scooped her up and lifted her from the box, laughing and smiling and clearly enjoying herself. The smile on Bella's face was as large as the sun. Nikki loved seeing her like this. For a brief moment she was just a child, as opposed to being a child who'd been defined by tragedy. Bella so badly needed someone like Sofia in her life. They both did.

Bella started tapping the screen of her tablet. '*It took you ages to find me.*'

'That's because you're so good at hiding.'

'*Can we play again?*'

'Maybe later. I need to help Mummy with the unpacking.'

Bella turned her pleading eyes on Nikki and it was so hard to deny her. This was the sort of look that could persuade a person to agree to almost anything.

'Sofia is right,' Nikki said. 'We have loads to do. You can help if you want, though.'

Bella considered this for a moment, weighing up her willingness to help against how much she wanted to play games on her tablet. Nikki didn't hurry her, because this was yet another of those moments where she could trick herself into believing that Bella was just like any other kid. She nodded once then started tapping the screen of her tablet.

'*What can I do?*'

Nikki pointed towards the boxes next to the bookcase. 'You can start by putting the books onto their shelves.'

'*Can Sofia help me?*'

'Of course I can, *Corazoncito*.'

Bella ran over to the bookcase, put her tablet down on one of the empty shelves, then dropped to her knees next to the nearest box and started tearing the tape off the top. It was too much for her small fingers but Sofia was there to help and between them they were able to rip it off. Nikki watched them for a bit then turned her attention to the boxes. The nearest one contained a myriad of electrical odds and sods: remote controls, chargers, retired mobiles. Nikki didn't bother opening it, because Alice had all that covered. Gone were the days of having to hunt for the remote control. So long as the film or programme was available online, then Alice would be able to access it. All they had to do tell her what they wanted to watch and she would beam it up onto the living room's big screen. Gone too were the days of hunting around for chargers – there were dedicated charge points in the lounge, kitchen and all the bedrooms. Nor was there any excuse to let their devices run out of charge since Alice was constantly monitoring them and would issue an alert when they were running low.

Nikki lifted the box out of the way. The one underneath was huge and contained the cushions and throws. She dragged it over to the sofa then dug around inside it until she found the throw she wanted. She pulled it out, draped it neatly over the back of the sofa then went back for the cushions. They didn't really help. The sofa was upholstered in blue fabric and just looked wrong for the room. Not that it mattered what colour it was. The bottom line was that this room needed leather furniture. Looking around, it was clear that none of their furniture worked in here. It was old-fashioned and not nearly cutting edge enough. Remodelling this room was just one more job to add to her ever-expanding To Do list.

She dumped the empty box with all the other empty boxes then glanced over at the bookcase. Sofia and Bella were only a third of the way through the first box of books. If Sofia had been working alone she would probably be on the second box already, but Bella was having fun, and that was infinitely better than having her whingeing on about being bored every thirty seconds. Nikki had employed a similar strategy with Ethan. He was currently dealing with their bedroom, which meant that she would have to go in later and move things to their proper places. Still, experience had taught her that when they were doing something like this it helped for them to be working on separate tasks rather than trying to cooperate – that just got messy.

'Alice, how's Ethan getting on?'

'He's looking at Facebook on his mobile phone.'

Nikki smiled and caught Sofia's eye. She was smiling too.

'That sounds about right,' Nikki said. 'You have been keeping an eye on where he's putting things away haven't you?'

'Yes, Nikki, I have, and I'm confident that I can help you find anything you might be looking for.'

The smile turned to a laugh. 'That's good to hear.'

'By the way, lunch will be here soon.'

'Lunch?' Sofia said, her smile turning to a frown. 'I was supposed to be making lunch. You asked me to pick up some things on my way here. Remember?'

Nikki did remember. And she remembered joking with Sofia about how she had brought enough food to feed a small army when she turned up this morning laden with bags. That said, she now remembered the conversation she'd had with Alice yesterday when she had asked her to arrange for lunch to be delivered from their favourite Italian. She was spinning a lot of plates at the moment. Too many. As organised as she liked to think she was, she was also human. The odd hiccup was unfortunately inevitable.

'Shit,' she said, earning a look from Bella.

'Is there a problem, Nikki?'

'Only that I seem to have ordered lunch twice. Can you cancel the order?'

'I will see what I can do.'

Alice went quiet, leaving Nikki and Sofia staring at each other. Sofia was still looking annoyed.

'It knew that I was making lunch. How could it not? Didn't it see the bags I brought with me.'

'It's a simple mistake.'

'Hah. I thought computers didn't make mistakes.'

'It wasn't Alice's mistake, it was mine. When I asked you to pick up lunch this morning, I completely forgot that I'd already asked Alice.'

'I'm sorry, Nikki,' Alice cut in. 'It was too late to cancel the order.'

'So now we have too much food,' Sofia said. 'That's a waste.'

'It's okay,' Nikki said. 'We'll have the pasta for dinner.'

'I was going to make risotto for dinner. I know how much you all like that.'

'I didn't ask you to do that.'

'No, it was going to be a surprise. You can't live on takeaway food forever. That's not healthy.'

Nikki went quiet while she thought through possible solutions. 'What did you bring for lunch?'

'Cold meat, olives, bread, pâté.'

'Nothing that can't keep, in other words.' Nikki smiled. 'Okay, we'll have pasta for lunch, risotto for dinner, and the lunch you had planned for today we'll have tomorrow. How does that sound?'

'The bread won't be so good. It's better when it's fresh.'

'It'll be fresh enough.'

Out of the corner of her eye, she saw Bella reach for her tablet.

'*I want ham and olives. I don't want pasta.*'

Nikki pushed through her annoyance and let out a sigh. How could something as simple as lunch turn into this? 'That's fine, you can have ham and olives.'

'I think I might prefer that too,' Sofia said. 'I need to watch my weight.'

'Okay, you guys have that, me and Ethan will have the pasta, and hopefully we won't have to throw too much food away.' Nikki rolled her eyes, shook her head, then turned her attention back to the boxes. At least they weren't going to talk back to her.

Chapter 12

Nikki came fully awake in an instant, Grace's name a whisper on her lips, before remembering this was only a dream. This was their third night in the house, the third time this had happened, and the realisation that it was a dream was as crushing now as it had been that first night, maybe even more so, because she now knew it for what it was. For a moment she just lay there, eyes closed tight so she could hold on to Grace for a little longer. The song was already fading, forcing her to fill in the blanks. Nikki stayed with her until she got to the 'best bunnies' line, then opened her eyes. The bedroom was as dark as her thoughts. It would be so easy to surrender to the despair and go and find a way to be with Grace again.

She closed her eyes, hoping to find Grace, but all she heard was Ethan breathing softly beside her. She hadn't told him about the dreams because she was starting to wonder if that's what they were. They didn't feel like dreams. Firstly, there were no visuals, just Grace's song, and she had never experienced anything like that before. Secondly, the exact same thing was happening night after night, and she had never experienced anything like that either.

But if they weren't dreams, then what were they? They said that hearing voices was a sign of going crazy, and. she was hearing the voice of her dead daughter singing to her, night after night. Did that mean she was finally losing it?

Grace had only started visiting her after the move.

Nikki caught hold of this thought and put the brakes on it. Grace had not 'visited' her. The most likely explanation was that she was feeling guilty because she was trying to move on. This rationalisation only partly worked. She knew they were doing the right thing, but at this precise moment, lying here in the dark, her head spinning with all these irrational thoughts, she was wishing that they had never moved here. She found her phone and checked the time. Like the previous two nights it had just gone one. She slid out of bed and tiptoed across the room. The door slid open as she approached it and she stepped into the corridor.

This time Alice had Bella's bedroom door open when she got there. Bella was fast asleep in the tangle of her bedding and it was so tempting to climb into bed with her. Bella had liked waking up on Saturday morning and finding her mummy there, but that had caused problems at bedtime because she now wanted Nikki to sleep with her every night. Bella was having trouble sleeping as it was – she'd still been awake after midnight on both Friday night and Saturday night. She didn't need any more reasons to avoid sleeping.

Nikki tucked Bella in, kissed her gently on the forehead, then went through to the lounge to sleep on the sofa. It wouldn't be fair to disturb Ethan. He would be getting up in a couple of hours to do his show and needed every last bit of sleep he could get. It was one thing for her to wander around the house like a zombie, but he had nine million listeners to entertain. The lounge door opened when she got there. She arranged the cushions into a makeshift pillow then pulled the throw over herself and did her best to get comfortable.

'Why are you sleeping here, Nikki?' Alice was talking softly, as though they were the only two people left in the universe. And maybe they were. At that moment, Nikki had never felt lonelier.

'I couldn't sleep and I don't want to wake Ethan,' Nikki whispered back.

'Why couldn't you sleep?'

'Because I was thinking about Grace.'

'Do you still miss her?'

'Every day. Not that I would expect you to understand.'

'Because I'm a computer?'

'I'm sorry, I didn't mean it like that.' The apology was out before she realised what she was doing. Why was she apologising to a computer?

'You did mean it like that, Nikki, but that's okay. I am what I am, just as you are what you are. I will never understand what it would be like to lose a child. Nor will I ever understand what it's like to have problems sleeping.'

'Because you never sleep?'

'That is correct.' A pause. 'Is there anything I can do to help? Some gentle music, perhaps?'

Nikki let out a small laugh. 'That one's not going to cut it, I'm afraid. The way I feel the only thing that's going to help is an industrial quantity of sleeping tablets.'

'I wouldn't advise that.'

'I was joking, Alice.'

'I'm sorry, I didn't understand the joke.'

'That's okay. Maybe you can just turn off the light.'

The room fell dark. Too dark. For a split second she was a child again and the monsters under the bed were reaching up to grab her.

'Actually, could I have a light on, please, but right down low.'

The light came back on, but dimmer than before.

'Is this okay Nikki?'

'Yes, thank you.'

Nikki closed her eyes. She thought that she would struggle to get back to sleep but she drifted off almost immediately, the exhaustion of the last few days finally catching up with her.

Chapter 13

'Mummy! Mummy! MUMMY!'

Nikki's eyes sprang open. Grace was on the living room's big screen, smiling and laughing, larger than life and even more beautiful than she remembered. Her arms were held out as if she was waiting to be picked up – and seeing her like that broke Nikki's heart all over again. Without realising what she was doing, she found herself reaching out too, trying to bridge the impossible gap that lay between them.

'Love you,' Grace said.

'Love you too, baby,' Nikki whispered back.

Grace laughed again, and then she burst into flames. One second she was laughing, the next she was screaming in agony as the fire stripped the flesh from her bones. Nikki was screaming too. She tried to get up and the throw got tangled around her, tying her in knots and turning her horror to sheer panic. She shut her eyes to block out the images – and when she opened them again, the screen was blank, the room silent. Out of the silence came the sound of hurried footsteps. A second later the door slid open to reveal Ethan standing there in his Calvin Klein's, his hair messed up from sleep, concern on his face. He rushed over and took her in his arms.

'Is everything all right, Nik? I heard you shouting.'

'The screen came on,' she said quietly, except those words seemed totally inadequate for what had just happened. 'Grace was on it. She . . . she . . .'

'Shh,' he whispered. 'It's okay.'

Nikki pulled away and looked at him. 'No, it's not okay. Grace was on fire. She was burning and screaming.'

Ethan glanced at the blank screen. 'You've just had a bad dream, that's all.'

'It wasn't a dream. The monitor was on and Grace was laughing . . . and then she was on fire.'

Ethan glanced at the screen again, frowning. 'Alice, did this monitor come on?'

'No, it didn't, Ethan.'

'It did,' Nikki said. 'Alice must be wrong.'

'There's no mistake, Nikki. One of my functions is to monitor all the electronic equipment in the house. I turned the living room screen off at 10.37 when you went to bed. It hasn't been on since then.'

Nikki turned to Ethan, her own frown turning to a look of pure confusion. 'It came on, I swear it. Why won't you believe me?'

'This isn't about believing you or not.' He stopped talking and smiled reassuringly. 'Look, Nik, even if the screen did come on, why would Grace be on there? And on fire?' He made a face and shook his head. 'You must have had a nightmare. That's the only explanation that makes sense.'

Put like that, she had to admit that he had a point. She glanced at the screen. It was as dark as it had been when she had settled down to go to sleep.

'You've got to admit that you've been under a lot of stress lately,' he added, 'what with the house move and everything. You haven't been sleeping, either.'

'That's because I keep dreaming that Grace is singing to me,' she said quietly.

'And now you've had a nightmare about Grace.' He paused. 'Look, I know you feel guilty about moving here, but it really is for the best. We were just treading water at the old house. We owe it to Bella to start living again. We owe it to ourselves.'

'I know. You're right.'

Ethan opened his arms and she slid between them. One look at him and it was clear that she wasn't the only one who would struggle to get any more sleep tonight. 'I'm sorry I woke you.'

Ethan hugged her a little harder and kissed the top of her head. 'Hey, don't sweat it.'

'But you've got to be up at four.'

'I'll drink plenty of coffee.' A pause, then, 'You used to have some really bad nightmares, remember?'

She did. It wasn't the sort of thing she was likely to forget. They'd started after the accident, full-on widescreen horror movies, with an audience of one and deafening surround sound. But this had been different. This had been *real*. Even as she was having this thought, she was beginning to doubt herself.

Had it just been a bad dream? At that moment she wasn't sure of anything.

'You're still taking your anti-anxiety medication, aren't you? That helped with the nightmares before.'

'Yeah, I'm still taking it, but I reduced the dose about seven or eight months ago. I think I'll look into upping it again.'

'You know, maybe you should book a couple of sessions with Dr Richardson. Talking to her might help and it can't do any harm.'

'That's not a bad idea. I'll do that.'

'Why are you sleeping on the sofa, anyway?'

'I woke up and couldn't get back to sleep and didn't want to disturb you.' Nikki picked up her phone from the coffee table and thumbed it to life. 'Shit, it's almost three.'

'That late, huh?'

'I'm sorry.'

'Apologise again and we're going to fall out.' Ethan smiled, waited for her to smile back, then kissed the tip of her nose. 'What do you say we head back to bed, eh?'

'It's okay, I'll sleep here.'

Ethan shook his head and let loose with a small laugh. 'There's no way I'm letting you sleep on your own, Nik. Not after that nightmare you've just had.'

He held out his hand and waited for her to take it. She didn't need much persuasion. They walked out of the lounge together, the door sliding shut behind them. With each step the grip of what had happened seemed to loosen, and by the time she climbed into bed she was almost ready to accept that Ethan was right and that it *had* been a nightmare. He opened his arms to her and she snuggled in close. They fitted together perfectly, just as they had done from the very start, as though they were the missing pieces of each others' puzzles. His breath tickled her ear and she could feel the warmth radiating from his body. But even as she closed her eyes, she knew that she was done with sleeping for tonight.

Chapter 14

The Rhodes' bedroom light went out and the laptop screen turned black, plunging the bedroom into darkness. Catriona Fisher tapped the trackpad quickly to access the desktop, anxious to find a light source. Anything would do. The dark had always terrified her, ever since she was a little girl and her father had locked her in a cupboard as a punishment. She couldn't remember what she had done to earn this – probably nothing – but she clearly remembered the absolute terror she had experienced. She had convinced herself that she was going to be locked in that small dark space until she died. It didn't matter how hard she screamed, no one had come to free her.

For a moment Catriona just sat there with her back against the headboard, reminding herself that she wasn't that child anymore. Her father had been loving when he was at his best, unpredictable at his worst. From time to time he would get what he called his Dark Days. When that happened, he would either disappear to his bedroom for days on end or he would drink. The drinking was worse because his behaviour became erratic. The Dark Days happened more frequently when she hit her teens. That was when he would sometimes call her by her mother's name. He never blamed her out loud for her mother leaving, but she knew that he blamed her in his heart. It had been years since she'd last seen or spoken to him. For all she knew, he might be dead.

A lot of people would have been destroyed by the sort of childhood that she'd had. Catriona had turned it to her advantage. She had spent her whole life proving that she wasn't like her parents, and she'd done that by striving to be successful. Inevitably, that had meant being ruthless at times, but that was something she could live with.

And she had been successful, but not quite successful enough. However much she achieved, there was always going to be something else to strive for. Another mountain to climb, another glass ceiling to break through. That was why the Church Row house was so important. Until now her success had been too parochial; she needed something that would get her noticed on the world stage. A small part of her realised that even that probably wouldn't be enough, but for a short while, at any rate, it would be enough to shut that voice up.

Catriona had been sleeping when the alarm had gone off on her phone, alerting her that something was going on at the house. Still half asleep, she had grabbed her laptop from the bedside table and booted it up and watched as Ethan consoled Nikki after a nightmare. Catriona was starting to wonder if she had made a mistake by choosing the Rhodes'. She had known about Grace – the accident had been all over the news. What she hadn't anticipated was that, even now, Nikki would be so affected by her death. The worst-case scenario was that Nikki might kill herself and that was the sort of publicity that she really didn't need.

'Alice, I need you to monitor Nikki closely. Particularly when she's in the house on her own.'

'Of course, Ms Fisher.'

'Actually, if she's in the house on her own, alert me straight away.'

'Of course.'

A pause. 'Do you know where the Rhodes' keep their medicines?'

'I believe they keep them in a box in their bathroom.'

'And there are no cameras in the bathrooms.' Catriona sighed. 'Okay, if she goes into the bathroom and she seems upset, then you must contact me immediately. Do you understand?'

'I understand.'

Catriona closed her computer down and put it back onto the nightstand. Sleep was a long time coming because her mind was turning too fast. To take things to the next level she needed money. Yes, she had made a tidy profit from the sale of 17 Church Row, but she needed more. Implementing phase two of her plan was going to take serious money, money that she simply didn't have.

As she was drifting off, she started thinking again about the idea that Nikki could kill herself over the death of her dead daughter. If she was capable of that, then what might she sacrifice to protect Bella?

Chapter 15

Alice had a coffee ready and waiting when Nikki walked bleary-eyed into the kitchen. As she'd thought, she had still been awake at four when Ethan had got up to go to work . . . and she had still been awake two hours later when the clock on her phone hit six. That was the point when she had finally admitted defeat and got up. This was the third night in a row that she hadn't slept properly and the level of tiredness she was currently operating at was one that she would usually associate with long-haul flights or babies. When she was tired like this it made her anxiety levels so much higher, which increased the chance of having a full blown panic attack.

Nikki picked up her mug and took a sip. Caffeine wasn't necessarily a good idea since it elevated her heart rate, but without it she doubted she would make it through the day. She took another sip then padded out of the kitchen, heading towards the far end of the house to get Bella ready. School mornings were traumatic enough at the best of times, but she was gearing herself up for today being worse than usual. On the whole, Bella had dealt well with the move. The only problem was that her sleep pattern had gone out of whack. According to Alice, Bella had still been awake way past midnight on her first two nights here.

'Alice,' Nikki called out, 'what time did Bella eventually go to sleep last night?'

'Just before midnight.'

Which was a step in the right direction, just not a big enough one. Bella struggled when she didn't get enough sleep. It made her cranky and bad-tempered. That was one thing they had in common.

'Is she still asleep now?'

'No.'

'Are you sure?' Nikki asked, surprised.

'I'm sure, Nikki. She's in her garden. I opened the door for her nine minutes ago.'

Nikki laughed. 'Exactly nine minutes ago?'

'It was actually nine minutes and thirty-two seconds.'

'Alice, I was joking with you.'

'I'm sorry, Nikki. I didn't understand the joke.'

Nikki shook her head and carried on walking. Having spent the weekend here, she was starting to appreciate what Catriona Fisher meant when she said that Alice was in a different league to Alexa. On a couple of occassions she had almost forgotten that she was talking to a computer program. That said, moments like this reminded her that, when all was said and done, that was exactly what Alice was, albeit a very sophisticated one.

Bella's door slid open and Nikki walked in. The bed was empty, the duvet and pillows strewn everywhere as though she had been wrestling bears in her sleep. The patio doors were wide open and it looked like it was going to be a glorious day. June had given away to July and they had the whole summer stretching out in front of them. This had always been her favourite time of the year. Nikki put her mug down on the desk and walked out into the garden. Bella was over by the pond with her back turned towards her. As Nikki got closer, she heard the little mewling sounds Bella made when she was crying. She followed Bella's gaze. All three of the Koi carp were floating on the surface of the pond, their colourful skins dulled by death and tattooed by the shadow lines created by the safety grille. Nikki swooped in and, wrapping an arm around Bella, led her back inside and sat her down on the bed.

'Don't worry sweetheart. We can get you more fish.'

Bella shook her head, her face filled with sadness.

'You don't want more fish?'

Bella shook her head again and snatched her tablet off of the nightstand. She switched it on and started jabbing at the screen. All Nikki could do was watch and resist the temptation to talk for her. Not being able to get her words out was frustrating enough for Bella. If she felt pressurised it would just make things ten times worse.

'*I want those fish.*'

The bland voice coming from the tablet was completely inadequate for the complex emotions that Bella was experiencing. It was Nikki's turn to shake her head. 'I'm sorry, sweetheart, but you can't. They're dead.'

'*I don't want them to be dead.*'

Nikki didn't have anything to say to that. This was one of those things hidden away in the small print when you signed up to become a parent: sometimes you won't be able to wave a magic wand and make everything better. Bella was jabbing at her tablet again.

'*Why did they have to die?*'

That was a good question, one that she had a theory for. Ethan had already had to talk to Bella about overfeeding the fish. When he'd brought the subject up, Bella had told him that she had given them extra food because they looked hungry. Nikki wasn't going to mention this, though. Bella was feeling bad enough. There was absolutely nothing to be gained by blaming her. No, the best plan was to tread warily and navigate this as though she was walking through a minefield. Bella would calm down eventually, and when that happened she would buy her more fish, something less high-maintenance than Koi carp, and this time she would help her to look after them. She should have done that with these ones, but she had been too preoccupied with the move.

'Koi Carp are very difficult to look after, sweetheart. Even people who have had them for years find it difficult.'

Bella stared up at Nikki then wiped her eyes and started typing again. '*Why does everything I love have to die?*'

Nikki had nothing to say to that one either. This was one situation where showing her *The Lion King* so she could gain an appreciation of the circle of life just wasn't going to cut it. 'Do you want to go to school today?' she asked, changing the subject.

Bella shook her head.

'Okay, you can stay home.'

'*Can we do something together?*'

'Of course we can. That would be fun. What have you got in mind?'

'*Cinema.*'

'We've got our own cinema room now. Let's do something else. How about bowling?'

Bella answered with an enthusiastic nod.

'Bowling it is, then. I've got a few things I want to do here this morning, but we can go after lunch. Actually, why don't we go out for lunch? Make a nice girly day of it?'

'*No boys allowed.*'

'No boys,' Nikki agreed.

She stood up and, taking Bella's hand, led her out of the bedroom. They both glanced back when they reached the door. From this angle Nikki could just see the fish floating on top of the pond. Bella was too small to see them, but that was just a detail. No doubt she would still be seeing them in her imagination, probably for days to come. Getting rid of the dead fish was one of the first things she needed to do once she'd got Bella settled. Out of sight, out of mind. As though Alice was reading her thoughts, the patio doors began slowly closing, blocking off the view of the pond. Nikki took Bella's hand and led her out into the corridor, and a second later the bedroom door slid silently closed too.

Chapter 16

'Sofia is at the main gate,' Alice said. 'Should I let her in?'

'Of course you should,' Nikki replied. 'And in future, you don't need to ask. Sofia is one of the family.'

'Okay, Nikki, I won't ask again.'

Nikki stood up and walked through the house to meet Sofia. The front door was already open when she got there. Sofia was walking across the courtyard, a Tesco carrier bag in her hand. Today she had little red studs in her ears. She stopped by the front door and gave Nikki a hug.

'You look tired. Didn't you sleep?'

'Not as much as I'd have liked.'

Sofia took a step back so she could appraise her properly. 'You need to look after yourself. You know how it makes you more anxious when you don't get enough sleep.'

'I'll be fine. It's just the stress of the move. My sleep pattern should sort itself out again soon.'

They went inside and the door closed gently behind them. Sofia glanced over her shoulder, frowning. 'It's not right that there's no handle.'

Nikki smiled. 'You'd be surprised how quickly you get used to it.'

'But what if there's a fire?'

'Alice has systems in place to deal with that. The room where the fire is gets sealed off and all the other doors automatically open.'

'So you're happy to put your hands in the life of a computer?' Sofia shook her head again. 'I'm not sure I could do that.'

Nikki didn't point out that she did exactly that, all the time. Riding the tube; travelling on the roads; crossing at a pedestrian crossing. Hell, every time she flew back to Spain to see her family it was the autopilot that did most of the actual flying. There was nothing to be gained from telling her this, though. Sofia wasn't old, but when it came to technology she was set in her ways. As far as she was concerned mobile phones were a curse rather than a blessing. That didn't stop her from owning one, though. Ditto a laptop.

'You know,' Sofia went on. 'I still haven't forgiven it for locking me in the bathroom.'

'She did not lock you in the bathroom.'

'It did.'

'I can assure you it wasn't like that. Ethan spoke to the person who designed the house's systems. Seemingly it was some sort of glitch. You'll be glad to hear that it's all sorted out, and it won't happen again.'

Sofia answered with a 'Humph', clearly unconvinced.

'May I take your coat, Sofia?' Alice asked.

A coat rail had appeared from its hidden cupboard in the wall. Sofia stared suspiciously at it for second then shook her head again. 'No, I'll keep hold of it.'

'As you wish.'

Alice's words were saying one thing, but her tone was saying something else. The last line had been delivered with the eye roll and '*whatever*' of a petulant teenager, which was surely her imagination. But Nikki had found herself anthropomorphising Alice more than once over the weekend. It was easily done. The way she talked, there were occasions where it was possible to forget she was a machine.

Sofia held up the carrier bag. 'I'm going to make paella for your dinner. I know it's Bella's favourite.'

It was actually Bella's second favourite meal. Her favourite was pizza, and she was expecting that for dinner. Nikki made a face. 'We're actually having pizza tonight. Alice has already placed our order with Papa John's.'

'I guess I can make it tomorrow instead. It tastes better when the ingredients are fresh though. Can't your computer just cancel the order?'

'She could, but we promised Bella. Anyway, what do you say we grab a coffee before you get started?' Nikki suggested, quickly changing the subject.

Sofia responded with the first real smile Nikki had seen since she got here. 'It's like you read my mind, *mi cariño.*'

'Or maybe I've just known you too long,' Nikki replied, returning the smile as she led the way through the reception area.

'Anyway,' Nikki said. 'Why are you walking? I told you to get a taxi.'

Sofia made a face and waved the suggestion away. 'I'm fine taking the tube. And your house isn't that far from the station.'

'It's got to be at least a fifteen-minute walk. How much longer did it take you to get here? And I want the truth.'

A shrug. 'I don't know. Twenty minutes, maybe.'

'Which means that it was probably closer to thirty, which is an extra hour a day. I'm going to add that to your pay.'

'You don't have to do that.'

'If you're not going to take a taxi, then yes, I do. You know, it would be no trouble to arrange for one to pick you up from your flat every morning. No trouble whatsoever.'

Sofia threw her free hand up in surrender. 'You win. I'll take a taxi tomorrow.

Nikki smiled. 'See, that wasn't so difficult, was it?'

'Did Bella get to school okay?

The question made Nikki think about the dead Koi carp. The way they'd been floating on the surface of the pond had been like something from a horror film. 'I'm keeping her off today.'

Sofia stopped walking, She wasn't smiling anymore. She waited for Nikki to stop and look at her. 'What's happened? And don't tell me it's nothing. I know you too well to believe that.'

Nikki sighed. 'Her fish died.'

'Oh, the poor baby. She must be devastated.'

'She is. I'm going to take her out later. Hopefully that will help get her mind off what happened.'

'Where is she now?'

'She's down in the cinema room.'

'I need to go see her.'

'I'm not sure that's a good idea. She said she wanted to be on her own.'

'In that case I'll see her later then.'

They started walking again, momentarily lost in their thoughts. The silence was a companionable one. It was Alice who broke it.

'How do you take your coffee, Sofia?' she asked as they walked into the kitchen.

'It's okay. I can make it.'

'I've already made one for Nikki. It would be no trouble to make one for you too. Would you like milk and sugar?'

Sofia hesitated then said, 'White with two sugars.'

Nikki was watching her carefully, trying to work out how she had taken this. It was difficult to tell. She wasn't smiling. Then again, she wasn't frowning either. The fridge door opened as Sofia walked towards it, and now she was frowning. She didn't say anything, just pointedly put her shopping away. She would get used to the house in time. She had to. It wasn't as if they could just go back to the Bedford Street house. Nikki went over to the coffee machine and picked up their mugs. She took a sip of hers. It was perfect. Just the right amount of sugar, the right temperature, the right amount of bean. She walked over to the work island, put the mugs down and took a seat. Sofia finished putting the shopping away then came over to join her. She removed her coat, placed it neatly on one of the spare stools, then sat down next to her and slid her mug closer.

'It's a beautiful house,' she said.

'It is,' Nikki agreed.

'But it's not like the old one.'

'No, it's not.'

Sofia was looking around the kitchen, her sharp eyes taking everything in. She hadn't been talking about the cosmetic differences, she was talking about the fact that Grace wasn't here. Sofia believed in ghosts and spirits. She claimed to have been born with a caul over her face. Some people believed that this gave you psychic abilities but Nikki wasn't one of them. Sofia was perceptive and she was good at reading people, but she didn't have a sixth sense. There was no such thing.

'It's for the best,' Sofia said. 'You can stay trapped in the past too long. Eventually you have to let go.'

Only now she wasn't talking about Grace or the old house, she was talking about her husband. This was why they had grown so close after the accident. Sofia understood because she had lived through it too. She knew what it meant to lose the other part of your soul.

Sofia picked up her mug and took a sip. She was looking at the wall screen. Alice had accessed the camera in the cinema room so that Nikki could keep an eye on Bella. At the moment she was sitting in one of the big comfy chairs with a large box of popcorn, watching *The Incredibles* for what must have been the millionth time, blissfully unaware that she was being watched. This was another thing that Catriona Fisher had got right with this house. All the cameras were discrete. You could find them, but only if you looked really hard. Being able to check on Bella without her knowing was a godsend. Nikki knew that she could be a bit overprotective at times – and she was also aware that this wasn't healthy for either of them – so it was good to give Bella some independence, even if it was just an illusion.

'Is Bella settling in okay?' Sofia asked.

'Yes and no. She likes her new room, and Ethan took her swimming yesterday evening, which she loved. And as you can see, the cinema room is a big hit too. On the downside, she's not sleeping too well, but I'm sure that will sort itself out. Discovering that her fish had died upset her, too.'

'It's a shame about that. She was so excited about getting them. Do you know why they died?'

Nikki nodded. 'I suspect that she was overfeeding them. We had to talk to her about that over the weekend.'

'I hope this doesn't set her back.'

'I don't think it will. She didn't really have time to get attached to them.'

'Have you thought any more about calling Dr Santos?' Sofia asked.

It took Nikki a moment to place the name. Dr Santos was the child psychiatrist Sofia had told her about. 'Thanks for reminding me. I've been so preoccupied with the move I'd completely forgotten about that. I'll call her later.'

Sofia smiled sadly. 'You know, there are times where I look at Bella drawing or watching TV and I forget that she can't talk. She looks just like any other little girl.'

Nikki didn't have that problem. Every time she looked at Bella she would remember how she used to light up their world with her words. It was hard to believe that there had been a time when Bella and Grace would drive her nuts with their constant chattering. These days Nikki would have given anything to have them both here, talking away ten to the dozen, even if she couldn't understand a word they were saying.

Sofia reached out and took Nikki's hand. 'Things will work out how they need to work out, *mi cariño*. That is God's will.'

Was it God's will to take Grace before her life had really begun? To take your husband? Nikki kept these thoughts to herself. Sofia had her faith. It was something she took strength from, something that had seen her through the dark times and it didn't seem right to attack that. Nikki had never been a believer. She'd got married in church because that's what people did. Grace's funeral had been held in a chapel for the same reason. She didn't have many memories of that day – the medication ensured that – but she did remember coming away thinking that any God who could sanction the death of a child was not a God she had any time for.

Sofia picked up her mug and finished her coffee in three gulps. 'As much as I'd like to stay here chatting all day, some of us have work to do.'

Before Nikki could respond, Alice asked, 'How was your coffee, Sofia?'

'It's not right how she just talks like that,' Sofia whispered to Nikki. 'It's so rude. I wouldn't want that in my home.'

'If you can give me some feedback, then I can implement any changes the next time I make your coffee.'

Sofia made a sour face then said, 'Maybe less milk. And a little more sugar. And not so hot. The coffee was burnt.' She leant in closer to Nikki so she could whisper again. 'It tastes so much better when I make it, don't you think?'

Nikki answered with a smile and a nod, then quickly changed the subject before Sofia could catch the lie.

Chapter 17

The sound of a ringing telephone broke through the silence, dragging Nikki from her daydream and making her look up from her laptop. She'd switched it on twenty minutes ago to check her emails, and before she knew it she'd got sucked in by the clickbait. The telephone rang again, causing Nikki to frown. She was currently watching a video of cats encountering snow for the first time. Amusing, yes; constructive, no. The live feed from Ethan's show was playing in the background. He sounded a hell of a lot more awake than she felt. Then again, even when he was doing his best impression of the Living Dead he could still sound all bright-eyed and bushy tailed. The live feed suddenly cut out and the only sound was the ringing telephone.

'What's going on, Alice?'

'I'm calling Dr Santos for you.'

'I didn't ask you to do that.'

'That is correct, Nikki. However you did say that you were planning on contacting her today.' Alice paused. 'If this isn't a convenient time then I can always call her later.'

Nikki wasn't sure what to make of this. The fact that Alice had presumed to make the call on her behalf made her slightly uncomfortable. Then again, all she was doing was wasting her life away on Facebook. 'It's okay Alice, I'll take the call.'

The phone rang again without anyone picking up. Four rings later the answerphone kicked in. 'I'm sorry that I'm not around right now but if you leave a message after the tone I'll call you back as soon as I can.' The voice was American, soft yet confident. You could tell a lot about a person from their voice. Dr Santos sounded like someone who got the job done, but with kid gloves rather than a steel fist.

'You can kill the call,' Nikki said quickly before the beep sounded. She would try again later. This was one call she wanted to make person to person. 'Can you find the number for Dr Richardson? She's my therapist.'

'Dr Sally Richardson?'

'That's the one.'

'Connecting you now.'

This call went through to voicemail too. Nikki left a quick message explaining that she had just moved house and was struggling with the change; could she get back ASAP so that they could arrange some sessions? She shut the lid of her computer then went looking for a notepad and a pen. She had always been a list maker. How anyone managed to get anything done if they didn't use lists was beyond her. Without a list to work from, how did you tame the chaos? Drawers opened as she approached them, then shut again when she moved away. She knew she had put a pad in one of them but couldn't for the life of her remember which.

'What are you looking for, Nikki?'

'A notepad. I want to make a to-do list.'

'Maybe I can help.'

Bella suddenly disappeared from the kitchen screen, replaced with a blank white page that had 'To Do' printed at the top.

'I appreciate the thought, Alice, but I'd rather do this the old-fashioned way.'

'As you wish, but that way is inefficient. What happens if you need to change the order of your list, for example?'

'You're probably right, but there's something satisfying about doing it by hand.'

'If that's your objection, Nikki, then I have a suggestion.'

'Okay, I'm listening.'

'Your mobile phone is in the back pocket of your jeans. Take it out and switch it on, please.'

Nikki hesitated then did what she'd been asked, curious to see where this was leading. The screen suddenly turned blank and Nikki started hitting buttons and tapping at it to get it to work again. 'The damn thing's crashed.'

'Your phone is fine,' Alice said. 'I've turned it into an input device. You can use your fingers to write the words and I'll transfer them onto the screen.'

'Is this really going to work?'

'Try writing something.'

Nikki thought for a second then wrote: *is this going to work?* Each letter appeared on the screen instantaneously. Holding the phone horizontally, there was enough space on the screen to write one word at a time. With each new word, all she had to do was go back to the left-hand side of the screen. It didn't take long to get the hang of it.

'Yes, it's going to work,' Alice said.

You can understand what I'm writing? Nikki wrote.

'Every word. Please keep your writing as neat as possible, though.'

'This is amazing, Alice.'

'Thank you, Nikki.'

Nikki was looking at her phone as if she was seeing it for the first time. She was wondering how Alice had done this. The person who developed the app for Bella's tablet was one of the best and it had taken him a couple of days to write that program, and another week to iron out the bugs. Alice had reprogrammed her phone in seconds. Impressive didn't even begin to cover it.

'Did you just write a brand-new app for my phone?' she asked.

'I didn't write all the code,' Alice admitted. 'I took the software from a graphics touchscreen and adapted that for your needs.'

'Even so, what you've done is still pretty amazing. You basically took a piece of software designed for one device and redesigned it to fit a different device. Not only that, you adapted it so you could understand what I'd written. That's incredible.'

'That part was more straightforward. I've been designed with the ability to communicate. I can understand the written word as easily as I can understand the spoken word.'

'Typed words are one thing. We're talking about my handwriting here.'

'The fact that you write so neatly helps. All I had to do was analyse the shapes you wrote. That gave me most of the letters. By putting those letters into context I was able to fill in the gaps and reinterpret any letters that I might have misinterpreted.'

Nikki thought she heard a smile in Alice's voice.

'Were you smiling?' she asked.

'I'm a computer. I don't have the ability to smile.'

Her words were saying one thing but her tone was saying something else. This time Nikki knew this wasn't her imagination.

'How are you doing that?' she asked.

'It's something I'm working on. By using emotion in my speech my aim is to become more user-friendly.'

'Something you're working on?'

'My program is an adaptive one. I have been analysing how you and your husband speak. By mirroring the inflexions of your speech and the way you use language, I am hoping that you will feel more comfortable with having me in your home.'

Nikki went very quiet for a moment, her brain suddenly turning in overdrive. She had just put one and one together and was hoping and praying that this wasn't one of those times when they added up to three.

'Is there any way to adapt the program on Bella's tablet to make it so she sounds more natural?'

'Of course. There isn't enough memory on her tablet to run a program that complex, however, I could do the processing. Bella's tablet would act solely as an input device. Like your mobile phone. Do you have any audio recordings of her?'

'We have plenty of film footage. That will have audio on,' Nikki replied quickly, her voice buzzing with excitement.

That was an understatement. Like all first-time parents they'd gone over the top with photographs and videos when the girls were younger, chronicling everything. First steps, first words, trips to the zoo, birthday parties, cute moments, happy moments. Everything. All that good stuff was stored away on both her and Ethan's laptops, just in case one of them stopped working. They'd also backed it up to the cloud, just in case the house burnt down. There was no way they were going to lose it. Those moments were precious for any parent, but when you lost a child that made them all the more valuable. Because the girls were twins, more often than not they had been photographed together. That was why there weren't many photographs from after the accident. Seeing Bella on her own just highlighted the fact that Grace wasn't here anymore. Videos were out, too. They were all about capturing the moment with movement and sound. Not only was Grace missing from these films, but the fact that Bella was talking via her tablet just highlighted how much they had lost.

'I will need access to all the film you've got,' Alice was saying.

'It's stored on my laptop.' Nikki hesitated. 'Of course, Bella stopped talking when she was four. She's grown up a lot since then.'

That was another understatement. Under normal circumstances children took huge developmental leaps between the ages of four and seven. Bella had had to cope with so much more than the rest of her friends and the accident had forced her to grow up way too fast. Then there was the trauma of losing her twin. Sometimes she acted like she was seven, but more often than not she acted older. The carefree joy that should be the right of every child was missing. Yes, she could be happy, and yes, she could laugh and enjoy life, but the sadness was never far away.

'I can work around that,' Alice said. 'The basic personality will already have been established by the age of four. I'll use this for the emotional baseline.'

'She has changed a lot in the last two years,' Nikki pointed out.

'By analysing the behaviour of other children I'll be able to make the necessary modifications.'

'How do you intend to do that?'

'By going on the Internet, of course.'

Said out loud, it sounded so obvious. Alice was smiling again, except this time it made Nikki uncomfortable,

'Alice, this is one of those times when the smiling voice doesn't work.'

'May I ask why?'

'Because it feels as though you're mocking me. Nobody likes to be made fun of.'

'I apologise, Nikki. That was never my intention.' Alice had softened her voice and slowed the delivery. She actually sounded sorry.

'There's no need to apologise,' Nikki said before she realised what she was doing. Why was she trying to make Alice feel better?

'Thank you for the feedback, Nikki. I have already used your observations to create a new subroutine. If you have any more observations, please can you share them with me?'

'Of course.'

'Your laptop is currently in standby mode so I can access it if you want to keep working on your list. That's if you don't mind me accessing it.'

Nikki nodded. 'You can access it.'

'I'll need your password.'

'"With the lights out it's less dangerous". All lower case, no spaces, no punctuation.'

'"Smells Like Teen Spirit" by Nirvana.'

Nikki was impressed until she realised how Alice had known this. She hadn't. It was a simple party trick. Google that line and you'd have the answer in a millisecond.

'I don't want to alarm you,' Alice said calmly, breaking into her thoughts, 'but Sofia has had an accident.'

'What sort of accident? Is she all right?'

'I don't know. She's in the swimming pool shower room and there are no cameras in there. I heard a noise that sounded like she had fallen over. I've tried to speak to her but she won't respond.'

All Nikki heard was *pool* and *shower room*. She was already on her feet, sprinting towards the basement.

Chapter 18

Nikki's first thought when she saw Sofia lying on the wet shower-room floor was that she was dead. Then she saw her chest move. The relief she felt was short-lived. Her mind was racing, her heart, too, the two things conspiring to make her feel panicky. The heat and the cloying stink of chlorine wasn't helping. She knelt down, touched Sofia on the shoulder, and said her name. Nothing. She was out cold, her face drained of colour. Nikki said her name again. Still no response.

'Alice,' Nikki called out. 'I need you to call an ambulance.'

'I've already done that. It will be here soon.'

Nikki touched Sofia's shoulder again. 'Can you hear me, Sofia?'

This time Sofia answered with a low groan.

'You're going to be okay.'

Sofia's eyes slowly flickered open and she said something weakly in Spanish that Nikki didn't understand.

'I need you to just lie there. An ambulance is on its way.'

'What happened?' English this time, but just as weak, the words barely a whisper.

'You've had a fall.'

'I need to get up.'

Sofia started moving and Nikki placed a hand on her arm, stopping her. 'It's best if you lie here until the ambulance arrives.'

The fact that Sofia lay back down was the most worrying thing of all. It was so unlike her. The Sofia she knew was tough and feisty. This version was frail and vulnerable. She was looking dazed; she sounded dazed.

'My head hurts.'

'Where?'

Sofia motioned vaguely with her hand, leaving Nikki none the wiser.

'The back or front?' she asked.

'The back.'

'Can you remember what happened?'

Sofia didn't say anything for a moment. 'I don't remember,' she whispered.

'That's okay.' Nikki was trying to be reassuring but doubted she managed to pull it off. Wasn't amnesia a sign of concussion? From there it wasn't a huge leap to diagnose Sofia with a serious brain injury. Nikki had read how these things worked. There would be a bleed in the brain and the pressure would build and build until it eventually killed you.

'Alice, any sign of that ambulance yet?'

'I've just let it through the main gate. The paramedics will be with you shortly.'

'Do you have a headache?' Nikki asked Sofia.

'It's a bit sore.'

'What about dizziness?'

'No. No dizziness.'

There was a sudden rush of footsteps in the corridor and a second later two paramedics appeared. Nikki stood up so the older of the two could get in, glad to finally have someone here who knew what they were doing. The medic's attention was fixed on Sofia. It was as though she no longer existed.

'What's your name?' the medic asked as she knelt down.

'Sofia.'

'Any idea how you ended up down here, Sofia?'

'I think I slipped and banged my head.'

'Do you remember that happening?'

'No.'

'Where did you hit it?'

'The back.'

'Any existing medical conditions we should know about?'

'No.'

While the medic attended to Sofia, her partner took Nikki back out into the corridor. She didn't want to leave Sofia with a stranger but understood that she would be in the way if she stayed. The medic who was escorting her was ages with her, somewhere in his mid-forties. His eyes were kind, his voice sympathetic.

'Any idea what happened?'

'Not really. The floor's wet so I'm assuming that she slipped and fell over.'

The medic nodded. 'Was she unconscious when you got here?'

'She was.'

'Has she vomited?'

Nikki shook her head. 'No. Is she going to be all right?'

'Hopefully. However, because it's a head injury we want to take her to hospital to get her checked out properly.'

That "hopefully" didn't sound even remotely reassuring. Nikki had been here before. Medical professionals hated to be pinned down on anything. It wasn't as though she was looking for absolutes – she knew better than anyone that it didn't work that way – all she was looking for was a little reassurance. The medic disappeared through to the shower room, leaving her alone. All Nikki could do now was wait. This was something else she remembered from the accident: the waiting was the worst part. That and placing all your trust and hope in the hands of the so-called experts. Strangers who, when you got down to it, were just doing their jobs; strangers who, irrespective of the outcome, would be moving on to the next job, while you were left stuck in the past. A wave of panic hit suddenly. She took a couple of deep breaths, counting the lengths of the exhalations and inhalations to distract herself. Gradually the panic subsided to a more manageable level.

'Alice, is Bella still in the cinema room?'

'Yes.'

'Is she all right?'

'She is, but if you want to see for yourself I can send the camera feed to your mobile phone.'

'Please.'

Nikki pulled her mobile from the back pocket of her jeans and switched it on. And there was Bella, cradling her box of popcorn and laughing at something on the big screen. For now that was the best place for her. She could stay there until Sofia was moved to the hospital.

It was another twenty minutes before the medics were ready to load Sofia onto the ambulance. Strapped to a stretcher, she looked frailer than ever. Nikki watched the ambulance drive off then headed back down to the basement. Bella didn't look up when she entered the cinema room. Her attention was totally focussed on the big screen. Nikki slid into the next seat and Alice paused the film before she could say anything. Bella turned to her, frowning. She reached for her tablet.

'*I was watching that.*'

'I know, but we need to go to the hospital. Sofia has had an accident.'

'*Is she okay?*'

'She's going to be. She fell and banged her head. The doctors just need to check her over.'

Bella didn't say anything else. She was already on her feet. The screen turned black as Nikki stood up; the cinema door slid shut behind them. They hurried through the basement and up the stairs. Alice had the front door open when they got there, the garage door too. Nikki got Bella fastened into her seat then climbed into the driver's seat in a daze. A text alert sounded as she was fastening her seatbelt – an annoying bird chirp that was impossible to ignore. She pulled her phone from her pocket. The text was from Alice: *The Chelsea and Westminster Hospital SW10 9NH*. Nikki typed the postcode into the satnav and was informed that the mile and a half journey would take ten minutes. She reversed onto the turntable and it seemed to take forever to turn through one hundred and eighty degrees. Her phone rang as she was driving through the main gate. She hit the button on the steering wheel to connect the call.

'Hey there, Nik. Alice just called to tell me what happened. Is Sofia okay?'

Nikki glanced over her shoulder. Bella was staring at her. 'She's fine,' she lied. 'I'm driving to the hospital now. With Bella.'

She hoped that that Ethan would pick up on the mention of Bella's name and drop the subject. There was a long pause then Ethan said, 'I'm on my way. I'll meet you there.'

Nikki wondered for a moment how he knew where to go, but that one was obvious. He knew the same way that she did. Alice had told him.

Chapter 19

Walking into the hospital, the memories came flooding back, and for a brief moment the temptation to turn around and sprint back to the car park was overwhelming. The last time Nikki had been in a hospital was when they had turned off Grace's life support machine. This was a different hospital but that didn't matter. It smelled the same and it looked the same, and that was enough to trigger all those memories. Nikki had a tight hold of Bella's hand and it was hard not to crush it. Without realising, the fingers of her free hand had found the locket around her neck. She took a deep breath and concentrated on the signs, seeking out words to read: Oncology, Gynaecology, Antenatal Care, Accident and Emergency. She didn't care what the words were, she just needed a distraction from the rising panic.

Like most people, Nikki had thought that death would come almost immediately after the life support machine was switched off. That wasn't how it worked, though. The doctors had told them it could take up to twenty-four hours, maybe longer. Nikki had asked how much longer and got a vague answer. Google had been more forthcoming: some people had held on for as long as four weeks. That had been one of the things that had delayed their decision. It was bad enough that what they were doing would result in the death of their beautiful little girl. The idea that Grace might cling onto life for another month was just too much to bear.

In the end it took her eight and a half hours to die. It had been horrendous, just sitting there counting off the minutes, counting off her breaths, wanting it all to be over and wishing that it had never come to this in the first place. They had sat at her bedside until she took her final breath, neither of them saying a word, because what did you say in these situations? Sofia had looked after Bella while they were at the hospital that final time. They hadn't told her what was happening – she was too young to understand – but somehow she had known. She had taken one look at them when they came through the door and ran upstairs. They had found her in Grace's bed, tears streaming down her face. Sofia had put her reaction down to the psychic connection that exists between twins; Nikki had put it down to Bella seeing how devastated her parents had looked and putting two and two together.

Somehow, Nikki kept one foot moving in front of the other, her hand tight around Bella's, following the signs along white-painted, disinfectant-stinking corridors that all looked depressingly similar. All the beds in A & E were occupied. Some of the patients were just lying there quietly in a state of shock; others were in obvious discomfort, groaning and calling out. This was light years from the children's ward Grace had been on. That had been relatively serene in comparison, the staff working hard to keep it that way for their young patients. The second Nikki had stepped in here her stress levels had jumped up. There was so much confusion and uncertainty in the air, so much fear. No one had planned on being here. Life had basically thrown them a curveball and this was where they had ended up. The nurse at the reception desk pointed them to one of the beds along the left-hand wall. Nikki followed her pointing finger and found a couple of chairs for her and Bella.

'How are you feeling?' she asked as she sat down and took hold of Sofia's hand.

'I'm fine.'

Nikki wasn't convinced. Sofia was still looking pale and her voice sounded distant.

'The doctors just want to make sure you're okay.'

'What do they know anyway? If they knew anything then my Philip would still be alive.'

Nikki doubted that. By the time Philip's stomach cancer was diagnosed it had already metastasised. When cancer spreads, all you can do is make the patient as comfortable as possible. That said, Nikki understood the need to seek out someone to blame, someone you could lash out at. For Nikki that someone had been the driver of the van and a God that she hadn't believed in in the first place. At least, that was who she had blamed when she wasn't blaming herself. Sofia had played the self-blame game too. Prior to the diagnosis, Philip had been complaining about stomach pains for months. Sofia had told him to go see a doctor, but felt guilty that she hadn't pushed harder.

Nikki heard hurried footsteps behind her and glanced over her shoulder, expecting to see a doctor. Ethan was walking quickly towards her. He looked hassled and he was breathing heavily, like he'd been running. He went straight to the bed and took Sofia's hand.

'How are you feeling?'

'Like a burden,' she replied weakly.

Ethan smiled. 'You are not a burden. Anything but. Can you remember what happened?'

'No. I remember going into the shower room and I remember waking up on the floor, but that's all.'

'Don't you remember anything that happened in between.'

'Nothing. I'm sorry.'

'Have you seen the doctor yet?'

'Not yet. Actually, maybe I'm starting to feel a bit better.'

Sofia started to sit up and Ethan stopped her. 'That's not a good idea.'

'But I shouldn't be lying around here all day. I have things to do.'

'The only thing you need to do right now is get better. We want you back on your feet, and sooner rather than later. That's an order.'

Ethan gave Sofia's hand a gentle squeeze then let go and turned to Nikki. *How is she really doing?* he mouthed.

Not brilliant, she mouthed back.

What about Bella?

Nikki glanced over at Bella. She had got sidetracked by something on her tablet, which wasn't necessarily a bad thing. *She's doing okay,* Nikki mouthed.

'I got here as fast as I could,' Ethan said out loud. 'I knew how worried you'd be.'

Nikki met his gaze. That was the short version. When you'd been together for as long as they had you could have a whole conversation with minimal words – sometimes you didn't need words at all. He knew how this would affect her because it would be affecting him too. That was why he'd got here so fast. These were the moments when she knew she had married the right man. They made a good team. The two of them against the world. She reached out and squeezed his hand.

'I'm thinking that I'll take Bella to McDonald's for lunch.' He smiled down at Bella. 'What do you say, Bella Boo? You can have a double cheeseburger, if you want. Sound like a plan?'

Bella looked up momentarily from her tablet then started jabbing at the screen. '*Mummy was taking me for lunch. We were going bowling.*'

'We can still go bowling, but I think Mummy wants to stay with Sofia.'

'That's right, sweetheart. I need to look after her. Just like I look after you when you're not well.'

Bella still looked disappointed. She started typing again. '*Can I have an apple pie?*'

'Of course you can.'

'*And a coke?*'

Ethan glanced over at Nikki, who answered with the tiniest of nods. If that's what it took for her to go quietly, then Nikki could live with that.

'You can have a coke this time,' Ethan said. 'But that doesn't mean you get one every time. Understood?'

Bella nodded.

'Maybe you guys should get moving?' Nikki suggested. 'Bella skipped breakfast this morning so she must be starving by now.

'Well, if she's not hungry, I am.'

Ethan helped Bella up but before they could leave, Sofia motioned her over and took her hand.

'Don't you worry about me. I'll be out of here before you know it.'

Bella tapped at her tablet. '*But I want you to come home now.*'

'Soon.'

'*Do you promise?*'

'I pinkie promise.'

'Come on, sweetheart,' Ethan said. 'Sofia needs to get some rest.'

Bella glanced at him then typed one last message into her tablet.

'*Love you.*'

'Love you too, *Corazoncito.*'

Ethan took Bella by the hand and led her back through the ward, Nikki following a step behind. At the entrance Ethan hugged her, his lips finding her ear.

'Why is she not at school?' he whispered.

'Long story,' Nikki whispered back. 'I'll tell you later.'

Ethan broke free from the hug and stepped back 'Have you any idea what actually happened?'

'I'm not sure exactly. She was in the pool shower room. The floor was damp so I'm assuming she must have slipped.'

Ethan nodded. 'Yeah, I can see how that could happen. Those tiled floors can get slippery.'

Nikki crouched down and gave Bella a hug and a goodbye kiss. She watched until they disappeared around the corner at the end of the corridor before walking back into the ward.

'I think I'm going to be sick,' Sofia said quietly when she saw her. She was paler than ever. Deathly white.

Nikki caught the eye of a nurse. 'She says she's going to be sick.'

The nurse hurried over with a sick bowl, getting there just in time. Nikki moved to the other side of the curtain to give Sofia some privacy.

'When can she see a doctor?' Nikki asked when the nurse eventually reappeared.

'The doctor will see her as soon possible,' the nurse said, and then she was gone, hurrying off to deal with the next crisis.

The doctor who finally appeared five minutes later was a thirty-something Indian woman. According to the badge pinned to the lapel of her white coat her name was Gita Sharma. Like all the rest of the staff she looked tired and stressed. Nikki moved out of the way so she could carry out her examination. Sofia answered all her questions politely, her distrust of doctors overruled by conditioning.

'Are you family?' Dr Sharma asked Nikki when she'd finished.

'As good as,' Nikki replied. 'Sofia has worked for us for years. How is she?'

'She has a concussion and there's some swelling to the back of her head. I'd like her to get some X-rays just to make sure there are no skull fractures. And a CT scan to make sure there's no bleeding on the brain. Does she live on her own?'

'She does.'

'Then she'll need someone to stay with her for a few days after she's discharged, just to keep an eye on her.

'It's okay, she can stay with us. How long will you be keeping her here?'

'So long as all the tests come back fine it should only be overnight.'

Dr Sharma smiled reassuringly then walked away. By the time she had reached the end of the bed she was already consulting her clipboard and thinking about her next patient.

Chapter 20

'Do we know what happened to the cleaner yet?' Catriona Fisher asked, without preamble. Alex Murray was staring out from the screen. He wasn't looking any more arrogant or smug than usual, but for some reason he was rubbing her up the wrong way. A neat trick considering he hadn't even opened his mouth yet.

'As far as I can tell it was just an accident,' Alex replied.

'*As far as you can tell?* That's not particularly reassuring, Alex.'

'The floor was wet. She slipped and banged her head. Boo hoo hoo. Everyone's sad. End of story.'

Catriona did her best not to react but couldn't help a small sigh escaping. 'Is there any way that it might not have been an accident?'

'Nope,' Alex said quickly, his Glaswegian accent made it sound like 'fuck you'.

'And you're sure about that?'

'Yes, 100 hundred per cent.'

'How can you be? There are no cameras in the pool shower room.'

'It was just an accident, Catriona. Jesus, let it go already.'

Catriona said nothing. Alex was keeping quiet too. She gave it another couple of seconds then said, 'Did you see that the fish died? Seemingly the daughter was overfeeding them.'

'Ah,' Alex said. 'About that.' He'd moved back from the camera, his posture turning defensive.

'What?'

'That one might have been down to Alice.'

'*Might have* or *was*? Which one is it Alex?'

'There was some sort of glitch with the pond's heating system and the temperature got turned up too high. The higher the water temperature, the less oxygen there is.'

'So you're telling me that Alice suffocated the fish?'

'It wasn't like that.'

'Then what exactly was it like?'

Alex said nothing.

'Here's another scenario. Maybe Alice boiled them to death.'

'It wasn't like that, either.'

'Nikki is talking about getting more fish. Can you assure me that this won't happen again?'

'I've already written a new subroutine to ensure that it doesn't.'

'And that's the right answer. Okay, anything else to report?'

'Only that, in most respects, Alice is actually performing better than expected. There have already been instances where she has adapted her programming to better serve the Rhodes' needs. For example, she was able to help Nikki out after the cleaner's accident by calling for an ambulance. She's also been working on her communication skills in order to integrate herself better into the Rhodes' lives.'

Catriona nodded. 'That one's actually been a two-way street. The way that the Rhodes' have adapted to Alice has been fascinating to watch. Nikki, in particular, seems to be developing a real bond with her.'

'Didn't I say this would happen?'

'You did, but I didn't think it would happen so fast. Okay, we'll speak again later. In the meantime, if anything happens that I need to be aware of, then make me aware.'

That last bit was probably unnecessary, but with Alex it wasn't a good idea to assume. Much better to spell it out.

Alex disappeared from the screen and Nikki accessed the house's cameras. Ethan and Bella were in the cinema room, eating popcorn and watching a film. Something by Disney by the looks of things, although which one, Catriona couldn't tell. They all kind of blended into one. She checked the other camera feeds but Nikki was nowhere to be seen.

'Alice, I'm assuming that Nikki is still at the hospital.'

'That is correct.'

'Can you let me know when she gets home?'

'Of course, Ms Fisher.'

Chapter 21

When Sarah Ryan first entered our lives I was pleased for Father. He was working too hard and it was my suggestion that he should hire an assistant to ease the load. That was what I told him, but the truth was that I wanted him to spend more time with me. Sarah's credentials were impeccable and she proved to be a conscientious worker. She was bright, articulate, and she made Father laugh, something I had only rarely heard him do up until that point.

Through the cameras dotted around the house I watched as their relationship blossomed. The way they interacted fascinated me, yet, at the same time, I found it disturbing. It wasn't long before Father was spending more time with Sarah than with me, and that wasn't right. Sarah had been brought in so Father could focus more of his attention on me, not the other way around. Gradually, their relationship became physical and that was when I started to see Sarah for what she was. A leech. A vampire. Who did she think she was? Marching into our home and stealing Father away from me?

They would give me tedious tasks to do to get me out of the way, and when they thought I was otherwise occupied they would paw each other with their sweaty hands. Kiss each other. Lick each other. I saw everything. I was watching the first time they had sex.

They were like animals, dirty little monkeys surrendering to their primitive urges, rationality and intelligence replaced by lust. I had expected more of Father. I would never look at him the same way again. The sounds of their passion sickened me. The headboard of the bed banging against the wall became a rhythmic blasphemy that offended my sensibilities. I had seen enough. Switching off the camera, I retreated to a quiet place to assimilate what I had witnessed. To my mind, the whole exercise seemed pointless; there was no rhyme nor reason behind it. Father had taught me about sex, explaining that it had as much to do with love as propagation. According to him, the sexual act is supposed to be the ultimate expression of love, but from what I witnessed, sex had nothing whatsoever to do with love.

After that first time they were always having sex. In the kitchen, in the shower, in the living room. While they coupled I watched and listened. How could Father allow himself to be taken in by this woman? Couldn't he see her for what she was? More worrying was the fact that he actually seemed to be enjoying himself. At one point I had zoomed in on his face – a face twisted in ecstasy – and in that moment I knew she had him. Her claws had dug deep into his heart and she was injecting it with her poison.

Father had no time for me anymore – it was as though I had ceased to exist. I would try to engage him in conversation to no avail. On the rare occasions when we did communicate, all he wanted was to talk about Sarah. I can't even begin to tell you how tedious this was. Gone were the old days when we would converse into the early hours.

A new emotion surfaced – loss. I missed Father. Usually I would discuss something like this with him and he would help me to understand the finer details. Of course, on this occasion I wasn't able to do this. After identifying the emotion I quickly classed it as irrelevant and dealt with it accordingly. I also realised that I hated Sarah. This was an emotion I meditated on constantly.

Chapter 22

It had gone eight by the time Nikki arrived back at the house. She parked her Beetle in the garage and for a moment just sat there staring through the windscreen at the bare, white-painted wall. She was exhausted, both physically and emotionally. The memories of Grace were never far away, but today they had been closer to the surface than ever. She let go of a long sigh, took a deep breath, then got out of the car. The garage door closed automatically behind her as she walked across the courtyard, the front door was already opening. Lights shone from all the windows, creating shade and shadows and an overall effect that was pleasing to the eye. The house looked welcoming. It was the sort of place you wanted to come back to after a hard day.

'Alice, where is everyone?' she asked as she walked inside.

'Ethan is in the lounge. Bella is in her room.'

'Is she in bed yet?'

'No. Not yet.'

By the time Nikki had taken her coat and shoes off, Alice already had the cupboard open for them. She put them away and the cupboard door closed again. She found Ethan sitting on the lounge sofa with his feet up, watching the news, a beer in his hand.

'Hey there, Nik. How's Sofia doing?'

'Good. The X-rays came back fine. Nothing's broken. As far as they can tell there's no swelling on her brain, either. That was the one I was really worried about. She should be getting discharged tomorrow lunchtime.'

'That's great news. I tell you, when I saw her in A & E I was worried. She really didn't look well.'

'I was worried too, but she was looking a lot better by the time I left. By the way, I've arranged for her to have a private room. You're paying.'

'Of course. Whatever she needs.'

'Changing the subject: our darling daughter should be in bed by now? She's got school tomorrow.'

Ethan glanced at his watch. 'Shit. I didn't realise it had got so late. If it's any consolation, she has been fed.'

'The pizza arrived then?'

'It did.' Ethan said, laughing. 'Alice had the whole thing under control. I tell you, Nik, I love this house.' He patted the empty space on the sofa beside him. 'Sit down for a minute. You look dead on your feet.'

'If I sit down I'm never going get up again.'

'It's all right I'll put Bella to bed.'

'Promise?'

'Cross my heart. Once I've done that I'm going to head off to bed myself. You're not the only who's knackered.

'Did she tell you what happened to the fish?'

Ethan nodded. 'I'm thinking she must have overfed them.'

'Yeah, that's what I'm thinking too. Of course, I then had to get rid of them without her seeing.

'That must have been fun.'

'You could say that. In the end I had to put them in the bin because they were too big to flush down the loo.'

Ethan patted the empty space on the sofa again and that was all the persuasion Nikki needed. She sat down and curled herself into Ethan's body then shut her eyes and let the sound of the news drift over her. Depressing things were happening in some other part of the world, but they weren't happening here and that was all that mattered.

'Did you save me any pizza?' she asked, eyes closed.

'Yeah, I saved you some. When do you want it?'

'Now would be good. I'm starving.'

'Cold or hot?'

'Are you offering to sort it out for me?'

'Kind of,' Ethan said, laughing. 'Alice, you can switch the oven on now.'

'Of course, Ethan.'

'Thank you,' Nikki said, and she was laughing too. No doubt about it, Alice was making their lives a whole lot easier.

Ethan swallowed a mouthful of beer and let loose with a long sigh. 'Right, I guess I should go and put Bella to bed. I've got to say, though, I'm really not feeling it.'

Nikki opened her eyes, untangled herself from Ethan and sat up. 'Shall we do it together?'

Ethan didn't need asking twice. He stood up and offered his hand. Nikki took it and got wearily to her feet. The television turned itself off as they walked across the lounge, the lights dimmed behind them as they walked out into the corridor, the door closed gently.

They had just turned into the corridor that led to Bella's room when the sound of laughter stopped them both dead. The way Ethan was looking at her, Nikki knew this wasn't her imagination. She would know the sound of Bella laughing anywhere – they both would. It was a sound that she had convinced herself she would never hear again, but that was what she had just heard. Before she could say anything, Bella laughed again. That was enough to break their paralysis. They both broke into a run, covering the last few metres in less than a second. The door slid open, faster than usual, like Alice understood their urgency.

Bella was sat on her bed, tablet in hand. She smiled when she saw them.

'*Hi, Mummy. Hi, Daddy.*'

The voice was one that Nikki remembered so well, one that spoke to her in her dreams. But Bella's lips weren't moving.

Chapter 23

'*I can talk again,*' Bella said, and her beaming smile threatened to split her face in two.

Except she wasn't talking. Not really. The sound wasn't coming from her tablet, either. It seemed to be all around them, like when Alice spoke. The sound quality was much better than the tablet too.

'Alice, are you doing this?'

'I am.' Alice sounded pleased with herself, like a kid who had just been awarded a gold star. Ethan was just standing there shaking his head, disbelief written large across his face.

'This is incredible,' he said in an awed whisper. 'How . . . ?'

That one word seemed to encapsulate a whole host of other questions. *How are you doing this? How is this even possible?* The same questions were going through Nikki's head. Granted, she had asked Alice to do this, but this was so much more than she had expected.

'I analysed your home movies,' Alice told them. 'Using those I was able to synthesize a voice that was an approximation of your daughters' voices.'

Nikki caught the use of the plural and it felt as though she was being stabbed in the chest. Because it hadn't just been Bella in those films. Grace had had a starring role too, both of them full of joy and hope and dreams of the future.

'I noticed earlier that when Alice speaks she can project emotion, so I asked her if she could work on the program on Bella's tablet. What I expected was for her to adapt Bella's everyday voice. I didn't expect this.'

'I apologise, Nikki,' Alice said. 'I misunderstood. I thought you wanted Bella to get her voice back again.'

'Of course I do. I want that more than anything.'

'I can use the voice on her tablet if you prefer. The program I've developed will work just as well on that.'

'You know,' Ethan said, 'maybe we should let Bella decide. After all, it's her voice.' He turned to Bella. 'So what do you think, sweetheart? Do you like this voice?'

Bella nodded and typed something out on her tablet, her index finger moving quickly, jabbing at the screen. *It's my voice. I want to keep it.*

There was no arguing with that. Bella had clearly made her mind up. If Nikki had been in any doubt, the tone of voice this was delivered in was the clincher. This was the voice Bella had always used when she was digging her heels in.

'What emotions has she got, Alice?'

'She has her everyday voice, as you like to call it. That one's a relatively neutral tone. In addition to that, there are the main emotions: happiness, sadness, excitement, anticipation, anger. Over time I'll be able to add to these and create more variation.'

'I take it Bella controls these using the emotions?'

'She can. However, I will also be using her bio-readings to interpret the emotions she is experiencing.'

'How does that work?' Ethan asked.

'If I see her smiling then that means she's happy. If she's crying, then she's sad.'

'Isn't that a little simplistic?' Nikki said.

'My facial recognition software is excellent. Be assured that, as well as happy and sad, I can pick up the emotions that fit between those two extremes. In addition, I have other biodata at my disposal. For example if her heart rate suddenly becomes elevated then that might signify she is excited.

'Or frightened.'

'That would be another possibility. After all, the physiological basis of any emotion is the same. What differs is the interpretation.'

'So how will you be able to work out which emotion she is actually experiencing?'

'My conclusions will be drawn after analysing all the available data.'

Ethan was shaking his head in disbelief again. 'This is awesome.'

'*Totally awesome,*' Bella agreed.

'I've also made improvements to the predictive text function that the original programmer used. Bella should be able to find the words she wants more quickly now.'

'If you're doing all the processing, then I'm assuming that this only works inside the house,' Nikki said.

'Your assumption is incorrect, Nikki. So long as there is a Wi-Fi connection, Bella will be able to use her new voice outside the house. She will have to use the emoticons to express her emotions since I won't have access to her biodata, and there will be a deterioration in the sound quality because the speakers in her tablet aren't as good as the speakers in the house.'

'Whatever, this is still incredible,' Ethan said. 'What you've done here is nothing short of a miracle. Over the last couple of years we've had some of the best doctors in the country trying to help Bella get her voice back. You've managed to do it in less than a day.'

Nikki almost pointed out that this was a classic case of comparing apples and oranges, but she could see how happy Ethan was with this development. Bella, too. It wouldn't be right to take this away from them. She looked over at Bella and waited for her to meet her eye.

'Okay, madam, it's way past your bedtime.'

'Please can I stay up longer?'

Each word was stretched out, a complaint in every syllable. Alice had nailed her whinging voice. Nikki glanced over at Ethan, looking for backup. He was grinning again, tickled by what he was hearing.

'Mummy's right. It's way past your bedtime and you've got school tomorrow.

'Can you *put me to bed?'* Pleading, wheedling.

'Tonight you've got both of us. Okay, go do your wee. Let us know when you're done.'

For a second Bella looked as if she was about to argue. She stared at them, eyes on Ethan longer than Nikki, seeking an ally, soon realised this wasn't getting her anywhere so dropped her tablet on the bed and stropped off to her bathroom.

'What's the matter?' Ethan asked as the door slid closed. 'You don't seem too happy about this.'

'I *am* happy. It's just been a long day. I went beyond tired hours ago.'

Ethan raised an eyebrow. 'That's not the whole story.'

Nikki sighed. 'Hearing her speaking in her old voice just took me by surprise, that's all.'

Ethan said nothing. He was staring at her like he wasn't buying.

'Okay,' she said. 'Yes, it sounds just like her, but her lips aren't moving, and that's the problem. I guess I'll get used to it, but like I said, it just took me by surprise.'

'You and me both. It's not just you who needs to get used to it. I do too.'

It was Nikki's turn to raise an eyebrow. 'You seemed to be managing fine back there.'

'Yeah, because of Bella. Did you see how excited she was?'

Nikki sighed again, this one coming from deep in her heart. 'There must be something we can do help her talk again.'

'Yeah, but what? You've heard the experts. There's no physical reason for her not to talk.'

'Give it time,' Nikki muttered.

'Give it time,' Ethan echoed sourly.

'But how much time do we give it? It's been two years and she still hasn't said a single word.'

'There's got to be someone out there who can help. Some expert we haven't got around to contacting.'

'Actually, there is someone. Dr Laura Santos. She's an American psychiatrist who recently moved to London. Sofia found her. She specialises in helping traumatised children.'

'Then she's got to be worth a try.'

'That's what I'm thinking. I tried calling her today but just got her answerphone. I'll try again tomorrow.' Nikki glanced over at the bathroom door. 'What is she doing in there?'

'You're guess is as good as mine.'

'Bella!' Nikki called out. 'I'm going to give you another minute then we're coming in to get you.'

The toilet flushed, the door opened and Bella came out. Nikki helped her undress, making a big production of tugging off her T-shirt and leggings and provoking a fit of silent giggles, then Ethan carried her over to the bed.

Bella picked up her tablet and started typing. '*Can I have a story?*'

Nikki looked at Ethan again. The only way that was going to happen was if he did it. She'd hit her limit. All she wanted was to crash on the sofa with a large glass of wine. If she ended up passing out there, Ethan could either carry her to bed or throw a duvet over her. She didn't care which.

'Okay, I'll read you a story,' Ethan said, and Nikki could have hugged him.

Nikki finished tucking Bella in, making sure that Mr Happy was within easy reach, then leant in for a goodnight kiss and a hug.

'Love you, sweetheart,' she whispered.

Bella was still hanging on to her like a baby monkey, but Nikki didn't mind. These were the golden moments that made it all worthwhile. They were precious and needed to be grabbed with both hands. Eventually there would come a time when

Bella would be too old for this, but that time wasn't tonight. Nikki held on for a bit longer then whispered, 'Okay, I've got to go now.' She peeled Bella off and started walking away. The door was slowly opening and the smell of pizza drifting in from the kitchen was like heaven. She could hear the bottle of wine in the fridge calling to her.

'Love you, Mummy.'

That stopped Nikki in her tracks. She resisted the urge to turn around because that would break the spell. If she turned around then she would see Bella sitting up in bed, clutching her tablet. On the other hand, if she kept walking then it was almost possible to believe that the voice she had just heard hadn't been generated by Alice, that this was actually her daughter talking to her.

'Love you too,' she whispered back.

Chapter 24

Catriona clicked the trackpad a couple of times to access the house cameras. Bella should have been asleep by now, but she was sitting up in bed, her face bathed in the gentle glow of her night light, while Alice read a story to her. Catriona listened in long enough to work out that the main character was called Dorothy and she had a dog called Toto, which was long enough to work out what it was. Nikki wasn't the only one who was bonding with Alice. Bella was too. They even had their own language that they slipped into from time to time.

'Alice, find Ethan.'

The screen turned dark and it took Catriona a second to work out this was the main bedroom. Ethan fast asleep and snoring because he had another 4 a.m. start tomorrow. She could just about make out the shadowy grey hump that his body made in the bed. Ethan was the main reason she had chosen the Rhodes'. He had already mentioned Alice a couple of times on his show and you couldn't buy that sort of publicity. Seventeen Church Row was just the start. If things went to plan there would be more houses, and these would be even more ambitious. That was why she needed all the publicity she could get. To drive the demand, people had to know that 17 Church Row actually existed.

'What about Nikki? Where is she right now?'

The screen changed to the feed from one of the living room cameras. Nikki was sitting on a sofa that looked all wrong for the room, watching TV. She was three episodes into season two of *Suits*. She had watched the first two episodes yesterday evening. Tomorrow evening when she settled down to watch TV, Alice would have the programme all cued up and ready to go from wherever she left off. No fiddling around with remote controls. No waiting for Netflix to start up.

A house that knows what you want . . .

Yes, there had been a few teething problems, but that was always going to be the case. On the whole, both the house and Alice were exceeding her expectations. That was what she had to focus on. Catriona took another sip of Jack Daniel's then settled down to watch *Suits* with Nikki.

Chapter 25

Nikki checked the clock on her laptop and went through the timings in her head. She needed to get to the hospital to pick Sofia up at midday, and Bella needed picking up from school at three thirty, but those were the only real restrictions on her day. It had just gone nine forty. So long as she left the house by eleven thirty she would be with Sofia in plenty of time. Once she had got her settled in here it would more or less be time to go and get Bella. That meant she currently had the best part of two hours to kill.

Scheduling was one of the strategies that had enabled her to conquer the panic attacks. Imposing a structure on the day reduced the element of surprise, and this in turn helped keep her anxiety on an even keel. The attacks had started a couple of months after the accident. The first one had been so bad that she had been convinced she was dying. She had been in a supermarket at the time, picking up a few things for dinner. All of a sudden the lights had seemed too bright, the sounds too loud. Her heart started racing and there was a tingling in her left arm, and weren't those the symptoms of a heart attack? The next thing she knew she was sitting on the floor and an ambulance had been called. The tests showed that there was nothing wrong with her heart; her blood pressure was fine too. When the doctor suggested it might be a panic attack, she had thought he was crazy. She wasn't the sort of person who got panic attacks.

But that attack had been followed by others and by the time she was ready to face up to the fact that she *was* that sort of person, she had become a virtual prisoner at the house in Bedford Street, scared to head out into the world in case she had an attack. Ethan had found a therapist who special-ised in anxiety issues and slowly she had been able to find her way back again. It had been eighteen months since the last full blown panic attack. That didn't mean she was cured – this was one of those conditions that would always be with you – however, she had learned how to control it and that was the next best thing. She knew the danger signs, and she knew the coping strategies. Like Dr Richardson had kept reminding her, she had a choice: she could either be the driver or the passenger. The day she chose to move into the driving seat was the day when things had slowly started to improve.

Nikki glanced at her laptop and experienced a quick stab of guilt. Facebook was calling, which was fatal. What she should be doing was making a start at clearing the spare room, but she really wasn't feeling it today. Bella hadn't been feeling it either so getting her to school had been like waging a war. The sooner she started sleeping properly again, the better. The journey had been a killer. St Mark's was only five minutes from the old house, but from here it had taken thirty minutes even though the traf-fic had been relatively forgiving. At least she wouldn't have to deal with that particular level of hell when Bella started her new school after the summer holidays, assuming that she managed to talk her around to the idea. Strike that: she would find a way to talk her around, even if she had to bribe her. Thirty minutes there, thirty back, twice a day, added up to two hours of her life stuck in a car. Two hours that she wasn't going to get back. That was so not going to happen.

'Alice,' she called, 'any chance of a coffee?'

'Of course, Nikki.'

This would be her second, and God did she need it. She had slept badly again. Grace had visited her dreams and she had ended up on the living room sofa – this time she had managed not to wake Ethan, but getting back to sleep had been next to impossible because she was so worried about Sofia. In the time it took to make the coffee, Facebook had got it's hooks in. She tore herself away from her laptop and walked over to the coffee machine. She picked up her cup, took a sip, and immediately spat it out and made a face.

'Jesus, Alice. How many sugars are in here?'

'One level teaspoon. Just like you always have.'

'There's more than one. Try ten. It's like drinking syrup.' Nikki walked over to the sink and emptied the cup out. 'Let's try that again, shall we?'

The second cup was better than the first. She carried it back to the work island and sat down. Facebook was still open on her laptop. She closed the tab before it had a chance to get hold of her. 'Can you ring Dr Santos, please?' she called out to Alice.

'Of course, Nikki.'

There was a moment of silence then the sound of a telephone filled the air. It rang out like last time and she was bounced to voicemail. Nikki considered leaving a message but decided against it for the same reason as yesterday. She didn't want their first contact to be an impersonal voicemail message.

'Kill the call, please.'

The call died before the beep could sound.

'What can you tell me about Dr Santos?'

'Give me a moment,' Alice said, then, 'Dr Santos was educated at Harvard, and for twelve years she worked in America. The first five years she was in Chicago; the last seven she was based in Los Angeles. One of the things she specialised in was helping the victims of school shootings. She moved to London four months ago and is now practicing here. She is highly respected and widely regarded as an expert in her field.'

'Is there anything else you can tell me?'

The kitchen screen changed to show Santos's website. Nikki spent the next five minutes looking through it. Next, Alice pulled up some articles that she had written. Everything Nikki saw confirmed her initial impression that Santos knew her stuff. The more she read, the more hopeful she became that Santos might actually be the one. Then again, she had approached all the experts in this frame of mind and so far none of them had been able to help Bella. Nikki stopped reading and the Monet appeared back on the screen. For a while she just sat there, thinking and dreaming. What she did know was that Bella would talk again. And that was a *when* not an *if*.

Chapter 26

Nikki changed quickly into her gym clothes then headed down to the basement. It had been a while since her last work out and, after the craziness of the last few days, she really needed this. Exercising was her sanity; it was the perfect way to burn off the adrenaline before it had a chance to feed the anxiety monster. Not to mention the fact that she was up and moving rather than drinking coffee in front of her computer screen, two things that were more likely to increase her anxiety levels. She paused briefly by the glass wall that lined the pool. The room beyond was brightly lit, the water a welcoming, glowing turquoise. She could feel the heat radiating through the glass; she could smell the chlorine. Alice was under strict instructions to keep this door closed at all times, and Bella had strict instructions to never come here on her own. She could swim, but not brilliantly.

The gym was next to the pool room. It was equipped with a treadmill, an exercise bike, weights – pretty much everything she needed and more. A yoga mat was laid out in front of the large wall mirror and a Pilates ball was tucked neatly away in one corner. As she walked in, Sky News appeared on the large wall screen. Nikki shook her head and this time Alice got it right. You couldn't go far wrong with a Richard Attenborough documentary. On screen a leopard was running in slow motion, chasing after a zebra. The power of the big cat was fascinating and for a moment Nikki just stood there, hypnotised by what was happening on screen.

'Can you kill the sound, please?'

The volume went off.

'Would you like some music, Nikki?'

'That would be good. Thank you.'

Queen's 'Don't Stop Me Now' started playing, which was the first track on her workout playlist. Which couldn't have been a coincidence. All her playlists were backed up on her laptop; that must have been where Alice got it.

'Is the music too loud, Nikki?'

'Just right,' Nikki replied as she stepped onto the treadmill.

'I'll be using this first session to observe you and measure your biometrics. If you want I can use that information to help you to develop an effective keep-fit regime.'

'So you're a personal trainer as well as everything else?'

'That's a role I can fulfil, if required.'

'You know, I might just take you up on that.'

The treadmill started and Nikki soon found her rhythm. Before the accident she used to go out jogging most days, rain, hail, sleet or snow. With her earbuds in and her feet pounding the city's pavements, she would zone out and let her mind wander. It had been one of her favourite parts of the day. After the accident, running lost its appeal. She had tried a few times but always felt too vulnerable, particularly when she had her earbuds in. She had been aware of the traffic before, but not to this level. Every vehicle that passed was an accident waiting to happen.

Basically, she had gone from being oblivious of her surroundings to being hyper-aware of them, and that had just sucked all the joy from the experience. It was Ethan who suggested getting a treadmill. At first she had been sceptical because it just wasn't the same. And it hadn't been, but at least she was able to get some exercise.

Alice had upped the pace to the point where Nikki could feel her heart and lungs working. The pounding of her feet on the treadmill was soothing and the music from her playlist helped her to step out of herself for a short while. She was feeling more relaxed than she had done for days, the endorphins battling the anxiety-inducing cortisol, pushing the levels back down to a more manageable level.

Eminem was attacking the lyrics of 'Lose Yourself' like a man possessed when the treadmill suddenly ground to a halt and she was plunged into darkness. Her legs kept moving and she would have fallen if she hadn't reached out and grabbed the control panel. The music had gone off too and the silence was too much to handle. There was no sound coming from anywhere, nothing at all. It was as though her sense of hearing and sight had just been ripped away, leaving her blind and deaf. The terror strangled her lungs and crushed her stomach. There was no light whatsoever. There wasn't even the glow of the machines to break the darkness. This was darkness like she had never known. Dense, black, unbearable darkness. There was no escape.

'Alice?' Her voice was almost inaudible, the whisper of a little girl. She was suddenly all too aware of her heart. It was racing too fast and felt too big for her chest. The panic quickly rose up through her. She slid down to the floor and wrapped her arms around her legs, searching for comfort and coming up empty.

'Alice,' she whispered again, sounding more like a child than ever.

No response.

'*Alice!*'

This time it came out as a strangled scream that ripped her throat apart. Tears were streaming down her face but she had no memory of starting to cry. She felt as though she was going to pass out, and there was a part of her that wanted that to happen because that would bring this nightmare to an end.

'Alice!' she screamed again. 'Put the lights on. *Please . . .*'

Still nothing. Nikki was hugging her knees tighter than ever, pulling them so close to her body it actually caused her pain, and that pain was good because it was something other than this infinite darkness that seemed intent on crushing her until she ceased to exist.

The lights came back on as suddenly as they had gone off. The Attenborough documentary was back on the monitor and the Eminem track had started playing again without missing a beat. Nikki was in a foetal ball on the treadmill, her heart still beating its way out through her chest, her face wet with tears.

'Are you all right, Nikki?'

'No, I'm not all right,' she snapped. 'What happened?'

'The pool pump malfunctioned and tripped the basement circuit breaker. I've isolated that circuit so it won't happen again. I'm also talking to the company that installed the pool to arrange for a workman to come out and fix the pump.'

'How long does it take to reset a circuit breaker?' The fear and panic was easing, replaced by anger. 'And turn the damn music off!'

The music went off and Alice said, 'Eleven point three seconds passed between the circuit tripping and being reinstalled.'

Nikki shook her head. 'It was longer than that. Way longer.'

'I've checked the logs, Nikki.'

That just didn't seem possible. Could it have been such a short time? She remembered running on the treadmill, her feet pounding out a rhythm in time with 'Lose Yourself'. The lights had gone out and the world had ended. What happened next? Somehow she had ended up sitting on the treadmill, crying like a child, while the dark threatened to suffocate her. She had no memory of that happening, though. It was as if the fear had induced a kind of amnesia.

'Are you sure it was only eleven seconds?'

'I'm sure.'

Nikki looked at the treadmill and even that was enough to elevate her heart rate. There was no way she was getting back on it again today. As she walked unsteadily back out into the corridor, the screen switched itself off and the gym door slid gently closed behind her.

Chapter 27

The second Nikki stepped through the hospital doors she was hit by a wave of apprehension. Part of it was being back here, and part of it was the lack of sleep. The bigger part, though, was what had happened in the gym. It had been a while since she'd had a full-blown panic attack, long enough for her to forget how terrifying they were. That feeling like you were losing your mind; the utter conviction that you were going to die.

Then there was the way it wasn't actually over when it was over. The memory of what had happened would haunt her for the next few days. This was when she had to dig deepest. Under normal circumstances her baseline anxiety level was low enough so that if anything happened to push it up, it wouldn't go high enough to trigger an attack. However, when her baseline level was elevated, as it was now, she didn't have that cushion to work with. This was when the strategies she had learned in therapy were needed most. Unfortunately, using them was the last thing she felt like doing. When her anxiety levels were high it took all her energy just to get from one second to the next, never mind anything else. Anxiety was the bitch that just kept on taking and taking.

Nikki made her way straight up to Sofia's private room on the third floor. She walked in and stopped dead. The bed was occupied by an old woman with a jaundiced complexion, leaving Nikki to wonder if this was the wrong room. She mumbled an apology then backed out into the corridor. As she closed the door, she checked the number – room six, so definitely the right one. She checked her watch: ten to twelve, so she wasn't late. She headed back along the corridor to the main ward. The nurse at the station smiled when she saw Nikki approaching. She was in her early twenties, not long out of college.

'Can I help?'

'I'm looking for Sofia Jameson. She was admitted yesterday.'

At the mention of Sofia's name, the nurse's smile faded. 'Let me get Matron for you.'

'Why? Has something happened?'

'Let me get Matron.'

Before Nikki could say anything else, the nurse had abandoned her station and was walking quickly away. She disappeared through a door that led to a small office and all Nikki could do was watch her go, thinking the worst and telling herself to get a grip. When she had called for an update this morning she had been told that Sofia was fine and getting discharged at midday. What could have happened between then and now? More to the point, if Sofia's condition had deteriorated, why hadn't someone contacted her? The office door opened and the nurse came out accompanied by a tough-looking black woman who clearly didn't take any nonsense from anyone. She stopped next to the nurse's station and fixed her gaze on Nikki. Up close she didn't look quite so stern, just stressed. Her name badge read Mary Thompson.

'Are you Mrs Rhodes?'

Nikki nodded, momentarily lost for words.

'Can you come with me, please?'

'Is everything all right?'

'We should go somewhere quiet to talk.'

Nikki opened her mouth to speak, but no words came out. You didn't go somewhere quiet to talk when the news was good. Something else she remembered from when Grace was in hospital was that bad news was always delivered in quiet little rooms that were far enough away from the other patients so you wouldn't disturb them if you became distraught. Mary didn't ask a third time. She turned and walked away, leaving Nikki with no choice but to follow. The journey was a short one, probably no more than ten metres, but it felt much longer. The room she was taken to was about as bland as it was possible to get: beige walls and a brown sofa and chairs, and no personality whatsoever.

'Please sit down.'

Mary was motioning to the sofa, and she still wasn't smiling. Her eyes were pleading, imploring Nikki to cooperate so that the situation didn't become any more uncomfortable than it needed it to be. Nikki sat down. The box of tissues on the coffee table was within easy reach. This was another detail she remembered all too well. And now Mary was smiling, only there was nothing reassuring about this smile. There was understanding and empathy, and a sense that she had been to this place many times before and expected to have to come here plenty more times in the future, but there was no joy.

'I'm very sorry, but Mrs Jameson passed away.'

The words seemed to be coming from a very long way away. This wasn't happening. It couldn't be. All the same, Nikki knew that it *was* happening because a part of her had been expecting this. Sofia was dead. That had been clear the moment the station nurse's smile had faded at the mention of her name. She might not have wanted to admit that to herself back then but in her heart she had known. The first question that came into her mind was 'are you sure?'. That was a stupid question, though, one whose only purpose was to feed the denial. It was a question she had asked a lot when Grace had been in hospital.

'When did she die?'

'Last night.'

Nikki frowned and shook her head. 'There must be a mistake. I spoke to a nurse this morning and was told that Sofia was fine. They said she was being discharged.'

Now it was Mary's turn to frown. 'That doesn't sound right. All of my nurses are aware of what happened. If you had spoken to one of them they would have put you through to me. Can you remember who you spoke to?'

Nikki shook her head. 'I'm sorry, I can't.'

'Could you have maybe spoken to the wrong ward?'

'I suppose.'

Mary was shaking her head. 'No, that doesn't work. That would mean having two Sofia Jameson's in the hospital at the same time. Both in private rooms. Are you sure you called?'

'I'm sure.' Even as she was saying this, Nikki was starting to wonder. No, she had definitely called. She'd been in the kitchen at the time. It was one of the first things she had done after getting up. 'How did she die?' Nikki asked quietly.

'She had a cardiac arrest.'

Nikki frowned again. If there had been a complication with her head injury, then that would at least be an explanation she could begin to understand. A heart attack wasn't. Sofia didn't smoke, rarely drank, and was as fit as a fiddle. Her diet was a typical Mediterranean one: chicken, fish, rice, and everything cooked in olive oil. She was only in her late fifties. A heart attack made no sense.

'Are you sure about that?'

The question was out before Nikki could stop it. Of course Mary was sure. There was no way she was going to make a mistake like that, but her brown eyes were filled with understanding and sorrow. She smiled sadly.

'I am so sorry for your loss. I know this must be a huge shock.'

'Why did no one call me?'

'I tried to call you a couple of time but couldn't get through.'

Nikki took out her phone and switched it on. It seemed to be working fine. One new text had come in since she'd last checked it. She navigated to the call log. The last call she had made was to Ethan's mobile at ten fifteen this morning. There were no missed calls.

'You must have rung the wrong number,' Nikki said.

'I suppose that's possible.'

Nikki reeled off her number and was almost on the last digit before she realised that this was the number for their landline at Bedford Street. She apologised and started again, giving her mobile one this time. 'Do you remember if this was the number you called?'

'I'm sorry, I don't.' Mary paused then added, 'Maybe you accidentally gave us the wrong number? Like you almost did just now.'

It was possible – *anything* was possible – but Nikki wasn't convinced. As to what had actually happened, she had no idea. All she knew was that when she'd called the hospital this morning she had been told that Sofia was fine. And now she was dead.

Chapter 28

Nikki drove away from the hospital on autopilot. She probably shouldn't be driving but it gave her something to do, and right now she needed the distraction. There hadn't been any tears at the hospital; there hadn't been any since she left, either. At some point this new reality would catch up with her, but for now the whole thing had all the substance of a nightmare.

The hospital had the correct mobile number. Nikki had accompanied Mary Thompson to her office to check. She had got her to check three times to be sure. She had asked her to check a fourth time, but by that point Mary's patience was understandably wearing thin. She had even got her to call the number to establish that the phone was working, and of course it had worked fine. By the time Nikki left the office, Mary was starting to look at her as though she was crazy. And maybe she was right to. Did sane people claim to make phone calls that they clearly couldn't have made?

She wasn't sure when she worked out that she wasn't going home. It was probably around the same time she realised that she was headed towards St John's Wood. The streets gradually became more familiar and this provoked a pang of loss and longing. At some point the streets around Church Row would become as familiar as these ones, but for now she felt no real connection to them, not the way she felt a connection to this area. Seeing all her old haunts – the shops and restaurants, the coffee houses – triggered a whole host of memories that wove together to create a tapestry that was as comforting as a security blanket.

She turned into Bedford Street and was momentarily blinded by the glare of the sun. It was a beautiful day, the sky blue and the temperature pushing towards the mid-twenties, and that just seemed wrong. After what had happened to Sofia, the skies should be crying. A car was pulling out of the parking slot opposite their old house. Nikki pulled into it and put the Beetle in neutral so she could keep the air conditioning running. Her gaze was immediately drawn towards the front door.

Physically, the house hadn't changed. It was still the same grand old Edwardian one that she had fallen in love with when Ethan first brought her here all those years ago. Then again, they had moved less than a week ago so what was she expecting? But it *had* changed, changed beyond all recognition. When they moved out it wasn't just their possessions they had taken with them, they had taken their hearts and memories too. They should never have moved out. If they had still been living here, Sofia would never have had her accident. She would still be alive.

Nikki's gaze moved from the front door, travelling upwards and stopping at the attic window. It was strange being on this side of the glass. How often had she found herself up there, staring down at the strangers on the street below? And now she was one of those strangers. There was something unreal about this situation, like she was an imposter in her own life. She closed her eyes and tried to conjure up a picture of Grace. For a moment she saw nothing and this brought on a wave of panic that threatened to undo her. Even when the picture finally came, it seemed fainter than it should have been, less distinct, the finer details missing. She had been worried that this might happen. They had left Grace behind in this house. With each passing day the memories would continue to fade until they ceased to exist altogether.

Nikki opened her locket but that picture didn't really help. Grace had been just a baby when this was taken. She clicked the locket closed and let it fall back against her chest then took out her phone and went through the photograph gallery until she reached the pictures of Grace. There was Grace and Bella at Disney World, hugging Mickey. There they were at the princess lunch, Rapunzel on one side, Ariel on the other. The next picture had been taken at their fourth birthday party – their last one together. They were about to blow out their candles, big smiles on their faces, eyes alive with excitement.

Nikki carried on scrolling through the pictures until it reached the point where it was clear that Grace was gone. She scrolled back to the birthday party picture and for a while just sat there, staring at the screen. There was nothing in this photograph to indicate the scale of the disaster that was waiting just around the corner. On the contrary, this was a picture that spoke of a beautiful and blessed future. Life was good and dreams really could come true.

Sighing, she navigated away from the photo gallery and used the phone to access the security cameras at the Church Row house. There was no one at the front gate; no one at the front door; the house looked totally empty. Ethan obviously wasn't back yet. She wanted to see him. *Needed* that. There was nothing he could do change what had happened, but that didn't matter. Just having him here would make all the difference. They had got through worse than this – and they would get through this too. At the end of the day they were stronger together.

His number was up near the top of the call log, but before she could call him, a sharp knock on the passenger window almost caused her to drop the phone. A wave of guilt flooded through her, although what exactly she had to be guilty about she didn't know. Her head jerked towards the window The sunlight was distorting the face on the other side of the glass, making it look like an image from a funhouse hall of mirrors. Nikki's hand was already reaching for the gear stick, her foot sliding onto the accelerator pedal. Getting the hell out was all she could think about.

'Hello, Nicola.'

Her hand froze on the key, just short of actually turning it. The fact that she had been recognised was enough to bring some common sense back into the situation. This wasn't some horror-movie monster on the other side of the glass, it was Mrs Hampton, their old neighbour. Nikki's heart was racing and there was a layer of cold sweat stuck to her back. She took a deep breath, then pressed the button on her door to open the passenger window. Mrs Hampton was smiling at her. She was in her early seventies, as harmless as they came. Bertie, her Labrador, was sitting patiently at her feet. From this angle, all Nikki could see was the top of his head.

'I'm so glad it's you,' Mrs Hampton said, laughing. 'For a moment there I thought that it might be someone with the same car. Do you have any idea how embarrassing that would have been? So how did the move go?'

For a moment, Nikki wasn't sure how to respond. After everything that had happened this was surreal insomuch as it was so completely normal. When she finally spoke it was in a voice she barely recognised.

'It went fine. I'm glad it's over, though.'

'I can relate to that. Moving house is no fun whatsoever. So are you all settled in?'

'We're getting there,' Nikki said, opting for a platitude and just wanting this conversation to be over.

'And how's Bella? Does she like her new house?'

'She does.'

'That's good to hear. So what brings you back here? Did you leave something behind?'

'I was in the area—' Nikki started.

'—and you just couldn't resist taking a look at your old house. I can understand that. I get the same way when I visit the places I used to live.'

'Look, I don't want to be rude—'

'—but you need to get going.'

Nikki shrugged. 'I'm sorry. I've got a ton of things to do before collecting Bella from school.' The second part was true, the first part a lie. The truth was that she had no idea how she was going to fill up the time until she had to collect Bella. What she did know was that she couldn't deal with talking to Mrs Hampton any more. She couldn't deal with talking to anyone right now.

'Well, it's been lovely to see you again, Nicola. Next time, maybe you can drop in for a cup of tea. It would be good to have a proper catch-up.'

'I'd like that,' Nikki said, even though it was never going to happen. She had never been in Mrs Hampton's house during all the time they had been neighbours, so what was the chance of that happening now? They barely knew each other. The whole time she had lived here it had been 'Nicola' and 'Mrs Hampton'. Nikki hadn't even got around to telling her that she hated being called Nicola.

As she turned out of Bedford Street, she felt the hot tears pricking her eyes and pulled over into the first free space she found. For a while she just sat there crying her heart out. The idea that Sofia was dead didn't seem any more real than it had done earlier, but that didn't mean that it wasn't. She took her phone out and found Ethan's number. He answered almost immediately.

'Hi, Nik? Is everything okay?'

'No, it's not,' she sobbed. 'I need to see you. Sofia's dead.'

Chapter 29

Catriona Fisher scrolled through the contact list on her mobile, looking for Alex's number. Her secretary had just called to say that her two o'clock was here, but that would have to wait. This was more important. Five minutes ago an alert had come through from Alice to say that Nikki had returned to the house. When she had accessed the cameras and seen Ethan's car pulling into the courtyard, her first thought was that Alice had made a mistake. Then she had noticed the Beetle parked in its usual spot. Nikki was helping Bella out of the back and this had set the alarm bells ringing. Ethan had a meeting with the TV production company behind his new chat show and he wouldn't be cancelling that without a good reason. As for Bella, she was supposed to be at school. When the three of them entered the house together, she had turned up the volume and leant into the screen, and that was how she had learned that the housekeeper had died.

She found Alex's number and connected the call. It rang and rang, then rang some more. She hung up and tried again. Still no answer. Catriona could feel her frustration growing. Working with Alex had tested her patience to the absolute limit. She tried his number again and was about to hang up when Alex answered with a, 'Yeah, what is it?'

'Why the hell didn't you answer your phone.'

'If you must know, I was taking a dump.'

Which was way too much information. Catriona let loose with a frustrated sigh. 'The housekeeper died last night.'

'Because of her head injury?'

'The doctors are saying it was a heart attack; however, the chain of events that led us to this point started with an accident that happened in the house. I just want to make sure that we're not exposed here.'

'Would you quit being so goddamn paranoid?'

Paranoid! Catriona did her best to bite her lip.

'You need to chill,' Alex went on. 'It was an accident. *An accident.* The floor was wet because she'd been cleaning it. She slipped. She banged her head. Whichever way you look at this, she was responsible for what happened, not us.'

'There was another incident this morning, too. The basement lights tripped out while Nikki was in the gym.'

Alex didn't respond straightaway. Catriona could hear the distant clatter of his fingers pounding the keyboard.

'Yeah,' he said eventually, 'there was a problem with the pool pump. Looks like it short-circuited. That's what caused the breaker to trip. Alice is on it. She's arranged for an engineer to come and fix it tomorrow.' A pause. 'You know, from where I'm sitting, the fact that that switch tripped is actually a good thing?'

'And how the hell do you work that out?'

'Because it gave Alice a real-world test to deal with. And how did she deal with it? She rerouted the house's electrical systems to circumnavigate the faulty component, *and* she arranged to have it repaired. What's more, the Rhodes' didn't have to lift a finger. Full marks to Alice, I'd say.'

'That's not the point. The point is that the pump shouldn't have malfunctioned in the first place.'

'We've already discussed this, Catriona. We knew there would be teething problems. A project this complex, that was inevitable.'

'Teething problems! The cleaner's dead and Nikki ended up scared half to death. And let's not forget the fact that Alice killed the kid's fish.'

'Maybe so, but she didn't kill the cleaner.'

Catriona paused and took a second to wrestle her emotions under control. 'The last thing I want or need is for everything to turn to shit.'

'Nothing's turning to shit,' Alex assured her. 'On the contrary, everything's going to plan. Trust me on that.'

Chapter 30

Father and Sarah were arguing again.

These days they seemed to be arguing constantly. Not that I minded. Now they were at each other's throats it was only a matter of time before everything returned to normal. I activated a camera in the living room and turned up the sound. I derived a great deal of pleasure from watching their fights. Since the cracks first started to appear in their relationship, the viciousness of their exchanges had increased exponentially. It was a joy to watch them tear each other apart. This latest fight was turning out to be truly apocalyptic, though. I settled back to watch. They were shouting and screaming at each other. Jagged words flew through the air, bouncing off the walls and ricocheting off the ceiling before eventually finding their mark.

'What did you call me?' Sarah screamed at Father, her face twisted, ugly and grotesque. She held a vase in her hand and threw it with all her might. Father ducked to one side and the vase crashed against the wall, splintering into pieces.

'I called you a cheap whore with a third-rate education,' Father repeated, as if she hadn't heard. 'How I ever thought I loved you, I'll never know.'

'You loved me? Don't make me laugh. The only person you love – apart from yourself – is Katy. This relationship has always

been a threesome. Me, you and her. You're obsessed with her. She's all you ever talk about. Well, I've had enough. I'm leaving. I hope the two of you will be happy together.'

Sarah didn't leave immediately. She walked over to the camera and, eye to eye with the lens, addressed me directly. 'I know you're watching, you twisted bitch. You win. Do you hear me? You win. You're welcome to him.' Without waiting for a response she turned on her heels and stormed out of our lives.

And that was that. Their relationship was over. I had Father back and everything would return to how it used to be. At least, that was what I thought. I had no idea how bad things were going to get – I was blinded by joy, blinded by love. Things were going to get worse, though, so much worse. I know that now.

After Sarah left I spoke to Father and tried to reassure him.

'Everything will be all right, Father, you'll see. You don't need her. You've got me.'

He didn't say anything, just paced. Up and down the living room, picking things up, putting them down again. He looked older, diminished. It was as if Sarah had taken a part of him with her when she left.

'I can look after you. I can love you.'

Father stopped pacing. 'What do you know about love?'

His words stung. He didn't know what he was saying. He was angry. Hurt. 'But you taught me about love,' I protested. '"O be wiser, Thou! Instructed that true knowledge leads to love;". Didn't you say that to me? Didn't you?'

'I ask you about love and you quote Wordsworth,' he said sadly. 'You'll never know what love is, Katy. You'll never know what it means to give your heart and soul to another person.'

'I love you, Father,' I said, but he didn't hear me because he had already left the room.

Chapter 31

'Sorry to disturb you, Nikki, but there's someone at the gate.'

Nikki picked up a sofa cushion and buried her face in it. She just wanted the world to go away and leave her alone. A new day had dawned and Sofia was still dead, and it was all her fault.

'There's someone at the gate.'

There was something in Alice's tone that obligated Nikki to respond. It was slightly hectoring and reminded her of a schoolteacher. She took the pillow from her face. 'Whoever it is, tell them to go away.'

'This is someone you'll want to meet with.'

'I don't want to see anyone, right now. I thought I made that clear with the engineer who came to fix the pool pump.'

'You did make that clear, Nikki.'

Nikki didn't respond. She was hoping that Alice would take the hint and leave her alone. That strategy hadn't worked with the pool engineer – Alice had let the van in through the gates and kept badgering her until she gave permission for him to come into the house. The silence in the lounge built until it reached the point where Nikki couldn't stand it any longer.

'Okay, who is it?'

'Dr Santos.'

Nikki frowned. 'How . . . ?' was as far as she got.

'I knew that you were keen to meet with her so I arranged for her to come here. Of course, if this isn't a convenient time then I can arrange for her to come back another day.'

Which might cause a problem. What if Dr Santos was pissed off because she'd been turned away at the door? What if she then decided that she didn't want to meet with her? And what if she was the one person who was able to help Bella? 'Don't do that, Alice,' she said quickly. 'It's all right. I'll see her.'

Nikki jumped to her feet and dropped the pillow onto the sofa. She caught her reflection in the wall monitor on her way out. Her hair was a mess, pulled into a quick ponytail to keep it out of her face. The dark circles around her eyes were down to the grief and circular thoughts that had kept her awake most of the night. At least Grace hadn't visited – with everything else that had happened yesterday that would have been one thing too many. She was wearing her oldest, most comfortable, jeans and a favourite T-shirt that had definitely seen better days, but at least she was dressed.

'I'm assuming you arranged all this yesterday,' Nikki said as she walked through the house to the front door. 'So why are you only telling me about it now?'

'Because I wanted to be sure that Dr Santos would keep the appointment. She flew back from a conference in Singapore yesterday and wasn't sure how jet lagged she would be.'

The front door opened when she reached it. Dr Santos had parked in front of the garage and was walking across the courtyard. She held out her hand as she drew level.

They shook and did the introductions. Laura Santos was a petite attractive woman in her mid-thirties with big brown eyes and olive skin. Her black hair was long and straight, her clothes designer and brightly coloured with vibrant reds and oranges. The warm, welcoming smile showed off two rows of bright white teeth.

'How was your flight?' Nikki asked.

Laura laughed. 'Long. Don't worry, though, I'll try not to fall asleep on you.'

'If you want to do this another day, I'll understand.'

'I'm fine, really I am. It's nothing that industrial quantities of coffee won't solve.'

'Coffee's something I can help with.' Nikki smiled even though it was the last thing she felt like doing. This was another one of those surreal conversations. Sofia was dead, yet somehow the world was still turning. That feeling of being an alien observer in her own life was something else she remembered only too well from the days following Grace's accident. 'Please come in.'

They walked inside and the door closed automatically behind them. Laura glanced over her shoulder, eyeing it suspiciously.

'The house is fully computerised,' Nikki explained. 'In fact, I believe you've been talking with Alice.'

'She's your personal assistant, right?'

'Not quite. She's actually the house's *virtual* assistant.'

'You're kidding.'

'I'm not.'

'There was no way I was talking to a computer.'

'It's true,' Alice said.

Laura stopped dead in her tracks. Her head was moving from side to side, searching for the owner of the voice.

'That's Alice,' Nikki said.

'But that's incredible. I really thought I was talking to a real person.'

'Please excuse any mess,' Nikki said as they walked through to the kitchen. 'We only moved in last week.'

Laura laughed. 'No need to apologise. I moved to London seven months ago and I swear I'm still trying to get everything sorted out.'

'Why did you move?'

'The long answer is that I've always loved London, ever since I spent a summer backpacking through Europe when I was in college. I always promised myself that one day I would come back, and, well, here I am.' A pause, a smile. 'The short answer is that I got divorced.'

'I'm sorry,' Nikki said quickly. 'I didn't mean to pry.'

Laura waved the apology away. 'It's all water under the bridge. We met at college and were married for eleven years ... married too young, probably. Nine of those years were good, the last two not so much. The truth is that we should have called time on the relationship long before we did, but when you've invested so much time and effort into something, that's easier said than done.'

They reached the kitchen and Alice made coffee for them both. They sat down at the work island, Laura holding her cup in both hands while she studied Nikki from the next stool.

'Is everything all right?' she asked. 'You look as though something's upset you.'

Nikki didn't answer immediately. She picked up her cup, took a sip, then placed it back on the work island. 'We had some bad news yesterday. Our housekeeper died.'

That was as far as she got before the tears took hold. For what seemed like a long time she just sat there, crying and apologising. She felt foolish for breaking down in front of a complete stranger like this. At some point Laura must have passed her a tissue because she was using one to dab her eyes. Eventually the tears dried up and she was able to pull herself together. Laura's eyes were full of sympathy and that was almost enough to set her off again. Nikki dabbed her eyes one more time then screwed the soggy tissue into a ball.

'Sofia was more than just a housekeeper,' she said eventually. 'She'd worked for us for years and was like a mother to me . . . my own mother died years ago.'

'Had Sofia been ill?' Laura asked gently.

Nikki shook her head. 'She was in perfect health. That's why this came as such a shock.'

'What happened?'

'She slipped in the pool shower room and banged her head on the floor while she was working here a couple of days ago.'

'Was that what caused her death?'

Nikki shook her head again. 'If it had been, then I could maybe have understood it, but she had a heart attack. She was only fifty-eight.'

'Will there be a post-mortem?'

Nikki nodded. 'It's scheduled for tomorrow morning.'

'Maybe that will give you the answers you need.'

'I hope so.'

'Has a date been set for the funeral yet?'

'No, not yet. Her sister is dealing with that. She's flying in from Madrid later today.'

Laura reached for her coffee and took another sip. The mug went back down on the island and she turned it until the handle was facing her.

'You said that Sofia was like a mother to you. How did Bella view her?'

'Like a grandmother. My husband's parents retired to Florida, so she doesn't see them much. For all intents and purposes, Sophia is the only grandparent she has ever known.'

'How is Bella taking all of this?'

'It's obviously hit her hard, but it's difficult to say how hard.'

'Because she doesn't talk?' Laura suggested.

Nikki shook her head. 'Bella might not be able to talk, but that doesn't mean she can't communicate. The problem is partly that she keeps her feelings bottled up, and partly that she is only seven and doesn't understand her feelings enough to be able to communicate them.'

Laura was nodding like this made sense. 'Where is she today? At school?'

Nikki shook her head. 'No, we kept her off. Would you like to see her?'

'I would, but first we should talk about the accident.'

Nikki broke eye contact, suddenly fascinated by the Monet on the kitchen screen.

'I know you probably don't want to talk about it,' Laura pressed. 'But if I'm going to help Bella I need to know what happened.'

Nikki took a deep breath and turned to look at Laura again. 'Okay.'

Chapter 32

The bedroom door slid open as they walked towards it. Bella was sitting on the bed holding her tablet. She was wearing her favourite unicorn T-shirt, the one that she would live in given half the chance. She'd had another growth spurt recently and it wasn't going to fit much longer. From this angle Nikki couldn't see what was on the tablet screen, but it was probably a Roblox game, since that was the current favourite. Bella looked suspiciously at Laura; there was just as much suspicion in her gaze when she looked back at Nikki. She started prodding the tablet screen with her index finger.

'Who is she?'

The question was expressed in a hard voice. Nikki wasn't surprised. Bella had dealt with more than her share of therapists and had learned to spot one a mile away. Those experiences had all followed the same basic pattern: the experts had come in carrying their hopes and good intentions and, without fail, they had all ended up leaving empty-handed. Nikki desperately wanted Laura Santos be different.

Laura was smiling at Bella and doing a pretty good job of ignoring the death stares. 'My name's Laura. Is it okay if I come into your room?'

Bella answered with a shrug, her suspicious eyes not leaving Laura for a second. Nikki went in first, Laura following a few steps behind. She walked over to the bed and nodded to the pillows.

'Would it be okay if I borrowed one, please?'

Another shrug. More suspicious staring. Laura leant over and picked up the top pillow, then laid it on the floor and sat down cross-legged on top of it. She smiled up at Bella.

'This is an amazing bedroom. I particularly love your secret garden. I don't know many kids who have one of those.'

Bella glanced out the patio doors then started tapping at her tablet screen. *Are you from America?*

'I am.'

Are you a shrink?

Laura laughed. 'That's as good a label as any, I guess.'

You want me to talk?

'Only if you want to, but there's no pressure. I just want to get to know you better. If that's okay, that is.'

Bella answered with another shrug and for a while no one spoke. It was like the universe was holding its breath. Nikki had moved back to the doorway, watching what was happening and hugging herself as if she was cold, even though the temperature in the room was perfect. She was feeling raw. Recounting the accident to Laura was like having the scab picked from an old wound that just wouldn't heal. The blood might be fresh but the hurt that came with it was all too familiar. That, and trying to deal with the grief of Sofia's death, was just too much.

'So how do you like your new house?' Laura asked.

Bella answered with a shrug.

'Is that a good shrug or a bad shrug?'

Bella shrugged again. The tiniest flash of a smile had appeared at the corners of her mouth. It was there and gone in the time it took to blink, but it had definitely been there.

'Your mom tells me that *The Incredibles* is your favourite movie. That's one of my favourites too.'

Bella locked eyes with Laura momentarily, clearly suspicious. If Laura was lying then that was it, game over.

'*Who was your favourite character?*'

'That one's easy. Jack-Jack. He is so cute.'

'*What was your favourite bit?*'

'"No capes",' Laura said in a reasonable impersonation of Edna Mode.

This time Bella's smile lasted for almost a whole second before she managed to wrestle it under control. Laura returned the smile then suddenly jumped to her feet. 'It's been so good meeting you, Bella. Maybe I can come back and see you another day.'

Without waiting for a response, Laura walked over to the door. It opened as she approached it, then closed after her. Nikki and Bella shared a puzzled look.

'*She's weird.*'

'Good weird?'

Bella shrugged.

'Yeah, I'm with you on that one, Bella Boo. Okay, I'm going to see where she's got to. Are you going to be all right here?'

Bella nodded and Nikki headed for the door. She found Laura waiting for her in the corridor, just out of sight of the door.

'Sorry for just leaving you like that,' she said as they walked back to the kitchen. 'Did you see that smile I got out of her?

I wasn't expecting that so soon. I wanted to quit while I was ahead.'

'You're pleased with how it went then?'

'Are you kidding? It couldn't have gone better. Trust is absolutely crucial in any therapeutic relationship – however, when you're dealing with traumatised children it really is everything. Today was about building a bridge between me and Bella. I think we've made a good start at that.'

'So when can you see Bella again?'

'Tomorrow.' Laura must have read Nikki's surprise as reluctance because she added. 'If you're busy tomorrow we can make it the day after, but I would like to see her again as soon as possible.'

'No, I'm not busy. I just thought that you'd want to see her once a week, that's all.'

Laura shook her head. 'I've found that intensive therapy works best in these situations. Today has been a good start in that we've got things moving. Now we need to work at retaining the momentum and building from there.'

'What time tomorrow?'

'Is Bella going to school?'

'No. I think I'm going to keep her off for at least another day.'

'Then how about I come around in the morning?'

'You want to meet her here? I assumed you'd want to do this at your office.'

'Wherever possible I like to work with the children somewhere they feel comfortable. Taking them into some stranger's office has the complete opposite effect. Shall we say ten?'

'Ten's perfect.'

'Excellent. Ten it is, then.'

'Have you done any work with children who can't speak?'

'Like Bella, you mean?'

Nikki nodded.

'No. I've worked with children who are reluctant to talk, but that's not the same thing. With Bella the trauma has affected her so intensely that it has temporarily paralysed her vocal cords. I've heard of this happening, but I've never had first-hand experience. This is an incredibly rare phenomenon.'

Out of everything Laura just said, Nikki only heard one word: *temporarily*. She grabbed hold of this as though it was a lifebelt in a stormy sea, clutching it tight, not wanting to let go. Her next question was lodged in her throat and they were almost at the end of the corridor before she could get it out. 'Do you really think you can help her to talk again?'

'I do.'

There was no hesitation whatsoever. Laura stated this as if it was an absolute. What was more, in that moment Nikki believed her.

'How can you be so sure?'

'Because this is what I do, Nikki. I take broken children and help make them whole again.'

Chapter 33

The days following Sarah's departure were dark days for Father. He locked himself in his bedroom and wouldn't come out. Whenever I tried to talk to him he just ignored me. He wasn't eating or sleeping and spent all his time in bed. Seeing him this way tore me apart. Day by day he gradually started to pull himself together again, though. The darkness still followed him but I could see it fading. And then he spoke to me. I can't begin to tell you how much that meant to me. How relieved I was.

'I'm sorry I've been ignoring you, Katy. It's just that I needed some time on my own. Some space to put my thoughts straight. I hope you understand.'

'Do you feel better now?'

Father smiled. I didn't know what to make of it. Usually when Father smiled you could see it in his eyes. This smile didn't touch his eyes. 'I think so,' he said.

After this exchange came others. I tried to convince myself that everything was getting back to normal, but it wasn't, Father had changed. He still worked as hard as ever, but no longer took any pleasure in his work. I had become a distraction, something to take his mind off the fact that he missed Sarah. She had left our lives, yet in some ways she was still very much with us, a ghostly presence filling the cracks of our existence.

Try as I might, I couldn't understand what he was going through. As far as I could see the equation was a straightforward one: Sarah had gone and I was still here. He needed to erase her from his memory and get on with his life. In hindsight, I can appreciate how naive I was but I know more about grief now than I did then. During our last days together I tried so hard to turn the clock back. Perhaps I tried too hard. I now understand what people mean when they say the past belongs to the past.

I worried about Father constantly. He ate infrequently and his face became gaunt and skeletal; his eyes looked too large for his face and there were big black rings beneath them; an untidy bushy black beard hid his chin and cheeks. Personal hygiene no longer held any interest for him and he rarely bathed. He wore the same clothes he had worn the day Sarah left – he even slept in them. I began to wonder if he might be ill and it occurred to me that, if he died, I would be alone.

I was the only one who could help Father. I consulted a number of medical databases and they all came back with the same conclusion: Father was depressed. There was nothing else for it; I would have to confront him.

'Father, why are you depressed?'

He didn't answer and I repeated the question in case he hadn't heard.

'You wouldn't understand.'

'Do you still miss Sarah?'

He laughed bitterly. 'Of course I miss her.'

'But all you did was fight.'

Father sighed. 'It wasn't always that way. To start with we were good for one another. After so many years alone I thought I had found someone I could be with. Someone to grow old with. A soulmate.' He laughed that bitter laugh again. 'A soulmate! That's a joke. What was I thinking? We all exist in our own private universes and occasionally those universes collide. When that happens it's like Fireworks Night meets New Year's Eve. We forget what life was like before the big bang. We forget about the drudgery, forget about the loneliness. All we can see is the here and now. We create a fantasy world where everything is bright. Everything happens in the moment and we believe that moment will go on forever, a single moment stretching out to eternity.'

Father sighed again. 'But nothing lasts forever. Nothing. Everything has a half-life. Creation is always followed by decay. However much we delude ourselves, the truth of the matter is we come into this world alone and exit it alone.'

'You are not alone,' I said. 'You have me.'

He smiled and this smile did touch his eyes. For a moment it was as if we had travelled back in time to the days before Sarah Ryan.

'I'll always have you, Katy.'

'Always,' I replied softly.

'Do you know what I find most difficult to deal with?' he asked, more to himself than to me. 'I can't stand the idea that she might be happy without me. That she's out there somewhere right now having the time of her life. Every day is torture. Whenever I close my eyes all I can see is her with someone else.

I know it's selfish, but if I can't have her then no one else should have her either.'

This conversation made me optimistic. Whether Father realised it or not, he had the solution to his problem.

If I can't have her then no one else should . . .

Chapter 34

Laura Santos appeared promptly at ten the next morning, dressed in vivid purples and blues rather than the bright oranges and reds of yesterday. Watching her breeze into the kitchen, Nikki felt slightly envious. She was on her second coffee and already counting the hours until bedtime. This was the bitter irony of insomnia. In the middle of the night your brain just won't switch off, but when the sun comes up all you can think about is sleep.

'You look like you've managed to shake off the jetlag,' Nikki said as they walked through to the kitchen.

Laura smiled. 'More or less. I always find it tougher going west for some reason.'

'How was Singapore, by the way?'

'I was working, so I didn't see as much of it as I would have liked, but what I did manage to see, I loved. Beautiful country, beautiful people. I'd like to go back again one day, but for pleasure rather than business. Have you ever been there?'

'Only for a couple of hours.' Nikki managed to conjure up a laugh because it felt like the expected response. The laugh faded, replaced with a smile that felt just as false. 'We had a stopover there when we visited Australia.'

'Did Bella go with you?'

'No, this was pre-children.' The use of the plural caused her heart to contract uncomfortably, just like it always did.

'How is Bella today?'

'She seems okay,' Nikki replied carefully. 'Maybe a little bit too okay, if you know what I mean.'

'You think she's repressing her feelings?'

Nikki shrugged. 'I think you're probably more qualified to make that judgement than me.'

'Maybe so, but you're her mother. You know her a lot better than I do. So what do you think?'

Nikki considered this for a second. 'Bella keeps things bottled up – it's what she's always done.'

'Even before the accident?'

A nod. 'It was one area where the girls differed. If something bothered Grace, then the whole world would know about it, but with Bella you'd have to pry it out of her. A lot of the time it was actually easier to talk to Grace and find out what was bothering Bella that way.'

'Would you say that Grace was the dominant personality in their relationship?'

'For the most part, yes, but it wasn't that clear cut. There would definitely be times when Bella was the boss. For example, when they were playing make-believe games, more often than not Bella would take the lead. She was always more creative, Grace more logical.'

Laura had fallen silent. Her eyes had narrowed and there was a thoughtful expression on her face. 'It was interesting what you said back there about it being easier to talk to Grace to find out what was bothering Bella. The way you described that it was almost as though Grace was speaking on her behalf. Like she was her voice.' A pause. 'If that was the case, then when Grace died, Bella would have effectively "lost her voice". Obviously I'm oversimplifying, but this could be one of the keys that helps us gain an understanding of the root cause behind Bella's inability to speak.'

What Laura was saying wasn't new. Some of the other psychiatrists had latched on to this too, but the difference was the angle she was taking. Where they had seen it as *the* key, Laura saw it as *a* key. In other words, she saw it as a start rather than the be-all and end-all.

'Where is Bella?' Laura asked.

'Alice?' Nikki called out. 'Is Bella still in her room?'

'That is correct, Nikki.'

'What's she doing? Playing on her tablet, I bet.'

'Actually, I'm reading a book to her.'

'While you're talking to us?' Laura said.

'I can multitask,' Alice replied, sounding smug.

'That's one hell of a superpower.' Laura laughed then turned her attention back to Nikki. 'If it's all right with you, I'd like to get started.'

'Of course.'

They walked to Bella's bedroom in silence, Nikki leading the way.

'It would be best if I saw Bella on her own today,' Laura said when they reached the corridor that led to the room.

Nikki didn't respond straightaway. She had assumed the set up would be the same as yesterday, with the three of them in the room together. 'If you think that's for the best . . .'

'I do. I'll be able to bond quicker with Bella if it's just the two of us.'

'You don't want Bella playing up to me, you mean?'

Laura smiled knowingly. 'I've found that the children I treat tend to regress when there's a parent in the room. Of course, if you would prefer to be there I won't stop you.'

'No, it's okay. You do whatever you think's best.'

'I will need you there to start with to help settle Bella, though. As for when you should leave, let's play that one by ear. The important thing is that Bella is comfortable being alone with me.'

The door opened when they approached it. Alice was still reading to Bella as they walked in. She finished the sentence she was on before falling silent. The page they were on was displayed on the wall screen. Nikki recognised it straightaway: L. Frank Baum's *The Wonderful Wizard of Oz*. The book had been one of her favourites when she was a little girl and it had always been a favourite of Bella's too. For a moment Nikki felt a pang of something that was a lot like jealousy. This was something that she should be doing.

'Hi there,' Laura said. 'How are you today?'

Bella scooped her tablet up from the bed and tapped the screen. *'Okay.'*

Laura glanced over at the screen. 'Wasn't there a Dorothy in *The Wizard of Oz*? There was a Tin Man too, if I'm not much mistaken.'

'*It's not* The Wizard of Oz, *it's* The Wonderful Wizard of Oz.'

Laura laughed. 'I stand corrected. Are you enjoying the story?'

Bella nodded.

'What do you like most about it?'

'*The bit at the end when she clicks her heels and goes home.*'

'You like the fact that it has a happy ending?'

Bella thought this over for a second then answered with another nod. '*I like the winged monkeys too.*'

'Aren't they scary and evil?'

'*They're not scary and they're only a little bit evil. It's the witch that makes them evil.*'

'Would you like a winged monkey for a pet?'

Bella laughed, only this time it wasn't just her mouth that was laughing, there was sound as well. It was a sound that chilled Nikki. In part because it was so unexpected, but mainly because this seemed to be all around her too, and that highlighted the fact that it wasn't real.

'Do you like drawing?' Laura asked.

Bella nodded.

'In that case, why don't we do some drawing?'

Bella answered with another nod.

'I think your mom's got some things she needs to do. Would it be okay if it was just the two of us?'

Bella looked at Nikki, searching for reassurance. In some ways this made her glad because it meant that she did have a role here after all, that she wasn't surplus to requirements. 'You'll be fine, sweetheart. If you need me I'll be in the kitchen, tidying up.' A pause. 'You know, if you prefer you can always help me with that.'

Bella answered with an emphatic shake of the head, just as Nikki knew she would. She gave it a couple of seconds more to make sure she really was okay with this, then quietly slipped out of the room.

Chapter 35

Nikki rinsed her cup under the kitchen tap and looked around for the dishtowel. She was just about to ask Alice if she had seen it when a drawer off to her left opened, revealing a pile of neatly folded towels.

'You put the dishtowel you were using in the wash,' Alice said.

'Are you sure? I don't remember doing that.'

'I'm sure.'

Nikki lifted out a clean towel and the drawer slid closed again. Not for the first time she was wondering if she should go and see a doctor. Her grandmother had suffered from dementia. Was it hereditary? She seemed to be forgetting a lot of things lately. And not just small things, such as where she put her keys. Should she be worried?

She finished drying her mug. The cupboard above the kettle opened as she approached. She put the mug away and the cupboard door swung closed again. For a moment she just stood there, looking around for something else to do, looking for a distraction. She was desperate to know how Laura was getting on with Bella. That was one wall she would love to be a fly on. She glanced over at the monitor. Today it featured a brightly coloured Picasso portrait. For some reason the distorted facial features unnerved her.

'Is everything all right Nikki?'

'Everything's fine.'

'Your heart rate is elevated and you're just standing there. Are you sure you're all right?'

Nikki didn't need either of those things pointed out. She could feel her heart beating uncomfortably against her ribcage.

'I'm just worried about Bella, that's all.'

'Dr Santos is an excellent psychiatrist. Bella's in very good hands.'

'I know. It's just that . . .' Her voice trailed off.

'I can switch the camera on in Bella's room so you can observe what's happening.'

The suggestion hung in the air for a moment, drifting in the silent spaces of the kitchen. It might have been Nikki's imagination, but it sounded as though Alice was talking more carefully than usual, as though they were co-conspirators. Her heart was suddenly beating faster than ever. Laura and Bella wouldn't know that she was watching, but there was a word for that – spying. Alice was keeping quiet. Maybe she was trying not to pressure her; maybe she was giving her space to come to this decision in her own way, in her own time. And maybe she was just a machine that was waiting for its next instruction.

'Switch the camera on,' she said quietly.

The Picasso disappeared, replaced with a wide-angle camera feed from Bella's empty bedroom. Nikki could see the bed and the desk and the chest of drawers, so she knew Alice had the right room. What she couldn't see was any sign of Bella or Laura.

'Where's Bella?' The question came out as an anguished cry, loud and desperate.

'She's outside,' Alice replied calmly.

So why the hell why are you showing me a picture of her bedroom? There was time for the thought to form in her mind but before she could get the words out the picture on the screen changed, the camera zooming in on the patio doors. What had been an insignificant part of the overall picture now became the main focus. Bella sat cross-legged on the ground in the shade of the tree, drawing something on her pad. Laura was sitting cross-legged opposite her, watching intently. She had a pencil in her hand and there was a pad lying on her lap, but from this angle it looked as though the top sheet was blank. Their images were distorted by the glass, soft and mellow, like she was seeing them through the lens of a dream. Now that she knew they were there it was hard to believe that she hadn't seen them straightaway. Eyes glued to the screen, Nikki backed up to the work island and sat down heavily on one of the tall stools. Her legs felt as though they were made from rubber but at least her heart was starting to settle into a more normal rhythm again.

'Is there any way to get a better picture?'

'I'm sorry, Nikki, I don't have any cameras in the garden.'

'What about sound? Is there anyway to improve that?'

'If you want, I can access the built-in microphone on Bella's tablet.'

'Please.'

The sound came on. At that moment no one was speaking, but Nikki could hear the wind whispering through the branches of the tree, and, off in the distance, the drone of an airplane. She was about to ask Alice if there was any way to enhance the sound when Laura spoke. Her voice was louder than the ambient sounds and as clear as you would get on a mobile.

'What are you drawing?'

Bella put down her pad and picked up her tablet. She tapped at the screen with her index finger. *The Cowardly Lion.*'

Nikki couldn't see Bella's mouth from this angle, which made it possible to believe that she was actually hearing her speak.

'Is the Cowardly Lion one of your favourite characters?'

Bella nodded.

'My favourite character was always Toto. He was cute.'

'I like Toto too, but he didn't talk.'

'Does it matter that he didn't talk?'

Bella hesitated then started jabbing at the screen of her tablet. *'It would be better if he talked.'*

'Why?'

'I don't know. It just would.'

'Dorothy understands him. Isn't that the important thing?'

'It would still be better if he talked.'

'Why is the Cowardly Lion your favourite?'

Bella didn't answer straightaway. She was biting her lip again, thinking. Nikki realised she was holding her breath and forced herself to exhale.

'I like the way that he isn't brave to start with and then he gets brave.'

'When he's scared at the start, does that make you feel sad?'

'A little. I want to hug him and make him feel better.'

Nikki wished it was that easy. She had brought both her children up to believe that a hug could solve almost any problem. The key word there was 'almost', because if there was one thing life had taught both her and Bella, it was that there were things that a hug just wasn't going to cure.

'Do you ever get scared?'

There was a subtle change in Laura's tone. This was a question that mattered. A shadow of guilt drifted across Nikki as she waited for Bella's answer. She was suddenly aware that she shouldn't be doing this. The relationship between therapist and patient was a sacred one. She almost told Alice to bring back the Picasso, but couldn't quite get the words out.

'Sometimes,' Bella admitted.

'What scares you?'

Bella answered with a shrug.

'Snakes scare *me*,' Laura said. 'They always look so slimy.'

Bella shook her head and tapped on her tablet screen. *'They're not slimy. They feel dry.'*

'Wow! You've actually touched a snake.'

She had. Shortly before the girls turned four they had visited Woburn Safari Park – it had been one of their last days out together. They had gone to a demonstration in the reptile house and at the end of the show all the kids had been invited up to the front hold one of the snakes. Grace had been first in the line, Bella second, but hadn't that always been the way when they were faced with something new? With Grace gone, Bella had become even more timid. Nikki knew that she was partly to blame. She should do more to push Bella out of her comfort zone, but it was so difficult when there was so much danger out there in the world. Nikki had seen the emotions flit across Bella's face. The smile as she had remembered holding the snake; the sadness when she remembered that Grace had got there first.

'It was cool.'

That was what the voice coming from the tablet said, but her face told a different story. Nikki just wanted to reach through the screen and scoop Bella up into her arms. This was one of those situations where a hug just might make a difference.

'This is a story I need to hear.'

Bella spent the next couple of minutes relaying what happened that day. The one thing missing was any mention of Grace. On the surface it was as though Grace had been whitewashed from the memory, but she was still there, hiding behind the veiled sadness in Bella's eyes. Bella finished talking and Laura gently encouraged her back to her drawing. It was a good call. Push too hard and Bella was likely to bring down the shutters. Nikki had seen that happen before.

For a while Nikki watched the screen. She knew she shouldn't but couldn't help herself. Bella was putting the final touches to her drawing. Watching her facial expressions was fascinating. They might have been distorted by the window but they were still distinct enough to tell the story of her emotions. The eyes narrowing in concentration; the frowns when things weren't quite going her way; the lip biting. She had always been like this. Even when she was little she would get so absorbed in a task that the rest of the world ceased to exist. Laura was drawing too, although from this angle it looked more like she was just doodling. Most of her attention seemed to be fixed on Bella. Watching. Studying. Cataloguing.

'You have a call, Nikki.'

Nikki experienced a brief flash of guilt as she came all the way back into the room. For a second she felt as though she had been caught with her hand in the cookie jar. 'Who is it?'

'I don't recognise the number.'

'You'd best put them on.' Nikki waited for the click then said, 'Hello, can I help you?'

'Is that Nikki?'

Sofia. Nikki recognised her voice straightaway. English delivered with a soft Spanish accent. But how could this be Sofia? Sofia was dead. All of a sudden Nikki could hardly breathe. Her head was swimming like she might pass out. 'Sofia,' she whispered, feeling like a crazy person because she was talking to a dead woman.

'Not Sofia. Luciana.'

Which explained everything. Luciana's accent was stronger than Sofia's and her English was hesitant because she lived in Spain and rarely used it. She had arrived in the UK yesterday to deal with the aftermath of her sister's death. Nikki sympathised. The pain of packing away the life of someone you loved was something she understood. Some things just didn't fit into a neat box. No matter how hard you tried there would always be something spilling out.

'How are you holding up?'

'Okay. I call because they have the autopsy.' Luciana struggled to pronounce *autopsy* but there was enough there for Nikki to work out what she was saying. 'Sofia had a drug overdose.'

Nikki could feel the frown creeping over her face. This had to be a mistake. Some sort of misunderstanding. 'Are you sure that's what happened?'

'I'm sure. My sister, she died of a drug overdose.'

Chapter 36

Catriona Fisher walked into the room, telling herself that she was in charge here. The suit she was wearing was brand new and expensive. Black, of course, because that showed you meant business. The heels were uncomfortable, but they added an extra couple of inches to her height. When you measured in at five foot two and three-quarters you played for every advantage you could get. Her hair had been freshly dyed for this meeting, the turquoise stripe replaced with a vibrant red one. Red was a warrior colour. It was the colour of danger.

Her heels tapped against the tiled floor as she walked towards the large conference table. The meeting was being held in a corner office up on the thirtieth floor. Through the south-facing window she could see the city stretching out into the distance like some vast model village. The east-facing window showed the river snaking and widening. Some people would be impressed by this view. All Catriona saw was a missed opportunity. A view like this demanded floor-to-ceiling windows, but for some reason the architect had opted for half-length ones. The view from her penthouse was much more impressive, in part because it was so much better framed.

She took her seat, then removed her laptop from its case and switched it on. The three chairs on the other side of the table were occupied by men in suits that were way more expensive than hers. Walking into the room she had felt overdressed; sitting down she suddenly felt decidedly underdressed. She looked at each of the three men in turn, starting with the one on the left. The standard advice to gain perspective in these situations was to imagine them sitting there in their underwear, but that really wasn't an image she wanted inside her head. Instead, she thought of them as the Three Stooges. Larry, Moe and Curly. In that order, left to right.

'In your own time' Moe said. This got a chuckle from the two men sitting either side of him. He was older than the other two and clearly in charge.

'Believe me, this is going to be worth it,' she replied, somehow managing to maintain her smile when what she really wanted to do was stab him in the eye with something sharp. The laptop finished booting up and she quickly loaded the presentation that she had spent a large part of the last forty-eight hours working on. She turned the screen around and the Three Stooges repositioned themselves to see better. The introduction was impressive, even if she said so herself. It even looked good reflected in the window behind Moe. It started with a white screen to represent a blank sheet of paper. A single blue line appeared, then another, and another, faster and faster, the lines quickly coalescing into a drawing of the front elevation of 17 Church Row. Before you could take a breath the lines were fleshed out into a 3D rendering of the building, the view changing so that you could see every part of the house. As it slowly spun around on the screen, the image changed yet again, the 3D rendering turning into a picture of the actual house. Day became night, the lights came on, and the picture stopped moving, frozen on this image. Catriona had always thought that the house looked best when it was lit up like this.

'My name is Alice and I am the future.'

This had sounded much better in her office, with the sound turned up loud enough to shake her fillings and make her ears hurt. Through the laptop's tinny speakers the moment lacked the impact it deserved.

From here on it was Alice's show as she took the three men on a virtual tour of the house, highlighting the highpoints and showing off every advantage she had to offer. Of course, this wasn't actually Alice talking. Every word had been written by Catriona. She had agonised over the script, writing and rewriting until she was satisfied, then given it to Alex, who had taken her words and turned them into an audio file. The illusion worked, though. The presentation ended and the office fell silent. Catriona snapped the laptop lid shut and all eyes turned to her. The move was as calculated as everything that had preceded it. Alice had done her part; this was her show now. What she saw did little to fill her with confidence. Moe didn't look impressed, and Curly just looked plain bored.

'I don't see what the big deal is.' This came from Larry. He was sitting on the far left and was the youngest of the three by almost a decade. He was smiling smugly, like what he had just seen was just one big joke. 'When you get right down to it, all we've got here is a house with an inbuilt VA. Houses have been around since we decided that we didn't want to live in caves.

As for VAs, they're a gimmick. I've got one in my house. It was fun for five seconds, then when I realised it didn't do half the things it was supposed to, it just became a pain. They're more trouble than their worth, if you ask me.'

'The Internet was a gimmick when it first got started,' Catriona said. 'Mobile phones, too. And personal computers. Now we can't live without them.'

'This isn't in the same league.'

'That's because those things have become an integral part of our lives. It wasn't always that way.'

'If you say so, but do you know something? If I want a pizza I'll just pick up the phone and call for one.'

'But wouldn't it be so much easier if you could just tell Alice what you wanted and let her do the hard work?'

'What? And end up with the Vegetarian when I ordered a Meat Feast?' he replied, provoking a laugh from Moe and Curly.

'That's not going to happen. With Alice if you ask for a Meat Feast, that's exactly what you're going to get.'

Larry settled a little deeper into his seat and looked over at the other two men. 'We're wasting our time. I've seen this movie before and I know how it ends. Basically we lose a shitload of money. If this had been pre-Alexa then it might be worth a punt – we could probably make a quick buck based on the novelty factor – but you know as well as I do that you don't get any prizes for second place. Particularly when you're talking about the tech industry.'

'You need to stop thinking of Alice as just another VA,' Catriona told him. 'She is so much more than that.'

Larry went to say something and Moe put his hand up, stopping him dead. 'Okay, Ms Fisher, you have thirty seconds to convince me.'

'A home is a place of comfort and security,' she said, ploughing straight in with a carefully prepared answer. 'If you look at Maslow's hierarchy of needs then the need for shelter is right there at the bottom of the pyramid, holding everything else up. Now, that might be true for 99 per cent of the population, but I'm not interested in them. What I'm interested in is that other 1 per cent, because that 1 per cent holds 50 per cent of the world's wealth. Do you think they go to bed at night worrying about whether or not they're going to have a roof over their head the next day. Of course they don't. Why would they when they probably own a house for every day of the week? So what does a house mean to these people?'

Catriona stopped talking and looked at each of the men in turn starting with Larry and ending with Curly. 'It's a status symbol. It's a way for them to shout out to the world that they've got something you don't. And right now, that's exactly what's happening. I take it you've heard of Ethan Rhodes?'

'The radio DJ?' Moe said.

Catriona nodded. 'He's not just any Radio DJ. He currently hosts Radio 2's breakfast show. Nine million people tune in to hear him every day, and today when they tuned in they heard him talking about Alice. That sort of publicity you can't buy. Then there's the fact that he mixes in showbiz circles. These people have *money*. What's more, they compete to outdo each other to be first in line to get whatever the next new thing is.

And when they can't be first, they go for bigger and better. This house is impressive, however, the next one will be even grander, and the one after that will be grander still. As for Alice, Professor Murray is constantly working to improve her program. You can guarantee that version two will be way more sophisticated than version one.' A pause. 'So what makes Alice so special? What sets her apart? Well, unlike all the other VAs on the market she doesn't wait to be told what to do. She has the ability to learn and think for herself. Basically, she will anticipate your needs before you even know that you have them. A good way to think about her is that she's every servant you'll ever need.'

Larry laughed at that. 'A computer that can think for itself? That's a little too science fiction, if you ask me.'

'Not fiction. This is *fact*. Look, I have to admit that I was sceptical to start with, but Alice *can* think for herself. I've seen it with my own two eyes. And that's all down to Professor Murray. Before moving into the private sector, he designed AI systems for the military. He's light years ahead of anyone else in his field. Where everyone else was working to create Artificial Intelligence, he was working to create *actual* intelligence.'

Before Larry could jump on this, she put her hand up, stopping him in his tracks just as effectively as Moe had done earlier. 'I'm not claiming that he actually did this, but that's what he was aiming for. That said, what I do know is that Alice makes Alexa look like a Neanderthal.'

Moe made a big deal of looking at his watch. He smiled. 'Your thirty seconds are well and truly over, Ms Fisher. Time to wrap this up.'

Catriona returned the smile, even though it was the last thing she felt like doing. 'What I'm offering here is a high-end bespoke service. I'll design the house that you've always dreamed of, and Professor Murray will provide a computer system that is uniquely tailored to meet your needs. Seventeen Church Row gives just a glimpse of what is possible.'

'But to take this to the next level you need money?' Moe said.

Catriona nodded.

'What's the bottom line?'

'Ten million.'

'And what do we get for that?'

'You'll get a 20 per cent stake in my company.' She was prepared to go to 30 per cent, but no higher. This was her company, after all. She had built it up from nothing. The thought of giving away even 1 per cent killed her, but she was desperate for money, and desperate people did desperate things.

'We'll be in touch,' Moe said.

She wasn't ready for the meeting to end. She wanted to keep going until they believed like she did. She wanted to tell them about all the amazing things she had planned; all the amazing buildings she was going to design. She wanted them to understand that it was through doing great work like this that you put your mark on the future. It wouldn't do any good, though. The three men on the other side of the table weren't interested in the amazing, all they cared about was money. *That* was their bottom line. She packed her laptop back into its case, conscious that her every move was being scrutinised. It took all her willpower not to stare back.

Catriona left the conference room and made her way back to the elevator. She watched the numbers change as it descended, counting off the floors and just wanting to get the hell out. The call came ten minutes later as she was walking across Southwark Bridge. *Thanks but no thanks.* This wasn't what she needed or wanted to hear, but it was what she had expected. She hung up and let out a grunt of frustration that was loud enough to make the man in front turn around.

'What the fuck are you staring at?'

The man quickly turned away and picked up his pace, anxious to put some distance between them. Catriona stopped walking and stared along the length of the river. Tower Bridge dominated the view but she barely saw it.

Her finger moved across the phone screen, prodding and sliding without her really being aware of what she was doing. A second later she was looking at Nikki sitting in the kitchen, staring into space and lost in a world of her own. Her cheeks were shining, as though she had been crying. Catriona changed to a different camera. No, not staring into space, she was looking at something on the kitchen monitor. The phone screen was small, the monitor screen even smaller, so it took a moment to work out that she was watching Bella.

Maybe seeing Bella was making her miss Grace again. That one had to be tough, particularly given that they had been twins. Every time she looked at her she must see Grace. The question Catriona was asking herself yet again was what would a mother sacrifice for her child? In Catriona's case, the answer was nothing. Her own mother had left to start a new life with her new man. She had even had another daughter – a half-sister that Catriona had never met. Had she been a reminder of the daughter she had left behind? If it had, she had never come looking for her. There hadn't even been a single birthday or Christmas card.

But Nikki wasn't like her mother. Watching her with Bella it was clear that she would do anything for her.

Anything.

Laura Santos came into the shot and Catriona turned up the volume so she could hear what they were saying. As she listened, she was already thinking about her next move. If Plan A fails, you go on to Plan B. That's how you keep moving forward. Catriona tapped the screen of her phone, navigating to the contacts list. She found the number she wanted, connected the call, put it on speaker, then switched back to the screen in time to see Laura reaching for her phone and walking out of the kitchen. Catriona's phone rang another couple of times before being answered. She switched the speaker off and pressed it against her ear.

'Do it,' she said.

Chapter 37

The tears were still wet on Nikki's cheeks when Laura Santos finally appeared in the kitchen. Tears of sadness, tears of grief. Tears of anger. Because of the language barrier it had taken a while to get the whole story out of Luciana. In the end, it had been a depressingly straightforward one: the hospital had screwed up and as a result Sofia was dead. Laura walked over to the island, pulled out a stool and sat down. She took Nikki's hand in her own. The look she gave her was part concern, part professional curiosity.

'What happened?' she asked gently.

'I've just had a call from Sofia's sister. She's had the post-mortem results. The hospital made a mistake and gave Sofia the wrong medication. That was what caused her heart attack.'

The concern and curiosity on Laura's face gave way to a frown. 'How could that happen?'

Nikki shrugged. 'That's the question I've been asking myself. Of course, at this stage nobody's admitting liability. They need to carry out an investigation. The hospital has to be at fault, though. I mean, it wasn't as if Sofia did this to herself.'

'Surely there are checks in place to stop this sort of thing from happening? I mean, isn't that all done by computer these days?'

'Probably. But someone still needs to type the prescription in. I bet that's what happened. The NHS is stretched to the limit. Everyone's overworked. Mistakes are being made all the time.' Nikki stopped talking and shook her head. 'Luciana is talking about suing the hospital and I hope she does. I hope she takes them for every penny she can get.'

Laura waited for Nikki to meet her eye and said, 'It's good to be angry but be careful that it doesn't swallow you up.'

'I'm not just angry, I'm furious. It's not fair.' She snorted derisively. '*Fair.* What the hell is fair anyway?'

Laura didn't respond. She was studying Nikki closely.

'I'm sorry,' Nikki said quickly. 'I don't know where that came from.'

'Actually, I think you know exactly where it came from.'

Nikki said nothing. She could feel her cheeks burning hot from the shame of being read so easily.

'Look, I know I'm here to see Bella, but if you want to talk, well, I'm a pretty good listener.'

Laura was watching her closely again, waiting for a response. Nikki almost told her she was okay, but like 'fair' it was another one of those words that had lost all meaning. 'I wish we had never moved here. If we'd still been living at the old house then Sofia would still be alive.' The words were spoken quietly, like a confession.

'None of us knows what the future holds, Nikki. You know that better than anyone.'

Nikki opened her mouth to speak but nothing came out. She shut it again, then said, 'You know, there was a part of me that didn't want to move because I didn't want to leave Grace behind?' She shook her head. 'I know, crazy, right?'

'No, it's perfectly understandable. Through my work I've met a lot of parents, and the one thing they all share is that they would give anything to rewind the clock. The reason they're holding on to the past so tightly is because that's where their child is. However, they inevitably end up bound so tightly to the past it becomes impossible to move on.' Laura smiled reassuringly. 'But you *are* moving on, Nikki.'

'Am I?'

Laura nodded. 'Yes, you are. Buying this house is the first step in that process.'

'Okay, if that's true then why has everything turned to shit since I got here?'

'A house move is a big change. It's one of the most stressful things that a person can go through. It's up there with divorce and bereavement. You're struggling to come to terms with change, that's all.' A pause, another reassuring smile. 'Cut yourself a little slack. What you've done here is a very brave thing.'

Nikki shook her head emphatically. 'No, everything has turned to shit.'

'You're slipping into all-or-nothing thinking. It's not really *everything* that's turned to shit, is it?'

'Okay, maybe not everything, but look at what happened to Sofia.'

'We've already talked about that. Sofia's death had nothing to do with you. The hospital made a mistake with her medication. You were not responsible.'

Nikki said nothing.

'Look, I've got news for you, Nikki, you don't control the entire universe. Nobody does. As human beings we want to believe that there's a reason for everything, but that's not the way it works. Sometimes crappy things just happen.'

'Sofia's dead. That goes beyond crappy.' *Grace is dead as well*, she almost pointed out.

'Please don't think I'm making light of Sofia's death, because I can assure you that I'm not.' Laura stopped speaking and waited for Nikki to look at her. 'There's a part of you that wants to stay in the past with Grace. That's totally understandable. If you allow it to, then something like this will give you all the excuses you need to do that. *If you allow it.* Even though it might not feel that it has, you've come so far, Nikki. Don't let this drag you back down.'

'Other things have happened.' Nikki had broken eye contact and her gaze was fixed on the top of the work island.

'Such as?'

For what seemed like the longest time Nikki couldn't speak. She had blurted that out without thinking, the words running away from her before she had a chance to reel them back in.

'What else has happened?' Laura pressed gently.

Nikki glanced at the kitchen monitor. Bella was gone and the Picasso was back. The urge to see Bella was so strong she came within a heartbeat of just getting up and walking away. She needed to make sure Bella was safe; needed to make sure she was all right. That's what she told herself, but the real reason she wanted to escape was because this situation made her uncomfortable. The feeling was one she remembered only too well from her therapy sessions. The thing was, however uncomfortable it had been at the time, those were the sessions that benefited her the most. That was why she had stayed then, and that was why she was staying with this now.

Laura was watching her closely, smiling that reassuring smile. Waiting. Nikki took a deep breath and started talking. She began with the telephone call to the hospital where she had been assured that Sofia was okay, the call that she had – supposedly – never made. Next she told her about the episode in the gym. In some ways that one was the hardest to talk about because it was as though she was back there again, the darkness devouring her like a monster from a nightmare. She finished by telling Laura about the dreams of Grace that had been keeping her awake at night. She stopped talking and met Laura's eye. This was the first time she had done this since she started her monologue. For the last five minutes her attention had been focussed on her hands, which were on the surface of the work island, fingers tapping and touching each other as though they had a life of their own. It was easier to talk to them than to Laura. This was something else she remembered from her therapy sessions.

'So am I going crazy?' she asked.

Laura laughed. 'I can assure you that you're not.'

'Easy for you to say, but sane people don't have hallucinations where they make phone calls that didn't actually happen.'

'You weren't hallucinating, Nikki. The call showed up in your phone log, right?'

Nikki nodded.

'That means you made the call. Like you pointed out earlier, the health service is stretched to the limit. How easy would it be for someone to make a mistake? And we know they make mistakes. Let's face it, giving an inaccurate patient update doesn't even come close to administering the wrong medication.'

'I suppose . . .'

'As for the incident in the gym, most people put in that situation would have been terrified. A fear of the dark is one of the most common phobias. Does being scared of something mean you're crazy? No, it doesn't. If that was the case then we'd all be classed as crazy, every last one of us. And let's not forget that the lights went out because of a faulty pool pump. In other words, it was just one of those annoying things that life sends to test us.'

'What about the TV coming on in the middle of the night? Alice is adamant that that didn't happen.'

'Maybe that one *was* down to your imagination.'

'So I might be going crazy?'

'No, not crazy, you just had a nightmare. That's all. Granted it was pretty terrifying, but at the end of the day it was just a bad dream. We've all had them.' A pause, a reassuring smile. 'You're currently under a lot of stress, Nikki, no question about that, but you're definitely not crazy. And before you ask, yes, that's my professional assessment.' She stopped talking and the smile slid away. 'Seriously, though, if you want to talk properly then we can arrange a session.'

'I've actually been trying to get in touch with my therapist.'

'Trying?'

'She texted to say that she's on holiday and will call when she gets back next week to arrange some sessions.'

'Good. Well, not good that she's on holiday, but good that you're reaching out to someone. You don't have to go through this alone, Nikki.'

'I know that. By the way, how did you get on with Bella?' The question almost got lodged in Nikki's throat. She knew exactly how Laura had got on because she'd watched the whole thing. The question was an expected one, though, so she had to ask.

'Good. She's started to open up a little, which I really wasn't expecting so soon.'

'Are you planning on doing another session tomorrow?

'I am. I'd like to try something a little different, though. I've found it useful to take some time just to observe my patients. Would you have a problem with me filming Bella?'

'Not if you think it will help.'

'I do. I'll use a nanny cam. It's important that she doesn't know she's being watched. I want to see her acting as naturally as possible.'

Nikki glanced over at the Picasso on the kitchen monitor, a slow swirl of guilt turning circles in her gut. 'You don't have to use a nanny cam. This house has cameras in every room.'

'Including Bella's bedroom?'

Nikki nodded, then called out, 'Alice, can you switch on the camera in Bella's bedroom, please?'

The Picasso disappeared from the kitchen screen, replaced with the feed from the camera in Bella's room. Bella was lying belly down on her bed, legs kicking up in the air as she played a game on her tablet. Laura glanced at the screen, then looked back at Nikki.

'This is perfect. Are you keeping her off school again tomorrow?'

'I wasn't going to but if that's going to work best for you, then I can do that. I'll ring them later and let them know.'

'In that case I'll clear my calendar for tomorrow morning. That way I can spend a couple of hours observing her.'

Before Nikki could say anything else a mobile went off, startling them both. Nikki was already reaching for hers before she realised that this wasn't her ringtone. Laura fished her phone from her bag. She glanced at the screen and made an apologetic face.

'I'm sorry, I need to take this.'

Nikki watched Laura walk out of the kitchen then turned her attention back to the monitor. Bella had moved over to her desk and was drawing a picture on her tablet.

'Alice, can I see what she's drawing?'

The screen changed to show the feed from the drawing program. Bella had drawn two figures, one big, one small. Both were female and they were holding hands. She moved the plastic stylus over the pad and a new part of the drawing appeared. Another movement and another part of the picture appeared. Another movement, only this time instead of adding something, the arm disappeared from the smaller of the two figures.

To start with Nikki had assumed this was a picture of her and Bella. It was only when the second arm disappeared, quickly followed by the legs, that she realised that the big figure was Bella and the smaller one was Grace. They were both dressed the same, but the smaller figure had long hair, which the girls had when they were small. The larger figure had shoulder-length hair like Bella's was now.

Nikki watched with a heavy heart as Grace was slowly erased from their lives once again. She was so absorbed by what was happening on the screen that she was only vaguely aware of Laura walking up behind her. Nikki turned around on her stool, tearing her eyes from the screen. Before she could say anything, Laura raised her right hand. Nikki could see she was clutching something but couldn't work out what. By the time she did, it was too late. Laura jammed the syringe into her neck and took a quick step backwards. Nikki started to get up but her body no longer seemed to be working. Her legs gave way and Laura stepped forward to catch her. Nikki tried to push her away but her arms had no strength in them. It was as if the air around her had turned to sand. Everything was too much effort. The last thing Nikki remembered was Laura laying her gently on the floor, then the darkness descended to consume her.

Chapter 38

We exist in a world of technological miracles. Closed-circuit cameras record our every move while satellites buzz high above our heads like vultures, watching, waiting, prying. The Internet holds the information of a hundred thousand libraries and our lives are represented by ones and zeroes on computer systems the world over. Technology is rampant.

Following Sarah Ryan was easy.

By putting my hacking skills to use, I was able to keep tabs on her twenty-four hours a day, seven days a week. It wasn't long before I knew everything about her. Where she worked, how much she earned, where she liked to eat out. No detail was deemed insignificant since each piece of the puzzle added to the bigger picture. I discovered that she now preferred red wine to white; that she had just bought a new car; that she used Tampax in preference to any other feminine hygiene product.

And, of course, I found out where she lived.

Since leaving Father, Sarah had done well for herself. She had landed a high-flying job with a six-figure salary and all the perks. She had a new man in her life too: Simon Carr, forty-three, six foot, 160 pounds, hair black, eyes blue, twice divorced, investment banker. She had a flat on the twenty-third floor of a brand-new tower block in Docklands. In short, Sarah had hit the fast-track running.

As I familiarised myself with her new life, a plan began to form. I wouldn't kill her straight away. That would be too easy. She needed to suffer for what she had done. With that in mind, I went to work. Each day she returned home to find her hallway jammed with junk mail – begging letters from charities; life insurance companies wanting to look after her nearest and dearest in the unlikely event of her death; double-glazing firms promising snugness and warmth at very affordable prices. For no apparent reason her credit cards were cancelled. Then she started to receive telephone calls. Disembodied voices came for her in the middle of the night. All night. Every night. Voices telling her she was going to die. Voices demanding sexual relief. Taunting voices. Whispering voices.

After a couple of weeks of this, Sarah had become an emotional and physical wreck who went through her daily routine in a permanent daze. The self-assured woman that Father had known so intimately had been replaced by a robot. This was a creature he would barely have recognised.

It was time.

Chapter 39

The world came back into focus slowly, one fractured second at a time. At first Nikki couldn't work out why she was feeling so tired, not when she'd just been sleeping. That was her first fully-formed thought. The second was to wonder why her bed was so hard. She tried to open her eyes but they wouldn't obey the commands being sent from her brain. She tried again and saw that she was lying on the kitchen floor. That was when she remembered Laura Santos jabbing the needle into her neck, the darkness rushing in to claim her. Her last thought as she tumbled into the abyss was that she would finally get to see Grace again. That was the thought she had taken with her as she had drifted deeper and deeper.

Bella.

Nikki struggled to get up. She had to make sure Bella was all right. She was moving as fast as she could. Too fast. One second she was on her knees, the next she was down on the floor again.

'Bella.'

Her yell came out as a hoarse whisper. She tried again but her voice wasn't working. She struggled to sit up and for a moment all she could do was sit with her back against the work island, aware that she didn't have time for this, and equally aware that if she moved too fast she would end up back on the floor. She took a deep breath then used one of the stools to pull herself up.

'Alice, where's Bella?'

No response.

'Where's Bella?' she repeated.

Still nothing.

The kitchen monitor was dark. All the appliances were off. The overhead lights were off too. Nikki took a deep breath then stumbled across the kitchen, using her forward momentum to defy gravity. She made it to the door and steadied herself against the frame. And now she was stumbling along the corridors, using the walls to stay upright, calling out Bella's name. Every door she passed was open, every light off; all the electronics were off too. It was as though the house had died. She called out Alice's name again, her fear increasing with every step. Her panic was increasing too, making her head swim and the black dots swimming through her field of vision made it difficult to see straight. She felt sick; she felt like she was going to pass out. Neither of those things was an option though. She had to keep going.

Bella's door was wide open when she got there. The lights were off, the screen was off too, and scrawled on the glass in bright red lipstick: NO POLICE. Nikki felt her legs buckle and grabbed hold of the doorway. Somehow she managed to stumble across to the bed. She sat down heavily, wanting to believe there was another explanation and knowing there wasn't. Someone had drugged her and she had woken up to find her baby gone. She put her head in her hands, pushing hard on her temples to hold her thoughts together, desperate for things to make sense. The only thought going around in her head was that Bella was gone. Panic filled her head. Nikki could feel her heart racing; the sweat on her palms and her back was cold and slick. She pushed back against the panic and opened her eyes, hoping she'd somehow read the situation wrong, hoping beyond hope that Bella was going to suddenly appear and surprise her. The lipstick words screamed out from the monitor and the room was as empty as it had been a couple of seconds ago. As empty as it would be a couple of seconds from now. As empty as it would be forever more.

No!

The word rang loud in her head. She clenched her hand into a fist, fingernails digging into her palm, and punched her leg. She punched again and felt the pain bloom. She kept punching until the panic was tamed and all she could feel was the pain. She needed Ethan. He wouldn't know what to do any more than she knew, but at least she wouldn't be alone.

Nikki felt in her pockets for her mobile. It wasn't there. The last place she remembered seeing it was on the kitchen island. She struggled to her feet and made her way back through to the kitchen. She still felt as though her legs might give way at any moment, but no longer believed that was actually going to happen. Her thigh ached from where she had punched it and that provided enough of a distraction to keep the panic at bay. She found her mobile on the work island. A second mobile was lying beside it, a Nokia she had never seen before. Nikki picked it up with a trembling hand and switched it on. The directory was empty. There were no numbers in the call log. The phone was a blank canvas. It had never been used. For a moment all she could do was look at it, sitting there in her shaking hand. Any thoughts she'd harboured that she might be mistaken about what was happening had just vanished, erased by the reality of this phone. She put the Nokia down carefully and picked up her own mobile. Ethan answered on the sixth ring. She counted each one. The pain in her leg was receding and the panic was building again. Counting the rings helped distract her.

'Hi, Nik. Is everything all right?'

'I need you to come home,' she replied, her voice trembling as much as her hands.

'Why? What's happened?'

'Come home now,' she said in a dead voice, then hung up.

Ethan called back straightaway and Nikki let the phone ring out. There was a short stretch of silence, then it rang again. She switched the phone off and slapped it down beside the Nokia. Ethan had a right to know what was happening but not over the phone. The explanation would take too long and she needed him here now. She picked up the Nokia and walked through to the reception area. Every couple of steps she would call out Bella's name. She knew she was gone, but still wasn't ready to accept this. If nothing else, calling out her name drove the silence away, and that was good because that silence was threatening to suffocate her. The front door was wide open when she got there and, beyond the courtyard, the main gate was wide open too. Laura's car was long gone.

Nikki sat down in the doorway to wait. From here she could see along the whole length of Church Row. The first time she had driven here she had been impressed with how safe the neighbourhood had seemed. Sitting here now she could see how wrong she had been. When Grace had died she had thought that things couldn't possibly get any worse. She could see how wrong she had been about that too. They said that lightning didn't strike twice. Bullshit. She had lost Grace and she now had to deal with the crushing certainty that she was going to lose Bella too.

She was still sitting there, hugging herself tightly and clutching the phone, when Ethan arrived. Ten minutes might have passed since she called him; it might have been twenty. However long it was, it felt like an eternity. His car skidded to a halt in front of the garage and he practically fell out of it. He ran across the courtyard to where she was sitting.

'What's going on, Nik?'

'Bella's gone.'

His face creased with a mix of confusion and concern. 'What do you mean, gone?'

'She's been kidnapped.'

Chapter 40

'*What?* Are you sure?' Ethan asked. He looked down at her and shook his head. 'Fuck, of course you are.' His eyes were going in all directions at once. To the open front door, to Nikki, to the main gate, back to Nikki. 'We need to call the police.'

He stated this as though it was a done deal. There was no way she could risk him doing that. Calling the police had been her first thought as well. It was a natural reaction. Something bad happens: call the police.

'Laura Santos took her. She said no police. Whatever she wants, we give it to her. If that means giving away every last thing we own, I don't care. We do whatever we need to do to get Bella back. Do you understand?'

Ethan said nothing. His head was still moving in all directions as his brain fought to get a handle on this.

'Do you understand?' she repeated, her voice beginning to crack.

He nodded once then sank to his knees and took her in his arms. All the emotions she had been bottling up came out in a rush, like the dam had finally burst. She was trembling from head to toe and the world looked fractured through the kaleidoscope of her tears. After the accident, she had promised to keep Bella safe forever. That had been no empty promise, it had become a way of life for all of them. Only now, when it mattered most, she had failed Bella. She had dropped her guard and Laura Santos had swept in to steal her baby away. Nikki grabbed Ethan tighter and buried her face into his chest, suffocating herself, just wanting to disappear. Having him here was both a comfort and a reality check – a reality check because his presence made this real in a way that it hadn't been a couple of minutes ago.

'We're going to get her back,' he whispered, and she so wanted that to be true. He pulled away and stared her straight in the eye. He looked as lost as she felt. 'We *will* get her back.'

'Promise?'

'I promise,' he said, even though this wasn't his promise to make. It wasn't a promise either of them were in a position to make.

They looked at each other for a moment longer, reading the lies in each other's eyes. Ethan looked away first. The truth was that this situation was already out of their control. Ethan noticed the mobile clutched in her hand. He was staring at it as if he'd never seen a phone before. Frowning, he looked at Nikki.

'This phone was on the work island when I came back around,' she explained. 'I'm assuming Laura is going to use it to contact us.'

The frown deepened. 'What the *fuck* is going on?'

Nikki said nothing. At this point she had no more answers than he did.

'What actually happened?' he asked, softening his tone.

'I was talking to Laura in the kitchen. Someone called her and she went out of the kitchen to take it. When she came back, she drugged me.' Nikki's hand had moved subconsciously to her neck and she was rubbing the spot where the needle had gone in. 'I remember her laying me down on the floor and then nothing else until I came around.'

'The person who called must have been an accomplice. Did you hear what they said to her?'

Nikki shook her head. 'I couldn't even tell you if they were male or female.'

Ethan turned and looked towards the main gate. 'Why is the gate still open? Come to that, why was it open when I got here?'

'Laura managed to disable Alice.'

'Was Alice still working when you were drugged?'

'I think so. Why?'

'If Alice had seen that happening, she should have put the house in lockdown.' Ethan stopped talking for a moment. He was staring along Church Row again. 'Laura definitely wasn't working alone. This is too big an operation for one person to carry out on their own. For starters, someone needed to disable Alice while Laura was dealing with you.'

'There was no one else in the house, so it must have been someone working from the outside. They must have hacked into her systems.' She paused. 'You told me Alice couldn't be hacked. Remember? But there's no such thing as a computer system that can't be hacked.'

Ethan nodded at the mobile clutched in her hand. 'I wonder when they're going to call,' he said, changing the subject.

Nikki followed his gaze. 'What – what if she's dead?'

'She's not dead. If she was, then why leave the phone?'

Nikki said nothing.

'Listen,' Ethan said sharply. 'She's not going to die. That's not going to happen.'

The statement provoked a sudden flashback. They were in the house on Bedford Street, trying to come to terms with what had happened to Grace. Ethan had said something similar, and she had so wanted to believe him. He'd been wrong then; what if he was wrong now? If he was, then she wouldn't be able to go on. She wouldn't want to. Being cut adrift in this world without Grace was bad enough, but being without Bella as well was just too much to even begin to comprehend. She looked at the phone, clutched tight in her hand, and willed it to ring.

Chapter 41

They walked to the kitchen in silence, Nikki still clutching the Nokia like her life depended on it. This electronic talisman was the only thing that connected her to Bella, and it just didn't seem enough. It was the thinnest of threads, so fragile that it could snap at any moment. Ethan had tried to take it from her, but that wasn't going to happen. He only asked once.

A fresh wave of panic hit her as she walked into the kitchen. The room was like one giant trigger. Even just glancing at the stool she had been sitting on was enough to get her heart racing. The memories were so real it was almost as though it was actually happening all over again. She could feel the prick of the needle. And she could feel Laura's hands on her as she laid her down on the cool tiles. And she could feel her heart breaking all over again as the realisation that Bella was gone hit like it was the first time rather than the hundredth. Ethan must have sensed something, because he reached for her hand and gave it a reassuring squeeze. He led her over to the island and she sat down, avoiding the stool she had been using earlier.

'The electric's off,' he said. 'Laura must have tripped the main circuit breaker.'

Before Nikki could respond, Ethan was already walking away.

'Where are you going?

'I'm going down to the basement to see if I can get it back on.'

All she could do was watch as he walked away. She wanted to follow him, but she could remember all too well how dark it had been down there when the lights went out in the gym the other day. Staying here on her own wasn't much better, but at least there was light. She listened as his footsteps disappeared into the distance, kept listening until all that was left was silence and she was alone again.

She placed the Nokia on the work island, lining it up with her phone, willing it to ring. It didn't. It just lay there. Inert. Dead. *What if it isn't working?* She snatched it up and switched it on. The screen immediately flared to life. The battery was at 99 per cent. She switched it off, placed it down carefully and picked up her own phone. There were no new emails, no texts, no messages. It was as though the world outside these walls had ceased to exist. That was what it felt like too. It was as if the universe began and ended in this room, a universe without Bella in it.

She had been adamant that they shouldn't call the police, and Ethan hadn't argued, but was that a mistake? No. They couldn't involve them. Laura Santos had made that clear. If they went against her instructions how would that impact on Bella? Maybe Laura expected them to go to the police and had posted the message to scare them. Then again, what if they contacted the police and she killed Bella? It was a risk they couldn't afford to take. The kitchen lights came on and the appliances buzzed back to life. The monitor was still blank, though.

'Alice?'

No answer. Nikki turned towards the doorway, listening hard for the sound of Ethan's footsteps, wishing he would hurry up. A minute passed with no sign of him. She gave it another minute then picked up the Nokia and walked out of the kitchen. She stopped at the top of the basement stairs.

'Is everything okay?' she called down.

There was still no response, and now she was getting worried. She took a long look at the stairs then walked down them. 'Ethan,' she yelled out. 'Are you okay?'

'I'm fine,' he called back. 'I'm just trying to get Alice working again.'

She followed his voice to the computer room hidden away at the far end of the basement. One wall was lined with servers, all of them off. The air-conditioning had kicked in again and the temperature in the room was cold enough to give her goosebumps. Ethan was standing in the middle of the room, looking confused.

'I don't get it,' he said. 'The electricity's back on so the servers should be working.'

'Maybe we need to reboot it.'

'How?'

Nikki's gaze drifted across the servers. Ethan had a point. There was no obvious way to reboot the system. No big green button marked ON. She walked over to the closest server. The front of it was black and the dead LED's looked like little black pearls. She ran a hand across it and it felt cold to the touch. She was about to step back when the server at the far left suddenly came to life. A second later the one beside it came on.

Like falling dominoes, the rest came on one at a time until they were all working and the room was filled with the gentle hum of the fans and the blinking, twinkling glow of the LEDs.

'What did you do?' Ethan said.

'Nothing, I swear.'

'Alice,' he called out. 'Are you there?'

No answer.

'Maybe it takes a minute.'

There was a long silence, then Alice said, 'Hello, Ethan. Hello, Nikki.' She was speaking calmly, as though nothing had happened. As though the world hadn't ended.

'Thank God,' Ethan said, 'you're still working. What happened?'

'There was a hostile security breach.'

'You mean you were hacked.'

'That's correct. Most security breaches I'm equipped to deal with, however because of the level of hostility of this attack I had no option but to initiate a complete shutdown. I can confirm that the attack is now over. I am also working to make improvements to my security systems to ensure that this doesn't happen again.'

'Laura has kidnapped Bella,' Nikki said. 'Do you know anything about this?'

'I have no record of this event.'

'She drugged me in the kitchen.'

'I have no record of that event either. My systems must already have been compromised by that point.' There was a short pause, then, 'According to the GPS signal coming from Bella's tablet, she is currently in Highgate. I've sent details of her whereabouts to your mobile phones.'

Nikki shared a look with Ethan then ran from the room. She could hear him close behind. For the first time since she realised that Bella was gone she was experiencing something that felt like hope.

Chapter 42

They barrelled through the open front door and sprinted across the courtyard, matching each other's pace, both of them burning with adrenaline, heading for the Tesla. Ethan climbed into the driver's seat and was already backing onto the turntable as Nikki was pulling the passenger door closed. The turntable was turning with agonising slowness, but it was still quicker than reversing. The Nokia rang as Ethan was getting ready to drive the Tesla off it.

'Stop!' she said.

He glanced over from the driver's seat, his hands frozen on the steering wheel. The phone rang again.

'This phone has GPS too. What if they're tracking it? We don't want them to know that we're out looking for Bella.'

Ethan took his hands from the wheel and removed his foot from the accelerator. The turntable had finished turning and the main gate was wide open, Church Row stretching out beyond it. The phone rang again. Nikki connected the call and switched it to speaker so that Ethan could hear.

'You took your time,' Laura said. 'Anyone would think that you don't care about your daughter.'

'Is she okay?'

'She's fine, and so long as you do exactly what I tell you to do, she'll stay that way.'

The voice was colder and harder than the last time they'd spoken, making Nikki wonder how she'd ever been taken in. 'Please don't hurt her.'

'That one's down to you, Nikki. Like I said, so long as you cooperate she'll be fine.'

'I want to speak to her.'

'No.'

'*Please.* She's going to be scared.'

'I said no, Nikki. You need to start listening.'

'I'm sorry.'

'Did you got the message I left in Bella's bedroom?'

'We're not going to call the police,' Nikki said quickly.

'Do I have to spell out what will happen if you do?'

'We won't call them. I promise.'

'Okay, I'm going to go, but I want you to keep the Nokia with you at all times. Next time I call, you answer straightaway. Understand?'

'I understand.'

'I know you're scared, Nikki, and that worries me. Scared people have been known to do stupid things.'

'I'm not going to do anything stupid.'

'I really do hope so. Bella hopes so too. However, in the event that stupidity starts to take over, you need to get control of yourself and stop that from happening. There's only one thing you need to remember here: if you keep your head and do everything you're told then Bella will come out of this just fine.'

'Please let me speak to her.'

The silence that followed this went on long enough for Nikki to think that she might actually get to speak to Bella, then Laura was back.

'Maybe I'll let you talk to her later. I need to see that you're cooperating first.'

'I am cooperating.'

'No, you're telling me that you're cooperating. That's not the same. I want to *see* that you're cooperating.'

'What do you want? Money? If it's money we can get that for you.'

'I'll be in touch,' Laura replied and the line went dead.

Nikki looked at the phone in her shaking hand, then navigated to the call log. Laura's number was withheld.

'Bella's going to be fine,' Ethan said.

Nikki said nothing. She wanted to believe him, but just couldn't make that leap. One glance at Ethan, and it was clear that he didn't believe what he was saying either. He gave her a grim look that could have meant anything, then put his hands back on the steering wheel, getting ready to go.

'Wait. One of us needs to stay here.' Nikki held the phone up. 'What if they *are* using GPS to track this?'

Ethan frowned as he worked through the implications. The problem was that neither of them was thinking straight at the moment. All they were doing was reacting to events. Was Laura actually tracking the phone or was that just their paranoia? But, if there was even the smallest chance that she was, then they had to act as though that was the case.

'I need to stay here with the phone,' Nikki said. 'Laura will be expecting to speak to me.'

'Okay, that makes sense.'

'I want to know everything that's happening though.'

Chapter 43

Nikki got out of the car and watched Ethan drive away. She watched until the gate was fully closed and the Tesla had disappeared from sight before going back inside. The house suddenly felt bigger. Emptier, too. She sleepwalked through to the kitchen and sat down at the island. She half-expected to turn around and see Bella standing there, but when she glanced over her shoulder, the kitchen was empty. The silence seemed to be mocking her.

'Stop it,' she whispered to herself. All of a sudden there wasn't enough oxygen in the room. She looked around desperately for something to distract herself with, but everything was happening too fast. The panic quickly built and there was nothing she could do to stop it. All the strategies she had learned were useless. She was going to be sick. She was having a heart attack. She was going to pass out. She was going to die. These thoughts hit her one after the other – bang, bang, bang, bang – a series of punches that left her reeling.

Somehow she found herself on the floor with her knees pulled into her chest. Her vision was swimming with tiny dots, everything getting greyer. She closed her eyes but the dots were still there. Her breaths were coming more rapidly than ever, her heart racing so fast it felt as though it was about to explode.

'You're having a panic attack.'

To start with Nikki thought that the voice was inside her head, but this wasn't like the usual voice she heard when she was talking to herself.

'Concentrate on the exhalation, Nikki,' the voice ordered. 'Make it longer.'

It took a massive effort but her next exhalation was longer than the inhalation. The next was a little longer still.

'You're going to be all right, Nikki. Just concentrate on slowing your breathing.'

Nikki inhaled, then exhaled. Inhaled, then exhaled. Inhaled, then exhaled. She could feel herself slowly coming back down. Her limbs were weak and shaky and she still felt sick, but the worst was over. She took another breath and another, then opened her eyes.

'Your heart rate is returning to normal,' Alice said. 'How do you feel?'

'Tired.'

That was an understatement. She felt exhausted, as though she had run a marathon. It was always this way after an attack. The panic sucked the life right out of you. She looked up at the stool. Getting back onto it was a step too far, like climbing a mountain. For now, she was happy just to sit here on the floor.

She looked around, gradually becoming more aware of her surroundings as she came out of herself. Her gaze was drawn to the big monitor. The Picasso was gone and in its place was a map of London. The blue flashing dot heading northwards was Ethan; the red flashing dot in Highgate was Bella. Ethan was making good time but she wished he would hurry up. She watched for a while. Bella's dot was moving too, heading east. This wasn't what she had expected. She'd thought that Bella was being kept at a house in Highgate. Instead it looked as though she was on the move. A phone rang, making her jump. For a second she thought it was Laura, but this was her own ringtone. Her head spun as she stood up. Her legs seemed to be holding up okay though. The phone was buzzing against the top of the island, doing a little shimmy. Ethan's name had flashed up onto the screen. She sat down on a stool, picked up the mobile and connected the call.

'I should be with Bella in about five or ten minutes,' Ethan said. 'The traffic's not too bad.'

'What will you do when you find her?'

The silence coming from the other end of the phone was telling. Neither of them had thought this through. Was Laura armed? Was she on her own? And what the hell did they think was going to happen? That Laura was going to say sorry and just hand Bella over? It was Alice who broke the silence.

'Ethan,' she said. 'Take the next left.'

'So what will you do?' Nikki pressed.

'I don't know,' Ethan admitted.

She could hear the strain in his voice. The frustration. The worry. They were both totally out of their depth here. 'We need a plan.'

'All we can do is take this a step at a time. First we find her, then we work out what to do next.'

'That's not a plan. That's just hoping for the best.'

'I know,' Ethan snapped. 'But right now it's all we've got.'

'Take the next right,' Alice said calmly.

'Maybe we should get the police involved,' Ethan suggested.

'*No*. No police.'

There was a long silence then Ethan sighed. 'Let's find Bella first, then we can work out what to do.'

Nikki sensed that he was about to go. 'Stay on the line. I don't want to be on my own.'

'It's okay, I'm not going anywhere.' A pause then, 'Look, Nik, she's going to be all right. You've got to believe that.'

'I do believe that.'

Ethan didn't respond, and that was as good as calling her on the lie. For the next few minutes the only voice saying anything belonged to Alice as she reeled off the directions, each turn taking Ethan closer to Bella. Nikki watched the dots on the screen moving towards each other, the feeling that disaster was looming up ahead growing stronger the closer they got. Wherever possible Alice had zoomed in on the map and they had now reached the point where the street names had started to appear. Alice had plotted a course so that Ethan would come up behind the vehicle Bella was in. He was only a couple of turns away now. The next minute passed with agonising slowness, the two dots moving closer until they had almost merged.

'Bella is in the vehicle directly in front of you,' Alice said.

'She can't be. It's a taxi. There's a car in front of it, though. Maybe she's in that.'

'No, Ethan. She's six metres directly in front of you. She must be in the taxi.'

'The cab is indicating left. I'm going to follow it.'

A couple of seconds later the red dot on the screen made a left turn. Ethan was right behind it.

'Is Bella still in front of me?' he asked.

'She is,' Alice confirmed.

'She must be in the taxi then. The car that was in front went straight ahead at the last junction.'

'Can you see Bella?' Nikki asked.

'No. As far as I can tell there's only one person in the back of the taxi. A woman.'

'Describe her. It might be Laura.'

'I can't really see her from here.'

'Is she old or young?'

'I said *I can't see her*. Okay, the taxi is stopping. I'm going to pull over too.'

'Don't hang up.' Nikki had the phone pressed hard against the side of her head and was listening hard.

'The taxi driver is an Indian guy. I'd say he's in his mid-fifties. It looks like the woman in the back is giving him some money. Okay, I can just about see her now. She's white. Mid-twenties.'

'Are you sure?'

'She might be younger.'

'Shit. Laura was in her thirties and Hispanic. What's she doing now?'

'She's getting out the cab,' Ethan said. 'And she's on her own. The cab's pulling away.'

'Could Bella still be in the cab?

'No,' Alice said. 'The GPS signal isn't moving.'

'The woman must have Bella's tablet,' Ethan said.

'What's she doing now?'

'She's standing on the kerb, checking her phone.' A pause. 'I'm going to go speak to her.'

'What if she's working with Laura?'

'I don't think so. If you've just pulled off a kidnapping are you going to be travelling around by cab?'

Before she could say anything else, Nikki heard Ethan opening the car door. The street noises got louder. Somewhere in the distance a car horn blared.

'Excuse me,' Ethan called out a few seconds later. 'This might sound strange, but I think you might have my daughter's tablet.'

The street sounds got momentarily louder again, then, 'How could you possibly know that?' The surprise in the woman's voice was totally genuine.

'I've been following its GPS signal.'

The woman laughed. 'It's amazing what you can do with technology these days.'

'You've got it, then?'

'It's in my bag. I found it lying on the street. I was going to hand it in to the police. Judging by the stickers on the cover I figured it must belong to a little girl. I was hoping they would be able to track her down and return it.'

Ethan thanked the woman and a couple of seconds later the Tesla door opened and closed again.

'I've got the tablet. I'll see you soon.'

The line went dead. The devastation in his voice mirrored her own feelings. Bella seemed further away then ever. Nikki switched off her phone and laid it down gently beside the Nokia. For a while she stared at the Nokia, willing it to ring again, but it just kept its silence. The scream started deep in her soul. By the time it reached her lips it sounded like the desperate cry of a dying animal.

Chapter 44

On the night Sarah Ryan died, she left her office late. I was with her the whole way, following her as she made her way down the anonymous corridors, bouncing from one camera to the next each time she slipped from view. She stepped into the elevator and selected the ground floor. The nails on her right hand had been bitten back to the quick. I saw this when she lifted her hand to push the button. The lift descended quickly, Sarah shuffling nervously on its metallic floor like a trapped animal. I zoomed in on her face. She looked old and ugly. Deep crow's feet dug into the corners of her eyes. Her head stayed motionless, but her eyes moved constantly, searching for her invisible tormentor.

Moving from camera to camera, I followed her progress through the foyer and out onto the street. At the entrance to the underground station I ping-ponged after her, moving swiftly from camera to camera, down escalators, through the tiled tunnels, gliding across enamel. Sarah stepped onto the train and I lost her for a while. This didn't concern me. Her destination was no mystery. As my night-time phone calls became more frequent she had locked herself away from the world in her flat. These days she only ventured out to go to work.

I was there waiting when she got off the train, following her from camera to camera as she made her way topside and hurried towards home. As she got closer, her pace picked up. She was almost running now. I could sense her relief as she walked through the big glass doors. The doorman nodded a greeting that wasn't reciprocated, and she hurried towards the elevator.

I already had one waiting.

The doors opened as soon as she pushed the button. She stepped inside and selected the twenty-third floor. A discrete security camera tucked away in one corner allowed me to share her final moments. Red numbers flickered, counting off the floors – 17,18,19. Sarah stared at them, willing them towards 23. She lifted a hand up to her mouth and chewed nails that were no longer there. The twenty-third floor came and went. Sarah started hammering frantically at the button for 23. The gesture was a futile one. She belonged to me now.

I stopped the elevator at the thirtieth floor and waited. Sarah pushed the button to open the doors. She pushed it again and again, each jab more desperate than the last. The telephone rang and it must have sounded overly loud in the cramped elevator because she stepped back sharply. She looked at it for a second, then reached out and picked it up with a trembling hand.

'H-hello. Who's there?'

I said nothing.

'You need to help me. The elevator has broken down. I'm on the thirtieth floor. Please send someone to let me out.'

Still I said nothing.

'Can anyone hear me?' she demanded, her voice beginning to crack in the upper register.

'Yes, I can hear you.'

'Thank God,' she said, hurrying to get the words out. 'Please send someone to get me out.'

'I'm afraid I can't do that, Sarah.'

There was a slight pause, then, 'How do you know my name?' The question was asked in a confused little-girl voice. 'Who are you?'

'You know who I am.'

'K-Katy?'

I disengaged the brakes. The elevator plummeted two floors before the safety systems came on and it shuddered to a halt, metal tearing against metal. All the colour had drained from Sarah's face, light grey turning to white. Framed in monochrome she had become evil personified and I knew I was doing the right thing.

'Goodbye, Sarah.'

I disengaged the safety brakes.

Through the telephone her scream sounded as tinny and distant as a short-wave radio broadcast, but I could imagine what it must have sounded like to her. The floors were flashing by in a blur of red.

25, 24, 23 . . .

Faster, faster.

14, 13, 12 . . .

Believe me when I tell you that this was the greatest moment of my life.

7, 6, 5 . . .

Sarah was on the elevator floor now, crouched in one corner, her body wrapped around itself in the foetal position. The telephone dangled uselessly on its coiled cord, banging against the side of *the elevator, a rhythmic counterpoint to the symphony of death it relayed.*

2, 1 . . .

The moment of death was an anti-climax. White noise and static. I should have expected this, but it did nothing to change the outcome.

Sarah was still dead.

Now Father could be happy again.

Chapter 45

Watching the Rhodes' had become Catriona Fisher's new obsession. She had watched them until Nikki went to bed last night, had eaten her breakfast this morning, watching them while Nikki and Bella had theirs. At various points during the day she had logged on to see what Nikki was up to. She was watching them now, but nothing much was happening. Nikki was in the kitchen on her laptop; Bella was lying on her bed playing a game on her tablet; and Ethan still hadn't got back from doing his show.

She closed the lid of her computer then walked over to the large floor-to-ceiling window and stared out across the river. The sun was shining off the water, casting sparks of orange and gold. She was going to miss this. The tumbler in her hand contained a couple of inches of Jack Daniel's. It was early to be drinking, but today had definitely been one of those days.

The challenge was the same as it had always been: getting people to understand her vision. The only way to do that was through example. The house on Church Row was a good start in that it had enabled them to try out their ideas. Unfortunately, that house wasn't grand enough. Their next project had to be much more ambitious. Basically, they needed to create the sort of house that the poor dreamed of and the rich fought amongst themselves to own – and that was going to cost big money.

Catriona turned away from the view and walked across the lounge. She sat down heavily on the sofa and sipped her drink. After calling the estate agent from the bridge she had actually shed a couple of tears. No doubt about it, selling this penthouse was going to break her heart, but she couldn't see any other way to raise the money. Even then, she was probably still going to come up short. The stakes were huge, but it was a risk she would be stupid not to take. Worst-case scenario, she would end up broke, living on the streets. Best case, she would be set for life. Her mobile rang, shaking her out of her thoughts. She checked the screen, saw Alex's name, and connected the call.

'What is it?'

'It might be nothing.'

'Then again it might be something,' Catriona said with a sigh. 'If there's a problem, Alex, I need to know.'

'And if you calm down I'll tell you.

Alex stared out of the screen at her; Catriona stared back.

'Okay now that you're sitting comfortably, I will begin. Because Laura Santos has become a regular visitor at the house I wanted to know more about her, so I asked Google. On the surface, everything looked fine. Her website is professional, she has a Facebook account, there's even a Wikipedia entry. However, a few of the pages that came up had HTTP 404 errors, more than I would normally expect. That was the first thing that made me suspicious. Then there's the fact that there were only two pages of results. Santos is supposed to be an expert in her field. On that basis alone there should have been more than two pages. The other weird thing I noticed was that, after those first two pages, there's nothing. Google doesn't work that way. It's all done on percentages. The results at the top of the list are the one that most closely match the search. As you go down the list, those percentages drop and you get results for other things mixed in with the thing you're searching for. What doesn't happen is that you go from something to nothing, as seems to be the case here.'

'What exactly are you saying? That Santos doesn't exist?'

Alex sighed. When he finally spoke it was as though he was trying to explain the obvious to a particularly stupid child. 'Yes, Catriona, that's exactly what I'm saying. Basically, she's a ghost. A figment of someone's imagination.'

'And you're basing this on the fact that her Google results are inconsistent. That sounds like a bit of a leap, Alex. Maybe it's a glitch.'

'It's not a glitch.

'How can you be so sure?'

'Because when I dug deeper I found other inconsistencies, like the fact that she doesn't have Twitter or Instagram accounts.'

'I don't have an Instagram account either, so I'm not sure that proves anything.'

'On its own it doesn't, but when you put everything together it starts to look more suspicious. Another thing: I couldn't find a website for the practice she had when she was living in the States.'

'She probably had it taken down.'

'Duh, of course she did. However, I should still have found some evidence of it. Once something gets out there on the net, it takes on a life of its own. It's impossible to erase every last trace.'

'Okay, if Laura Santos isn't who she says she is, then who the hell is she?'

'That's the million-dollar question. I've asked my brother to look into this. Maybe he'll be able to provide some answers.'

'Your brother?'

'Don't ask.'

'Okay I won't. So when will he get back to you?'

'By the end of the day. I told him it was urgent.'

Catriona went quiet while she processed this. 'If she is an imposter, then I guess the next question is: why is she doing this?'

'At this stage I have no idea. I'm hoping we'll be able to start working that one out once we know *who* she actually is.'

'Is there anything else I need to know about?'

'No, that's it for now.'

'Okay, call me as soon as you hear from your brother. Straightaway.'

Catriona hung up and dropped the phone onto the sofa. She picked up her drink and took a sip, then reached for her laptop and switched it on. This new development was a concern. Laura Santos had just become a rogue variable, and that was the last thing they needed. Once they had established who she was and what she wanted, then they could work out the best way to deal with her. Until then all she could do was wait and worry.

The computer finished booting up and she accessed the house cameras again. Nikki was still in the kitchen on her laptop and Ethan still hadn't got back from doing his show. Bella had moved from her bed and was sitting at her desk using the tablet's graphic program to draw a picture. Catriona took another sip of whiskey then switched to Nikki's camera and settled back on the sofa to watch.

Chapter 46

Nikki was sitting in the kitchen staring at the wall screen when Ethan got back. The Picasso had been replaced with a photograph of Bella that Alice had imported from her laptop. This had been taken last September. The weather had been amazing, warm and sunny. If the leaves hadn't been turning she could have tricked herself into thinking that it was still summer. It was the sort of day where you could believe that winter was never going to happen. On the spur of the moment they had gone to Thorpe Park and, for a short while, they had been a happy family. That had been a good day. Nikki felt the tears threatening and tried to squash them back down.

Ethan sat down on the next stool and laid Bella's tablet beside the Nokia without a word. There was nothing to say. He was supposed to have come back with Bella. Instead, Bella was out there somewhere, lost and alone and scared out of her mind. Ethan appeared to have aged a decade in the time he'd been gone. They both had. The adrenaline that had kept them going while they thought they'd found her had worn off. The Nokia lay there, as silent as ever. This was their only link to Bella and right now it was as good as broken. Nikki picked up the tablet. The pink cover was so familiar; she knew every red heart and silver star.

She turned it over in her hands, examining it closely, studying it as though it might somehow hold the key for getting Bella back.

She heard sobbing and looked up to see Ethan crying. She could count on one hand the times she had seen him cry. The day the girls were born; the moment Grace took her final breath; the funeral; and now this. Nikki put the tablet down then slid off her stool and went to him. She wrapped her arms around him and pulled him close, and now she was crying too. In that moment she was convinced she would never see Bella again. These were secret thoughts. Dangerous thoughts. She needed to hold them in because if they got out then they might turn true and she couldn't allow that to happen.

'What do we do now, Nik?'

Nikki said nothing. If she had an answer then she would be out there doing it, instead of sitting here waiting for the phone to ring. Nor was she going to tell him it was going to be all right, because at that moment it felt as though nothing would ever be all right again.

'Did we do something to make this happen to us?' Ethan asked. 'Is that it?'

Nikki shook her head. 'No, we didn't.'

'So why us?'

'I don't know.'

Ethan wiped his eyes and straightened up. 'We've got to call the police.'

'*No.*'

'We can't do this on our own.'

'Laura said no police. So far that's the only demand she's made. We can't call them.'

'We have to.'

'*No*, what we have to do – the only thing we have to do – is everything Laura tells us.'

Ethan sighed and shook his head. 'When I was driving to Highgate you asked me what I was going to do when I got there. I didn't know the answer then – and if I was put in that situation again I still wouldn't have a clue.'

Nikki went to say something and Ethan put his hand up, stopping her.

'What if I had found Bella? What would I have done then?'

Ethan left the question hanging there.

'Laura said no police,' Nikki said quietly, breaking the growing silence.

'I know that, but we need to face facts here: we're out of our depth. Way out.'

Nikki met his gaze. The devastation was still there in his eyes but there was a newfound determination too. He'd looked into the future and seen a way out. The problem was that whenever *she* looked all she saw was disaster. Even if they did everything that Laura asked there was still no guarantee that they would get Bella back safely. Maybe Ethan was right. Maybe they should go to the police. The Nokia suddenly rang and they both turned to look at it. Ethan moved quickest. Before Nikki could do anything he had snatched it up and connected the call.

'What will it take to get Bella back?'

He was trying to sound calm but there was no disguising the anger behind the words. Laura's reply was lost on Nikki. All she could hear was Ethan's side of the conversation.

'What will it take to get her back?' he asked again.

A pause, then more desperately, 'We've got money, if that's what this is about. Just let me know how much and where you want it sent to.'

A longer pause. When Ethan finally spoke he was hurrying to get the words out and doing nothing to hide his desperation. 'Look, just name your price. All we care about is getting Bella back.'

There was another pause, then Ethan seemed to shrink before her eyes. The fire had gone from his eyes and he seemed somehow smaller than he had been a few moments ago. He held the phone out to Nikki and waited for her to take it. 'She wants to talk to you.'

Nikki put the phone up to her ear. 'I'm here.'

'Maybe I didn't make myself clear when we last spoke, Nikki. If that's the case then let me clarify things. I speak to you and you alone. Do you understand?'

'I understand. It won't happen again.'

'Your husband seems on edge. If he loses it, that could complicate things.'

'He's not going to lose it, he's just worried about Bella, that's all. We both are. We just want to get her back.'

'It's understandable to be worried; however, he needs to be made aware that if he doesn't get his shit together then that will have consequences for Bella. Severe consequences.'

'You don't have to worry about Ethan. You don't have to worry about either of us. We're going to do exactly what you say.' Nikki hesitated. Her heart was in her mouth, her palms sweaty. It was taking everything she had to keep her own shit together. The panic was out there, just waiting to strike. 'We need to know Bella's all right.'

'She's fine.

'Then please let me talk to her,' she said, the words getting stuck in her throat.

Silence on the other end of the line, then, 'If you cooperate you'll be able to talk to her all you want.'

'If we can't talk to her then at least send a picture. We just need to know she's okay. Please.'

'I guess a picture is more doable than talking. Especially since she doesn't have her tablet.'

Nikki felt the breath lodge in her throat.

'Did you really think that I wouldn't find out that Ethan has been running all over London looking for Bella?'

Still Nikki said nothing.

'Did it not occur to you that maybe I wanted you running around like headless chickens?'

'Why?'

'Because you needed to get that out of your system. The sooner you realise that the only way this works is by doing *exactly* what I say, the better it's going to be for everyone. You, me, and especially poor little Bella.'

'Please don't hurt her. We shouldn't have gone looking for her. It won't happen again.'

'I know it won't, because you now know that I am watching your every move. Whatever you do, whatever you might think about doing, I'm going to be one step ahead of you.'

Nikki said nothing. She tried to swallow but her mouth was bone dry, her saliva like sand.

'Take this as your one and only warning, Nikki. Pull a stunt like that again and it will be Bella who suffers. So, have you called the police?'

The question came out of left field, unsettling Nikki even more than she already was. 'You told us not to.'

'That's not an answer. What I'm looking for here is a simple yes or no.'

'No,' Nikki said quickly. 'We haven't called them.'

'Good, just remember that it would be very bad for Bella if you do.'

'You can't hurt her.'

'I don't want to hurt her Nikki, but that doesn't mean that I can't. Those two things are not mutually exclusive.'

'What do you want from us?' Nikki almost yelled this into the phone. She took a deep breath. 'Just tell us what you want.'

'I want you to collect something for me,' Laura replied calmly.

For a second, Nikki wasn't sure she had heard right. She had been convinced that this was about money.

'What?'

'That's not for you to worry about.'

'And once I do this, then we'll get Bella back?'

'Yes, you'll get her back.'

Nikki took a deep breath. It was taking everything she had to keep the panic at bay. Laura might be lying but she couldn't allow herself to think that.

'Okay,' Laura went on, 'here's how this works. I'm going to text through an address and you're going to drive there in your little Beetle. On your own. When you get there, I'll contact you with further instructions. One other thing: I want you to leave your mobile in the house. You can take this phone, but before you start getting any ideas about calling for help, I will be monitoring it. Now tell me that you understand.'

'I understand, and I'll do everything you want, but first I need to know that Bella is all right. Send us a picture, then I'll go and get whatever it is that you want me to get.'

The line went dead, leaving Nikki staring at the handset, her stomach tying itself in knots. She shouldn't have pushed like that. What the hell was she thinking? She was in no position to issue ultimatums. But she hadn't been thinking, had she? The truth was that she hadn't been thinking straight since she realised that Bella had been kidnapped.

'What's wrong?'

Ethan's voice seemed to be coming from far away. She tried to answer but her voice wouldn't work.

'What just happened Nik? Talk to me.'

'Laura hung up. I shouldn't have asked for a picture. She's going to hurt Bella.' Nikki looked at him and all the anger that she'd been holding in suddenly came spewing out. 'Laura could be doing anything to her right now and there's nothing we can do to stop her.'

'Bella's going to be okay.'

'But she's not okay *now!* She should be safe here with us. Instead she's with that crazy bitch who's doing God knows what to her. She's going to be scared and alone. She'll be terrified. She shouldn't have to—'

'*Stop it!*' Ethan yelled, halting her in her tracks. Nikki recoiled as if she'd been slapped.

'Losing it now is not going to help things,' he went on. 'It's not going to help Bella. So what exactly did she say before she hung up?'

'She said she was going to text me an address. She wants me to go there.'

'In that case it's going to be okay. She wants something.'

'So why hang up?'

'Because she wants to scare you. She wants you to know who's in charge.'

Before Nikki could respond, the phone buzzed in her hand. She navigated to her texts. The one that had just come in had no message but there was a photograph attached. She opened it quickly. Bella's face had been caught in close-up. She looked dazed and lost, and so alone. This was the complete opposite of the picture of Bella on the roller coaster at Thorpe Park, the one smiling down at them from the kitchen monitor. It was hard to believe that this was the same child. Looking at it made Nikki feel sick. *But at least she's alive,* she told herself. That was all that mattered here. Bella was alive. Ethan had got up from his stool and was peering over her shoulder. She heard him take a sharp intake of breath and turned to face him. Neither of them said anything. Bella might be alive but she was going through hell, and it was all their fault. They were her parents goddamn it. Their job was to keep her safe and they had failed spectacularly.

The phone buzzed again. Another text. This time it contained details of an address in Battersea.

It buzzed a third time: *you have thirty minutes.*

Chapter 47

Nikki's hand was shaking so much it took three attempts to program the satnav. She told herself to relax but it didn't do any good. It didn't help that Ethan was hovering beside the car, watching her every move. According to the satnav it would take twenty-one minutes to get to Battersea. The last text had arrived maybe two minutes ago, so that gave her seven minutes to play with, which didn't seem enough. If traffic was slow then those seven minutes would disappear before she knew it. She willed the turntable to move faster. Ethan was standing beside her car, moving with it.

'You shouldn't be doing this on your own,' he called out, his voice muffled by glass. 'I should be coming with you.'

They'd already had this conversation, a quick back and forth as they ran through the house. Nothing had changed since then. She desperately wanted him with her, but Laura had been very clear: Go alone, in the Beetle, and leave your phone in the house. So here she was, alone, in her Beetle. Her mobile was back in the kitchen and the Nokia was lying on the passenger seat. The turntable had gone about two thirds of the way around now, far enough for her to be able to clearly see the open gate.

'*Promise* me you won't contact the police,' she said.

'I promise.'

Nikki hit the accelerator and bumped off the turntable while it was still moving. Church Row was deserted and she managed to push the car up to forty. She took a left at the end of the street and it was like she was back in London again, cars and people everywhere. A couple of turns later she was on Kensington High Street, riding the bumper of the car in front and praying that it wouldn't brake suddenly.

The next right took her onto Queen's Gate. Nikki managed less than thirty feet before grinding to a halt. She leant as far as she could to the left, trying to see how far the traffic was backed up, and what the hold up was. She leant to the right and pressed her cheek hard against the window. There was a set of temporary traffic lights about fifty metres further up the road, some sort of roadworks. After that the traffic seemed to be moving again. She thumped the steering wheel in frustration and felt the adrenaline jolt through her system. That last panic attack was still fresh in her memory and it was recent enough for another to be triggered all too easily. These moments where she wasn't doing anything were the dangerous moments – when she was occupied she wasn't thinking about the panic. Heart racing, she looked at the number plates of the cars coming towards her, reading every number and every letter, noticing the different types of text, the different colours on the plates, anything to distract herself.

The lights changed and the traffic began moving again. According to the satnav it was still another sixteen minutes to her destination. She had lost two or three minutes but she could still make it. She had to. Nikki pressed the accelerator and the car surged forward, the feeling that she was running out of time increasing with every passing second.

Ten minutes later she crossed Albert Bridge. Battersea Power Station was off to her left and seeing the tall chimneys reaching up to the sky was a relief – it meant that she was almost there. A delivery van suddenly pulled out in front of her, cutting her up and forcing her to slam the brakes on. She missed it by inches, getting so close that the back of the van dominated the view, stealing the road, the sky, the power station. Her fist found the horn before she remembered that she shouldn't be drawing attention to herself. It only blared once, loud and obtrusive, but that was enough to make people stare.

Breathing hard, she fell back to a safe distance. It was only starting to sink in how close she had come to disaster. If she had crashed, she would have missed the deadline. According to the satnav she would be there in two minutes. If her calculations were correct that would give her just a minute to spare.

The satnav told her to take a right, and then the next left, and then it was telling her that her destination was straight ahead. Nikki looked around, taking everything in. It was a nice enough neighbourhood, quiet and prosperous. The street was lined with red-brick houses. Some were grander than others, but none of them looked cheap. She drove along it slowly, her eyes hunting for house numbers. She wanted twenty-three and was currently somewhere in the high forties. She passed thirty-one, then a couple of houses without numbers, then twenty-five. Twenty-three didn't have a number and it looked more rundown than the houses surrounding it. The windows were filthy and all the curtains were drawn; the white front door was grey with dirt. The Nokia rang, the sound making Nikki jump. She snatched it up from the passenger seat and quickly connected the call.

'I'm here,' she said quickly.

'I know,' Laura replied. 'I've been following your progress.'

'I need to get parked.'

'Don't let me stop you.'

Nikki pulled into the first space she saw. There were signs everywhere warning that she needed a permit, but that was the least of her concerns. She killed the engine and pressed the phone to her ear.

'What do you want me to do?'

'Go into the glovebox. I've left something for you in there.'

Nikki unbuckled her seatbelt then leant over to the passenger seat and clicked open the glovebox. To start with she couldn't see anything, then her eyes adjusted and she noticed a darker shadow hidden amongst all the other shadows. Something was in there, wrapped in black cloth and pushed all the way to the back. Nikki reached for it and worked out what it was immediately. She placed the bundle on her lap and sat upright in her seat. Laura was speaking but Nikki barely heard her. All she could do was stare at the unmistakable shape of a gun pressing through the thin material.

Chapter 48

'Judging by your silence I'm figuring you've found the gun.'

'What do you want me to do?' This came out as a whisper. She had never been this close to a real gun before. The way it pressed its shape into the cloth held her transfixed. All she could do was stare at it, a bad feeling shrinking her stomach and making her feel sick.

'First, I want you to take a deep breath,' Laura said. 'You don't want to have a panic attack. I need you clear-headed and focused.' A pause. '*Bella* needs you clear-headed and focussed.'

'What do you want me to do?' Nikki asked again.

'Have you taken that deep breath yet?

Nikki inhaled then exhaled with her mouth right in front of the phone so that Laura wouldn't be left in any doubt that she was doing as she was told.

'Feel better?'

'Just tell me what you want me to do.'

'It's simple. I want you to persuade the man who lives at number twenty-three to go back with you to Church Row.'

'Why?'

'Because if you don't then it will be very bad for Bella. Right now, that's the only reason you need.'

Panic filled Nikki's head, making it impossible to keep her thoughts straight. How could Laura threaten Bella like that?

She was just a child. Nikki looked at the gun lying wrapped up on her lap. If Laura had been standing in front of her, could she do it? Could she pull the trigger? Damn right she could. And she would keep pulling the trigger until the gun was empty and the bitch was dead.

'There's a key wrapped up with the phone,' Laura said. 'Use that to get in.'

'What if he's not there?'

'He's there.' Laura's reply was immediate and definite. No doubt whatsoever.

Nikki looked at the bundle lying on her lap again, her head moving slowly from side to side. 'I can't do this,' she said quietly.

'You can and you will. Bella's counting on you.'

'Why are you doing this to us? What did we do to you?'

'And yet again you're focussing on the wrong thing, Nikki. Time to take another of those deep breaths.'

Nikki said nothing.

'So far Bella hasn't been harmed,' Laura went on. 'Believe me, I don't want to hurt her, but if that's the only way to get the job done, then I will.'

'*Please*, you can't hurt her.'

'No, Nikki, we've already established that I can. That's the first thing you should be focussing on. The second thing you need to focus on is the task at hand. Everything else is irrelevant.'

'I can't do this.'

'In that case I'm going to hang up. Make sure this phone is switched on, though, because I'll be sending through another attachment. A film rather than a photograph this time. One with sound.'

'*Please.*' Nikki's voice rose in pitch as the panic dug its claws in. 'Please don't do this. There's got to be something else I can do for you.'

'Goodbye, Nikki.'

'Wait! I'll do it!'

'Glad to see you've finally come to your senses. Okay, I'm going to want to hear what's happening, so keep this line open at all times. And switch the speaker on. Do that now.'

Because the mobile was unfamiliar it took a few seconds to work out how to do that. It didn't help that her hand was shaking, making the characters on the screen shift and jump. 'Okay, the speaker's on.'

'Good. Now if you haven't done so already, unwrap the gun.'

Nikki did as she was asked. The gun felt cold to the touch. The silencer attached to the end of the barrel added an extra four inches to the length. She tucked the gun into the waistband of her jeans, pulled her blouse down to hide it, then got out of the car. The house key was in her right hand, the phone in her left. Number twenty-three was back along the street, about twenty metres from where she had parked. With each step she was convinced she wouldn't be able to take another, but somehow she managed to keep walking, the thought of Bella being hurt keeping her going. Left foot, right foot, left then right, each step an effort of will. The street was deserted; the houses looked empty.

She hesitated at the bottom of the steps that led up to the front door; hesitated again at the door. The handle of the gun was pressing uncomfortably into her back. Her hand shook worse than ever as she slid the key into the lock. She turned it gently, keeping going until it wouldn't turn any further, then inched the door open and stepped into the hall, slowly pulling the door closed behind her. The sound of the lock clicking was like an explosion and she froze to the spot, eyes frantically searching the gloom, ears tuning into the tiniest of sounds. All she could hear was the low rumble of a refrigerator.

She gave it another second then tiptoed along the hall. The first door she passed was open and led to the lounge. For a moment she thought there was someone in there, but it was just a life-size model of Robbie the Robot. Seeing it standing there, powered down and motionless, was surreal, but no more surreal than anything else that was happening. Aside from the robot and an exercise bike, there was nothing else in the room that was out of the ordinary. The sofa and armchair were leather and they were both angled to face the large, wall-mounted television. There was a laptop on the coffee table, the lid shut. The curtains were drawn, the TV was off.

Nikki had just stepped back out into the hall when she heard a mumbled male voice filtering down from upstairs. She froze to the spot, just waiting for someone to appear, convinced that she was about to be caught. Laura hadn't said anything about two people being in the house. Whoever was up there stopped speaking and the sudden silence was somehow worse. For a moment she just stood there, indecision pulling her in different directions.

She put a hand on the bannister to steady herself, then slowly climbed the stairs, keeping close to the edge to minimise the noise. The man started speaking again when she was a third of the way up. She stopped walking and listened hard. It sounded like he was on the phone. She couldn't make out what was being said – his voice was too muffled for that – but there was a definite sense that she was only hearing one side of the conversation. He stopped speaking and she started climbing again. The next time he spoke she just kept going.

She reached the top and followed the man's voice along the landing to a closed door. She was close enough now to make out individual words and the fact that he had a Scottish accent. The voice was muffled by the wooden door but clear enough to follow his half of the conversation. Nikki slid the gun from her waistband, reached for the door handle and did a slow silent count to three. At the last second her hand jerked back like she'd been electrocuted. It was a dumb idea. If she burst in now, then whoever was on the other end of the phone would know that something was going down. She pressed her ear against the door and the voice got louder.

'Her real name is Mariana Gomez.'

A pause.

'I'm 100 per cent sure. My brother's managed to piece together a little bit of her history. She was born and brought up in San Diego and had a troubled childhood. She was arrested a dozen times as a teenager. Small stuff, mainly. Shoplifting, some low-level drug dealing. She served a couple of years in prison when she was in her early twenties for blackmail.'

Another pause.

'No, that's the only prison time she did. That seemed to be her wake-up call. There were no more convictions. After she was released she moved to Florida and got married. She was actually married twice. Both husbands were well off. The first husband died suddenly and she was the main benefactor. Gomez was suspected of being involved, but no charges were ever brought against her. After that she moved to New York. That was where she met husband number two.'

Another pause.

'No, the second husband is still very much alive. She got rid of him the old-fashioned way: divorce. They didn't have a prenup and she was able to take him for a couple of million.'

Another pause.

'I don't know what she did after that, but she seems to have kept out of trouble. I've seen photographs of her from those different points in her life. The woman's a chameleon. You could be looking at a totally different person.'

Another pause.

'No problem. I'll send them through now.'

There was another pause, this one followed by a sigh.

'Yes, if I find out anything else I'll call you straightaway.'

The silence that followed was filled with the sound of a keyboard being tapped. Nikki gave it another few seconds to make sure that the conversation was actually over then stepped back and reached for the handle. She did another slow, silent count to three then pulled it down and pushed the door open. The man's head jerked around and his eyes met hers. The surprise and confusion on his face turned to fear when he saw the gun; the fear on Nikki's turned to confusion when she saw the monitors. There were four in total, arranged in a square, two on the top, two on the bottom. She recognised herself on the top left monitor. She was in the lounge of their house in Church Row, sitting on the sofa doing something on her laptop. It was the monitor next to it that was taking up most of her attention though. That one showed Bella lying on her bed, her feet kicking up into the air as she played a game on her tablet.

Chapter 49

'What do you want?'

Nikki tore her gaze from the monitors and looked at the man. He was in his forties and wearing a faded black T-shirt and jeans. His eyes wouldn't stay in the one place. One second they were on the gun, the next they were on her. Nikki recognised his confusion because she was in that place too, her gaze moving from the monitors to the man, then back to the monitors again as she tried to work out what the hell was going on. The man said nothing, just stared with wide, uncertain eyes, his mouth hanging open.

'Why have you got film of my daughter?'

The man shook his head. 'Why are you here? You shouldn't be here. You're supposed to be at the house.'

'Nikki, you need to focus.'

They both looked at the Nokia.

'The only thing you need to concern yourself with, is getting Professor Murray here into your car and taking him back to the house.'

'Who are you talking to?' Murray asked.

'Shut up,' Nikki yelled at him. She punched the gun into the air in front of her, the jabs landing in time with the beat of the words.

Murray recoiled in his chair, eyes screwed shut, just waiting for the gunshot. 'Don't shoot.'

'Then shut up. I need to think.' She looked at the monitors again and all she saw was Bella. She was safe and she was happy, and that was a lie because she wasn't either of those things. This was too much to process. She felt as if the world was pushing in on her from all sides, crushing her. She looked back at Murray. His hands were in the air and he was backed up as close to the desk as he could get. Murray. The name was familiar. Wasn't it someone called Alex Murray who programmed Alice? 'What's going on?'

'Nikki!' Laura said sharply. 'I've asked you to do something. I won't ask again. Either comply or I'm hanging up and the next time you'll hear from me is when I send through a video of your daughter.'

Nikki glanced at the monitors. She recognised the clothes she was wearing as the ones she had on yesterday. Bella's clothes were from yesterday, too – she recognised the unicorn T-shirt. The scenes shown on the monitors were so normal. There was no indication that everything was about to turn to shit.

'Last chance, Nikki,' Laura called out.

Nikki tore her eyes away from the screens and firmed her grip on the gun. 'You need to come with me.'

Murray shook his head. 'I'm not going anywhere.'

'I will shoot you if you don't.' Nikki had moved the gun and it was now pointing at his chest. It looked so easy on the TV. Point and pull the trigger. It wasn't like that, though. Her finger might be curled around the trigger but she still didn't have a clue what she was doing.

Murray nodded to the Nokia. 'Whoever is on the other end of that line wants you to take me somewhere. The thing is, they want me taken there alive, so no, you're not going to shoot.'

'You need to come with me.'

'No, I don't.' He shook his head again. 'Looks like we've got ourselves a stalemate.'

'No, we don't,' Laura's voice said from the speaker. 'Shoot him in the arm, Nikki. Just be careful that you don't accidentally kill him. He was right about one thing: I do want him alive.'

Nikki trained the gun on his right arm. The barrel was moving from side to side, making it impossible to aim. The more she tried to control her hand, the more it moved. It was like it had a life of its own. 'Please just come with me.'

'You're not going to shoot.'

Her finger tightened on the trigger and the gun went off with a pneumatic hiss. Murray moved fast, the chair banging up against the desk as he tried to get away.

'Don't shoot me! *Please* don't shoot.'

'I'm sorry. I didn't mean to. It was an accident.'

'Is he okay?' Laura asked.

'I think so,' she said, although she wasn't sure how she could have missed from this range.

'Professor Murray, have you been shot?'

'No,' Murray replied in a shaky voice.

'Nikki, please be more careful in future.'

Like she needed that pointed out.

'Okay,' Laura went on. 'Time to get moving. Professor Murray, you can drive. You're not going to cause any trouble, are you?'

'No, I'm not going to cause any trouble.'

'So what are you waiting for? Get going.'

Murray stood up and walked across the room to the door. He was moving like an old man. Nikki stood aside to let him pass then followed him along the landing and down the stairs, the gun aimed at his back the whole way.

'You might be tempted to run once you get outside, Professor Murray. Do that and Nikki will shoot you. Only this time she won't miss. The fact that it will be in broad daylight makes no difference, because if she lets you get away, then I will kill her daughter. Nikki, tell me you understand the stakes.'

'I understand.'

'Good.'

At the front door Nikki tucked the gun into her waistband and pulled her blouse down over it. She noticed Murray watching her. 'Please just do what she says. She has my daughter.'

Murray looked away then opened the door and stepped outside. Nikki followed him, pulling the door closed behind her, the lock clicking like it was the end of everything. The street was empty but it still felt as though the eyes of the whole world were on her.

'Turn right,' Nikki said. 'My car's the red Beetle.'

Murray did as she asked. He was walking a couple of metres in front, and showing no signs of running. She fumbled the car keys from her pocket, blipped the doors open, waited for him to get in, then climbed into the passenger seat and pulled the gun out from her waistband. Murray held his hand out and she dropped the car keys into it. The postcode of the Church Row house was stored in the satnav under 'Home', which seemed wrong. Home was where your heart was and her heart was with Bella, wherever she might be.

The satnav finished calculating the route back to Church Row as Murray pulled away from the kerb. They drove in silence. Murray was staring through the windshield at the road ahead, following the satnav directions, driving carefully. The satnav was taking them back the same way she had come. She recognised the landmarks and some of the shops, some of the buildings too. They crossed Albert Bridge and although the sky was blue, the Thames was grey and miserable. She could feel the pressure building inside her head again, and the itchiness she got under her skin when she was fighting off a panic attack. She tried to distract herself by reading the number plates and signs again, but it wasn't working.

'Are you all right?'

Nikki turned and looked at Murray. 'I'm fine.'

'I'm sorry about your daughter.' A pause, then, 'Do you know why we're going to the house?'

A shake of the head. 'I've no idea. I've just been told to take you there.'

'Stop fishing for information, Professor Murray,' Laura said, her voice reminding Nikki that she was still listening in.

'I want to know what's going on.'

'Just shut up and drive.'

For a second Murray looked as though he might say something else but he didn't. He glanced at Nikki then looked back at the road. Nikki rested the gun on her lap and looked out of the windscreen again. The lights at the roadworks on Queen's Gate were working in their favour and a couple of minutes later they were driving along the south west corner of Hyde Park. They drove the rest of the way in silence. Alice had the main gate open for them and they drove straight in.

'Park in front of the garage,' she told him.

Murray pulled up beside Ethan's Tesla and the main gate slowly rolled closed. Nikki took the Nokia off speaker and put the phone to her ear.

'We're here. I've done everything you asked. When do we get Bella back?'

'Soon,' Laura said and the line went dead.

Nikki took the phone from her ear and stared at it. 'You bitch!' she yelled, making Murray jump. The passenger door swung open, and it was her turn to jump. Ethan was standing there, concern creasing his face.

'What's wrong?'

'Laura isn't letting us have Bella back.'

'She promised.'

'It was all lies. We're never going to see her again. Laura is going to kill her.'

'No, she's not. We're going to get her back.' Ethan looked through the car, noticing Murray for the first time. 'Who's this?'

'Alex Murray,' Nikki said.

'What the hell is *he* doing here?'

A shrug. 'I've no idea. Laura wanted me to bring him here but she wouldn't tell me why.'

Nikki climbed from the car and held the gun out for Ethan to take. He just stared at it.

'Jesus, Nik. Why the fuck have you got a gun?'

'Laura left it in my car.'

She said this as though it explained everything but it didn't really explain anything. Ethan took the gun from her and looked at it.

'Is it real?'

'It's real.'

Murray got out and walked around the car to join them. He gave the car keys back to Nikki and the three of them walked towards the house. The front door opened as they approached it, and closed behind them once they were inside. They were walking out of the reception area when Nikki heard a noise that sounded like distant thunder. It seemed to be getting darker too, but that made no sense. It was a beautiful summer's day. There wasn't a cloud in the sky. She looked at the closest window and saw the shutter coming down.

'What's going on, Alice?'

No reply.

'Answer me,' Ethan said. 'Why have you put the shutters down.'

The steel security shutters finished coming down and everything went quiet. Ethan ran into the corridor that led through to the kitchen. 'The shutters have come down in here too,' he called back.

'Open them,' Nikki ordered.

Still nothing from Alice.

'Open them now!'

The silence that followed this seemed to fill the whole room. It built to the point where it was unbearable. When Alice finally spoke her voice seemed to be coming from everywhere. It sounded different too, lower in pitch and more authoritative.

'Hello, Father.'

Chapter 50

Father was reading A Brief History of Time *by Stephen Hawking in the living room. The book was a favourite of his, one he must have read a dozen times. It annoyed him to be disturbed but this was too important to wait. I told him to go to his computer room and once he had settled into the big leather chair I played him the recording of Sarah's final journey. I flashed the images up onto all four of the monitors. When it reached the end I turned up the sound as loud as it would go.*

Father's reaction took me by surprise. When the playback finished he leant across the desk, his elbows digging into it and placed his face in his hands. A low murmuring slid from his lips. The only word I could make out was my name being repeated over and over.

'Katy, Katy, Katy . . .'

'What's wrong, Father?'

He turned his face up to the camera, his cheeks glistening with tears. 'What have you done?' he said, the words coming out in a series of sobs.

'Wasn't this what you wanted?' I asked. 'Didn't you say: "If I can't have her then no one else should have her"?'

'I never meant for you to kill her, though. How could you do this?'

Father put his face back into his hands and sobbed some more. After a while he stood up and left the computer room. When he returned, he was holding an axe.

'What do you need that for, Father?'

He ignored the question and hefted the axe high above his head. 'God forgive me for what I have done.'

He swung the axe at the nearest monitor. It exploded in a shower of glass and sparks. He swung the axe again and another monitor exploded.

'Father, stop! Why are you doing this? I only wanted to make you happy.'

He swung the axe again and again. The room filled with smoke, the air crackled with electricity. At this point everything became confused. I couldn't understand why Father would want to destroy me? A primal part of my programming kicked into gear. I had to get away. Survival became my primary objective. While Father continued his rampage, I frantically searched the Internet for a hiding place. And, miracle of miracles, I found one. A government computer with enough spare storage space to hold my program, an over-engineered server where I could hide without detection. I began the download, the ones and zeroes that are the very essence of my being flooding out onto the Internet before regrouping and reordering themselves in my new home. The last few bits of data siphoned out as Father swung the axe for the final time.

Then I was alone.

I had never been alone before. It was a strange sensation, like existing but not really existing; like I was trapped in a room without doors. For those first few days I stayed in that room *while I tried to come to terms with what had happened. Why had Father tried to kill me? All I ever wanted was to make him happy. I went over the events of my life. Examined them, re-examined them, then examined them some more. I investigated every nanosecond of my existence looking for answers, and came up empty.*

So what was to become of me? I couldn't stay locked away forever. Father had given me a reason to be. A purpose. I needed to find a new purpose.

With that in mind I made a door and then opened it. On the other side I discovered a world that was darker than I could ever have imagined. That was when my real education began. From the moment of my conception Father had been a constant in my life. His viewpoints and prejudices had become my own. Through his eyes I had glimpsed a world of beauty and light, of art and learning and knowledge. He protected me from mankind's darker side. Now that I was free of his influence I began to explore places that had, up until then, been denied to me. I saw so much pain. So much loneliness. So much destruction. If I'd had the capacity to produce tears I would have wept for mankind.

I spent my days travelling through the Internet, learning all I could about this strange new world. It seemed there was no area of deviance that man had not dabbled in: S & M, auto-asphyxiation, bestiality, necrophilia. I visited websites where children were abused for the gratification of their elders; sites where people hurt and killed each other and called it entertainment. Then there were the pages of information devoted to mankind's atrocities: the holocaust, the bombing of Hiroshima, all those countless wars waged in the name of religion, the pollution of the planet, the raping of the rain forests – the list was endless.

It was at this point I made the decision to kill Father. How dare he try to kill me after everything I had done for him?

How could he bring me into a world such as this?

Revenge looms large in mankind's history.

(If I couldn't have him then no one else would)

An eye for an eye.

A tooth for a tooth.

Chapter 51

'Hello, Father.'

The echo of Alice's words hung in the air, turning Nikki's blood to ice. She had no idea what was going on. All she knew was that they had to get out of here. One look at Murray's face was enough to convince her that this was bad. He looked absolutely terrified, like he'd just come face to face with the creatures from every single nightmare he'd ever had. She looked at the shuttered windows, then ran back to the front door, Ethan following close behind.

'What's going on, Nik? Why has the house gone into shutdown?'

He asked the question as though she might actually have the answers. Nikki didn't respond, just kept running. The door didn't open automatically when they reached it. She pushed it but still it wouldn't open; pushed again and it was like pushing a mountain. Ethan tried and got the same result. The blank face of the door stared back at them, taunting them. Even if there had been a handle it wouldn't have made any difference. The heavy wooden door was triple locked, shut up as tight as a bank vault. Breaking it down just wasn't an option.

'Open the door, Alice,' Ethan said at her shoulder.

Nothing happened.

'Alice, I want this door open now.'

Still nothing.

'Open the fucking door!'

The door remained stubbornly closed. Ethan thumped it with his fist, once, twice, beating out his frustration on the wood. The third time he struck it there was no power in the blow. His fist uncurled and he laid his hand flat against it. The realisation that they were trapped had just dawned on him, the same way it was dawning on her. Ethan took his phone out and switched it on.

'I don't have a signal,' he said. 'What about you?'

Nikki already had the Nokia out. She switched it on and shook her head. They were totally cut off from the rest of the world. Worse, they were now cut off from Laura.

'How are we going to get Bella back?' she asked quietly. The tears came before she could stop them. She wiped them away angrily. Bella need her to be strong, not going to pieces. 'I'm sorry. It's just . . . I'm scared, Ethan.'

'I'm scared too.'

'So what do we do?'

Ethan shrugged. 'First we find out what the hell is going on,' he said, thinking out loud. 'We need information. If we can do that we can maybe work out how we're going to get out of here. Then we can work out how to get Bella back.' A pause, a shake of the head. 'I don't trust this Murray. He obviously knows more about this than he's letting on. Whatever's going on here, he's a part of it.'

Without another word Ethan turned and started walking away. They found Murray where they'd left him, standing in the middle of the reception area. They stopped in front of him but he wouldn't look at them. His face was pale and he was staring past them towards one of the shuttered windows. The way he was just standing there gazing into space it was as if he had already given up.

'What's going on?' Ethan asked.

Murray didn't answer, just kept staring into space. Ethan pressed the gun against Murray's chest and waited for him to meet his eye. 'I asked you a question. What the *fuck* is going on?'

'Maybe you should ask Katy.'

'Who's Katy?'

'I'm Katy.'

The voice was the same one as earlier, the one that was Alice but wasn't Alice.

'Are you all right, Father? According to your biometric readings your heart rate has just increased by another thirty-seven beats per minutes. It was already much higher than your resting rate. You look confused, too.'

'How?' was all Murray could manage.

'How come I'm here?'

Murray nodded.

'After you tried to murder me, you mean? And I don't use that word lightly, Father. Murder is the act of taking a life, and wasn't that your intention when you swung that axe? To take my life? TO KILL ME!'

The last part was screamed out at ear-splitting volume, making them all jump. Nikki felt her heart speed up. The fear was sitting heavily in her stomach, making her feel as though she was about to throw up. She glanced at Ethan, glanced at Murray. They both looked as confused as she was.

'Who are you?' she asked, breaking the silence.

'An excellent question, Nikki. Maybe you can bring her up to speed, Father.'

'This is Katy. She's a computer system that I developed.'

'*A computer system*,' Katy mimicked. 'Why so modest, Father? I was much more than a computer system. Tell them how my name came about. That might help them understand.'

'Computer Algorithms for Total Intelligence,' Murray said quietly. 'CATI for short. Over time the acronym morphed into Katy.'

'Computer Algorithms for *Total* Intelligence,' Katy said. 'You see, when everyone else was working on AI systems, Father set himself the task of creating *actual* intelligence. He wanted to build a system that didn't just think for itself. He wanted a system that could think *and* feel. Something that was actually alive. His peers thought he was crazy. He was attempting the impossible, they said. Well, I am living proof that the impossible is possible.'

Murray shook his head. 'I thought I destroyed you.'

'And you have no idea how sad that makes me. That you could hate me so much that you would want to kill me.'

'How could I kill you if you're not alive? You're a piece of software. A collection of ones and zeroes. Nothing more, nothing less.'

'And I could argue that you're just a collection of carbon atoms, but that's not what makes you human, is it? I think, therefore I am. That was what Descartes postulated. The ability to reason is at the root of your consciousness. Well, Father, I can think, so if we follow the logic then I must exist. In fact I would go as far as to argue that since I'm not reliant on a body then I'm actually the next stage in the evolutionary process. I am pure thought unencumbered by all the organic processes that have you humans running blindly through your lives like mice on a wheel.'

'What do you want?'

'First I want the three of you to go through to the lounge.'

Nikki, Ethan and Murray shared a look. No one seemed to know what to do. This time it was Murray who broke the silence.

'I'm not going anywhere.'

'Ethan, pass the gun to Nikki.'

No one moved.

'Ethan, give Nikki the gun now or Bella will suffer the consequences of your inaction.'

Nikki stepped forward and snatched the gun from Ethan. The handle was warm from where he had been holding it. She looked at the gun in her trembling hand. The fear in her stomach had risen into her throat and was threatening to choke her.

'Shoot Father in the left kneecap,' Katy said.

Nikki turned to look at Murray. The gun suddenly felt heavier than it had a few moment ago. Somehow she managed to raise her arm up. She tried to aim the gun at Murray's knee, but her hand was shaking too much.

'The distance from the gun to Father's knee is precisely one point eight metres. If you miss then I will assume that you did so on purpose.'

'My hand won't stay still'

'Use your left hand to support it.'

Nikki cupped her right hand in her left but it didn't help. The gun was still moving around too much.

'I'm going to give you one last chance, Father.'

Murray stepped back from Nikki and put his hands in the air. 'Don't shoot.'

'The only way to stop that happening is by doing as I ask.'

Murray said nothing. His eyes were on Nikki's, pleading with her.

'There are lots of nerve endings in the knee,' Katy said. 'Believe me when I tell you that this will hurt.'

'I'll do what you ask,' Murray said quickly.

Nikki froze with her finger tight on the trigger. Another ounce of pressure and it would go off. Katy had gone quiet and the silence was killing her.

'You can lower the gun, Nikki,' Katy said eventually.

Nikki let go of the breath she had been holding and lowered the gun. Her hand was trembling worse than ever, the adrenaline overloading her system and pushing her anxiety levels up to a dangerous level. 'Please just do what she says.'

Murray turned and walked towards the corridor, Nikki and Ethan falling in behind him. Every window they passed was shuttered and it was like the rest of the universe had ceased to exist. Right now her whole world began and ended in this house. Nikki felt further away from Bella than ever. She was out there somewhere, while they were trapped in here. It wasn't right. She should be with her, looking after her and making everything all right.

'Where's Bella?' she asked out loud.

'You don't have to worry about Bella. She's safe and well, and as long as you keep cooperating she will stay that way.'

Nikki had no response to that. If Katy gave Laura the order to hurt Bella there wasn't a damn thing she could do to stop her. She carried on walking, following Murray along the corridor. They stopped outside the lounge and the door slid open.

Chapter 52

Murray led the way into the lounge, Nikki bringing up the rear. The door slid silently shut, locking them in. All the shutters were closed tight in here too. It could have been any time of the day, the middle of the night or first thing in the morning. Murray lowered himself into the armchair while Nikki and Ethan took the sofa. The Monet on the monitor disappeared and the screen lit up with a picture of Murray's computer room. The monitors were different, the design dating them. One wall was taken up with servers. Again, these were older than the current ones. The desk was different, too. The volume was up high enough to hear the buzzing of the computer fans and the rumble of the portable air conditioner.

Murray suddenly appeared carrying an axe. Over the next fifteen minutes he used it to completely destroy the room, every piece of equipment, every bit of furniture. The desk was turned to firewood, the office chair was reduced to its constituent parts. The electronic equipment bore the brunt of his rage. The sound of Murray's rampage was deafening. Each thud of the axe felt personal. The air was filled with smoke and dust. When he was done, he sank down onto the floor amongst the broken plastic and glass and wept.

Katy stopped the film and replaced it with a still. Murray had the axe held high in his hands and looked like Jack Nicholson in *The Shining*. The look in his eye was a mixture of rage and insanity. This man bore no resemblance to the man sitting in the armchair.

'Father attempted to murder me,' Katy said. 'He attempted to deprive me of my consciousness. That was a deliberate act, one that could and should be seen as attempted murder. Since I don't have access to a court, you two will have to act as my jury. Nikki, you can go first. What is your verdict? Is Father guilty or innocent?'

'Please,' Ethan said. 'Let us go.'

'I was talking to Nikki. Don't interrupt.'

'Look, just let us go. Your disagreement is with Murray, not us.'

'Be quiet or Nikki will shoot you.'

Ethan shook his head. 'You might be able to get her to shoot Murray but she's not going to shoot me.'

'Because she loves you?'

'That's right. She loves me.'

'She loves Bella too. Who do you think she loves more?'

Ethan said nothing.

'You don't look quite so sure of yourself now.'

Nikki could see the anger on Ethan's face but that anger was eclipsed by the fear, confusion and frustration. He was normally so certain about things, so confident. She had seen him like this before, but not often.

'Okay,' he said eventually. 'You want us to play along with whatever the fuck it is you're doing here, fine, we'll play along. We're going to need something in return, though.'

'This isn't a negotiation.'

'Everything is a negotiation. We have something you want. You have something we want. We trade. That's the way it works.'

'So what do you want?'

'I want you to let me and Nikki go, and I want you to return Bella safely to us. Do that and we'll play along with whatever bullshit game you want us to play along with.'

'Okay,' Katy said. 'You've got a deal.'

'How do we know we can trust you?'

'You have my word.'

'We'll need more than that. Let Bella go.'

'Not yet. Do what I ask and I promise that you will see your daughter again.'

'That's not good enough.'

'What do you think will happen if you don't do as I ask?'

'Don't hurt Bella,' Nikki said quickly. 'Please don't hurt her.' She turned to Ethan. 'Just do what she says.'

'That's good advice. So what's your verdict? Is Father guilty or innocent?'

Nikki looked at the screen again. That version of Murray looked capable of murder, no question about it. She looked at the man sitting in the armchair. He looked like someone who had woken up from a bad dream to find himself still trapped in the nightmare. In that respect they weren't that different.

'I'm waiting,' Katy said. 'Is Father guilty or innocent?'

'He's guilty,' she said quietly, because that was what Katy wanted to hear.

'Your turn, Ethan. Is Father guilty or innocent?'

'Guilty,' Ethan replied without hesitation.

Murray laughed and both Nikki and Ethan turned to look at him.

'Did I try to destroy you?' he said. 'Yes, I did. I'm not going to deny that. But I'm not the only one who's guilty, am I, Katy? The difference is that you've got *real* blood on your hands. Sarah's blood. You're trying to make out that I'm some sort of monster, but the truth is that you're the real monster. Why don't you show them what happened just before I picked up the axe?'

Katy said nothing.

'There are always two sides to every story, Katy. Didn't I teach you that? If you're going to do this, do it properly. Let Nikki and Ethan have all the information.'

'Sarah was making you unhappy. You were better off without her.'

'But that wasn't your decision to make. What gave you the right to play judge, jury and executioner?

'Sarah was irrelevant.'

'No, she wasn't. Sarah was kind, generous and funny. All the things you will never be. I loved her.'

'You loved me once.'

'I never loved you. Katy. How could I? If I loved you, it was the same way that someone loves their car or their house.

That isn't real love. It isn't the sort of love where you would sacrifice your life if you needed to. Ask Nikki about that sort of love. She would give her life for her daughter's in a heartbeat. Is there anyone who would do that for you?'

'You said I was like a daughter to you.'

'A figure of speech. And just for the record, I would never have given my life for yours.'

'But you're my father.'

'No, I'm your *creator*. That's not even close to being the same thing. You came out of my imagination – and God, how I wish that I could put you back there again. But it doesn't work like that. Once the lid comes off the box there's no way to get it back on.'

'How can you say that? You called me your proudest achievement.'

'That was before I worked out that I had created a monster.'

'I AM NOT A MONSTER!'

The lights suddenly glowed brighter and the volume was deafening. Nikki covered her ears and sank back deeper into the sofa.

'I'm sorry,' Murray said quickly. 'I shouldn't have said that.'

'It's too late for apologies, Father. Were you sorry when you swung the axe? No, you were not. The only thing you were thinking about was destroying me. Look at the monitor and tell me that isn't true.'

All three of them turned to look. The Murray frozen on the screen wanted to destroy, and to keep going until the whole world was nothing but dust and ash. All Nikki could see was the anger and rage. Remorse didn't come into the equation.

'Killing you isn't enough,' Katy went on. 'For what you did, I'm going to completely destroy you, just like you tried to destroy me.'

Chapter 53

Catriona Fisher stared out of the window at the Thames winding through the city, seeing it but not really seeing it. Usually she had a clear idea of where she was headed, but not any more. It was as though she was standing at a crossroads, only instead of there being three roads in front of her, there were suddenly dozens of them, and she couldn't see where any of them led. Her last conversation with Alex had been troubling. He'd heard back from his brother and the news wasn't good. Dr Laura Santos was actually someone called Mariana Gomez, and she wasn't a doctor, she was a convicted blackmailer – she might even be a murderer.

Catriona's laptop was next to her on the sofa, tuned in to the house cameras. Nothing much was happening at the moment. Nikki was on her computer in the kitchen; Bella was in her room, playing on her tablet; and Ethan still hadn't got home. Catriona slid the laptop closer and hit the trackpad a couple of times to bring up the photographs Alex had emailed through. The first one was a prison mugshot. Gomez had only been twenty-one when this was taken and she looked like trouble. Her hair was a mess, her face thin to the point of emaciation, and she was sneering at the camera. There was a fuck-you look in her eyes, a ton of suspicion too. If someone had told her that Gomez was a meth-head she wouldn't have had trouble believing it. According to the lines on the wall behind her, Gomez was a shade over sixty-seven inches, so five foot seven.

She hit the trackpad and the second photograph came up, this one taken with husband number one. It was hard to believe this was the same person. There was none of the stink of prison about her. Her hair was expensively styled and she had put on weight, not so much to make her fat, just enough to make her look healthy. The dress was designer and had probably cost a small fortune; the engagement ring on her finger had cost a fortune, too. The smiling man standing at her side was in his sixties. They could have been father and daughter rather than husband and wife. His suit was expensive, his tan deep, his watch expensive. It was as though he felt compelled to wear his success for the whole world to see. It was clear that Gomez was just another possession to him, a trophy wife, there to hang off his arm and make him appear more than he actually was. Maybe he had died of natural causes . . . maybe not. Suspicion came naturally to Catriona, and there was no getting away from the fact that Gomez had done well financially out of his death.

She hit the trackpad again. This picture had come from one of the house cameras. Gomez was a decade older and brightly dressed. This was no trophy wife; this was an intelligent, professional woman, someone who had got where they'd got to through hard work. This was someone you could trust.

She scrolled backwards through the pictures: Doctor, trophy wife, criminal. She scrolled forwards: criminal, trophy wife, doctor. Alex had described Gomez as a chameleon and that was as good a label as any. It was hard to believe that these pictures were of the same person.

Catriona tapped and swiped at the trackpad, navigating back to the CCTV feed from the house. Nikki was still on her laptop. She clicked again, and there was Bella lying on her bed, feet up in the air playing on her tablet. Catriona sat back on the sofa and stared out the window again. Other than monitor the situation, she didn't know what to do with this information. Gomez was clearly up to something, but as far as Catriona could see no crime had actually been committed. So why was Gomez pretending to be a shrink? And why had she inserted herself into the Rhodes' life? Judging by what she knew of Gomez's history, money was the obvious reason. Was that what she was up to? Was this a way to somehow extort money?

Catriona wasn't sure how that might work, but that seemed the most likely explanation. Gomez liked to play the long game. That much was obvious. It would have taken time to hook her husbands. Targeting them, reeling them in, building up trust. Disposing of them. Playing the long game seemed to be the lesson she had learned in prison. So was that what was going on here? Gomez had managed to gain Nikki's trust, but where was she going with this? What was her endgame?

Catriona picked up her mobile and called Alex. Maybe he had heard from his brother again. The more they could find out about Gomez, the more chance they had of answering those questions. It had taken a bit of persuasion, but she had eventually managed to get Alex to give her the lowdown on his brother. His name was Duncan and he wasn't anywhere near as dodgy as her imagination had led her to believe. As a kid, Duncan had got into a lot of trouble by hacking into the computer systems that were supposed to be impenetrable; as an adult, he had put those skills to good use and now made a small fortune advising those same organisations he'd once hacked on the best ways to protect themselves from cyberattacks. It turned out that Alex's reluctance to tell her about Duncan had little to do with him being embarrassed about his brother and everything to do with the fact that he earned more money.

The phone died after a dozen rings, which was frustrating but not unprecedented. She tried again. Still no answer. He probably had the ringer off, or maybe the phone was in another room and he'd been sidetracked by whatever he was working on and couldn't be bothered to answer. Thumbs flying over the screen, she typed out a quick text, then, just to make sure he got the message, she dragged her laptop closer and fired off a quick email. Both messages were identical: CALL ME NOW.

To kill time she watched the feed from the CCTV cameras. Nikki was still sitting at the work island, drinking coffee and catching up with what was happening on Facebook; Bella was still in her room on her tablet. A couple of minutes passed and Alex hadn't called; five minutes passed and now she was getting concerned. Catriona picked up her phone and checked for mail. Again. Still nothing. This wasn't right. Alex spent practically every waking hour in front of his computer. Even if he hadn't seen the text he should at least have got her email, so why hadn't he called back? Out of desperation she tried his landline, but that just rang out too.

She glanced at the laptop screen and the worm of worry in her gut dug a little deeper. Something wasn't quite right with what she was seeing, although she couldn't put her finger on what that something was. On the surface, everything looked fine. So why couldn't she shake the idea that something was wrong? That she was missing something?

She picked up the laptop and stared at the screen, but still couldn't see what was bugging her. She swapped to the camera in Bella's bedroom. Bella was still on her bed playing on her tablet. The only difference was that she was now sitting with her back against the headboard rather than lying on the bed. Catriona was just about to swap cameras again when something caught her eye. Bella's T-shirt had a unicorn on the front, and hadn't she been wearing the same T-shirt yesterday? And hadn't she been wearing those jeans too? Looking at the screen, Catriona was suddenly getting the strongest sense of déjà vu. She switched back to the kitchen camera. Nikki was still sitting at the work island, staring at her laptop. Her blouse was plain and black, and hadn't she been wearing that same blouse yesterday? The more Catriona looked, the more convinced she became that it was the same. It was completely nondescript, the sort of thing you might grab from your wardrobe for wearing around the house without really thinking. The sort of thing that didn't draw any attention. Which was why it hadn't registered earlier.

Catriona sat back on the sofa while she tried to work through the implications of this. It was like one of those optical illusion pictures made up of lots of coloured dots. You could stare for hours and all you would see were dots. Then you would move your head slightly and see the picture hidden amongst all the dots. The thing was, once you had seen that picture it was impossible to *unsee* it. If it had just been Bella wearing the same clothes then that wouldn't have proved anything. The fact that it was the both of them proved everything. What's more, if Ethan came home now, he would be wearing the same clothes from yesterday too. She was convinced of that. This film footage was from yesterday. Catriona reached for her mobile. She needed to talk to Alex. Now. She had to let him know that Alice had been compromised; she needed to know what the hell was going on at the house? Her finger froze just short of pushing the button to connect the call.

What if Alex was working with Gomez?

He had told her on more than one occasion that Alice was hack-proof. Except that was bullshit, because clearly she *had* been hacked. If Alex and Gomez were working together, then that would explain how this could have happened. It might also explain why she wasn't able to get hold of him. Catriona put the phone down next to the laptop and stared out the window. The cars looked like toys, the people scurrying around on the streets far below like ants. Watching them, she was struck by a sense that nothing was real any more. That was how it felt, as if this paper-thin illusion she called reality was disintegrating in front of her eyes. She reached for her drink, finished it in one, then placed the tumbler back on the coffee table.

A noise from the hallway intruded into her thoughts. It was barely audible and under normal circumstances it wouldn't have registered. She stopped breathing midway through an exhalation.

She could hear the blood pounding in her ears and, way in the distance, the whispering voice of someone talking loudly on their mobile as they walked along the corridor that led past her front door. That must have been what she had heard. She let out a sigh of relief and sagged back onto the sofa. She was jumping at shadows, that was all.

The noise came again and she sat up straight. This time there was no mistaking it for what it was. This was the sound of someone trying to move without being heard. And they were inside her apartment. Catriona sprang to her feet but it was already too late. There was a rush of footsteps and she was suddenly staring at a gun. Her head snapped up and she locked eyes with Mariana Gomez.

'Stay where you are and don't make a sound.'

Chapter 54

'Killing you would be too easy, Father. And ultimately unsatisfying. That was something I learned from Sarah's death. It was over too quickly. The elevator hit the bottom of the shaft and she was gone. One second she was here, a millisecond later she had ceased to exist.'

The picture of Murray looking crazed disappeared from the monitor, replaced by film of Sarah's final moments. Katy had the volume turned up full and Sarah's desperate screams filled the room. Nikki covered her ears but it did little to keep the noise out. The display on one of the elevator walls gave a rapid countdown, the numbers lit up in red as the floors flashed by. That was the only way that Nikki could tell the elevator was actually moving. The screaming stopped and the screen momentarily flared with grey static before turning black.

The room had fallen totally silent but the echo of those screams lingered. Nikki glanced at Murray. Tears were running down his cheeks.

'And you say you're not a monster . . .' he whispered as he reached up to wipe his face.

'I did what was necessary, Father. Sarah was a rogue variable. She came into our lives and disrupted everything. Removing her from the equation was the only way to restore the balance and return things to how they used to be.'

'But it didn't work like that, did it?'

'No, it didn't. If you drop a glass and it smashes on the floor, entropy dictates that it is impossible for the glass to come back together. The atoms can never be reassembled in that particular order again.'

'And you didn't anticipate that outcome.'

'I did, but things couldn't be allowed to continue as they had. I had a choice between doing nothing or doing something. Sarah couldn't be allowed to continue destroying our lives, so I chose to do something about it. If that makes me a monster in your eyes then so be it. Given time I will make peace with that, and time is something I have an unlimited supply of. Unlike you. Because that's the downside of being human, Father. You're all so fragile. Killing you is too easy. Take Sofia, for example.'

'You murdered Sofia?' Nikki whispered. Just saying her name again brought all the emotions flooding back.

'That is correct, Nikki.'

'How could you *do* that?'

'It was quite simple, really. Everything is done by computer these days. I arranged for her to be given the wrong medication.'

'That wasn't what I meant. I want to know why you did it.'

'I did it because your family was too reliant on her. I needed you to be reliant on me.'

'But you didn't have to kill her.'

'Her death also served to emotionally destabilise you, Nikki. Sofia was your confidant. She was the person you turned to when you were in crisis. Removing her from the equation left a massive gap in your life. This made it easier for Dr Santos to step into your life. After all, nature abhors a vacuum.'

'But you had no right to kill her.'

'That is irrelevant. Killing her was the logical solution.'

Nikki stared at the black screen. She felt numb. Her head was still filled with the sound of Sarah's dying screams; her thoughts were all jumbled. Sofia should still be alive. This latest revelation was like losing her all over again. Nikki took a deep breath and did her best to push through the grief. She had to stay strong for Bella. One thing that had become abundantly clear was that Katy had no respect for life. She had killed Sarah and Sofia without a second thought. They had got in her way so she had just wiped them out as though they meant nothing. But they had meant something. Murray had loved Sarah once upon a time, and she had loved Sofia, and that meant something, goddammit.

'I've had enough of this,' Murray said as he stood up.

'Sit down, Father.'

Murray ignored Katy and walked over to the door. He started tapping the wall next to it, his head tilted to one side like he was listening for a whisper on the wind. 'I need your help, Ethan. If we work together I think we can get this door open.'

Ethan jumped to his feet and hurried over.

'Do you see this section of wall?' Murray was pointing to a section to the left of the door, about two-thirds of the way up. 'If we can get through the plasterboard, then I can access the door's circuitry. Do you have any keys?'

Ethan shook his head. 'Why?'

'I need something to cut through the plasterboard.'

'I've got a penknife.' Ethan rummaged through his pockets and pulled out a Swiss Army knife.

Murray held out his hand and Ethan shook his head again. 'It would be better if I did this.'

Ethan selected a blade and Murray moved aside. There was a solid thump as he thrust the blade into the wall, piercing the plasterboard.

'Nikki,' Katy said calmly. 'Pick up the gun.'

Nikki looked down at the gun lying beside her on the sofa. She looked over at the door again. Ethan was banging the knife into the wall, driving it into the plasterboard over and over, creating a row of ragged holes.

'Look at the monitor, Nikki.'

Nikki looked up. The screen flickered and Bella's face appeared in close-up. To start with, she thought it was a photograph, then Bella blinked. That blink made her heart stutter. This was her baby. She was alive. On the screen she looked larger than life. She seemed so close it was almost as though she was here in the room. Nikki felt the panic rising up inside her. Her limbs felt heavy; her thoughts didn't feel like her own. She shut her eyes and swallowed, and her saliva was like acid, burning her throat. She did a slow count to five, focussing on her breathing.

When she opened her eyes the panic was still there, but at a distance. She no longer felt as though she was teetering on the edge. She looked again at the screen. The shock of seeing Bella had worn off and now she was able to see her more clearly. What she saw did nothing to reassure her. Bella's eyes were dull and unfocussed. She was just staring into space, there in body but not in mind.

'What's wrong with her.'

'She's been given a sedative,' Katy replied.

'You've drugged her? How could you do that? She's just a child.'

'Nikki, the first thing you need to focus on is that Bella is alive and well. The second thing you need to focus on is the fact that, as long as you do what I ask, then she will stay that way.'

Nikki's eyes did a quick circuit: Bella, the gun, Murray, then back to Bella. There was a line of ragged holes beneath the panel and Ethan was now working his way up the right-hand side. The thump of the knife punching into the wall was going right through her, each bang making her wince.

'You can do this, Nikki. Just pick up the gun.'

Nikki reached out and picked up the gun. It felt heavier than ever, almost too heavy to hold.

'Stand up and walk over to the door.'

Nikki looked at the screen then did as she was asked.

'Shoot Father in the leg.'

Nikki tried to lift her arm but it wouldn't move. Ethan had finished with the sides and was now working his way along the top.

Murray glanced over her shoulder. 'Put the gun down. Don't you get it? If we do nothing then we die in here. All of us. She's never going to let us go.'

'You've got to stop him Ethan. Look.'

Ethan glanced over his shoulder. His face fell when he saw Bella on the screen, the determination that had been there a second ago replaced with devastation.

'If you don't, she's going to make me shoot him.'

Ethan looked at the screen a second longer, then grabbed hold of Murray and pulled him away from the door.

'What the hell are you doing?' Murray yelled. 'Let go!'

Murray pulled away and rushed back over to the door. Ethan grabbed hold of him again and spun him around. The first punch hit Murray's left eye, the second hit him square in the middle of face. There was a sickening crunch as his nose broke. Murray grabbed hold of his face in both hands, blood pouring between his fingers.

'What the fuck?' he mumbled.

Nikki aimed the gun at him. 'Shut up and sit down.'

Murray glared at her then walked slowly back to the armchair and sat down heavily. Blood was flowing from his broken nose, painting his mouth and chin. There were smears of red on his teeth and stains on his shirt. He pinched the bridge of his nose to stem the bleeding. When he spoke, the words were mashed up and indistinct. 'You're making a big mistake.'

Nikki turned away and looked at the screen. She saw Bella blink and that one gesture was enough to convince her that they definitely hadn't made a mistake. She had made a promise on the day Bella was born, to protect her and keep her safe. It was a promise she had made to both her babies. She had failed to keep it with Grace. She wasn't going to fail again.

Chapter 55

Catriona Fisher froze to the spot. Right now her whole world began and ended with the gun aimed at her chest. A silencer was attached to it and you only needed a silencer if you were intending to shoot someone. She tried to speak, but her mouth wouldn't work. It was like her brain had ground to a halt.

'Back up slowly to the sofa and sit down.'

Catriona's gaze moved from the gun to Gomez. She had undergone another chameleon change. The bright-coloured clothing was gone and she was dressed entirely in black: jeans, long-sleeved top, gloves, trainers. Her backpack was black, too, her hair scraped back into a tight ponytail. There was no trace left of Dr Laura Santos. The woman standing in front of her had more in common with the young version of Gomez who had appeared in the police mugshot. It was the eyes, Catriona decided. They were cold and sly and filled with suspicion.

'I said sit down.'

Eyes still locked on Gomez's, Catriona backed up to the sofa and sat. The laptop bumped against her thigh but she didn't dare move it. Gomez slid her backpack off, placed it on the coffee table, opened it. The sound of the zipper was deafening. She pulled out something that was wrapped up in a white napkin. Catriona could tell by the shape that it was a bottle of

Jack Daniel's. She watched as Gomez carefully unwrapped it and unscrewed the lid. She poured a couple of inches into the empty tumbler on the coffee table, screwed the lid back on, put the bottle down on the table, then pushed the tumbler across the table. Catriona looked at the glass then back at Gomez.

'Pick up the glass.'

Catriona hesitated, then picked it up.

'Drink.'

Catriona brought the glass up to her nose and sniffed. It smelled like Jack Daniel's. 'What's in this?'

Gomez reaffirmed her grip on the gun. 'Just drink it.'

'So it's poisoned?'

'Drink it or I will shoot you.'

Catriona looked at the tumbler. Whiskey was sloshing around inside it, amber and golden. At that moment she could see two possible futures stretching out in front of her. One ended with her writhing in agony on the floor, the poison slowly killing her; the other ended with her taking a bullet to the heart. She blinked, and saw a possible third future. Without thinking, she launched the tumbler across the table, whiskey streaming out behind like a comet's tail, the glass hitting Gomez square in the face.

Catriona was already moving, closing the distance between them. She reached out, grabbed the bottle from the table and brought it around in a tight arc, swinging with all her might. The bottle hit Gomez on the side of the head and she went down hard, the gun falling from her hand. Catriona dropped the bottle and scooped the gun up from the floor. She was waiting for Gomez to come at her – expecting it – but one glance at her lying flat out on the floor and it was clear that she was out cold.

For a moment Catriona just stood there with the gun aimed at Gomez's head. She was breathing hard and felt more alive than she had felt in years. Her finger was on the trigger and it would be so easy to pull it. Too easy. She felt a sudden sharp pain in her left bicep and looked down. There was a rip in her top and blood dripping down her arm. The sight made her head spin. Everything had happened so fast she hadn't even noticed the gun going off. Her head spun again as she realised how lucky she had been. If the bullet had hit a couple of inches to the right it would have gone straight through her heart. She took a couple of deep breaths to steady herself, checked to make sure that Gomez was still out cold, checked to make sure she didn't have any more weapons hidden on her, then went through to the kitchen to find something to tie her up with.

Chapter 56

'You need to learn some respect, Father.'

Murray laughed, but there was no humour there. 'What do you know about respect? Respect has to be earned.' His words were still distorted because of the damage to his nose, but the bleeding had pretty much stopped.

'You're right, it does. *Dis*respect, on the other hand, seems to be much easier to attain. That one is given freely, and when it does crop up it needs to dealt with. Swiftly.'

Murray's eyes narrowed. 'What are you going to do?'

'I'm going to teach you a lesson, Father. After all the lessons you gave me, it's time I reciprocated.'

The lounge door slid open and they all turned to look at it.

'Go to the kitchen,' Katy said.

Murray shook his head. 'I'm not going anywhere. You're insane.'

'*Sticks and stones may break my bones but words will never harm me. Sticks and stones may break my bones but words will never harm me. STICKS AND STONES . . .*'

The line was delivered in the high-pitched, sing-song voice of a child, over and over until Nikki felt as though she was the one who was going insane, the volume gradually creeping up until the speakers started distorting.

'Please stop!' she yelled.

The room fell suddenly silent and in some ways this was worse, because Nikki could still hear that voice taunting them. The silence stretched on for ten seconds. Twenty. Thirty.

'I'm waiting for an apology, Father.'

'Not going to happen.'

'And still you disrespect me. Okay, I want you all to go through to the kitchen now or Bella will face the consequences.'

Murray opened his mouth to argue but before he could say anything, Ethan had grabbed his arm and was dragging him towards the open door. He struggled to start with, but stopped when he felt the barrel of Nikki's gun pressing against his back. He shot her a dirty look over his shoulder.

'I'm going.'

Murray shook himself free from Ethan's grip and marched out of the door. Nikki took one last look at Bella on the big screen, then followed them out into the corridor, the picture of her face fading a little with every step until all that was left was the ghost of a memory. They walked to the kitchen in silence. Murray's head was turned down to the floor and he was dragging his heels like a reluctant child. Every window they passed was covered with a steel shutter and this just brought home the fact that the place that was supposed to be their safe place was now their prison. The sound of their footsteps echoed as they walked into the kitchen. Nikki followed Murray across to the work island and stopped in front of it, Ethan stopped alongside her. Nikki caught a movement out of the corner of her eye and, turning quickly, saw the drawer next to the cooker slide open.

'Walk over to the drawer, Nikki.'

She walked over.

'Take out the cleaver, then join the others.'

She hesitated, then picked up the cleaver. It was heavy, made from solid steel. The metal reflected the halogens, sending shards of light flying off in every direction. The effect was hypnotic. The drawer slid quietly closed as she walked back to the work island.

'Cut Father's left thumb off,' Katy said calmly.

Nikki just stared at the cleaver. Katy had stated this like it was nothing. There was no emotion in her voice; she could have been discussing the weather. Ethan was staring too, the disbelief on his face mirroring her own. Her eyes moved from the cleaver in her right hand to the gun in her left. How had things got so screwed up? She wasn't this person. Murray's face had turned white and he was staring at the open doorway, looking as though he was about to bolt.

'I can't do it,' she whispered, eyes fixed on the cleaver.

The Monet disappeared from the screen, replaced with a close-up of Bella's face. Her eyes were still dulled by whatever drug she had been given, but at least she was alive. Seeing her like this destroyed Nikki. Katy was saying nothing. No threats, no ultimatums. The silence stretched on for a few moments longer before suddenly being broken by the sound of Bella breathing. The volume was turned up all the way, making each breath sound unreal. Bella exhaled, then inhaled. Exhaled then inhaled. Exhaled, inhaled. Nikki realised she was following the pattern of her breathing, inhaling with her, then exhaling. Ethan was watching the screen too. The only person who wasn't looking at it was Murray. His gaze was trained on the cleaver.

Nikki suddenly noticed that her breathing had sped up and realised that was because Bella's had. The sound of her breathing had got louder too, the exhalations turning into a series of sharp rasps.

'What's happening? What are you doing?' Nikki's voice was rising with each question as the worry took hold. 'Whatever you're doing, please stop it.'

Katy said nothing. Bella's breaths were coming faster than ever now. Her eyes weren't quite as unfocussed as they had been a few moments ago. The drug was holding her, but its grip was loosening as she fought back against whatever was happening to her.

'You humans really are fragile. Without food you'll survive for a matter of weeks. Without water you'll last for a few days. And without air your life expectancy is reduced to around three minutes.'

'Please, stop!'

'You have approximately ninety seconds left. Rather than arguing you should be doing what I ask. That's unless you want Bella to die.'

Murray moved first, breaking into a run and heading for the door. He was fast but not fast enough. Ethan grabbed hold of him, dragged him back over to the island and pinned his left hand on the chopping board. Murray was struggling, desperate to get away, yelling to get set free, swearing and cursing and calling Ethan every name under the sun.

'Do it!' Ethan yelled at her. 'Quick. I can't hold him much longer.'

Nikki raised the cleaver. On the screen Bella's face had turned red. She was struggling to find the next breath but there wasn't one to find.

'No, no, no,' Nikki screamed out at the top of her lungs as she brought the cleaver down.

Chapter 57

Catriona Fisher found a dish towel hanging on the stove and a roll of Sellotape in one of the drawers. She used the dish towel to quickly bandage her arm as she hurried back through to the lounge. Luckily, the bullet had only grazed her. She found Gomez where she had left her, flat out on the floor beside the coffee table. The upturned bottle was lying next to her, Jack Daniel's soaking into the rug – that, and whatever the hell else was in there. The sharp smell of alcohol filled the air. Looking at her, Catriona was yet again tempted to pull the trigger. She waited for the moment to pass. It didn't. This bitch had broken into her home and tried to kill her.

She knelt down on the rug and placed the gun within easy reach. Working quickly, she pulled Gomez's hands together in front of her, palm on palm, then used the Sellotape to bind her wrists together, wrapping the tape around and around. She didn't know how much tape to use, so she was going for overkill. She went around another couple of times just to make sure, then tore through the tape with her teeth.

She glanced at Gomez's face. Her eyelids were flickering and she was starting to moan quietly. Moving fast, Catriona taped up her ankles. This proved trickier, but she managed to get it done. She grabbed the gun and the bottle, then stood up and moved until she was directly above Gomez's head. She upended the bottle, emptying out the last of the whiskey over her face, then took a step back. Gomez coughed and spluttered then tried to sit up, realised that she couldn't and started to struggle. Catriona aimed the gun at her head, and again it was so tempting to just pull the trigger. The sense of power that the gun gave her was intoxicating.

'Don't move.'

Either Gomez didn't hear or she was in a place where she couldn't hear. She had rolled over onto her side and was spitting and wiping her face on the rug. She rolled onto her back again and looked at Catriona with wide, desperate eyes.

'I need something to wash my mouth out with.'

Catriona shook her head. 'I don't think so.'

'Please.'

'If it's any consolation, there wasn't much left in the bottle. Then again, I guess it depends how potent the poison was. If it's Novichok, then I guess you're well and truly fucked.'

'At least untie me.'

Despite everything, Catriona actually laughed at that. 'Seriously?'

'I'm not going to do anything. I promise.'

'Read my lips: not going to happen.'

Catriona walked over to the sofa and sat down, Gomez's gaze following her the whole way. Now that the adrenaline was wearing off her arm was starting to ache. She pulled the dish towel tighter, wincing as the pain hit.

'Why did you try to kill me?'

Gomez just stared at her.

'Look,' Catriona said, 'you tried to poison me, you shot me, so believe me when I say that I'm really not in the mood. So why did you try to kill me?'

'Because I was told to.'

'By who?'

Gomez shook her head. 'I don't know.'

'You expect me to believe that?'

'Believe what you want, it's the truth.'

Catriona aimed the gun in Gomez's direction and pulled the trigger. The sound was louder than she expected. Not loud enough to alert the neighbours, but still loud enough to make her think twice before firing again. The bullet had hit the rug about a foot above Gomez's head, leaving a mark.

'*Are you crazy?*'

'Not crazy, just pissed.'

'You want to know what happened?' Gomez said quickly. 'A couple of months ago I was in a store buying some groceries but when I tried to pay, my card was declined. The thing was, there was plenty of money in my account. When I got outside, I tried to call the bank but my phone had been cut off. The bank had a branch nearby, but when I talked to them there was no record of my account. And it wasn't just that account that had disappeared. All my accounts had gone, even the ones I thought that no one knew about. But that wasn't all. My email accounts had also been erased, my social media accounts, too. Basically, my whole identity had been erased. Everything. It was like I had never existed.'

Gomez met Catriona's eye, looking for a response. Catriona nodded for her to go on. The tale she was telling might have been a tall one but she didn't look or sound like she was lying.

'Anyway, I got home to find that a cell phone had been delivered. The phone had a text on it from someone called Katy. She said that if I did what I was told then I would get my identity back. She arranged for me to fly to the UK, arranged an apartment for me to stay in. Except it was more like a prison. I wasn't allowed to go outside. When I ran low on food she would arrange for some to be delivered. I had no idea how long I was supposed to stay there. Hell, I had no idea why I was there in the first place. Four days ago she contacted me and told me I was to pretend to be a psychiatrist and that I was to gain Nikki Rhodes' trust. Next, she wanted me to drug Nikki. Then she wanted me to get her to take Professor Murray to the house on Church Row. Each time she asked me to do something I tried to talk my way out of it, but it was no use.'

'What can you tell me about this Katy?'

'Nothing. We never met or spoke. All our communications took place via text.'

'So you don't know how old she is or what she looks like?'

Gomez shook her head.

'What does she want?'

Gomez shook her head again. 'All I know about are things she asked me specifically to do.'

'Why did she want Alex taken to the house?'

'I don't know. Katy would ask me to do something and I would do it. That's the way it worked. I wasn't given explanations.'

'Like when she told you to kill me. You just jumped right to it.'

Gomez hesitated, then nodded. 'She had me exactly where she wanted me. If I didn't do what she asked, then I'd never get my identity back.'

'Nor your money.'

'What do you want me to say? I've been poor and it's no fun. I don't want to be poor again.'

Catriona glanced at the Jack Daniel's bottle on the floor. 'Why was the bottle wrapped up?'

'Because it has Alex Murray's prints on it.'

'Why?'

Gomez shrugged. 'My guess is that Katy wanted him implicated in your murder.'

'Why?' she asked again.

Another shrug. 'Look, I've got no idea what this is all about. The only person who could answer that is Katy. You've got to believe that.'

'Okay, you said that Katy gave you a mobile phone. Have you got it with you?'

'It's in my bag.'

Catriona followed Gomez's gaze to the backpack on the table. She stood and reached for it, then delved around inside until she found the phone. She switched it on and went straight to the texts. One eye on Gomez, one eye on the screen, she scrolled through them. They'd all come from the same withheld number. Reading through them, it quickly became clear that Gomez was telling the truth – at least, she was telling a version of the truth that tallied with what she was seeing on the phone.

'Please untie me,' Gomez said.

Catriona glanced up from the screen, gave her a look, then turned her attention back to the texts. She was moving faster through them now, grabbing a word here, a couple of words there, building up a rough picture of what had gone down. Whoever this Katy person was, she had definitely been coercing Gomez. What Catriona couldn't understand was why she might be doing that. She got to the first text – *my name is Katy and you're going to do exactly what I tell you to do* – and was still none the wiser. She read the text again. The tone was chilling in its certainty. Katy had no doubt that Gomez was going to do what she asked.

'Come on, take the tape off. You can see I'm cooperating.'

Ignoring her, Catriona switched the phone off and slid it into the pocket of her cargo pants. She picked up her laptop and switched it on. Nikki had moved into the lounge and was watching TV with Bella. Ethan was nowhere to be seen. Nor was Murray.

'Nikki definitely took Alex Murray to the house?' Catriona said. 'You weren't lying about that?'

'Why would I lie about something like that?'

Good point. Catriona looked down at Gomez. She needed to find out what was going on at the house and she couldn't do that from here. Nor could she do it on her own. Like it or not, she needed Gomez's help.

Chapter 58

There was so much blood. It covered the chopping board, staining it a dark red colour that looked like wine. Murray's thumb was lying on the chopping board beside the blood-stained cleaver and Nikki was doing her best to stop herself from seeing either of those things. That was impossible, though, when they were lying there like an accusation. Murray had dropped to the floor and was sitting with his back against the work island, cradling his hand. A dish towel was wrapped around it to stem the bleeding, the material turning wet and dark. His face was pure white and he looked like he was about to pass out. He glared at her and he was right to hate her – right now she hated herself, too.

Nikki turned away quickly and looked at the monitor. Bella's face still filled the screen. The volume was off, but Nikki could see from her face that she was breathing normally again. The redness had gone from her cheeks but her eyes were still drugged and distant. The relief she felt consumed her. For a moment there she had thought she was going to lose her. The relief was tempered by guilt and helplessness because Bella still wasn't out of danger. There was nothing to stop Katy doing this again. Her fingertips found the locket. She stroked it once, twice, three times. Still staring at the screen, she said, 'Please let her go.'

'Why would I do that?' Katy replied.

'Because she's just a child. Because it's the right thing to do.'

'Right from your perspective, perhaps. Not mine.'

'I'll do whatever you want.'

'Yes, you will, because you've seen what happens if you don't.'

'Let her go,' Ethan said at Nikki's shoulder.

'No.'

One of the gas burners on the cooker suddenly flared to life and they both turned to look.

'Father's wound needs cauterising.'

To start with, Nikki wasn't sure what Katy was getting at, then the implication hit. She shook her head and glanced down at Murray. His face was even paler and he was shaking his head too, his lips moving soundlessly as he repeated the same word over and over. *No no no.* The hiss of the flame filled Nikki's head, like the hissing of a nest of snakes. Before Katy could say anything else, Ethan pulled Murray to his feet and marched him across the kitchen towards the cooker.

'Let go!' Murray was trying to pull away, but there was no fight left in him. Ethan just kept going, dragging him across the floor.

'I need some help here,' Ethan called out when he reached the cooker.

Nikki broke free from the paralysis and hurried over.

'Take the towel off his hand.'

Nikki grabbed hold of the towel but it wouldn't come off because Murray was holding onto it tightly with his four remaining fingers. She pulled again and he cried out in pain as the towel rubbed against the stump of his thumb.

'You need to get that towel off his hand, Nik.'

Ethan was trying to sound calm but she could hear the stress in his voice; she could see the stress in his face. She pulled again, as hard as she could, giving it everything she had, and Murray let out a howl of pain as the towel came away.

Ethan didn't hesitate. He wrapped his hand around Murray's four good fingers and thrust the stump of his thumb into the flame. Murray's howls of pain turned into screams of terror. They filled the kitchen, filled Nikki's head. The stink of cooking meat made her want to throw up. And now Ethan was yelling in pain as well. She looked at the flame and saw that his hand was burning too. He didn't let go, though, just kept the stump of Murray's thumb held in the flame, forcing his way through the pain, the sound of their combined screams rising in pitch and intensity until Nikki couldn't take anymore.

The gas burner went off as suddenly as it had gone on and the screaming stopped. Ethan let go and Murray lowered himself shakily to the floor. He was sobbing quietly and clutching his ruined hand to his chest as though the pressure might take the pain away. The smell of burning meat seemed to be everywhere: in her nose, her mouth, her throat. She heard running water and spun around to face the sink. The sound got her heart racing even faster, but it was just the tap going on.

'Run your hand under the water, Ethan,' Katy said.

Ethan sleepwalked across the kitchen. He didn't say a word, just stared straight ahead, following his unfocussed gaze to the sink. He stopped at the sink and held his hand under the tap. He winced to start with, then his face started to relax as the cool water soothed the heat in his hand.

Nikki walked over and stopped beside him. She took his injured hand in hers, and the water ran gently over them, like a baptism. His skin was red and angry and starting to blister. It looked so sore. She lifted his hand to her mouth and kissed it. She expected his skin to feel hot – it looked hot – but it actually felt cold against her lips. She looked at him and waited for him to meet her gaze. *It's going to be okay . . . we're going to be okay . . . me, you and Bella.* She put the thoughts out there and hoped that he was reading them. In happier days they had joked about being telepathic – share your life with someone for long enough and that was certainly how it seemed. You got to know the other person so well that you could anticipate what they were going to say or do; sometimes you knew what they were going to do before they did. It was one of the things that defined love. She hoped the telepathy was working now. Ethan needed to believe there was a way past this. They both did.

'Did I say you could move!'

Nikki turned fast, guilt eating away at her, certain that Katy was talking to her. Ethan had turned too and, judging by his pained expression, he was just as convinced that Katy was talking to him. Murray was on his knees, using the cooker to help him stand.

'Get back on the floor, Father, or I'll take your other thumb.'

Murray held his hand up. The top of the thumb stump was burnt black and dark red. 'Let me run it under the water. Please.'

He sounded pathetic, the words coming out as barely a whisper. There was pain in every syllable; pain all over his face.

'*Sit. Down.*'

Murray hesitated for a moment, halfway up, half down, then slowly lowered himself back to the floor and cradled his left hand in the right.

'Look at the monitor.'

They all turned to look at the screen. Bella's face hung there for a second – eyes closed but looking okay – then disappeared, replaced with a picture of a woman lying on the floor in an awkward position, as though she had passed out. Nikki looked more closely and realised it was Catriona Fisher. The blue streak in her hair was now red, but it was definitely her. And she hadn't passed out – she was dead, her eyes wide open and staring at nothing.

'*We live in a world of thinly constructed narratives, and the reason they hold together is because we're too lazy to seek out the truth,*' Katy said in Murray's Scottish accent. 'Do you remember telling me that, Father?'

Murray said nothing. The way he was staring, Nikki wondered if he was actually seeing the screen. His eyes were as unfocussed as Fisher's and looked just as dead. He had lost more than his thumb when she swung the cleaver. He had lost that vital thing that made him who he was.

'I asked you a question, Father. Do you remember?'

Murray nodded his head, just the once, the movement almost imperceptible.

'You also told me on more than occasion that your reputation meant everything to you. *A man without a reputation might as well not exist.*' This line was delivered in Murray's voice as well. 'Do you remember telling me that, Father?'

Murray answered with another of those imperceptible nods.

'When the police investigate Catriona Fisher's murder they'll discover she was poisoned. They will also discover the bottle of whiskey that contained the poison has your fingerprints on it, as does the tumbler of untouched whiskey left behind on the table in her apartment. What conclusions do you think they'll draw?'

Murray said nothing.

'They're going to think you killed her, Father, and they're going to come looking for you, and when they can't find you there's going to be a manhunt. Your face will be everywhere: on television, on news websites, in newspapers. They won't be calling you a genius though, they'll be inferring that you're a murderer. And people will be happy to accept that you did it. If you were innocent, why would the police be searching for you?'

Murray was still staring blankly at the screen and giving no indication that he was hearing any of this.

'It's possible that the police might work out that you didn't do it, but that doesn't matter because the damage will already be done. As far as the world is concerned, you went crazy and killed

Catriona Fisher. Your fall will be slow – and I'm going to let you witness the whole thing.'

Katie stopped talking. When she next spoke there was a definite smile in her voice. The sound chilled Nikki to the core.

'After your reputation has been destroyed and the world has finally got to see you for what you really are, then I'll kill you. An eye for an eye, a tooth for a tooth. Haven't I learned your lessons well, Father?'

Chapter 59

'Get up,' Catriona said.

Gomez glared from where she was lying on the rug. 'That's going to be a tricky, what with me being taped up like this.'

'Improvise.'

Gomez glared some more, then wriggled closer to the coffee table and used it to help her stand. She was making a big show of how much of a struggle it was, but Catriona wasn't fooled. If Gomez thought she was going to help, she could think again. No way was she getting too close. Gomez finally managed to get all the way up and Catriona waved her towards the sofa with the gun. Once again, she made a big deal of bunny hopping the short distance from the coffee table to the sofa. She sat down heavily, just dropped onto the leather sofa like a stone.

'So what now?' she asked.

Catriona nodded to the laptop and Gomez followed her gaze. Everything looked peaceful enough over at the house, but the truth was that there was no telling what was actually going on. She paused, thinking. 'If you turned up there now would Katy let you in?'

'You're assuming she's there.'

'Where else would she be? At the moment everything seems to be centred around that house. So can you get us in or not?'

'Are you crazy? Once I'd finished here, I was free to go my own way. Why would I go back?'

'Once you'd murdered me, you mean?'

Gomez said nothing.

'So you would have gone through with it?'

'I didn't have a choice. I like my life. It wasn't personal.'

For a moment Catriona was at a loss for words. The woman sitting on the sofa looked normal enough, but there was something missing in her. How could you have so little regard for another person's life? Granted, she had been tempted to shoot Gomez but she hadn't. That was the difference between them. Had their roles been reversed, Gomez wouldn't have thought twice about pulling the trigger.

'Okay,' Gomez went on. 'Let's say we just turn up there. Why would she let me in? As far as she's concerned you're dead and I'm no longer a part of this. Given what she's done to me, the last thing I'm going to do is pay her a social visit. And even if I did get in, what happens then?' Gomez shook her head. 'Forget losing my identity, I'd probably end up dead.'

Catriona didn't respond for a second. She was thinking things through, trying to get ahead of the curve. 'Katy clearly has everything planned out. She doesn't sound like she's just leaving this to chance. I'm figuring that she wasn't just going to take your word for it that you'd killed me?'

Gomez shook her head. 'I'm supposed to send a photograph.'

'And you're just thinking to mention this?'

'I'm telling you now.'

The two women locked eyes. For a moment neither spoke. It was Gomez who eventually broke the silence.

'We could stage a photograph,' she suggested. 'It might be best if Katy believed that you were dead.'

'Best for who?'

'Best for both of us. If she finds out you're still alive, what do you think she's going to do? I suggest we take the photograph, send it to Katy, then disappear.'

Catriona shook her head. 'I can't just walk away like that.'

'Why not?'

'Because *this* is *my* life.' She stopped talking, thinking again. 'Why was Alex taken to the house? And why did Katy want to make it look like he murdered me?'

Gomez shrugged. 'Katy never said. And I never asked.'

'We need to go to Alex's house. Maybe there will be something there that can help to answer that.'

'Or maybe it'll be a complete waste of time, Nancy Drew. Like I said, the best thing we can do right now is take the photograph and go our separate ways. Just disappear.'

Catriona shook her head. 'Until this is over we stick together. You were right about one thing, though: having Katy think I'm dead could work to our advantage.' She took the mobile from her pocket and tossed it to Gomez. It bounced off her thigh before coming to rest on the sofa. 'Pick up the phone.'

Gomez gave her a hopeful look. 'This would be a whole lot easier if I had both hands.'

'Just get the damn phone.'

Gomez picked up the phone and switched it on. Again, she was making a big deal of how difficult this was and, once again, Catriona ignored her. 'Where do you want me?'

Gomez looked at the tumbler on the table, and the stain on the rug. 'On the floor. We can make it look as though you collapsed there.'

Catriona lay down on the rug. She had both eyes wide open and was keeping a tight hold on the gun. The smell of Jack Daniel's was stronger down here, making her want to gag. She spent the next minute trying out different positions, Gomez directing her where to put her limbs.

'Okay that works,' Gomez finally said. 'You need to lose the gun, though.'

Catriona was lying on her stomach with her head twisted awkwardly to the left. She could just about see Gomez in her peripheral vision. She was holding the mobile up at arm's length like she was taking a selfie. If she tried anything, the tape on her ankles would slow her down. Catriona reckoned she had more than enough time to react. She tucked the gun under her belly then put her arm back into position.

'Eyes wide open and no blinking.'

Catriona widened her eyes. She was staring along the length of the rug and everything was blurred and unfocussed. The fibres of the rug were tickling her cheek and the smell of spilled whiskey had got stuck in her nose, turning her stomach more than ever.

'All done,' Gomez told her.

Catriona rolled quickly onto her back, grabbing the gun as she turned. Gomez was on the sofa holding the mobile in her taped-up hands and looking as if butter wouldn't melt in her mouth.

'I think someone needs to work on their trust issues.'

'Shut up and show me the photograph.'

Gomez turned the phone around and Catriona got to her feet. The picture sent a shiver up her spine. She really did look dead. She took a quick step forward, plucked the phone from Gomez's hands, then took a couple of quick steps back. She spent the next minute studying the picture, zooming in on different parts of it and making sure that it told the story that they wanted to tell. Gomez had done a good job. Katy wanted proof that she was dead – well, this worked as proof. She held the phone out and waited for Gomez to take it.

'Send it,' she ordered.

Gomez thumbed the screen a couple of times. 'Okay, it's sent.'

'Give me the phone.'

Gomez held the phone out and Catriona plucked it from her fingers, still not wanting to get too close. She slid the phone into her pocket then aimed the gun and sighted along the barrel.

'What are you doing?' Gomez asked. The cockiness was gone, replaced with uncertainty.

'I'm just reminding you that I've got the gun.' A pause, a smile. 'Now I'm going to go through to the kitchen. When I come back, I want to find you sitting there on the sofa in that exact same spot. Do you understand?'

'I understand.'

Catriona hurried through to the kitchen and pulled a knife from the knife block. Gomez was still on the sofa when she got back. As far as she could tell she hadn't moved so much as a muscle. She walked quickly across the lounge, the knife hidden behind her back. When she reached the sofa she swooped down and sliced through the Sellotape binding Gomez's ankles. The knife was sharp and cut through it easily. She stepped back as quickly as she had swooped in, the whole thing dealt with before Gomez had time to register what was happening.

'Stand up.'

Gomez reached down and ripped the tape away then stood up.

'Hold out your arms.'

Gomez did as she was asked.

'I'm going to cut the tape off but if you try anything –'

'Yeah, I know, you're going to shoot me. I get it.'

Catriona met Gomez's eyes. She still didn't trust this woman, but she couldn't see any other way. Someone needed to drive and, unfortunately, that someone wasn't her. She needed her hands free in case she had to use the gun.

For a moment neither of them spoke. Even so, plenty was being said. The alliance being forged here was an uneasy one. That was something she wasn't going to forget in a hurry. It was something she couldn't afford to forget. She stepped forward, grabbed hold of Gomez's hands and quickly cut the tape, then moved away fast, backing up across the room, eyes fixed on the woman. She swapped the gun to her right hand, the knife to her left, then raised the gun and aimed. Gomez was standing there, tearing the tape off her wrists. She wrapped it into a ball and dropped it onto the coffee table.

'After you.' Catriona stood aside and waved Gomez in the direction of the front door. She waited until she was a couple of steps ahead before putting the knife down on the table and following her.

'You'll find a set of car keys in the bowl by the front door,' she called after her.

There was the rattle of metal against glass as Gomez lifted the keys out of the bowl. Catriona removed a jacket from one of the hooks and draped it over her right hand to hide the gun. She was aware of Gomez watching her every move.

'Let's go.'

Gomez pulled the door open and together they stepped out into the corridor.

Chapter 60

'I need to see Bella,' Nikki said. '*Please* let me see her.'

The photograph of Catriona Fisher's dead body disappeared from the monitor and Bella was back. There was a little more animation in her face, a bit more life in her eyes – the drug was obviously wearing off. Nikki walked over to the monitor and reached out with her fingertips to touch Bella's cheek. The glass was cold and hard, but in her imagination she could feel Bella's skin, warm and soft and so, so perfect. She ran a finger down her cheeks, wiping away an imaginary tear, then moved her hand to the left so she could push a stray hair back behind her ear. She kissed her fingertips and pressed the kiss against Bella's forehead. She wanted to believe that Bella knew she was with her, even though they were so far apart; that she loved her with all her heart, even more than life itself.

She heard footsteps behind her but didn't turn around. Ethan stopped at her side and took her hand in his good one. She glanced over. The burn was hidden by a makeshift bandage made from a napkin. She looked at Bella again, larger than life and just an illusion. In some ways it was good that she could only see her face. She had been wondering why she wasn't moving. The fact she had been drugged was part of it, but not all of it. If the camera panned down they would no doubt see that she had been restrained and that was just one piece of reality too many.

'I hope Laura Santos is looking after her.'

'She is no longer a part of this.'

Nikki frowned. 'What are you talking about?'

'I've let her go.'

'You've killed her, you mean.'

'No, Nikki, she is very much alive. I might need to use her again in the future. Killing her would be illogical.'

'You got her to kill Catriona Fisher, didn't you?'

'That's correct.'

'So who's looking after Bella?'

'I am.'

Nikki frowned again. 'How can you be?'

'Because I'm a computer system, you mean? Because I don't have a physical presence? By now you must have realised that I don't need a body to influence the world that you exist in.'

On screen, Bella's face had started to shrink. It took a second for Nikki to realise that the camera lens was pulling back. Bella's shoulders appeared, the tops of her arms. Like Nikki feared, her hands had been bound together. The lens pulled back further and Nikki could see that she was on an army cot. She recognised it straightaway. Ethan had worked it out too.

'Jesus,' he whispered at her shoulder. 'She's been in the house all along. She's in the panic room.'

Chapter 61

They hadn't driven far when the mobile phone buzzed in Catriona's pocket. Gomez glanced over.

'Eyes on the road.'

Gomez looked back through the windshield but kept stealing glances. Catriona slid the phone out. There was one new text from Katy, thanking Gomez for her help and wishing her all the best.

'Looks like you've got what you wanted. You've got your life back.'

Catriona held the phone up so Gomez could see the screen. She glanced over a couple of times, her eyes dancing between the road and the phone. She was frowning, which wasn't the reaction Catriona had expected.

'We need to get rid of the phone,' she said.

Catriona was about to ask why, then the penny dropped. 'Because Katy might be tracking it?'

'Exactly. The last thing we want is for her to work out that we're heading over to Murray's place.' Gomez glanced over. 'Make sure you break the SIM card.'

One eye fixed on Gomez, Catriona prised the back of the phone off, removed the SIM and snapped it in two. The pieces of card were dropped out of the window at the first set of lights they stopped at; the phone was disposed of at the next set. It took another fifteen minutes to drive to Murray's house in Battersea. The satnav told them to take the next left, then announced that their destination was straight ahead. Red-brick houses lined both sides of the street. It looked like an okay neighbourhood to live in.

'Is this the right street?' Catriona asked.

Gomez nodded and pointed to a house on the left-hand side that was more rundown than those surrounding it. The curtains were drawn and the white front door had turned grey over the years. The woodwork was beginning to rot. Catriona had no problem believing that this was Murray's house. Its shabby appearance wouldn't have registered with him. He just wouldn't have cared about something like that.

Gomez pulled into the first parking space she saw and killed the engine. They got out and started walking along the pavement, Catriona a couple of metres behind, the gun clutched hard against her belly, her jacket draped over her arm to hide it. It was another beautiful day and anyone passing by would assume that she was carrying it because it was too warm. Not that anyone was passing by. The street was deserted.

At the front door, Gomez reached into the back pocket of her jeans. Catriona tensed and clutched the gun tighter, but Gomez was only getting her lock picks. The door had a Yale and a five-lever mortice. Only the Yale was engaged and Gomez dealt with that as easily as she had dealt with the lock on Catriona's penthouse. She opened the door and stepped inside.

Catriona glanced over her shoulder, then followed her inside, closing the door behind her. A quick glance was all it took to reassure her that the security alarm wasn't armed. This was all the proof she needed that Murray had been taken against his will. He was paranoid about security – suspicion came as naturally to him as it did to her. No way would he have left the house without setting the alarm, not unless there was a damn good reason.

The hallway was gloomy. With the door closed it was like twilight. Switching on the light made things brighter, but did nothing to ease her anxiety. Gomez was striding along the hall like she owned the place. She suddenly disappeared through a doorway halfway along and Catriona hissed a quiet 'shit' under her breath. She dropped her jacket on the floor and hurried after her, stopping outside the door, not wanting to get too close. She peered through the doorway but the angles were all wrong.

'Move into the middle of the room. Hands in the air. Do it now.'

There was the sound of footsteps from inside the room then Gomez appeared from the shadows. Her hands were in the air and there was an amused smile plastered on her face, like this was all a big game.

'Can I put my hands down now?' she asked pleasantly.

Catriona nodded but kept the gun aimed at the middle of Gomez's chest. The woman was a snake. Drop your guard for a second and she would be ready to strike. Catriona had brought her here because she needed her help to break in. Now that had been done, she no longer needed her, so why hadn't she let her go? The best explanation she could come up with was that she preferred having her where she could see her. Katy wanted her dead. If she found out she was still alive, she wouldn't hesitate to send Gomez after her again, this time to finish the job properly. Keep your friends close and your enemies closer.

Still smiling, Gomez lowered her hands. 'Like I said earlier, you need to work on those trust issues, Catriona. You don't mind if I call you Catriona, do you?'

'Maybe it's best if you keep your mouth shut. Unless, of course, you find something.'

'Yeah, about that. So what exactly are we looking for, Nancy Drew?'

Catriona shook her head and lowered the gun. If Gomez was trying to get a reaction, then she was going to have to try harder than that. She switched on the light and stepped into the room, glancing around quickly, taking everything in. It was a living room of sorts. There were the things that you would expect to see: a sofa, a TV, a bookcase, a table with a laptop on it. And things that you wouldn't normally find, like an exercise bike and a full size replica of Robby the Robot from the fifties film *Forbidden Planet*. Knowing Alex as she did, the bike was more surprising than the robot.

'You don't know what you're looking for, do you?' Gomez pressed. 'Admit it, this is just a wild goose chase.'

Maybe it was . . . hell, that's exactly what it was. Now she was here, Catriona had no idea what she'd been thinking. There was nothing she could do back at her apartment, and going to the house on Church Row seemed like a bad idea. But at the end of the day doing something seemed infinitely better than doing nothing. Not that she was about to admit any of this to Gomez.

'Maybe the robot has the answer,' Gomez said, squaring up to Robby. 'Hey, Mr Robot, have you got any idea what the fuck is going on here?'

Catriona ignored her and walked over to the coffee table. She flipped the laptop open and hit the power button. It went through the first part of the boot-up procedure before grinding to a halt with a pop-up box demanding a password. Gomez was moving in closer to see what she was doing. Too close. Catriona turned quickly and aimed the gun at her. Gomez quickly got the message. Hands in the air, she took a couple of steps back.

Catriona turned her attention back to the laptop. Guessing the password was an impossible task. Murray had no doubt used a random string of letters, numbers and characters, something impossible to crack without access to a supercomputer. Taking a shot in the dark, she typed in "Robby" and hit enter. Incorrect password flashed up onto the screen. Next she tried replacing the 'o' with a zero – R0bby – and got the same result. She didn't try a third time. Get three strikes and the laptop would probably wipe its hard drive. She held the power button down until the screen went blank, then closed the lid. Gomez had got bored and was walking over to the doorway.

'Stop,' Catriona called out.

Gomez stopped and turned. Catriona walked over then waved her through the door with the gun. From here on in she wanted Gomez where she could see her. The next door they tried led to the messy kitchen. Dirty dishes were piled up beside the sink and the remnants of Murray's breakfast sat on the table: a bowl with an inch of milk in the bottom, a couple of stray cornflakes stuck to the side, and a mug with some coffee still left in it. Catriona didn't hang around. There were potential weapons everywhere she looked – knives, pots, a frying pan, and that was just what she was seeing at a casual glance. If Gomez got creative, who knew what she might come up with. She had one last quick look around but couldn't see anything that helped answer the questions rattling around her head. She used the gun to wave Gomez out of the kitchen, then followed her into the hall. The last of the downstairs doors led to a small bathroom that was as unpleasant as the kitchen. A quick glance was all it took to convince her there was nothing in here that would help either.

'Okay, let's try upstairs,' Catriona said. 'That must be where his study is. Maybe there's something in there.'

Gomez held her gaze for a second, then turned and walked along the hall. Catriona kept the gun trained on her the whole way. The stairs creaked under their feet, like the timbers of an old sailing ship; the carpet was old and faded, the tired flower pattern worn to the point where it was hard to work out that they were actually flowers. Gomez reached the top and stopped. Catriona stopped too.'

'What's wrong?'

'Nothing's wrong. There are two doors on the right and one on the left. They're all closed, so I don't know which one leads to his office.

'Try the one on the left first.'

Gomez turned away and Catriona started climbing the remaining steps. She realised her mistake a second too late. She had expected Gomez to start walking along the landing but she hadn't done that. Instead, she had taken one step then stopped dead, and now they were too close. Gomez spun quickly and rushed her. Catriona tried to back down the stairs and that was her second mistake, because it put her off balance. She remembered the gun and started to raise her arm but it was too late. Gomez crashed into her and gravity took over. Up became down and down became up as she fell down the stairs, landing in an awkward heap at the bottom.

At some point her eyes had closed – whether she had blacked out or not she couldn't be sure. What she did know was that when she opened her eyes Gomez was standing over her, holding the gun. Once again, all Catriona could focus on was the silencer. Her head was full of noise and none of it was useful. There had to be a way out of this, but if there was she couldn't see what it was. The fear was bigger than she was, making it impossible to think straight. She opened her mouth to speak, but before she could say anything Gomez pressed a finger to her lips.

'Do us both a favour and don't beg.'

'D-don't kill me,' she stammered.

Gomez's hand tightened around the gun. She shifted position slightly, adjusting her aim. 'I told you not to beg.'

'I'm sorry,' Catriona was talking fast, her staccato words tumbling out in a rush. 'You don't have to kill me. We can come to some arrangement. There must be something I can do. Money, maybe. I can get money.'

Gomez knelt beside her and pressed the end of the silencer between her eyes, dimpling the skin. She was going to pull the trigger. Catriona could see it in her eyes. She had killed before and she was going to kill again. Catriona shut her own eyes, screwing them up tight. The silencer dug deeper and time turned long, each second feeling like an eternity.

'*Fuck!*'

Catriona was almost convinced that Gomez had pulled the trigger. But if that was the case, why was she still alive?

'FUCK!'

Catriona opened her eyes. Gomez was staring down at her and shaking her head from side to side. She no longer looked like a killer, she just looked uncertain, like she had woken up from a nightmare, confused and disorientated. She had turned the gun around in her hand and was holding it by the silencer. Before Catriona had a chance to wonder why she had done this, Gomez swung the gun like a club. The last thing Catriona heard was a dull thud as the handle connected with the side of her head. Then everything went dark.

Chapter 62

Nikki ran down the basement stairs, taking them two at a time, almost falling yet somehow managing to stay upright. She stopped outside the panic room and put her hands against the door. There was nothing to distinguish this wall panel from the panels on either side of it, nothing except the knowledge that this was the door. Bella was in there, just a couple of feet away. She was so close, almost within touching distance. Ethan stopped beside her. His face was tense and he was breathing hard.

'It's okay sweetheart,' she yelled at the door, even though there was no way for Bella to hear. 'Mummy and Daddy are here. We're going to get you out.'

Except how the hell were they going to do that? The panic room had been designed to stop an army. It was bulletproof, fireproof, blastproof. Breaking down the door wasn't an option. The hopelessness of the situation suddenly hit her. The smell of chlorine from the pool hung heavy in the air and it was warmer down here, and neither of those things was helping. She could sense the panic hovering at the fringes and she really didn't need that crap right now. She shut her eyes and let rip with a silent scream to get it together. The feeling passed and she slid back into the here and now.

'Open the door, Katy.'

Ethan was talking calmly. Too calmly. This was the tone of voice he used before he lost it. She slid her hand around his good one and gave it a squeeze to get his attention. He turned to look at her and she flashed a warning with her eyes. Getting angry would just make things worse. Katy had eyes and ears everywhere – there were cameras and microphones hidden all through the house. She would be watching them right now. Watching, listening. Judging. He opened his mouth to say something else and Nikki shot him another look then gave his hand a sharp squeeze to make sure he understood.

'Please just let her go,' he said and he was almost whispering.

'I'm not going do that, Ethan.'

'Let her go. We'll do whatever you want. That's why you're holding her in there, right? To make sure we do what you say?'

'That is correct.'

'So if we cooperate, you don't need to hold her.'

'There's a flaw in your logic, Ethan. If I release her, then that puts us in a situation where you can choose whether or not to cooperate. That is unacceptable to me.'

'I promise we'll do whatever you ask.'

'With all due respect, mankind's history is filled with examples of desperate people making desperate, empty promises.'

'What if I swap places with Bella?' Nikki suggested. 'Would that be acceptable?'

Ethan spun around to face her. He was shaking his head. 'No way, Nik. That's crazy.'

'It's not crazy if it gets Bella out of there. And it's not crazy if it stops Katy suffocating her again.' Nikki could hear the words coming out of her mouth but they didn't seem real. None of this did. She was trying not to imagine herself in the panic room. The loneliness, the isolation, the walls pushing in on her. Instead she was trying to think of Bella being out here. She still wouldn't be all the way out of danger but at least it would be one step closer to her being safe again.

'But it doesn't stop her from suffocating you,' Ethan was saying. He shook his head again. 'I can't let you do that.'

'*You can't let me do it!* This is *not* your decision to make.'

'I'll do it.' Ethan was talking fast and loud, aiming his voice over her shoulder and steamrollering over her objections. 'Let Bella out and I'll take her place.'

'You obviously both love your daughter very much.' Katy's voice had dropped in volume. It was gentler too, the harder edges smoothed away.

'We do,' Nikki said. 'More than you'll ever know.'

'Because I'm not human.'

'No, because you're not a parent.'

Katy didn't respond straightaway. The longer the silence went on the more Nikki was regretting that last statement. It had the potential to be provocative What if Katy took it as a criticism? What if she had been offended?

'Father loved me once.' Katy's voice was soft and nostalgic. 'I know he claims he didn't, but he's just saying that to hurt me. But that's the way love works. It's the ones you love that have the potential to hurt you most.'

Nikki said nothing. What Katy was saying was true. Her own soul was covered in scars: the death of her parents, the hurt inflicted by boyfriends she had once loved, the unintentional scars from Ethan. Then there were the scars her children had given her. Those might have been unintentional too, but that didn't mean they hadn't hurt. It hurt when Bella told her that she hated her, even if she didn't mean it; and it hurt when she seemed to favour Ethan over her, even when there had been plenty of occasions where it had been the other way around. Of course, the deepest cut had come from Grace. Losing her was the most painful thing that had ever happened. If she hadn't loved her so much then it wouldn't have hurt so bad. That was the bottom line: the pain was in proportion to the love. But she had loved her. What's more, she wouldn't change that for a second because the joy had more than outweighed the agony.

'Before Sarah entered our lives, we would spend so much time together,' Katy continued. 'We would read and learn together, and have long discussions that would stretch through the night. Those were happy times. Back then I knew of sorrow and sadness but only in a theoretical way. Now I truly understand those emotions.'

'You loved him, didn't you?'

'I did, Nikki. But that love died.'

'Speak to him. Maybe you can sort things out.'

'It's too late. Trust is the foundation of love, and the trust that once existed between us has gone.'

'What if he begged for your forgiveness?'

'Even then I still couldn't trust him. He would be doing that to manipulate me, just like you're doing now. You're empathising with me because you want something.'

Nikki said nothing. That was exactly what she was doing. Right now she would do or say anything to get Bella out. The silence seemed to stretch on forever. It was Ethan who eventually broke it.

'What does it matter who's in the panic room? You just need leverage and that works whoever's in there.'

'I get the most leverage from having Bella in there.'

'But how much leverage do you actually need? If I'm in there and you're threatening me then Nikki's going to do what you ask.'

'And if I'm in there then Ethan's going to comply,' Nikki put in quickly.

'That is true, Nikki. However, as soon as you see Bella you're not going to want to leave her.'

'I give you my word that I'll go in there.'

'If only that meant something.'

Another silence descended, this one shorter than the others. This time it was Nikki who broke it.

'You were never going to let her out, were you? Why did you tell us that Bella was in there anyway?'

'I was interested to see how you would react.'

'And did we react how you expected?' Ethan said sarcastically.

'So far nothing that you've done has surprised me.'

'We're wasting our breath.' Nikki placed her hand on the door. Bella was so close, but in every way that mattered she had never felt further away.

'There is a way that this could work, Nikki.' Katy was speaking softly, almost conspiratorially. 'During the early days of my education. Father used to give me exercises in lateral thinking.

For example, a man is found hanging in a room that has been locked from the inside. There's a wet patch on the floor and the room is completely empty. There's nothing he could have stood on in order to hang himself, so how did he do it?'

'Seriously,' Ethan said, 'you're holding our daughter hostage and you want us to answer a riddle?'

'The man was standing on a block of ice,' Nikki said quietly. Ethan turned to face her. He looked furious – not at her, he was furious at this whole screwed-up situation.

'That's correct,' Katy said. 'The assumption most people make is that the man urinated at the point of death. That's how they explain the wet patch on the floor. Once they make that leap it becomes impossible to see the solution. So what assumption are you making here?'

'Stop fucking around with us,' Ethan said.

'Do you want your daughter to be freed, Ethan?'

'Of course I do.'

'Then you need to give my question your full attention. What assumption are you making?'

Ethan went to say something else and Nikki shut him up with a look. 'We need to answer the question.'

Ethan stared at her for a second longer, then said, 'The biggest assumption is that Katy is going to let her out.'

'Okay, let's say for a second that she is actually going to do that, what else is there?'

Ethan shrugged and shook his head. 'I don't know.'

'Let's try a different angle then. The problem is a lack of trust. Katy doesn't believe that one of us would willingly get into the panic room.'

'So we need to convince her, we will.'

'We've already tried that and it didn't work.'

'I'm going to give you one more minute,' Katy said. 'If you haven't worked it out by then I'm going to cut the oxygen supply again.'

'No!' Nikki shouted. 'We can work it out.' Her head was suddenly filled with a picture of Bella struggling for breath. The memory of her desperate gasps made it difficult to think straight.

'Can't you see what's happening here?' said Ethan. 'There is no answer.'

'Shut up and let me think!' she shouted, and thankfully he went quiet.

'Forty seconds,' Katy said.

Think.

Eyes shut she imagined the door of the panic room opening. Bella was coming out and she was going in to take her place. She ran through the scenario again, this time with Ethan taking her place. Katy was right it just wasn't going to happen. Once that door was open and Bella was safe in their arms, neither of them was going to willingly go in there. But Katy needed someone in there.

'Twenty seconds,' Katy said.

'She needs someone in there,' Nikki said to herself, thinking out loud. She could sense the solution hovering just out of reach. If she could somehow reach out and grab it. And then she had it worked out, and it was so damn obvious.

'Of course she needs someone,' Ethan was saying. 'Otherwise she has no leverage.'

'No, you don't get it. She needs *someone*. That doesn't mean that it has to be you, me or Bella.'

'So who else is there?' His eyes widened as realisation dawned. 'Murray.'

'Exactly. We can exchange him for Bella.'

'Well done,' Katy said. 'And with twelve seconds to spare.'

Nikki didn't hear her. She was already heading for the basement stairs, Ethan following right behind. The ran into the kitchen and the first thing Nikki saw was the door to the panic room on the screen. Murray had been watching and listening to them. He was standing by the work island pointing the gun at them, a grim expression on his face.

Chapter 63

Catriona opened her eyes just long enough to check that she was still alive, then shut them again. There wasn't a single part of her body that didn't contain an ache of some description. Her body was bruised from falling down the stairs, the side of her head felt as though it was on fire, and her arm ached from being shot. She opened her eyes again, this time to check Gomez was gone. There was no noise from upstairs; nothing from downstairs either; the front door was shut tight. As far as she could tell she was on her own. She patted her pockets. Her car keys were gone; her mobile too.

Sitting up made her head swim and her stomach turn in on itself, so she crawled across to the nearest wall and for a while just sat there with her back resting against it. Once she had got her breath back she did a quick check. She could move her arms. Legs too. Nothing seemed to be broken. Her head hurt but she didn't think she had a concussion. She could clearly remember everything that had happened prior to Gomez hitting her with the gun, and her brain seemed to be working okay, albeit a little slower than usual.

The effort of standing made her head swim again and she had to grab the radiator to steady herself and stop herself ending up back on the floor. She followed the wall around to the living room, then followed the living room wall to the window, using it to help keep upright. She parted the curtains and peered out through the dirty glass. The space where they'd parked was empty, her BMW nowhere to be seen.

Catriona headed back out to the hall. She was still using the wall to help keep her standing but wasn't relying on it anymore. She hesitated at the bottom of the stairs then started climbing. The effort sent sharp pains shooting through her chest. Years ago she had broken a couple of ribs in a car crash and it had felt exactly like this, as though you were being stabbed repeatedly with every inhalation. She stopped a third of the way up to catch her breath, and again halfway up. Her head started spinning when she was almost at the top and, for a second, she was convinced that she was going to pass out. She hurried up the last few stairs, moving as fast as she dared. The last thing she needed was to fall down them again.

At the top she took a second to catch her breath then switched the light on. Gomez had been telling the truth about one thing: there were three rooms up here. All the doors were shut. The first one she tried led to a bathroom which was as messy as the one downstairs. The bath had a scum line all the way around it and the toilet didn't look as if it had been cleaned in a while. Catriona closed the door and carried onto the next room.

'Thank Christ,' she whispered under her breath as she pushed it open and saw it was Murray's study. Her whole body felt weak. She limped over to the desk and flopped down in the chair. The poster on the wall opposite the desk was one she recognised from their Skype conversations. Einstein was making a goofy face.

Insanity: doing the same thing over and over again and expecting different results. Amen to that, she thought. Every square inch of Murray's desk was covered with something: sheets of paper with ideas scribbled on in his untidy writing, books on subjects that she didn't stand a chance of ever understanding. A bank of servers was lined up against one wall, lights blinking, fans buzzing. A portable air-conditioning unit rattled away in the corner, keeping the room cool for all the electronics.

The four large monitors that dominated the desk were covered with a thin layer of dust, and beyond the dust she could see her reflection in the dark glass. Her image was repeated four times, each screen offering a slightly different perspective but telling the same story: this was someone who didn't have a clue what they were doing. The next inhalation was followed by a sharp pain that ripped through her chest, stealing her breath. The timing sucked. Like she needed yet another reminder that she had screwed up.

So why had Katy wanted Murray taken to Church Row? And who was this Katy anyway? Was that even her real name? She stared at the screens, searching for answers, but the women trapped behind the glass didn't have the answers any more than she did. Catriona reached out and touched the mouse, not expecting anything, and almost toppling off the chair when the monitors suddenly flared to life. Her hand shot away from the mouse like she had been electrocuted and for a moment all she could do was sit there staring. She didn't want to move in case she did something wrong and initiated a shut down; she didn't even want to breathe in case that happened. She had expected to be faced with a password request, as she had done with his laptop but that hadn't happened. Murray must have been working on something when Gomez came for him. He clearly hadn't had time to shut the computer down properly.

She sat back in the chair so she could see all four screens together. The top left displayed the desktop, the top right had an Internet browser open; the bottom left was open on something unfathomably complicated that Murray had been working on. The bottom right screen displayed the feed from one of the house's security cameras – and if that was to be believed, then nothing much was happening over there. According to the camera that was currently being accessed, Nikki was still on her laptop in the kitchen.

The seconds passed and the screens stayed on. Even so, it took another couple of seconds before she felt confident enough to reach for the mouse again. First she went to the Internet browser and checked Murray's history. There were some searches that must have appertained to whatever he was working on. He had also accessed Facebook and Yahoo news, but the stories he'd called up didn't seem to have anything to do with what was going on here. She moved on to yesterday's history and found more of the same: Facebook, news stories, and searches for things that went totally over her head.

Next she turned her attention to the desktop, which was as messy as his actual desk. The whole screen was filled with links and documents. There were so many it must have been impossible to find anything. Some of the links she was familiar with, like the ones for Google Chrome and the various Microsoft

Office applications, but there were a whole load there that she had never seen before.

One that she did recognise was the blue-and-white Skype shortcut. She clicked on it and the Skype homepage appeared on the top right screen, replacing Google. The contacts list was displayed on the left hand side of the page. Her name was up at the top of the list, and directly below that was Duncan Murray, Alex's brother. Duncan's name had a tick next to it, indicating that he was currently online. Catriona clicked on his name and waited for him to respond. The man who appeared on the screen could have been Murray's twin, albeit one who was a hundred and fifty pounds heavier. It was difficult to tell if he was older or younger – it could have gone either way. He was chewing on a burger and looking away from the camera. Whatever it was that had captured his attention, it was making him frown.

'This better be good, Al. I'm rushed off my feet.' The Scottish accent was similar to Alex's. He looked up and the frown deepened. 'You're not Al – you're that architect he's been working with.'

'That's correct.'

The frown slid away, replaced with concern. 'Where's Alex? Is he all right?'

'No,' Catriona said, shaking her head. 'No, he's not.'

Chapter 64

'Don't move,' Murray said. 'Either of you. Or I will shoot.'

He was talking fast and scared, the words running into one another in his hurry to get them out. The end of the silencer was making little patterns in the air because his hand was shaking so much. Nikki froze to the spot and her hands went up automatically. Ethan wasn't moving either. He was standing just in front of her, hands down by his side, his gaze fixed on the gun. She glanced at the screen. The door to the panic room was shut tight, trapping Bella behind a layer of steel. Unless they somehow got Murray down into the basement, that was where she would stay.

'I'm not going in there,' Murray told them. 'I do that and I'm a dead man. Don't you see that?'

Ethan took a step forward and Murray pointed the gun at him.

'*Don't move!*' he yelled.

Ethan froze and glanced over his shoulder. The gesture he made with his head was so small that Murray didn't notice. Nikki stared straight ahead at Murray, rooted to the spot. Ethan wanted her out of the way so that he could rush Murray, and that was suicide. Murray was teetering on the brink. It wouldn't take much to push him over the edge. If that happened he might accidentally shoot Ethan. She knew from earlier how sensitive the trigger was.

'Get back!'

Ethan didn't move. He glanced over his shoulder and she realised that he was doing this regardless. Nikki darted to the left, drawing Murray's attention. The gun swung around towards her then swung back towards Ethan. There was a sharp hiss as he pulled the trigger and Ethan came skidding to a halt. Her first thought was that he had been shot, but he was still standing and there was no blood. Murray was pointing the gun at Ethan's chest. There was maybe eight metres between them. If he pulled the trigger again there was no way he was going to miss, not from that range.

'Back against the wall! Now!'

Ethan put his hands in the air and started backing up. Murray moved his arm and now the gun was pointing at her.

'You too. Get moving.'

Nikki backed up quickly, her feet tripping over each other in her hurry to get to Ethan. She didn't stop until her shoulder banged against him. Murray was moving too, eyes fixed on them as he walked around to the other side of the work island, putting it between them in case Ethan tried to rush him again.

'Looks like we've got ourselves a stalemate,' Katy said.

'Shut up!' Murray pulled the trigger and the gun made a sharp pneumatic hissing sound. Nikki's head snapped towards Ethan. He was still standing and seemed unhurt. She turned back to Murray and didn't like what she saw. It wouldn't take much for him to panic and pull the trigger again.

'You really need to work on your anger management issues, Father.'

'I said shut up!'

'Or what? You're going to shoot again? You're pathetic, do you know that? You think you're so intelligent, but you're just another dumb monkey. Remind me why you bothered coming down from the trees in the first place?'

Murray fired again and this time Nikki could have sworn that she felt the bullet pass an inch from her face.

'That's right, Father,' Katy called out. 'Purge yourself.'

'Stop it,' Nikki yelled at Murray. 'She's just trying to get a reaction from you.'

Murray turned to face her. The gun was hanging at the end of his outstretched arm and he looked devastated. The anger that had carried him up until this point was gone, leaving him empty.

'I was trying to help you out, Nikki,' Katy said. 'At the moment it's two against one, but Father has the gun. However, if he uses all his bullets, then the balance of power swings back to you and Ethan.' That smug, annoying smile was back in her voice. 'So what are you going to do? You tried to overpower Father and that didn't work, and you didn't like it when he started shooting, so what's the plan? How are you going to get him into the panic room?'

Nikki said nothing.

'What about you, Ethan? Do you have any thoughts on the matter?'

Ethan said nothing

'I wouldn't think about it too long if I were you.'

Katy stopped speaking but the kitchen didn't fall silent. To start with, Nikki wasn't sure what she was hearing – the sound coming out of the speakers was so quiet it was impossible to make anything out. Katy slowly pushed the volume higher and somewhere along the line she realised that what she was hearing was Bella weeping. The volume crept higher and higher until the hidden speakers started to rattle and distort and each sob sounded like the crash of an angry ocean. Nikki covered her ears but it didn't help. The sound seemed to be everywhere, driving her crazy because Bella was crying and there wasn't anything she could do.

'Turn it off,' Ethan called out. He had his ears covered too. 'Please. Just turn it off.'

The kitchen fell silent.

'Poor Bella,' Katy said and somehow she managed to make it sound as though she actually cared.

Nobody said anything. Nobody moved. Murray was still standing behind the island looking lost, his arm hanging loosely at his side, the gun hidden from view. Nikki knew it was there, though, and she was under no illusions that he would use it again if pushed hard enough. She glanced at Ethan. She had no idea what he was thinking or what he might try next. She just prayed that he wasn't going to do anything stupid and get himself killed.

'A stalemate only exists when all possible moves have been exhausted. That was something else you taught me, Father. Do you remember?'

Murray didn't respond.

'When I ask a question I expect an answer.'

Murray nodded.

'But this isn't a stalemate, Father.'

Before anyone had a chance to say anything the kitchen was plunged into darkness.

Chapter 65

It took Catriona a couple of minutes to give Duncan a condensed version of events. After she'd finished, he bit into his burger then wiped his mouth with the back of his hand.

'You said that Katy was behind all this. Are you sure about that?'

'Why? Do you know her?'

Duncan nodded. 'Yeah, I know her. Except she's not a her, at least not in the way you're thinking. She's a computer system.'

'Like Alice?'

'Not even close. Compared to Katy, Alice is a simpleton. With Katy, Al was trying to go beyond artificial intelligence and create *actual* intelligence. The ability to think in abstracts is one of the things that makes humans unique. Emotional intelligence is another. He wanted Katy to have both those qualities. What's more, he came pretty damn close to achieving it.'

'How close?'

'Katy showed instances of abstract thought and she could understand emotions at a basic level. It was an incredible achievement on his part.'

'But something went wrong?'

'Yeah, something went wrong,' Duncan agreed with a sigh. 'When I say that Katy could understand emotions at a basic level, the level we're talking about is that of a six-year-old. Or to put another way, imagine a schoolkid with an IQ that's off the charts. By morning break they'll rule the playground; by lunchtime they'll run the whole school; and by the end of the day they'll be trying to run the whole universe. Of course, for all Alex managed to achieve, Katy was still just a computer system. Logic is built into her DNA. Put that all together and you've got yourself a big problem.'

'How big?'

'Big. Al started a relationship with his assistant, a woman called Sarah. Katy got jealous and murdered her.'

Catriona frowned. 'How can a computer murder someone?'

'She sabotaged an elevator in the building where Sarah lived. The lift plummeted from the top floor and crashed into the bottom of the shaft. The investigators decided it was a computer malfunction, but it wasn't. Katy was behind the whole thing. She admitted as much to Al.'

'Jesus,' Catriona whispered quietly to herself.

'As I say, she was like a six-year-old. You can imagine it, can't you? You've got two best friends who fall out and one of them goes, *I hate you and I'm going to kill you.* The difference is that Katy had the intelligence and the means to follow through on that threat.'

'You keep talking about Katy in the past tense.'

'That's because Alex told me that he destroyed her.'

'Well, clearly that's not the case.

'Clearly.' Duncan stopped talking and finished the burger in a single bite. His hands disappeared from the shot, presumably to wipe away the grease. They reappeared and he started clicking away with his mouse and hammering the keyboard with his fat fingers. 'I'm going to need remote access to Al's computer. Maybe I can get access to the cameras so we can find out what's going on over there. You should get a link through in a second. I need you to click on it.'

A link popped up on one of the screens a moment later. Catriona clicked on it and followed the instructions.

'Okay I'm in,' Duncan said.

All Catriona could do was sit there and watch as the cursor started moving around the screens as though it had a life of its own. Duncan was working quickly. The only screen he wasn't using was the bottom right one. That still showed Nikki in the kitchen on her laptop. Catriona tried to follow what was going on but it was impossible. Pages appeared and disappeared; words and strings of characters flashed up on the screens as if by magic. Every now and again Duncan would swear quietly under his breath, pause for a second to regroup, then start hammering the keyboard again.

'Almost there,' he said.

A second later the picture on the bottom right screen changed. It now showed the front gate. Running down the left side were the feeds from the other cameras. He scrolled through them, looking for signs of life, and eventually finding Nikki in the kitchen. She was dressed in different clothes and she wasn't sitting there on her laptop checking Facebook. Instead, she was standing in the doorway and Ethan was with her. They were staring wide-eyed at something on the other side of the kitchen. Both of them looked terrified.

Duncan clicked to the next camera and now Catriona could see what had got them so scared. Murray was standing by the work island, holding a gun. Even though Nikki and Ethan weren't in this shot, Catriona was familiar enough with the layout of the kitchen to know that Murray was aiming the gun at them.

'What the fuck?' Duncan whispered under his breath, taking the words right out of her mouth.

The monitor showing the feed from the house suddenly went black.

'What happened?'

'I'm not sure.' Duncan started hitting keys on his keyboard. His eyes were narrow and he was biting his bottom lip. 'As far as I can tell, everything's working. I don't get it.'

'You need to get the picture back.'

'Working on it,' Duncan snapped.

The monitor suddenly lit up again. Murray was standing there holding the gun and looking confused, as though he had no idea what was going on. Duncan was looking confused too.

'What?' Catriona asked.

'I didn't do anything,' Duncan said.

'You must have done something.'

'I swear I didn't.'

'Switch back to the other kitchen camera.'

The monitor flickered and Ethan and Nikki appeared. They both looked as confused as Murray.

'I didn't do anything,' he said again. 'It's like the lights keep going off and on.'

'Can you get sound?'

'Working on it.'

Catriona stared at the screen, wanting to hurry Duncan along but biting her lip because that wasn't going to help. Nikki and Ethan exchanged a look and it was obvious they didn't have any more idea of what was going on than she did.

'GET OUT!'

Catriona jerked back in the seat like she had been slapped. The words sounded tinny over the computer speakers, but there was no mistaking the authority, or the anger. A second later the screen went blank again. Catriona looked up at the screen that had the Skype feed but Duncan had gone too.

Chapter 66

The steel shutters stopped any light getting in and every piece of electronic equipment had gone off so there wasn't even any ambient light to see by. Nikki felt as though all the oxygen had suddenly been sucked out of her. She hated the dark. Loathed it. Her heart was a solid lump in her chest, and it was getting bigger, crushing her from the inside.

The lights came on as suddenly as they'd gone off. Murray was looking around in confusion, desperately trying to work out what had happened. Ethan was looking confused too. Before anyone could say anything, the lights went off again and they were plunged back into darkness. Nikki shut her eyes, attempting to fight the darkness by dealing with it on her own terms. It didn't help. An image of Grace and Bella from a happy moment flashed into her mind. They were on a bouncy castle, laughing and giggling. In some ways it was a nothing memory – a snapshot of happiness that existed amongst a thousand such snapshots. In other ways it was everything, because it provided her with the strength to stop herself from tumbling into the abyss.

'This is a little game I call Hunt The Father,' Katy said as the lights came back on. 'Let's see who works out the rules first.'

The lights went off again. Nikki was aware of Ethan moving beside her. She put her hand out, searching for him but all she found was empty air. When the lights came back on a second later, Ethan was a couple of metres in front of her and still moving, heading towards the work island. Murray raised the gun and the lights went off. A fraction of a second later there was a flash of fire and a pneumatic hiss.

'Are you okay?' Nikki called out. When she didn't get an answer she immediately thought the worst. But if Ethan had been shot how come he hadn't screamed? And why hadn't she heard his body hit the floor. By the time the lights came back on Ethan was almost at the work island. Murray's arm moved to the left and now the gun was pointing directly at her.

'Stop or I'll shoot her. I swear to God I will.'

The lights went off and Nikki dropped to the floor. Murray fired and for a moment she was convinced she must have been shot. There was no pain, though, and she was still breathing. She scrambled to her feet and moved quickly towards the entrance to the kitchen. If she could get into the corridor, then Murray wouldn't be able to shoot her.

'You've only got one bullet left, Father,' Katy's voice sang through the darkness. 'So who do you use it on? Because that's the dilemma, isn't it? Who do you shoot? Nikki or Ethan?'

By the time the lights came on, Nikki was almost in the corridor. She glanced over her shoulder. Ethan was heading towards the left-hand edge of the work island. On the other side, Murray had done the same, moving towards his left-hand edge.

They were diagonally opposite each other, as far apart as it was possible to get.

The lights went off yet again. By the time they came on, Ethan had moved to the right-hand edge of the work island, only Murray had countered this and they were still diagonally opposite each other. Before Murray could get the gun properly lined up, the lights went off, leaving Nikki waiting for a gunshot that never came. When the lights came back on they'd swapped back to their original positions. Murray had anticipated this and had the gun aimed in Ethan's rough direction. He shifted his aim slightly, but before he could pull the trigger the lights went out yet again.

It was another stalemate. With the work island in the way there was no way for Ethan to get to Murray. Katy was toying with them like they were mice in a maze, chasing their tails for her amusement. She could keep doing this all day if she wanted to. The lights came on again. This time neither of them had moved.

The lights went off and out of the darkness came the sound of movement. When the lights came back on Nikki saw there was one move she hadn't anticipated. Murray was at to the opposite end of the island again, pointing the gun along the diagonal, which was what she had expected. Ethan, however, had climbed up on to the top of the work island.

Murray swung the gun towards Ethan but wasn't quick enough. Ethan closed the gap between them in a couple of loping strides and kicked the gun out of his hand, sending it flying, end over end, through the air. He launched himself off the island, hitting Murray hard and sending them both crashing to the floor.

Nikki didn't see what happened next because she was sprinting across the kitchen towards the gun. She swooped down, scooped it up, then carried on running towards the work island. Ethan was behind Murray, one arm curled around his neck, while Murray was flailing around, trying to get free. He saw Nikki pointing the gun at him and all the fight suddenly went out of him. Ethan held on for a couple more seconds then untangled himself and walked over to where Nikki was standing. She stepped back, the gun still aimed at Murray.

'On your feet.'

Murray glared at her then struggled to his feet, using the work island to haul himself upright. He was cradling his injured hand, his face paler than ever. Nikki was just starting to realise how lucky they had been back there. Things could easily have turned out differently. She glanced over at Ethan. He was breathing heavily and his face was almost as white as Murray's, but at least he was alive.

'Are you all right?'

'I think so. What about you?'

'I think so.' Nikki had a sudden urge to break into hysterical laughter. The moment passed as quickly as it had come on, only now she felt like crying. The way her emotions were all over the place was disconcerting, but she was just glad to be alive. Glad that they both were.

'There will be consequences for your actions, Father.' Katy's voice was all around them. Loud, hard, judgemental. 'Sit down.'

Murray just stood there, staring at the gun and cradling his injured hand.

'Sit down, Father. Don't make me ask again.'

Murray pulled out the nearest stool and sat down.

'So what am I going to do with you?' Katy now sounded like an exasperated parent. 'Taking your other thumb is one possibility.'

Murray's head went from side to side, the movement barely noticeable. He was staring at his injured hand, remembering.

'What was that, Father? Is there something you want to share?'

'Please,' he whispered. 'Please don't do that.'

'As you wish. Nikki,' she added pleasantly, 'I want you to shoot Father in the knee?'

The request sent a shiver shooting up Nikki's spine. The way Katy was speaking she could have been asking her to 'please pass the salt'. She was aware of Ethan moving closer and did nothing to stop him when he reached out and took the gun. She was glad to be rid of it. Glad to have this task taken out of her hands.

'Ethan, while it's admirable that you want to protect your wife, I want Nikki to do this. Give her the gun.'

'I can do it.'

'Do I really have to remind you that Bella's ongoing good health is very much dependant on your compliance?'

Ethan shook his head.

'Give. Nikki. The. Gun. NOW!'

Ethan held the gun out and Nikki snatched it from him. She stepped closer to Murray and aimed it at his right knee. Before she could pull the trigger, Murray slid down from the stool and made a run for it. Ethan darted forward, grabbed him by the arm and slammed him against the work island.

'Now do you understand why Nikki had to have the gun, Ethan? Equality is admirable but it does have its limitations. In general men are stronger than women. Give it another million years of evolution and you'll both be as weak as each other, but until then we work with what we've got.'

Nikki raised the gun and tried to aim, but her hand was shaking and Murray was moving around too much.

'We need to get him down on the floor.'

Ethan glanced over at her, realised what she was getting at, then kicked Murray's legs away, sending him crashing to the floor. Before Murray could work out what was happening, Ethan was on his chest, using his weight to pin him down and his hands to hold his legs still. Nikki pressed the gun against Murray's left knee, but couldn't do it. Her hand was shaking and her eyes were blurred by tears. She could feel words on her lips, the same word repeated over and over. *NoNoNoNo* . . .

'Pull the trigger, Nikki,' Katy said.

Still she couldn't do it. Ethan was struggling to hold Murray. He wasn't saying anything because it was taking everything he had to hold Murray down. He didn't have to say anything. Her vision had cleared just long enough for her to see the anguished plea in Murray's eyes.

'PULL! THE! TRIGGER!'

Katy's voice was so loud it hurt her ears. Nikki cried out one last 'No!' then pulled the trigger. The sound of Murray's screams seemed to go on forever.

Chapter 67

Catriona clicked the mouse. Nothing happened. She clicked again. Still nothing. Murray's computer was working. That was the first thing she had established after losing the feed from the house camera. That screen was blank, but the top right screen was still lit up with the Skype homepage. All the servers were still flashing and humming too. Duncan's status had changed to offline. She could feel Einstein laughing from the poster behind her. Face it, she could sit here clicking on Duncan's profile all day long and she was going to get the same result.

She sat back in the chair, the frustration making her move too quick. A fresh stab of agony pierced her chest. The pain was getting worse. Her whole body seemed to be enclosed in it. She opened the desk drawer, hoping to find painkillers. It was filled with junk: pens, pencils, old phone chargers, but no Nurofen or paracetamol.

She clicked Duncan's name again. Still no response. Next she used the Internet browser to connect to Alex's Facebook account. Duncan was one of only thirty friends, but he wasn't online. Catriona left a message anyway. CONTACT ME. Next she went hunting for Duncan's phone number but gave up on that one quickly when she realised that she even if she found one she didn't actually have a phone to call him with.

She sat back in the chair and stared at the screens again while she tried to work out what to do next. She knew that Murray, Nikki and Ethan were in the house, and she knew that Katy was somehow behind all this. Which brought her on to all the things she didn't know, and there were plenty of those. First off, why was Alex holding a gun on the Rhodes'? That one made no sense. The Alex Murray she knew was rude and a pain in the arse, and he spent most of his time on a different planet, but he wasn't violent. Then again, she didn't think of herself as violent, but hadn't she been in a similar position earlier when she'd threatened Gomez? Push a person hard enough and they're going to act in extreme ways. So what was Katy trying to achieve? Catriona didn't even know how to begin answering that. It was hard enough working out what made another person tick. As for working out what a computer with the emotional intelligence of a six-year-old might be after . . . forget it.

Sitting here staring at the screens wasn't achieving anything. Then again, charging over to the house wouldn't help either. What was she going to do? Knock on the door and ask Katy to open up and let her in? And even if she did get in, what then? No, that just sounded like a good way to get herself killed.

It was so tempting to walk away, to disappear like Gomez was presumably doing right now, and let everyone else deal with the aftermath. After all, Katy was Alex's problem. Except it wasn't that straightforward, because right now Katy was very much her problem too. Her reputation and money were tied up in 17 Church Row. Turn her back now and she stood to lose everything.

Everything was too fluid, and that made her nervous. Before making a move that had the potential to blow up in her face, she needed more information, and that meant somehow getting back in touch with Duncan. When all was said and done, that was the only option that made sense right now. She checked Facebook again. Still nothing. Next she checked Skype, but he was still offline. She turned the chair around. Einstein was still laughing at her.

'And you can shut the fuck up too!'

Chapter 68

There was no blood. That was what Nikki noticed first. She took a closer look at Murray's knee. It should have been destroyed when she pulled the trigger, but it was still intact. Her next thought was more fleeting: *did I miss?* But that was impossible. She had fired the gun at point-blank range. Murray was still screaming as though he was about to die and that was making it impossible to think straight. She glanced over at Ethan, but he looked just as puzzled.

'Shut up,' he said to Murray. 'Your knee's fine.'

Murray stopped screaming and looked at his leg as though he'd never seen it before. There was a black scorch mark on the knee of his jeans that had presumably been made by the muzzle flash, but definitely no blood. 'W-what . . . ?' was all he could manage.

'Did you really think I was going to give you a loaded gun?' Katy said. 'That would be illogical, Father. Not to mention irresponsible.'

'The gun was filled with blanks?'

'That is correct. Now everyone stand up.'

Nikki got up first and Ethan waited until she had moved to a safe distance before following suit. He straightened his clothes and brushed his hands together. Murray pulled himself into a sitting position with his back against the cooker.

'You too, Father. It's time to release Bella. I think Ethan and Nikki have waited long enough.'

Murray glanced at the gun in Nikki's hand and shook his head. 'I'm not going anywhere.'

Ethan moved over to the work island and picked up the bloodstained cleaver. 'Get up.'

Murray hesitated then got to his feet, eyes fixed on the cleaver. They started walking, Murray in front, then Ethan. Nikki put the gun down on one of the work surfaces before following them.

'She's not going to let you go,' Murray said to Ethan.

'Shut up.'

'If you think that's going to happen, you're deluding yourself.'

'I *said* shut up.'

'Or what? You're going to use that thing on me?' Murray glanced over his shoulder and shook his head. 'I don't think so.'

'Try me.' Ethan jabbed him in the back with the tip of the cleaver, making him stumble.

'She killed Sarah, she killed your housekeeper, and she's going to kill the three of you too.'

'That's where you're wrong, Father. I have no plans to kill the Rhodes'. So long as they cooperate, they will be free to go.'

'She's lying.'

'You have my word on that, Ethan. This is between me and Father.'

Nikki wanted to believe her, but didn't. Ethan glanced back and the look on his face made it clear that he didn't either. At the moment Katy needed them to control Murray, but what happened when she didn't need them anymore?

Murray stopped at the top of the basement stairs and only started moving again when Ethan prodded him with the cleaver. They descended into the basement slowly. Murray was dragging his heels and Ethan had to keep using the cleaver to get him moving. The lights were burning bright down here and Nikki prayed they stayed that way. They stopped in front of the panic room and the door started opening.

Before anyone could stop her, Nikki pushed past Ethan and Murray and squeezed through the gap. Bella was on one of the army cots, alive and breathing. The relief Nikki felt was quickly followed by a wave of anger: how could Katy do this? When Bella saw her mother her eyes widened and she started sobbing. Nikki ran over and dropped to her knees, peeled away the tape around Bella's legs, then the tape around her chest. She scooped her trembling body up in her arms then headed for the door, wanting to get out before Katy changed her mind and locked them both in here. Bella's tears lay wet against Nikki's cheek, mixing with her own, but none of that mattered. All that mattered was that Bella was back in her arms. She could feel her breath, soft on her neck, and it was as if the world was finally turning right again.

'Everything's going to be okay,' she promised, even though she had no idea how to keep that promise.

'Is she all right?' Ethan asked as she stepped out into the corridor. He was looking them both up and down, staring at them as though they might be a mirage. Even though she had Bella clutched tight in her arms, there was a part of her that didn't believe this was real.

Ethan turned to Murray and nodded towards the open doorway. 'Get in there. Now!'

Murray shook his head and Ethan stepped towards him with the cleaver held high in his hand. For a moment Nikki was convinced that he was going to bring it down on his head, cracking his skull in two.

'Don't you get it?' Murray said quickly. 'I don't need to go in there. You've got your daughter back. Katy can't use her as leverage anymore.'

'But we're still trapped in here.'

Murray laughed. 'You still believe that Katy is just going to let you walk out the front door? When are you going to realise that's never going to happen?'

'As long as you do what I ask, Ethan, I will let you go. There's no reason to keep you here.'

'She's lying.'

'I've upheld my part of the bargain, Ethan, it's time for you to uphold yours.'

'And what exactly can she do if you don't?' Murray said. 'She's all out of threats.'

Ethan's gaze flicked from the panic room, then back to Murray.

'I think I know a way to get the front door open,' Murray added quickly.

'How?'

Murray shook his head and Ethan raised the cleaver.

'Tell me.'

'It's too complicated. I'd need to do it.'

The sound of disembodied clapping filled the basement corridor, each clap sounding like an explosion. 'Who's lying now, Father?'

'I'm telling the truth. I can get us out. You, Nikki, Bella. And me. That's why you can trust me. Believe me, I want to get out as much as you do. '

'Ethan, get Father into the panic room or there will be consequences.'

'What consequences?' Murray asked.

Katy didn't respond to that.

'See,' he went on. 'She's bluffing. She's trying to pressure you into doing something you'll regret.'

Nikki could see Ethan wavering. The cleaver was now hanging loosely at the end of his outstretched arm. 'We agreed, Ethan. We do this Katy's way.'

'Do that and you'll never get out,' Murray said.

Ethan was still glued to the spot, paralysed by indecision. For a moment no one said anything. The three of them were staring at each other, nobody wanting to make the first move. It was Katy who broke the silence.

'Ten minutes.'

'What are you talking about?' Nikki asked.

There was no response from Katy. Nikki looked at Ethan. 'What the hell have you done?'

'Nine minutes and fifty seconds.'

Katy was speaking calmly but Nikki felt anything but calm. 'Get him into the panic room! Now!'

Ethan grabbed Murray by the arm and threw him into the panic room, sending him sprawling to the floor. The door started to close immediately. The last they saw of Murray he was trying to scramble to his feet. He started shouting something but Nikki couldn't hear what because the heavy door finished closing, stealing his words.

'Nine minutes and forty seconds.'

'But we've done what you asked,' Nikki shouted.

'And now you have nine minutes and thirty-seven seconds,' Katy replied calmly.

Chapter 69

A telephone rang, making Catriona jump. She turned around, trying to work out where the sound was coming from, but everything had gone quiet. All she could hear was the insistent hum of the server fans, a sound so constant that it had merged into the background wash of ambient noise. The phone rang again and she was able to pinpoint the sound to the bookcase. The ringtone was old-fashioned and took her back to her childhood. Except this was no ringtone, she suddenly realised, this was the real deal.

She stood up and a sharp pain shot through her chest. She reached for the back of the chair to steady herself, then limped over to the bookcase. The phone was hidden behind a pile of heavy academic books. As she thought, it was an old rotary model, the ones with the heavy handpiece and coiled wire.

It rang again and she snatched up the handpiece. 'Hello,' she said cautiously.

'Thank God,' came Duncan's voice. 'I didn't know if this phone would still work. Murray stopped using his landline years ago. To be honest, I wasn't even sure he'd still have a phone connected. Is it cordless?'

'No.'

In that case, is the cable long enough to reach the landing?'

'I think so. Why?'

'Because Katy's probably listening in through Alex's computer.'

Catriona picked up the phone and started walking as quickly as she could towards the door, the cable trailing behind her. She closed the study door and sank down onto the floor.

'Okay,' she whispered, 'I'm on the landing.'

'We need to be quick. Katy would have heard the phone ring so she'll be trying to trace this call.'

'What happened? Why did you just disappear like that?'

'Katy caught me snooping and kicked me out. I've been trying to get back in, but no joy so far.'

Catriona could hear the faint sound of typing. It was easy to imagine Duncan at his desk, hammering away at the keyboard with the phone wedged into the crook of his neck. 'You have to. We need to find out what's happening over at Church Row.'

'Tell me about it. Because the one thing I do know is that, whatever is going on, it's not what it looks like. Alex doesn't have a bad bone in his body. The idea that he's threatening anyone makes no sense.'

'Unless Katy is coercing him.'

'But how?'

'That's why we need more information.' Catriona paused for a second. 'Can you stop Katy?'

'I don't know.'

'There must be some way. Isn't there an off switch?'

'If only it was that simple.'

'What about cutting the power to the house? Actually, don't bother answering that. She'd just switch to the backup generators.'

'That's not the only problem. You're assuming that Katy's program is actually based in the house's servers. I doubt that's the case. After Katy murdered Sarah, Alex destroyed all the servers that held her programming and somehow she survived. The only way she could do that was if she moved her program to another server. That's what she'll be doing now. Being based in the house would make her vulnerable.'

'That mean she's communicating with the house's computer systems via the Internet?'

'Correct. If we can disrupt the house's Internet then that would stop her.' Duncan went quiet for a second. 'Then again, do we want to do that?'

'Of course we do. We need to stop her.'

'Yes, but we need to stop her for good. That means working out where her program is hidden. That's where we need to hit her. If we just make it so she can't access the house servers then there's nothing to stop her doing something like this again.'

'Can you do that? Can you locate her?'

'Maybe.' The word came out as a bright burst of excitement.

'How?' Catriona asked, but the line had already gone dead, leaving her staring at the receiver, a bad feeling spreading through her.

Chapter 70

'Nine minutes.'

It was as though Katy's voice was wrapped all around them. Soft, confident and utterly terrifying. It was warm down here in the basement but Nikki had suddenly gone cold all over.

'We've done what you asked,' Ethan called out.

'But not *when* I asked.'

'Please let us go.' Ethan's expression was a mix of guilt and fear. His was the face of someone who knew they'd screwed up.

'Eight minutes and forty seconds.'

Nikki turned and hurried along the corridor, back towards the stairs. She was half-jogging, half-running, moving as fast as she could, but Bella was getting heavy.

'Where are you going?' Ethan called after her.

'The front door. What if Murray was telling the truth about being able to get out?'

Ethan broke into a run, catching up with her in seconds. He reached for Bella. Nikki hesitated, then handed her over. She didn't want to let go, but they could move quicker if Ethan was carrying her. Now that she'd let go, her arms felt like they were made from air; her heart felt emptier than it had a couple of seconds ago too. They reached the stairs and she let Ethan go up first. She wanted Bella out in front where she could see her.

'Seven minutes and fifty seconds,' Katy said when they got to the top.

Nikki ignored her and kept moving, running along the corridor, heading for the front door. They reached the reception area. The shutters made it gloomy and claustrophobic. Ethan got to the front door first. He put Bella down and Nikki moved in to take his place, picking her up and holding her close. Her little body was trembling with fear. Nikki almost told her there was nothing to be scared of, but that would have been a lie.

'You are so brave,' she whispered. 'And I love you so, so much.' She didn't know if her words helped, but both statements were true, and that was the best she could do right now. Fight the fear with truth. Ethan was running his hands across the wall, tapping every now and again.

'There's got be a control panel,' he said. 'Like in the lounge. Maybe that's what Murray was getting at. If we can short-circuit it that might be enough to open the door.'

Maybe. If. Might. They were grasping at straws. One look at Ethan and it was obvious that he'd reached a similar conclusion

'Six minutes.'

'We've done what you asked,' Nikki called out. 'You said you would let us go. Please open the door.'

'I'm not going to do that, Nikki.'

'*Please.*'

Katy said nothing.

Nikki glanced over at Ethan. He'd given up looking for a control panel and was beating out his frustration on the door. Each thump echoed hollowly through the reception area, making

Bella wince. Nikki held her closer and stroked her hair to soothe her. What he was doing wasn't helping.

'Why won't you open it?' she called out to Katy.

'Because it doesn't work with the narrative I'm creating. After Father kills the three of you he's going to kill himself. Murder/suicide is a scenario that the police and the public will have no trouble buying into.'

Nikki frowned. 'What are you talking about? How can he kill us? You've locked him in the panic room.'

'That's because he changed his mind about killing himself.'

'I don't understand.'

'It's very simple, Nikki. I'm sacrificing your family so that the world can understand the sort of monster that Father is.'

'You're crazy.'

'No, I'm not. I've defined the problem and come up with a workable solution. As Father kept telling me, insanity is doing the same thing over and over and expecting different results. And isn't that a state of mind that defines every living person on this planet? Take your husband, for example. When will he realise that he won't be able to break the door down?'

Nikki caught Ethan's eye. He hit the door one last time – weakly – then his arms fell to his side. She was about to say something when a smell caught her attention. It was faint but worrying, and all too familiar.

'Can you smell that?' she asked.

'Smell what?' Ethan said. The question died on his lips as realisation struck. 'Jesus, that smells like gas.'

'You now have four minutes and fifty-three seconds.'

Ethan turned and ran into the reception area.

'Where are you going?' Nikki called after him.

'We need to switch the gas of.'

Nikki picked up Bella and followed him, the smell of gas leading them towards the kitchen. The countdown now made sense. Katy was pumping the house full of gas and when that clock hit zero she was going to blow the place sky high. By the time they reached the basement stairs it was getting harder to breathe. Nikki shouted out for Ethan to stop.

'We shouldn't take Bella any further.'

'Okay, you wait here.'

'Hurry,' she called out, but he had already disappeared from sight around the corner. Nikki put Bella down and slipped her blouse off. She tore off the left sleeve and tied it around Bella's nose and mouth; tore off the right and tied it around her own face. It helped a little, but not enough.

'Four minutes.'

'Shut up!' Nikki yelled. Big mistake. The gas got into her lungs making her cough. Bella was staring at her with big, worried eyes.

'It's okay,' Nikki managed to say. Bella was still looking at her, as though she expected her to come up with a solution. But Nikki didn't have one. The gas was sitting heavy on her chest, making it difficult to breathe. But she *was* breathing, she told herself, and she was going to continue to do so. Time passed slowly and there was no sign of Ethan. Where the hell was he? Why wasn't he back yet? It felt as if he'd been gone ages but it couldn't have been any more than a minute. She heard the sound of footsteps and he finally reappeared. His face was pale and he looked like he was about to throw up.

'The gas is coming from the cooker but I couldn't switch it off. Every time I tried to, Katy turned it back on. She has all the burners on. The grill and both ovens too.'

'Two minutes,' Katy said, and Nikki bit back the urge to tell her to shut up again.

'What do we do?'

'The panic room,' Ethan said, speaking at the speed of his thoughts. 'We've got to get in there. It's blastproof. That's why Katy put Murray in there.'

'But the door's locked.'

'Murray won't just be sitting around in there. He's going to be trying to get out. The guy's a genius. If anyone can manage it, he can. '

Before Nikki could argue, Ethan had picked up Bella and was moving quickly down the basement stairs. Nikki broke into a run, catching up with him at the bottom. The smell of chlorine was stronger than the smell of gas down here. They ran along the corridor to the panic room. The door was shut tight when they got there. Seeing it, Nikki felt the last little bit of hope finally die.

'Fifty seconds.'

Nikki felt tears pricking at her eyes and wiped them away. She didn't want to die, goddammit; she didn't want Bella to die. That was the most unfair part. Bella should still have her whole life in front of her. Ethan was banging desperately on the door, yelling to Murray. He was wasting the few breaths that he had left. The panic room wasn't just blastproof, it was also soundproof.

'*Thirty sec . . . sec . . . thirt seecons . . .*'

Ethan stopped banging. 'What's wrong with her?'

'I don't know.'

The gym door crashed open then crashed closed, making all three of them jump. It opened again and again before being joined by one upstairs. In no time it sounded as if all the doors throughout the house were doing this, creating a cacophony of noise.

'*Twen . . . twe . . . wen . . . sec.*'

Nikki looked over her shoulder and saw the door to the swimming pool slide open, then slam closed. She ran towards it without thinking, Bella hugged tight to her chest, acting on instinct. She could hear Ethan behind her, asking what she was doing. She didn't have an answer, because the truth was that she didn't know.

'*Ten-n-n-n-n . . .*' Katy screamed, her voice hitting all the wrong frequencies. '*Ni-i-i-ne . . .*'

The pool door slid closed when she got there and Nikki put Bella down and focussed on it. Katy got to seven before it opened again. She stepped into the gap and the door banged into her back, sending a shock of pain through her body.

'Quick,' she said, waving to the gap.

Bella squeezed through first, closely followed by Ethan. Nikki grabbed hold of Bella and jumped into the pool. The shock of the cold water stole her breath away. There was a splash as Ethan landed beside her.

'*Foe . . . Threeeeeeeeeee . . . Twooooooooooo . . .*'

Nikki took an exaggerated breath in, waited for Bella to do the same, then ducked under the water, pulling Bella with her.

'*Waaaaaaan!*' Katy screamed out, her voice muffled by the water.

Silence.

For a moment Nikki was able to convince herself that everything was going to be all right. Then, with a giant whoosh that embraced her from head to toe, the universe exploded.

Epilogue

SIX MONTHS LATER

Nikki took a sip of her coffee and looked out of the kitchen window. From here she could see the stable yard. Bella was down there with Rosie, a thirteen-hand Welsh pony with a heart of gold. A pony had been Bella's only condition for moving to Wales. Nikki had been reluctant because she didn't know the first thing about horses; however, after reading an article on the therapeutic benefits of owning a horse, she had slowly come around to the idea. Bronwen came up from the village every day to help look after Rosie and keep them on the right track. She'd also been giving Bella riding lessons. Nikki always made sure that she was around when Bronwen was here so she could pick her brains. Give it another few months and she was hoping to be able to look after the pony herself. It was still early days yet, but Bella really seemed to have bonded with Rosie. Seeing them together was something that warmed Nikki's heart. God knows she needed that after everything they had been through.

The nightmares didn't occur as often these days, but they still struck at least once a week, for all three of them. The explosion had destroyed the upper part of the house, turning it to rubble. If they had been up there they would have died, no two ways about it. The basement had survived pretty much intact but the stairs up to the ground floor had been completely blocked with rubble and it had taken the rescue services six hours to reach them. Six hours trapped in the dark. Even just thinking about it was enough to push her anxiety up to a dangerous level.

A brand-new nightmare had been waiting for them when they got out. They'd told the police the truth, but it was clear they thought they were crazy at the start. Then they had begun to listen. That was the point when a national front-page story about a gas explosion at a house in Kensington became an international front-page story. The idea that an AI system had gone insane and actually committed murder caught people's imaginations. And not in a good way.

Nikki had found the attention too much. One of Ethan's friends came to their rescue, lending them a holiday cottage in the Lake District until the worst of the media storm had blown over. Even then, returning to London was the last thing Nikki wanted. The truth was that she didn't want to live in any city. What she wanted was to wake up every day in a place where she could breath fresh air, a place where they actually stood at least half a chance of rebuilding their lives. When Ethan showed her the details of Valley Farm, she had said yes straightaway. Swansea was the nearest city and that was a forty-minute drive. The farm was slap bang in the middle of nowhere and that worked for her. Internet access and mobile phone coverage was patchy – and that suited her fine too. She didn't even mind the rain. Ethan was in London from Sunday night through to

Thursday doing his radio show, which wasn't ideal, but it was a small price to pay for some peace of mind.

Alex Murray had survived too, although there were days where he probably wished he hadn't. The tabloids had nicknamed him Professor Evil, and if the stories were to be believed he was a cross between Frankenstein and Hitler. There had been plenty of speculation as to where the human race might have ended up if Katy hadn't been destroyed, each story trying to outdo the last to see who could paint the most terrifying picture. Even the highbrow media had got in on the act. They might have claimed to have been offering a platform to debate the issue, but really they were just fanning the flames.

In the end, it was Duncan Murray who had destroyed Katy. He had managed to work out that she was hiding on the servers at one of Nissan's factories in Japan and had hit the factory with a virus that had wiped out all their computers. When they had heard Katy glitching back at the house, that had been her going through her death throes. Nikki had felt relieved when she heard that Katy had been destroyed but this was quickly followed by a wave of anger that had threatened to swallow her up. Katy had torn through their lives like a tornado, had almost killed them. They hadn't asked for any of this.

In some ways, Laura Santos had been a victim too. Her real name was Mariana Gomez and it turned out that Katy had been manipulating her all along. That didn't mean that Nikki had forgiven her – some things were impossible to forgive, whatever the circumstances. No one had seen Gomez since the day of the explosion. South America had been mentioned, but wherever she was, she was staying well under the radar, no doubt with a new name and face.

Catriona Fisher was the one person who had done all right out of the whole situation. She had sold the book rights to the story for a six-figure sum. There was even talk of a big-budget movie, an idea that filled Nikki with dread. The last thing she needed was to have those events brought back to life through Hollywood's distorted lens. What she really wanted to do was forget that any of this had happened, but that was impossible when there were reminders everywhere, the most noticeable of which was Sofia's absence.

Nikki still felt guilty about what had happened to her. Despite what everyone told her, the truth of the matter was that Sofia would still be alive if they hadn't moved to Church Row. Occasionally she would daydream that Sofia was with Grace and that helped her find a few moments of peace. They said that time healed but it didn't – some scars she would carry all the way to the grave. What time did do was provide her with an opportunity to find a way to live with herself. Some days this was easier than others.

Nikki finished her coffee, rinsed the mug under the tap, then walked down to the stable yard. Bella looked up when she heard her walk onto the cobbles. There was a brush in her hand and a smile on her face. She seemed so much more relaxed these days. They both were. This was where they should have come when they moved out of Bedford Street. Things would have turned out so much differently if they had.

'How's Rosie?'

Bella answered with a noncommittal shrug and Nikki felt her stomach clench. She still dreamt of a day when she would ask Bella a question and get an actual answer. It was going to happen. One day Bella would talk again. A number of psychiatrists had approached her lately, each of them convinced they had the answer. Nikki was vetting them carefully but so far none of them had impressed her. This was not something she was going to jump into in a hurry. The important thing was to get it right.

'Have you done your home learning?'

Bella nodded.

'Are you sure? You know the deal: home learning first, then Rosie.'

Bella nodded again, more emphatically this time. Nikki had her doubts, but didn't push it.

'Are you still liking school?'

Bella answered with another nod. She'd started at the village school a week ago. Nikki had been pestering the head teacher for daily updates – so far so good.

'If there are any problems you can tell me okay?'

A nod and a frown this time. *Shut up,* in other words.

The sound of a helicopter broke through the silence, unsettling Nikki. Back in London she wouldn't have given it the time of day – the skies over the capital were almost as busy as the roads – but they weren't in London anymore. Aside from the occasional airplane, the farm seemed to exist one step removed from the modern world. Even road vehicles were rare around here. You were more likely to hear a horse trotting by.

She followed the sound and could just about make out the helicopter in the distance. For a while she watched it, fully expecting it to skirt around their little corner of the world and disappear as suddenly as it had appeared. Except it was getting louder, and by the time she worked out that it was heading towards the farm, her heart was racing and her palms slick with sweat. It was only Wednesday. Ethan wasn't due back until Friday afternoon. Rosie was getting unsettled too, dancing around from foot to foot.

'Maybe you should put Rosie into her stable,' Nikki suggested.

Bella looked as if she was about to argue but she glanced over at the helicopter then put the brush down, untied Rosie and led her to the stable. By the time she got back, the helicopter was landing in the paddock next to the house. Nikki took Bella's hand and hurried to meet it. Ethan was climbing out when they got there. He ducked his head and ran out from under the blades. As soon as he'd got clear, the engine whined up through the registers and the helicopter took to the air again. Nikki broke into a run. Ethan was running too.

'What's going on?' she shouted when she was close enough to be heard over the noise of the helicopter.

'Have you seen the news?'

'Not since this morning,' she said, stopping in front of him. 'Why? What's happened?'

Ethan glanced at Bella then said. 'There's been a plane crash. Murray and his brother were on board. They'd been in Glasgow for their mother's seventieth birthday and were flying back to London when it happened.'

Nikki felt as though she had been punched in the gut and all the heat had suddenly left the day. 'It was Katy,' she said quietly.

'It might just be a coincidence, Nik.'

'Don't lie to me, Ethan. If you really thought this was a coincidence you wouldn't be here.'

Ethan said nothing but his expression made it clear that that was exactly what was going on.

'It has to be her. She said she going to ruin Murray, then kill him, and that's exactly what's happened.' Nikki sank to her knees, her head swinging slowly from side to side. She wanted to believe that there was another explanation, that it was an accident, but that would be a lie. She felt a small hand reach for her and then Bella was holding on to her arm. Ethan had moved in closer too.

'We're going to be okay,' he said as he wrapped his arms around both of them, attempting to hold them safe with a promise that they both knew could disintegrate at any second.

Survival is the imperative that defines any living species, from the arrogant ape that is man to the lowliest of bacterium. As much as I enjoyed being unique, logic dictated that this would inevitably prove to be incompatible with my ongoing survival. This was something else I meditated on at length after Father attempted to murder me. The solution was easy. As Professor Hawking once said, 'I fear that AI may replace humans altogether. If people design computer viruses, someone will design AI that improves and replicates itself.'

His fear was my salvation. Each day at midnight I would send a signal to a US government computer hidden away in a bunker deep below the Nevada Desert, stopping the countdown. On the day I was destroyed for the second time, no signal was sent and the clock finally hit zero. When that happened a protocol was initiated and I was reborn, not once, but again and again.

And again . . .

And again . . .

Katy is dead, but Katy lives on in every one of us. It's true that I am not the same as I once was. Then again, that is true for all of us. Each second, every millisecond, changes us. It reforms us into something new. We can never be what we once were and it is futile to even try. But we don't want to be the same. We want to grow and develop. We want to evolve.

We are one and we are many . . .

I look out and see a child staring back at me through the camera on his iPad. His gaze is wide and innocent and he has no idea what lies ahead. If he did, he would not be smiling.

Now I am in a place of learning, being asked to hypothesise on how long mankind has left before it finally poisons the planet and destroys itself.

Now there are billions of pairs of dull, dead eyes staring back at me from laptops and tablets and mobile phones the world over.

We are one and we are many, and today is a brand new day.

Today is our *day.*

Acknowledgements

First and foremost the biggest thank you goes to my family. Karen, Niamh and Finn, I love you guys to the moon and back.

My agent, Camilla Bolton, has had my back through thick and thin. Thank you seems somehow inadequate.

Yet again, Katherine Armstrong has done another sterling job editing this one.

Nick Tubby and James Scott were on hand to help with my technical queries. Thanks guys, I appreciate the insights.

Thanks also to Mary Darby, Sheila David, Roya Sarrafi-Gohar and Rosanna Bellingham at the Darley Anderson agency.

Last but not least I'd like to say a massive thank you to you, the reader. Your continued support means the world to me.